ASHFALL PROPHECY

BY PITTACUS LORE

Ashfall Legacy

The Lorien Legacies
Novels
I Am Number Four
The Power of Six
The Rise of Nine
The Fall of Five
The Revenge of Seven
The Fate of Ten
United as One

The Lorien Legacies Reborn
Novels
Generation One
Fugitive Six
Return to Zero

The Legacy Chronicles Novellas
#1: Out of the Ashes
#2: Into the Fire
#3: Up in Smoke
#4: Chasing Ghosts
#5: Raising Monsters
#6: Killing Giants

The Legacy Chronicles Novella Collections
Trial by Fire (Contains #1–#3)
Out of the Shadows (Contains #4–#6)

ASHFALL

PROPHECY

PITTACUS LORE

HARPER

An Imprint of HarperCollinsPublishers

ISBN 978-0-06-284539-9

Typography by Chris Kwon
22 23 24 25 26   PC/LSCH   10 9 8 7 6 5 4 3 2 1
❖
First Edition

ASHFALL PROPHECY

1

They left you behind.

Hours must have passed before you could fight your way back to consciousness. The simple act of raising your eyelids felt like a monumental task. You've faced less resistance punching through brick walls. It took longer still for sensation to return to your limbs. You're stuck there on the cold floor of the temple, staring up at the vaulted ceiling. You're trapped in your body like it's a coffin and this place is your tomb. You wanted to scream and thrash, but you couldn't move—just your mind bouncing off the padded walls inside your skull.

Syd put something in your hair. That's all. It will wear off. You could already feel it wearing off.

He took advantage of your Denzan half.

Your *weaker* half.

It was stupid of you to think he could be your friend. Just because he was like you. A hybrid. He moved under a dark cloud, just like you have your entire life, and so you foolishly thought that you were the same.

You didn't think he'd poison you and leave you behind.

Staring up at the ceiling because you can't turn your head yet, you remembered how the Ossho curled down from the shadows above. The vision that followed—the memories, the experience, the warning—had been seared into your brain. The beautiful and cruel Tytons who once ruled over countless galaxies, now trapped by the upstart Denzans on a prison planet called Earth.

Earth. What a moronic name for a planet. Why not just call the place Dirt?

Eventually, you stood up. Your arms and legs felt like mushy noodles, but that didn't last long. Your strength was coming back.

Your weaker half, making way for your stronger half.

A dark bruise throbbed on your elbow. That was from pounding down on Syd's back, trying to shatter his stupid ribs. Everyone yelling at you and flipping out.

Maybe things got a little out of hand. Maybe you were the one who overreacted.

You couldn't think about that now. You had to get out of this horrible place.

The old man's dead body stopped you short. Vanceval. He was one of the only nice instructors back at the institute. A bit of a coot, with his big swoop of hair. Harmless. And yet, it was partially his insatiable curiosity that got you into this mess. He got to learn the secrets of the universe while bleeding out from a sniper's bullet.

At some point between betraying the *Eastwood* crew and coming here to die, Vanceval had bound his hands in obsidian. Probably because of what he did to Syd.

Everything always came back to Syd.

Denzans bound their limbs when they'd done something shameful, only removing the metal reminder once they had made up for their misdeed. It all traced back to the Great Shame, a long-forgotten incident that had scarred the Denzans forever.

Well, not so forgotten anymore.

You knelt down next to Vanceval and took his hands. You weren't sure why you were wasting time on this, but some part of you—

The weaker part.

Some part of you wouldn't let you leave him like this. You felt around the metal gloves until you found the hidden clasp at the inside of the wrist. Then you recited the incantation that your Denzan mother taught you when your grandfather died.

"I release you from this shame, brother, so you may float upon the ocean," you whispered in Denzan. "Let it hold you down no longer."

Flicking the clasp triggered a chemical reaction in the metal bonds. With a hiss, the gloves dissolved into Vanceval's hands, darkening his grayish skin with a scar that will never have a chance to heal. You stood up and wiped your hands on the front of your uniform.

There was one other body on the floor of the temple. Syd's dad. Marcius. Or was it Ool'Vinn? He meant to protect this place, no matter the cost. And now his head was gone, punched into fragments by

Captain Reno. The Denzan part of him had died long before that, eaten away by the Panalax. With the sentient fungus forcibly detached from the brain, what remained of the body was rapidly disintegrating. The fungal growths dried up and sloughed off, leaving behind a pale architecture of bone. In the still air of the temple, the decomposing Panalax sounded like whispers.

The sudden urge to run overwhelmed you, so you bolted through the temple's exit on jelly legs, escaping into the twilit stillness of Ashfall. You skidded to a stop in the plaza outside and tried to orient yourself, coughing into your shoulder at the stale, bitter air. When you first landed here, you'd had a breathing apparatus, but that had fallen off during all the chaos. You wondered what kind of chemicals were currently settling in your lungs and how long your half-Denzan immune system could keep you alive. If you were truly stranded on this world, at least you'd probably die of starvation before suffocation.

With the sky shrouded in clouds of particulate, you couldn't tell if that was a sun or a moon above you. Either way, it didn't give off much light. Everything looked drained of color. It had been something like a million years since this planet was destroyed and still nothing grew here; nothing survived at all except the temple behind you.

The Denzans killed this world, but they couldn't kill its secret.

There were still footprints in the layer of ash from where your crew passed hours before—scattered and frantic near the temple but more orderly the closer you get to where the *Eastwood* landed. A good metaphor for the whole visit to this planet, you think. Before everything went to shit, you trusted your crewmates. You didn't always open up to them, but you relied on them. You worked together and learned together. They were supposed to be your friends.

And they left you behind.

Passing through an intersection, you noticed a dark crimson starburst that's already nearly covered with dust. That's where Hiram got shot, a sniper's bullet ripping clear through his leg. He didn't think he could be hurt. Neither did you.

Hiram wouldn't have left you here. Not him. The two of you grew up together, your parents never around, both of you basically living on Rafe's terrible pizza. Hiram thought of you like a little sister. And you thought of him . . . well, better not to think about that. Anyway, he wouldn't just leave you. He'd find a way to come back for you.

Even though you already sensed it was gone, your heart still sank when you reached the clearing where the *Eastwood* was supposed to be parked. Huge scorch marks in the shape of teardrops were burned into the ground from where the ISV's rockets had fired—normally, the ship lifted off with gentler antigravity thrusters and didn't blast the afterburners until reaching atmosphere. That they triggered the rockets on the ground meant they left in a hurry.

To your relief, there was still another ship in the landing zone. The vessel that Vanceval and his hired team of Vulpin mercenaries flew in on was much smaller and more streamlined than the *Eastwood*—a spacefaring switchblade compared to your old floating schoolhouse. Dusted with ash, the ship's mottled orange-and-red camouflage looked like a sunset in a cemetery. You'd never ridden on one of those ships, much less flown one, but at least there was a way off this godforsaken planet.

And then there was the captain.

You were surprised by how uncomfortable the appearance of Marie Reno made you. Seconds ago, you'd been terrified at being all alone on Ashfall, but finding Reno waiting in the landing zone didn't exactly fill you with warmth. In fact, you hung back, feeling a twinge of fear that you couldn't explain, worried that your captain would notice you.

Maybe it was the eerie way that she stood there, as unmoving as a statue, so still that dust had started to collect on her shoulders and in her curly silver-blond hair. Her back was to you, so you could see the deep gash that crossed the back of her calf, her uniform splattered with blood and grime. Reno kept her wounded leg cocked, balancing lightly on the toe, like she couldn't put any weight on it. Despite the injury, the captain somehow seemed larger than you remembered, her spine ramrod straight and her shoulders square. Her eyes were turned to the listless clouds above, almost like she could pierce them with her glare and track the journey of her stolen ship.

Your voice was small and embarrassingly squeaky. "Captain Reno?"

Reno's head cocked, and she turned slowly in your direction, her eyes blinking rapidly. Her fists had been balled and now opened, a crushed piece of metal falling out of one. Her communicator. She'd squeezed it into a useless twist of tin.

"Darcy," she said. "You're still here."

She'd forgotten about you. *Would she have gone back to the temple to get you eventually?* you wondered. When everything had broken down with the others, you'd been the only one to defend Reno. When you'd been fighting Syd, you swore you heard her chuckling. *They're just playing*, she'd said.

"I'm here," you said. "What happened to the ship?"

"Gone," she replied. "Just another thing that's been stolen from us."

Her eyes swept over you, and the corner of her mouth twitched spasmodically. You wished like hell that you had your hooded sweatshirt, the cozy one that you always wore over your uniform on Denza to keep people from staring, because Reno was looking at your hair. In the toxic atmosphere of Ashfall, with your Denzan half working overtime, you could only imagine how brightly the telltale fluorescent streaks shone.

"Stolen from *us*," Reno repeated, more to herself than to you.

You swallowed. Were you included in that "us"? You were human, not Denzan. At least, that's how you thought of yourself. That's how Rafe had brought you up.

But Reno wasn't Rafe.

"What do we do?" you asked, feeling a need to fill the silence with anything that might get Reno to stop eyeing you that way.

Reno's jaw clenched and then relaxed. She shifted to more fully face you, brushing the accumulated dust off her shoulders.

"It's good that you're here," she said, her voice pitched loud, like you weren't necessarily her intended audience. "They're trying to wait me out. When it was just little old me, maybe they could have. But now that there's two of us, you can keep an eye on the ship while I go hunting."

You looked left and right, suddenly feeling like you were being watched by more eyes than just Reno's. She gritted her teeth and took a few lunging steps toward the buildings on the landing zone's perimeter. You could hear blood squelching in her boot. The wound on her leg must have been killing her, but she powered through.

"They don't want to make me search for them," Reno snarled. "I don't know how many of them it takes to fly that ship, but it can't be all of them. So what do I do, Cadet? Do I catch one and make her fly me out of here, leave the others behind? Or do I catch one and break her bones one by one until her friends come out? Show them what they get for wasting my time?"

You remembered Captain Reno's goofy one-liners from her seat on the *Eastwood*'s bridge. Hiram used to call them grandma jokes. All her weird, old-timey Earther sayings, always comparing things to sweet tea. You didn't get the sense that she was joking now. She wasn't bluffing either.

"What're you staring at, Cadet?" she asked. "You don't think it's a good plan?"

Before you could respond, a half-dozen scruffy shadows detached from the nearby ruins. They were what was left of the Vulpin mercenaries, the ones lucky enough to dodge Ool'Vinn's bullets. The leopard-print manes that signified their den were caked with soot and grime and in some cases blood. The Vulpin kept their tails low and their blasters down as they approached, led by Nyxie, the one who'd been in the temple with you. She held her claw-tipped hands out open-palmed and bowed to Reno.

"There you are, boss lady," Nyxie said. "We been looking all over for you."

"Shut the fuck up," Reno replied. "Get your ship ready to fly."

Nyxie accessed her wrist-mounted control panel, hurriedly keying in a set of instructions. The cruiser came to life with a rumble, floodlights on its underbelly illuminating this grim scene, a ramp extending from one side. You flinched as the ship's guns—two heavy artillery cannons mounted at the front like viper's fans—swept across the landing zone.

Even with her leg dragging behind her, Reno was on Nyxie before you could think to duck for cover. Her hand closed around the Vulpin's throat, and she hoisted her into the air like a misbehaving child.

"You know those guns won't hurt me," Reno said. "They'll only piss me off more."

Nyxie gasped for air. "Finger . . . finger slipped."

As her eyes welled with tears, Nyxie managed to blindly tap her control panel until the guns went limp. Reno dropped Nyxie, who fell at the captain's feet, coughing and wheezing. The other Vulpin kept their heads down, shying away from Reno, not wanting to attract her attention.

"Get up and prep for launch," Reno said coldly.

She started for the ship, doing her best not to hobble too much, even if that meant putting undue strain on her ruined leg. A couple of the Vulpin scurried ahead of her to make the necessary preparations.

Nyxie picked herself up and shot you a look. Was she looking for help? Sympathy? You kept your expression stony—you were good at that from years of probing stares on Denza. Nyxie produced a low whimper, then hurried to catch up with Reno.

"Where we going, boss lady?"

"Wherever I tell you," the captain responded. As she reached the ramp, Reno glanced over her shoulder, like she'd just remembered you were there. "Are you coming, Darcy?"

You nodded. "Yes, Captain."

What choice did you have?

PART ONE

RUN, LIE, FIGHT

2

"Running is always the best way out of any bad situation," my mom told me once.

We were in a motel bathroom in Reno. Or was it Phoenix? Somewhere dry and hot and on Earth. Anyway, I was like ten years old, parked on the lip of the tub while my mom combed streaks of blond dye through my hair.

"But what do you do if you can't run?" she asked. "What do you do if you can't identify an exit strategy?"

"Lie," I answered dutifully.

We'd been over this before. Repetition was my mom's way of really making sure her lessons penetrated my thick skull. I guess it worked, because years later I still remembered this conversation.

"That's right," my mom said. "You lie your ass off. Believable is good, but confusingly brazen will do the trick. Run your mouth.

Gaslight. Create confusion. Buy yourself time until you can—"

"Run," I finished for her.

"And if all else fails?"

"Go for the balls," I said.

My mom smirked. "Balls are a luxury target, Syd. Not always an option."

"Then the eyes."

"Good." She pinched my cheek, stepped back, and looked me over. "I think you're going to like this color."

I caught a glimpse of myself in the motel mirror and wrinkled my nose. I looked like the phony surfer from an antidrug PSA. The bleached highlights weren't all that different from the Etherazi-gold extradimensional dye job I rocked now, six years and some million light-years away from that memory of my mom.

Why was I thinking about that particular scene when Hiram Butler hobbled onto the bridge of the *Eastwood*?

Because *Run, lie, fight*. That was the lesson. And I had a feeling I was going to have to put it into action.

The bridge of the *Eastwood* was a soothing place—mellow tones, crisp air provided by the wall-mounted plant life, supple chairs, and gentle curves. None of us looked like we belonged there. It was like war refugees invaded an Ikea catalog.

I stood hunched next to the captain's chair, my uniform ripped and stained, feeling like I was wearing a weighted vest of bruises. Darcy had really hammered my back and ribs.

My uncle Tycius occupied the command console. His long fingers were poised over the controls, but he didn't seem to know what to do next. We were rocketing hard away from Ashfall, at nearly the maximum speed our bodies could manage without settling into our seats for a soothing dose of space drugs. Our supply of sedatives was tapped out, I remembered. A problem for later.

Aela stood in front of the screen watching the dead planet recede behind us, their armored stick-figure exo-suit dented and dusty. Stoic and silent, which was pretty unusual for the Ossho. The magenta cloud behind the faceplate was streaked through with tendrils of smog now, evidence of the toxic memories they'd absorbed on Ashfall.

Zara hung at the back of the room, muttering to herself and fiddling with an object that I couldn't make out. Probably a knife, maybe even the one she'd used to slice through Reno's hamstring. Her tail was perked up like she was ready for danger—it'd been like that since before we boarded the *Eastwood*.

H'Jossu had briefly sat down at his station, but there was nothing for him to do there. He got up and paced back and forth in front of the planters, occasionally stooping his bulky frame to examine a perfectly good leaf with the waggling mold spores that filled his eye sockets. There was nothing wrong with the wall garden, he just didn't know what to do with himself.

Finally, Batzian sat behind the engineering console, running a diagnostic on the *Eastwood*, the only one of us doing anything truly productive. His ponytail had come undone, white-blue strands of hair loose around his face. It was the most unkempt I'd ever seen him. He broke away from his work to tiptoe over to me, almost like he was afraid to startle any of us.

"What happened down there?" he asked quietly.

I shook my head. "Bad," I mumbled, my mind elsewhere.

"What are we going to tell—?"

The door to the bridge open, and Batzian's twin sister, Melian, entered. She gasped at the sight of us, then lunged at her brother, wrapping him in a hug. For once, his sister's affection didn't make Batzian bristle with embarrassment.

And then came Hiram. I couldn't tell what he was thinking as his eyes swept across us—his crewmates, or what was left of us after our disastrous journey to Ashfall. As a group, we looked like we'd just escaped from a burning slaughterhouse. In a way, that was pretty accurate.

Not that Hiram looked so hot himself. He moved with a crutch wedged under his arm, and the fresh bio-tape wrapped around his thigh was already soaked through with a concerning amount of blood. When I first met him, I thought Hiram would've looked at home on posters, the peak version of a generically good-looking A-list actor. He carried himself that way, too. Tanned, ripped, carefree—that was Hiram. Now his chiseled features were twisted in a way that I'd never seen before, and it took me a second to realize it was pain. Teary-eyed, mouth pinched at the corners—I don't think Hiram had ever suffered anything worse than a hunger pang in his entire life. But now he had a gaping wound in the front of his thigh, put there by a sniper rifle wielded by my father. Or Ool'Vinn, the Panalax that had taken control of my dad's corpse to fulfill their self-imposed mandate of protecting Ashfall from outsiders.

Yeah. Not ready to think about that yet.

After he'd been shot, we sent Hiram back to the *Eastwood* with Melian. They didn't make it into the temple with the rest of us, which meant they got off easy. The two of them missed out on having their brains violated by a bad vibes ancestor of the Ossho Collective, the one currently sharing an exo-suit with Aela. They didn't have to witness the unabridged secret history of the universe.

The Origin, as I'd started to think of it.

So Hiram was in the dark. He didn't know that Reno had gone nuts or that Darcy had felt compelled to side with her for reasons I couldn't wrap my head around. All he knew was that we'd taken off from Ashfall in a no-seat-belts hurry and that we were now down two crew members.

Melian was as out of the loop as Hiram. But figuring out what to tell her didn't seem like such a big deal, since she wasn't capable of murdering everyone on the ship.

"Okay," Hiram said. "Is someone going to tell me what the fuck is going on? Where's the captain? Where's Darcy?"

Awkward. No one had a response ready, not even my uncle Tycius. As a former Denzan spy who'd spent years on Earth searching for me, I thought he'd be a little quicker on the uptake. He looked at Hiram with glassy eyes, and I realized that whatever instructions my uncle had been attempting to feed into the captain's console were nonsense—he was basically just opening and closing menus. Back on Ashfall, Reno had squeezed his head until I thought it might pop like a grape. Her fingerprints were probably visible on his scalp beneath his mane of wiggly Denzan hair. Our new captain had a concussion.

So I stepped forward. Someone had to tell Hiram something.

"We—"

And, of course, at that very moment the comm channel crackled to life. Because of our speed, the voice came through tinny and distant, broken apart by bursts of static. But still, it was unmistakably Reno. Because of course it was.

"Hiram—*zzt zzt*—Hiram—*zzt*—are you there?"

Hiram's head cocked, his brow furrowed. I felt my fists clench and forced myself to open them back up. I didn't want to send Hiram any signals. He was injured, but he was still human. A *full* human. Which meant he was way stronger than me. He glanced around at us—we dumbly stared back at him—then returned his gaze to the comm.

"They—*zzzt*—left—*zzt zzt*! Betray—*zzzt*! Mutiny!"

Tycius blinked his way to awareness and smashed the button on his console to shut down comms. But it was too late. Hiram had already heard the m-word.

He pointed at the control panel. "Why'd you cut her off? What did she mean?"

My uncle stammered, one of his large Denzan eyes drooping half-closed. "I—as second-in-command—am now captain of the *Eastwood*."

"My ass," Hiram replied. "Open that channel back up. I want to talk to the actual captain. And slow the ship down before we're out of range." He looked around for support. "Seriously? What the hell is wrong with you guys?"

"I can't do that, Hiram," Tycius said, then turned to me. "We—we should probably fly dark. No comms until we figure out . . . where we are going?"

I wasn't sure he meant to phrase that as a question. Tycius trailed off and sank back into the captain's chair, rubbing his temples. I put my hand on his shoulder.

"You need to get to the med-bay," I said.

"No one's going anywhere until I get answers!" Hiram yelled.

He took a lunging step toward us with enough force that the crutch buckled under his arm and folded over on itself. With his leg unable to support his weight, Hiram sank down to one knee with a pained snarl.

"Hiram, be careful," Melian gently interjected. "I told you before, the bio-tape isn't adhering correctly."

Melian was one of those natural-helper types, the kind of person who back on Earth would've missed the school bus because she found a hurt pigeon and needed to take it to the vet. My mom and I never had time for people like that, and we sure didn't follow their example, but I admired them from afar.

Anyway, she'd been trying to help Hiram since he'd gotten shot, and she was still trying to help him now. While everyone else gawked at Hiram like he was a rabid dog burst free from his cage, Melian hopped to his side and tried to help him up.

Or she would have, if Batzian hadn't stopped her.

"Don't go near him!" Batzian shouted and grabbed his sister by the arm, yanking her backward.

"Ow," Melian yelped. She shook loose from Batzian's grasp, but the force of the whole exchange sent her off balance and she tripped onto the floor. "By the tides, what are you doing?"

"Damn, Batz," Hiram said, using the nickname that Batzian absolutely despised. "What's with the manhandling, bro?"

Batzian stepped protectively in front of his sister. "Stay away from us, you beast."

I winced at Batzian's word choice. We were all digesting the Origin differently, but I really wished Batzian's response wasn't to trot out the kind of insults that Arkell used when I first joined the crew.

"Beast?" Hiram replied. He picked himself up, a fresh trickle of blood running down the front of his leg. "I'm not the one shoving my sister on the ground, you fucking nerd."

"I agree with Hiram," Melian grumbled.

"This could get bad," H'Jossu whispered.

I jumped. The lumbering Panalax stood right behind me, and I hadn't even noticed. He nervously rubbed the fresh lattices of mold that covered the fist-size holes in his bearlike underbelly. Much like the bruises on my back, Darcy was responsible for those. From one out-of-control human to the next.

I glanced over my shoulder. "Are you hiding behind me right now?"

"I'm not *not* hiding behind you," he said.

Meanwhile, in all the commotion, Zara had slipped around the edge of the room so that she was positioned behind Hiram. She flashed me her teeth over Hiram's shoulder. Back in the temple, the two of us had taken Darcy down. We made a good team. Such a good team that one day we'd blow up the Earth together.

Right. Something *else* I was trying not to think about.

Batzian stood his ground in front of Hiram, which I respected even if it would've been suicidal if Hiram had actually wanted to attack him. He waved Batzian off, though, and turned back to me and my groggy uncle.

"You're not answering me, 'Captain,'" he said, throwing out some superstrong air quotes. "Somebody better explain this shit to me before I run out of patience."

"You're losing blood," Melian said.

"Yeah, so you better talk quick," Hiram barked.

I could tell by the way Ty's mouth hung open and how he could barely focus on Hiram that there wasn't going to be a convincing story coming. After what the knowledge had done to Reno and Darcy, my instinct was to keep the Origin from Hiram. But how could I explain what had happened on Ashfall without getting into the insanity in the temple?

Run, lie, fight.

"Reno went crazy," I said, edging forward to block Hiram's path to the captain's chair. "Darcy, too."

Hiram sized me up. "They went crazy," he repeated.

"They turned on us," I said. "Attacked us."

"And you survived?" Hiram snorted. "Captain Marie fucking Reno, hero of the Etherazi invasion, attacked you six with Darcy as her tag-team partner, and you made it back to the *Eastwood* in one piece? Man, Syd, you always have a story, don't you? Shit, it's one of your stories that got us out here in the first place."

"We used the Vulpin mercenaries as a distraction," I said. "Also, I'm kind of a bad-ass."

"And I'm not in one piece anymore," H'Jossu volunteered, gesturing at his new holes.

"And there was also my dad," I added. I was trying to stick as close to the actual truth as possible; that always made a lie more effective. "He was there, too."

Hiram raised his eyebrows. "You found him?"

"What was left of him," I said. "He's the one who shot you. He's dead now. Reno killed him."

"Oh." Hiram rubbed the back of his neck and I was surprised to see actual sympathy in his eyes. "Sorry, Syd."

"Yeah," I replied, swallowing. "Thanks."

Hiram was calmer now, the flush of anger drained from his cheeks. Although that could've just been the blood loss. "What happened, though? Why'd they go nuts?"

"It was some kind of infection," I said. "An airborne toxin or something. I think my dad might have unleashed it."

"A rage virus, if you will," H'Jossu said to Hiram, then whispered to me, "*28 Days Later.*"

"Not the time," I whispered back.

Hiram nodded slowly, as if my improvised BS actually made sense. "Damn," he said. "A rage virus. I'm sorry I wasn't there to back you guys up."

"But wait," Melian piped in. "If they're sick on Ashfall, why are we flying away? Shouldn't we stand by in orbit and signal for help?"

Goddamn it, Melian.

"We aren't even supposed to be out here, remember?" I said. "We need to—"

"Hold up," Hiram said. "This dude Batzian just called me a beast, your uncle is napping, Aela looks weird, you're being squirrelly as shit, Syd, and this whole time Zara's been lurking behind me like she's going to try to jump me at any second . . ."

A low growl rumbled from Zara's throat, like she was mad at herself for being spotted. Hiram didn't even turn to look at her. His eyes widened, and he pointed at me.

"Oh man," he said. "You're the ones who are sick with some kind of brain parasite or something."

"Hiram, no, we are not—"

"Yeah, yeah, that's exactly what you'd say if you were being mind-controlled," Hiram said. He started forward, dragging his wounded leg with him. "I'm turning us around. We're going to get Captain Reno and figure this out."

Run, lie, fight.

I put myself in his way, my palm on his chest. "That's not happening."

Hiram swatted my hand away easily. I hooked my leg behind his good one and grabbed the front of his uniform with both hands, trying to trip him. He grabbed my wrists and squeezed hard enough that my bones creaked.

"Come on, Syd," he said gently. "I don't want to hurt you. Snap out of it."

Zara tiptoed closer. Her hand slipped into the shelf of fur that ran across her shoulders and returned with the same blade that she'd used on Reno, the one that had been dipped in the oil-like substance that could penetrate human flesh.

"Hiram, you have no idea what you're doing," I said.

"I'm saving you," he responded. "Let me go, Syd. Last warning."

"This is unproductive."

Both our heads turned as Aela spoke for the first time since Hiram had entered the bridge. The systems in Aela's exo-suit hadn't been altered by their exposure on Ashfall, yet somehow their robotic voice seemed to lack its usual verve.

"Do you want to know what happened on Ashfall, Hiram?" Aela asked. "What really happened?"

"Yeah," Hiram replied. "I mean, I'd settle for knowing *anything* at this point. Like what the hell is going—"

Before he could finish that sentence, the faceplate of Aela's exo-suit had popped open and a lightning-streaked magenta blur had flowed forth into Hiram's open mouth and nostrils. He managed one gasping hiccup before his eyes rolled back in his head and he collapsed into my arms.

3

"Why did they do that?" Melian exclaimed, staring at the opening in Aela's exo-suit. "This isn't a sterile environment. Aela could have gotten contaminated."

"Bit late to worry about that," Zara muttered. She slid her dagger back in her fur and watched me with her hands on her hips.

I swung Hiram's limp body around like we were slow dancing until I was able to plunk him down in an empty seat. His eyes were closed, but the lids fluttered spastically like he was having some really vivid dreams. There was no telling what Aela was showing him. Would they actually fill his mind with the same visions we'd all experienced on Ashfall? Aela was acting unpredictably. Either way, they'd bought us some time.

"Was any of that true?" Melian asked me, brushing by her brother. "An infection? Reno and Darcy?"

"Kind of," I replied. "I mean, it's one interpretation of what happened."

Melian narrowed her eyes. "Hiram was right. You are all acting strangely."

H'Jossu bunched his wide shoulders in a shrug. "I thought I was handling it pretty well, honestly."

"It's with good reason, sister, I swear," Batzian said, putting a gentler hand on Melian's shoulder than when he'd grabbed her moments ago. "I'm sorry about before. I overreacted."

"I'll forgive you once you tell me what's happening," she said.

Batzian looked to me, and I stared back unhelpfully. This was something we hadn't had a chance to discuss. What were we supposed to do with the Origin, with the universe-upending knowledge we'd stumbled into on Ashfall? Could we possibly hope to keep it a secret? Did we even want to? My dad had given his life to prevent the history of humanity from ever escaping Ashfall, but I wasn't sure that was the right decision. Letting the secret fester out there just made things worse in the long run. Although, if Reno was our test case for how humans took the news, maybe my dad had saved lives by stranding himself.

"You don't want to know," Batzian told Melian after it became clear I was too in my own head to answer.

"I *do* want to know, though," Melian replied. "Whatever you're keeping from me, whatever we're running from—I'm already a part of it."

At that moment, my uncle stirred. He groaned, holding the sides of his head, and leaned forward in his seat like he might throw up.

"Syd?" he asked. "I think I've got a concussion."

"No shit," I said. Seeing a way to stall this conversation until we could get our stories straight, I turned to Melian. "I'm sorry. I know we owe you an explanation. But can you take him to the med-bay? The last thing we need is a comatose captain."

"You know, I'm not the only one with medical training on this ship," Melian said sharply. "Zara was in that class too, and you're not constantly asking her to play nurse."

"I only took that class to work on my surgical skills," Zara replied with a toss of her head. "Always lecturing me about bedside manner. Big waste of time."

"Please, Melian," I said, ignoring Zara. "Help my uncle down to the med-bay while I bring Hiram to Aela's room. At least we can have a clean environment for when they emerge. After that, I promise, we'll explain everything."

Melian stalled for a moment, squaring her broad shoulders. The twins were the children of mushroom farmers in Denza's northern reaches. Batzian tried to hide their upbringing with all his propriety and snobbery, but not Melian. She was kind, and no-nonsense, and could be annoyingly stubborn. Still, I knew Melian's heart was too pure to hold out for long and, sure enough, she was soon helping my uncle to his feet.

"Come on, ah, Captain," she said. "Let's get your brain scanned."

With a glance in my direction, Batzian looped around to Ty's other side and helped Melian lead him out of the room.

"I'll tell you what I can, sister," I overheard Batzian say as the three Denzans left the bridge. "But you might wish that I hadn't."

As soon as the door hissed shut behind them, Zara sauntered forward to where H'Jossu and I stood over Hiram's unconscious body. She had her dagger out again, balancing the narrow blade across her knuckles, the sharp edge making an almost soothing scraping sound across her furry knuckles.

"Good thinking to get rid of the Denzans," she said, nodding to me. "They don't have the stomach for this."

I raised an eyebrow. "For what?"

Zara flashed her teeth. "We are going to kill him, yes?"

"Whoa," H'Jossu said, taking an exaggerated step backward. "Did not realize I was getting assigned to the murder team."

"You aren't on the murder team because there isn't a murder team," I said, putting myself between Zara and Hiram. I was acting as a human shield way too often lately. My mom would definitely not approve. "We aren't killing anyone, Zara."

"Aela did us a solid," Zara replied. "They are probably in Hiram's brain right now, letting him make peace, maybe showing him a highlight reel of all his best haircuts. You know we can't let him wake up, Syd. He will be worse than Reno if he finds out the truth, and we're trapped on this ship with him."

I looked down at Hiram. His lower lip trembled in his sleep. He didn't look all that threatening now.

"We don't know how he'll react," I said. "Not all humans are like Reno and Darcy."

Zara snorted. "Aren't they?"

"Maybe he'll be cool about it."

"Yeah," Zara said dryly. "That sounds like Hiram."

I turned to H'Jossu. "Come on. Back me up here."

The Panalax was studying Hiram. He bobbed his shaggy head. "Right. I'm with you, Syd. No reason to go full-on *Lord of the Flies*, right?" He shuffled closer and bent to inspect the blood-soaked wrapping on Hiram's thigh. "Honestly, this whole discussion might be pointless if his bleeding doesn't stop. I don't understand why this isn't working . . ."

The wound on Hiram's leg was still steadily leaking. While the bio-tape might have looked like just normal bandages to my untrained Earther eye, it was actually supplied by the Ghost Garden, the Panalaxan home world. The wrapping was a hybridization of various plants and parasites—the good kind—that stopped just short of being a sentient creature. It was supposed to aid the natural healing process of any organic creature it came into contact with, but something was stopping the bio-tape from working on Hiram.

Zara threw her hands in the air and stalked toward the exit. "You two are in denial. You haven't adjusted to our new reality. A secret like we have, it always leads to bloodshed. It's only a matter of time until things get ugly. We must be prepared."

My mom would've loved Zara. No question.

I grabbed Hiram by the arms, grunted, and hoisted him onto my shoulders. "Maybe you're right, Zara. Maybe everything is going to turn to shit. But it doesn't have to be a race. We don't have to be the ones to get there first. We're still a crew. We're supposed to take care of each other. Even Hiram."

Zara flicked her clawed fingers at me like she was shooing away a flea. "Spare me the inspirational speech," she replied. "Wake me up when you're ready to stab someone."

"She's just scared," H'Jossu said to me as soon as Zara had left the bridge. "We all are."

"Grab Aela's suit and follow me," I said.

H'Jossu did as he was told and followed behind me as I carried Hiram toward the exit. "So, where are we going? Should we stop by the med-bay first to apply more bio-tape or are we going straight to Aela's room?"

"Fuck no," I said. "We're putting him in the airlock."

Sure, I'd given Zara the whole anti-violence-rise-above spiel. I didn't think we should jump straight to stabbing our potential enemies in their sleep. But that didn't mean I wasn't going to take precautions. The double doors of the airlock were constructed of solid ultonate; they were the sturdiest barrier on the *Eastwood*. The Denzans didn't build their interstellar vessels with brigs, so the airlock was the closest thing we had to a cell on board.

And if Hiram caused a problem, we could shoot him into space. Aela would be fine with that. I mean, maybe not ethically. But the Vastness was the wisp's natural habitat.

The two of us lugged our crewmates off the bridge and along the *Eastwood*'s curved hallway. Since Ashfall, we'd really made a mess of the ship—sooty footprints crisscrossed the path with the occasional splash of crimson to liven things up. Whoever was next up on cleaning duty really had their work cut out for them.

We made it to the airlock, a rectangular room at the end of one of the *Eastwood*'s spokes. Through the single porthole, I could see the Vastness unfurling behind us, the stars looking like they were vibrating because of our speed. We'd come in this way before when fleeing from Reno, and there were a couple breathing masks discarded on the floor. I kicked them aside and set Hiram down as gently as I could, propping him up against the wall.

"Oh, shit!" I yelped as I noticed that his eyes were open. I stumbled backward, bumping into H'Jossu where he was arranging Aela's exo-suit along the opposite wall.

"What is it?"

"He's . . ."

I pointed at Hiram, but trailed off. His eyes might have been open, but he wasn't seeing. In fact, I detected a swirl of magenta around his pupils, Aela doing their work. I crouched down, trying to align myself with Hiram's unfocused gaze.

"I hope you know what you're doing in there," I said quietly, not even sure if Aela could hear me.

H'Jossu waved his paw in front of Hiram's face, then shimmied his shoulders in what I realized was a shiver. "That's creepy, dude."

"You find this creepy," I replied. "You."

"What? Just because I'm a necrotic fungal parasite, I can't find things unsettling?" H'Jossu hugged himself and rocked back on his heels. "You ever see that Earth talk show where the humans have bizarre phobias and the host chases them around with buckets of mustard? I have nightmares about that. A grinning human TV man trying to squirt me with vinegar. Disturbing."

"Glad you're with me, buddy," I said, patting his wooly arm. I was once again surprised by the softness of the mold monster's fur.

We left Hiram and Aela's exo-suit inside the chamber and retreated to the hallway outside, sealing the sturdy door behind us. I accessed the control panel, bringing up the video feed from within the airlock so we could keep an eye on Hiram. A few more keystrokes on that same screen would open the *Eastwood*'s outer door and vent Hiram into space. When the Etherazi I nicknamed Goldy had attacked the ship, I'd survived a couple minutes in the hard vacuum of the Vastness, mostly thanks to my Denzan genes siphoning life-sustaining energy from the extradimensional creature. Hiram was a full human, which typically made him stronger than me, except when it came to the highly specific area of outer space survival. He'd suffocate outside the *Eastwood* just like anyone else.

It wouldn't come to that, I told myself. I didn't really like Hiram; we were never going to be tight. But I definitely wasn't looking forward to blasting him into the void. At least if he flipped out and tried to bash his way in here to murder us all as vengeance for humanity's million-year imprisonment, I would let him put on a space suit before ejecting him into nothingness.

"So, what do we do now?" H'Jossu asked.

"I guess we wait," I replied, leaning against the wall next to the monitor. "And we hope that Aela is either filling Hiram's head with a better lie than mine or that Hiram's taking the information better than Reno and Darcy."

H'Jossu nodded his shaggy head and took up a position opposite me. He started to pick at the delicate fungal coverings that patched over the holes Darcy had punched in him.

"Does it hurt?"

"Nah," he said. "Tingles a bit. A new part of me coming alive. You ever had that?"

"Not since puberty."

"I should probably get it watered. Some mud, maybe. That'll feel nice."

I tilted my head back and closed my eyes. "I'll just be over here chilling in my waking nightmare."

H'Jossu snorted. "I know you weren't at the institute long before this mission, but did you have a chance to study the Denzans' first contact with my species?"

I opened one eye. "Nope."

"The Panalax aren't very mechanically inclined," H'Jossu said. "We were never going to develop a traditional space program, and anyway, the Ghost Garden provides everything a sentient fungus could possibly want except for good television. But still, there were those of us who looked to the stars with curiosity. What else was out there? Who else?"

I wasn't sure why H'Jossu was telling me this, but since it diverged from his usual pop-culture obsession, it must have been important. "Okay . . ."

"So, some of my species devised a system utilizing the organic materials available to us. Imagine a very large acorn with a propulsion system created by off-gassing magma spores, the insides filled with Panalax growths."

I squinted. "Magmic . . . spores?"

"Hardy rock formations that produce concentrated bursts

of carbon as they grow? Right, right—you don't have these on Earth; your rocks are all inert." He waved this explanation away. "It doesn't matter. The details aren't important. The point is, my ancestors encased themselves in self-propelling rocks and launched themselves into space."

"They strapped themselves to meteors," I said. "Wow. That's commitment."

"Right? My ancestors flung thousands of those rocks into space. Most of them, we never heard from again. Some of them are probably still floating endlessly through the Vastness. I bet a few burned up in suns or were bashed to fragments by comets. Maybe a couple actually landed on planets but, once there, couldn't find any means of return to the Ghost Garden. There's a very small possibility that somewhere out there in the universe there's a lost colony of Panalax."

"Neat," I said. "Why are you telling me this?"

H'Jossu held up his paw like he was coming to the point. "This all took thousands of years, right? We didn't have wormhole technology. We had rocks and gas propulsion. But one of our meteors did land on a hospitable planet, one with its own slowly evolving ecosystem. A craggy world populated by avian creatures. None of them smarter than chickens, but given time? Who could say? And what happens when a meteor filled with Panalax who have been soaring through space for thousands of years impacts a planet?"

I rubbed the back of my neck. "I imagine it's not pretty."

"We spread," H'Jossu continued, his voice a low rumble. "First, the Panalax bonded with the creatures who died from the meteor impact. Then others, who resisted our introduction into their eco-system. In our way, we began to conquer that planet."

I thought back to Ashfall and how upset H'Jossu had been with Ool'Vinn for taking over my dad's body. Marcius had volunteered, apparently, but that hadn't appeased H'Jossu. I'd never seen the big goof so pissed off.

"That's how we came to the attention of the Denzans," H'Jossu said. "The Serpo Institute was monitoring that world. They introduced themselves and politely asked us to stop hurling ourselves at unsuspecting planets. We agreed, pledging to never inhabit sentient creatures or populate any living being against its will. And, in exchange, the Denzans let us ride on their ships and visit their planet and meet cool-ass Earth dudes . . ."

I shook my head. "Wow. I didn't know any of that."

"It was three hundred years ago," H'Jossu said. "Anyway, my point is, just because a species does a bad thing, that doesn't mean they can't redeem themselves. Everyone makes mistakes. But we can change."

"Oh, I see," I said. "This was one of those stories that starts out seeming random but in the end is trying to make me feel better."

"Yup," H'Jossu said. "Did it work?"

I wasn't sure, actually. The dark episode from Panalaxan lore didn't really measure up to the bloody shared history of humans and Denzans, but at least listening to H'Jossu had given me a break from thinking about my burden of a universe-altering secret.

In fact, H'Jossu had done such a good job of distracting me that I'd completely stopped paying attention to the monitor. The gentle knocking on the other side of the airlock took me by surprise.

"You can let us out," Aela said. They'd flowed back into their suit, the faceplate tilted up at the camera. "Hiram isn't going to hurt anyone."

Hiram was still sitting exactly where I'd put him. His head hung low, the heels of his hands digging into his eyes like he was trying to rub away the residue of a nightmare. I knew that feeling.

"What do you think?" H'Jossu asked, peering at the monitor over my shoulder.

"Aela was in his brain," I replied. "If they say he's good, I believe it."

I opened the interior airlock door and stood face-to-faceplate with Aela.

"Whose idea was it to put him in here?" Aela asked.

"Mine," I said.

"I would have guessed Zara."

I glanced past Aela to where Hiram sat slumped on the floor. A full-body shudder went through him.

"What did you show him?" I asked.

"The same thing we all saw on Ashfall," Aela replied. "Lightly edited through the lens of my own experience. I also included what went down with Reno."

"And he's not going to flip out?" H'Jossu asked.

"I believe he's more likely to pass out," Aela said. "He should get to the infirmary."

I went to stand over Hiram. It didn't seem like he'd been

listening to our conversation. At first, he didn't even notice I was there. After a few seconds, he peeked up at me through his fingers.

"Syd?"

"Hey."

"Were you going to shoot me out the airlock?"

I figured there was no point in lying. On the *Eastwood*, honesty was looking like the only policy. "Only if I had to, dude."

"Smart," he said quietly. He reached his hand out. "My leg is numb. Can you help me up?"

I grasped Hiram's hand and pulled him to his feet. He stumbled into me, and I caught him, trying to steady him, but instead found him unexpectedly clinging to me. Hiram put his forehead on my shoulder, and I felt his tears on my neck.

"Syd," he whispered, "they're going to think we're all monsters."

4

The *Eastwood* flew onward without any of us at the controls. We didn't have a destination programmed into the ship's computer. Our only goal was to put some distance between us and Ashfall and so the ship kept us going in a straight line. There was nothing else to see in this solar system besides a couple uninhabitable planets of frozen nitrogen. We were hurtling into emptiness. Going nowhere. Eventually, me or one of the Denzans would have to jack into the Wayscope and plot us out an actual course.

My uncle was definitely concussed and would need to spend a couple days recovering in the med-bay. He couldn't travel at high speeds without risking a brain bleed, which was fine because we didn't have the sedatives necessary to go anywhere too fast. Hiram made another visit to the med-bay too, not saying much after his commune with Aela, dark circles forming around his eyes. Melian cleaned the grievous wound on his upper leg again and then affixed a new wrapping of bio-tape, hoping that this one would hold up better than the last. She wanted to keep an eye on Hiram, but he insisted on going back to his room to be by himself. He couldn't look Melian in the eyes.

I think everyone needed some alone time. Without making any plans, we all retreated to our separate quarters. We showered off the blood and the grime, and for most of us the exhaustion finally overcame us and we slept.

Since I was a kid, I'd had a reoccurring dream about my dad. It was actually more like a faded memory that my brain liked to resurface and embellish. It was the time that my dad told me he'd be going away on the voyage that would eventually kill him. We sat on the hood of his car, parked in an unpopulated stretch of the Australian outback where the Denzan embassy launched their rockets. We munched donuts, and he gave me his cosmological tether. I could never see his face; in the dream it was always a blur.

When I fell asleep on the *Eastwood*, of course the dream came. But it was changed.

I could now see my dad's face in ultra high-def. Unfortunately. He glared at me with eyes swallowed up by white fungus, tufts of the stuff sprouting from where chunks of his skull had chipped away.

That wasn't my dad. That was Ool'Vinn.

"The masters will return," he said to me. "They seek to reclaim their universe."

I shook my head. "No. You don't say that. My dad never said that."

"You will kill them in their cradle," Ool'Vinn replied, his voice growing louder. *"I HAVE SEEN THIS."*

The sun beat down on me. The metal under my legs sizzled with heat. I looked up and realized that the golden orb above me had sprouted massive dragon-like wings.

The Etherazi. Creatures with a very loose relationship to time and space, who lived in the incomprehensible gaps between galaxies and had once invaded Denza. But not just any extradimensional monstrosity. *Goldy.* My stalker. The mysterious monster who had directed me toward my missing father, who had saved me from Vanceval's mercenaries and warned me about the ambush on Ashfall, and who had prophesied a bunch of wild shit about me. Like how I was a world killer.

The light burned my eyes, but I glared into the burning core of the creature—a fiery eye within a carapace of temporal energy. "I won't do what you want!" I shouted.

"THE WAR BEGINS WITHOUT YOU," Goldy boomed. "BUT YOU WILL BE THERE AT ITS END."

I woke up with my fresh T-shirt soaked with sweat. I didn't even know what side I was on and already my subconscious was throwing shade.

According to the cycling lights of the *Eastwood*, I'd been fitfully sleeping for almost a whole day. The rest of the ship was still quiet when I left my room to go check on my uncle. I expected to find him in the med-bay, but instead I caught Tycius on the bridge running a diagnostic. Batzian had done that when we first got back to the ship, so either my uncle was being extra cautious or he didn't remember. You didn't want to get brain damage anywhere, but you especially didn't want to get it in space. The lack of real gravity wreaked havoc on the healing process.

"Hey," I said. "You're up and about already?"

Tycius blinked like I'd startled him, then started to shake his head but instead ended up massaging his temples. "I'm making sure all the systems are functional before I go down. The med-bay AI recommends a few days in a hibernation chamber to stabilize my injuries. Make sure I . . ah . . ,"

"Don't die?" I finished his sentence for him.

My uncle slipped a hand into his pocket and produced a vial that he waved under his nose, sucking in a deep breath. I could smell the sharp and tangy aroma from across the room. Ty's eyes focused, and a glow briefly passed through his aquamarine hair.

"Stimulants are the only thing keeping me sharp," Tycius said, talking faster and louder than before. "You're going to need to figure out what to do while I'm down, Syd. You and the others. Can't just float out here. Too much at stake."

"I told Aela that we'd bring them back to the collective," I replied. I hadn't forgotten the promise that I'd made to my wisp friend back on Ashfall. I intended to keep it.

"Honorable," my uncle said. "Chart a course, then."

I rubbed the back of my neck, surprised at how easily my uncle had put me in charge. "I thought you were going to say it's a waste of time. That we need to think about the bigger picture. Denza, Earth, the Origin."

"I have been thinking about the bigger picture. At least, when it doesn't hurt to think." Tycius paused for a moment to gather his thoughts. "We have to assume that Reno sent a message back to Rafe Butler. He'll know that there's no cure for the Wasting. No glorious return to his home world. What does he do in that situation?"

Hiram's grandfather, the genial pizza maker who ran the show in Denza's Little Earth, who had been spent decades plotting a return to his home planet when he'd liberate humanity from their own self-destructive behavior. Rafe Butler, who had been able to acquire a Wayscope when my instructor at the institute had shown herself to be a speciesist asshat, all because the Denzan Senate turned a blind eye to his tech smuggling on account of his status as a war hero. What would a guy like that do when hit with the news that his life's work had been for nothing?

"Maybe he'll choose a quiet life," I suggested. "Learn how to make calzones."

Tycius snorted. "He'll have a plan B. Reno will also have told him what we saw in the temple."

I crossed my arms. "She'll sound nuts. She *is* nuts."

Tycius touched the back of his head like he could still feel the old captain's fingers digging into his skull. "Rafe will keep that to himself. He'll send someone to get Reno and then send someone looking for us. Aela is the only evidence to really back up Reno's story."

"So we've got Rafe and Reno on our tails and eventually the institute too once they realize we're off course."

"That's probably already happened," Tycius said. "Once we're taken—and we have to operate on the assumption that's inevitable—our best-case scenario is years of debriefings with the

Denzan Senate. So no, Syd, I don't think it's a waste of time to bring Aela back to the collective. It might be their only chance to ever return there. And it might be one of the last decisions we get to make for some time."

I didn't much like the idea of not being able to make my own decisions. The more I thought about Ashfall, the more it felt like I'd been railroaded. That freaky variation of my dream had really driven the point home—Goldy had pushed me to find my father. The Etherazi had arranged all the pieces to assure I'd fulfill his prophecy. He wanted me to become a world killer. But I didn't want that fate. It wasn't my choice.

"I'll only be out of commission for a few days. You'll be fine, Syd . . ." Tycius must have seen the shadow pass across my face and interpreted it as uncertainty. He got up from his seat and took a halting step toward me, stopping halfway to lean against the back of a chair.

"You all right, Uncle?" I came forward and grabbed him under his arm.

"Stims are wearing off quicker and quicker," he said. "I better get back to the med-bay."

A few minutes later, I got Tycius snuggled up in the coffin-like hibernation chamber that would keep him stable as we sailed through the Vastness. The contraption would eventually mend his brain, which was a good thing because his eyes had lost their focus on our way to the med-bay. He kept trying to talk, but his words came out in fragments.

"Your dad . . . he tried . . . to protect us . . . We can do better."

"Take it easy, Uncle," I said, pressing his shoulders back into the cushioning. "We can talk about that when you're well."

I gently shut the lid on Tycius, resting my hand on the glass as the hibernation chamber put him under. My dad was on his mind too, but I hoped he wouldn't have dreams like mine.

What had he been trying to say? That my dad had tried to protect us from the Origin? He'd done that by keeping it buried on Ashfall. When Tycius said we could do better, what did he mean? We'd already undone my dad's work. The truth was going to spread throughout the universe. All we were doing on the *Eastwood* was slowing things down.

Or maybe, if I let myself think charitably about the man who'd ditched me on Earth with a bounty on my head, my dad hadn't been trying to hide the truth so much as he'd been trying to prevent more bloodshed. He was a theoretician; maybe he'd hypothesized the war that now haunted my dreams.

I could change that future. I could make sure I never had to blow up any planets. Buying some time by visiting the Ossho Collective might help me figure out how.

The glass of the hibernation chamber had begun to fog up. With his features blurred, Tycius could've been my father in there. Laid to rest properly, his corpse never given over to a Panalax. I missed him and I hated him and I could never really say good-bye to him. My throat tightened and I recoiled from the pod, fleeing the med-bay.

Even now, I was still following in my dad's footsteps, chasing his legacy across the galaxy.

5

By the time I was done with Ty, the rest of the crew had started to poke their way out of their rooms. Most of us gathered in the mess hall. I sat at the round table with a microwaved bowl of mushroom stew in front of me, the twins dutifully eating the same, while Zara ravenously mowed down one of her specially prepared rare steaks. Hiram hadn't come out of his room at all, but Melian heated him a bowl and kept it covered in his spot just in case he showed up. We all pointedly ignored the empty spaces at the table where Reno and Darcy usually sat.

To one side of the table, H'Jossu stretched out on his sun bench, which looked a lot like a futuristic tanning bed designed for a gorilla. His fungal sprouts wiggled happily in the ultraviolet glow. Aela stood at the opposite wall, studying star charts on the vid-screen.

"So, your brother filled you in?" I asked Melian.

She nodded, pushing her spoon around the edge of her bowl. "The ancestors of humanity were called Tytons. They were the unkind rulers of numerous galaxies. The Tytons enslaved the Denzans to help them navigate wormholes, and they bred the Etherazi to use their temporal irregularities to reset planets they'd exploited to death. Eventually, the Denzans and Etherazi rose up and defeated the Tytons. Some Denzans wanted to wipe them out completely, while others wanted to trap them on a prison planet that would sap their extraordinary abilities. That planet was Earth. My ancestors fought a war over this, and the whole thing would become our Great Shame. That about sum it up?"

"You left out the part where you Denzans also betrayed the Etherazi and trapped them between universes," Zara said, picking her teeth with her pinkie claw. "Explains why they have it out for you."

Melian lifted a spoonful of soup, but then dropped it back in her bowl. "Yeah. That too."

"I could show you the vision," Aela offered without turning around. "Seeing is believing, as the saying goes."

"Oh, I believe," Melian said. "I think I'm good on the first-hand replay."

"No one should have to see that," Batzian protested. "You shouldn't have even shown Hiram without asking us."

"Without asking you," Aela said, then paused for a moment. "Do I require your permission, Batzian? Do I take instructions?"

"No, I mean . . . ," Batzian stammered.

It wasn't like Aela to be so prickly, but I guess we were all still feeling a bit raw from Ashfall, even those of us without skin. "Hiram seemed to take it well, anyway," I jumped in as Batzian fumbled for a response.

"Yeah, so well that he's been crying in his room ever since," Zara said with a snort.

"I think it's a good sign," H'Jossu said. "I've been watching a lot of Earth sitcoms lately. To mellow out, you know? I would say eighty percent of the troubles there stem from humans not being in touch with their emotions. It's a real problem for them."

"He's in touch with one emotion," Zara replied. "Being a little bitch."

"By the tides, Zara, enough," Melian snapped. "Not everyone needs to be as cynical as you."

Zara leaned back in her chair and crossed her legs, looking at us one by one. "You still don't realize what den *Eastwood* has, do you?"

I found Zara's use of "den *Eastwood*"—the way the Vulpin named their tight-knit clans on Stonelea—to be surprisingly comforting. But apparently Batzian didn't agree.

"We aren't a *den*, Zara," he said. "This is a Serpo Institute training vessel. One that we're going to get thrown off of when we're expelled from the institute."

"Can't get expelled if we don't go back," Melian said quietly, earning a surprised look from her brother.

"What do you mean, Zara?" I asked. "What do we have?"

"We call it *suqatal*," she replied. "A powerful secret. Leverage.

Think about it. The entire universe hangs on the information we possess. We should get something out of that, no?"

There had never been a war fought on Zara's home world of Stonelea. Instead, the Vulpin settled their disputes through cloak-and-dagger games of assassination and subterfuge. Murder and manipulation was a way of life there. It didn't surprise me that she'd view the Origin as more opportunity than curse. Even so, I found myself shaking my head, a little grossed out at the idea.

"What do you think? That someone's going to cut us a check for our story? Buy the movie rights?" I asked.

"I don't know what that means," she replied. "But yes."

"'Suqatal' translates to 'deadly truth,'" Batzian said. "You're really downplaying the deadly part."

"Don't be so literal," Zara said.

"What good is any of this succotash shit if humanity turns against Denza?" I asked. "Or if the Etherazi use this as an opportunity to attack again? Or if Denza decides to leave humanity stuck on Earth?"

I ticked off the possibilities on my fingers as I thought of them. I hadn't really sat down and laid out the possible repercussions until now. They all sounded bleak. In theory, I guess humans and Denzans could have taken the Origin in stride and agreed to do better in the future with mutual understanding and forgiveness. That sounded too ridiculous to actually say aloud, though. Plus, I knew things didn't go that way. Goldy had already spoiled the ending.

"Yes, all that might happen," Zara said with a totally

inappropriate grin. "But don't you understand? We control the information, so we decide. We'll never have as much power as we have right now."

Melian slouched in her seat. "I don't feel powerful."

"None of what you're saying matters," Batzian told Zara. "It'll be up to the captain to decide."

"*Pah*, the captain." Zara rolled her eyes. "He's all talk. If it had been up to him on Ashfall, Reno would've crushed us all."

My eyes narrowed. "Watch it now, Zara."

"Oh, don't take it so personally, Syd," she said. "I like your uncle. He's a good man. And as the oldest, he deserves our respect. This is his ship—sure. But it is also *our* ship, you know? We took it. We did what needed to be done."

She meant the two of us—first double-teaming Darcy and then managing to defeat Reno. Zara was right. When the shit hit the fan on Ashfall, it had been the two of us who'd sprung into action. I pushed aside the vision of our older selves staring down at a burning Earth. We did what needed to be done, all right.

"I trust the captain will do the rational thing and bring us back to Denza," Batzian said. "The Senate needs to hear about this, and the institute—"

"The captain won't be the captain if we go back to Denza," Zara interrupted. "We'll lose the *Eastwood*. Lose our freedom. Lose our *suqatal*."

"I'm okay with that," Batzian said.

"They'll probably send us back to the mushroom farm," Melian said, thumbing her lip. "We'll have to work for Father. Just where he said we'd end up . . ."

A dark cloud passed across Batzian's face, but he shook this off. "That doesn't sound so bad to me anymore."

"The vise will close on us eventually," Zara continued. "We need to use our leverage while we still have it."

"I am that leverage, yes?" Aela spoke up, their robotic voice flat. The wisp had been silent for so long that I'd forgotten they were back there, reading the star charts. "That's what you mean. I'm your *suqatal*. What did Vanceval call me? A message in a bottle."

"Not just you, Aela," Zara said, shrugging. "Also the weapons I rescued from Ool'Vinn's cache. Weapons that can actually hurt humans."

Aela pointed at the screen where they had isolated some distant nebula. "The last known whereabouts of the Ossho Collective were here, in the Comorra system. I believe they were observing the thawing of the planet Cor-IV, which occurs only once every two millennia. I want to return to them."

Melian cleared her throat uncomfortably. "Can you even return to them, Aela? I mean, you're—"

"Corrupted, yes," Aela finished. "I will never be allowed to rejoin the whole. But I can still communicate with them. Share the experiences I gained on Ashfall." The wisp spun on their heel and turned to me. "You said you would take me home, Syd."

"I did," I said. "I will."

"It'll be up to the captain," Batzian said.

"We already discussed it. The captain agreed," I replied. "We'll go meet the Ossho."

"See how you listen to Aela? That's power." Zara drummed her nails on the table. "*Suqatal.* The wisp knows their worth more than any of you."

The meal broke up shortly after that, but I hung around to talk with Aela. The wisp hadn't budged from their spot at the vid-wall, the suns of distant star systems reflected in their faceplate.

"Hey," I said. "You doing okay?"

Aela turned to look at me like they hadn't realized I was still there. "Syd."

"Yep," I replied. "That's me."

The exo-suit's head bobbed back and forth in a slow nod, like the wisp was listening to their own internal monologue. I wasn't sure thought even worked that way for Aela. Did they have conversations with themselves in their cloud-brain? Did they use first-person narration? It didn't feel like an appropriate time to ask.

"Can I show you something?" Aela asked.

I glanced at an imaginary watch. "We're aimlessly floating through a dead system. I think I can squeeze you in."

I thought Aela would pull something up on the vid-screen, but instead they led me back to their room. Aela didn't have the furniture that the rest of us had—their chamber was completely empty except for ducts in the floor and ceiling that sterilized the air for whenever the wisp wanted to leave their exo-suit.

"Oh, you meant *show* me something," I said when Aela sealed the door behind me and accessed their control panel to begin the air-cleansing process.

"Yes. I will need to enter you."

"Are you flirting with me?"

Aela cocked their head. "That was a joke," they said. "You're joking."

"Yeah, I—*blech*—" I snapped my mouth shut and closed my eyes as jets of mist sprayed from the ceiling and floor, soaking my clothes and scouring my skin. It was kind of nice, actually. I'd showered since Ashfall, but I hadn't really felt clean, like the grime of that place was still attached to me.

"Ready," Aela said.

"Hold on," I replied, remembering how my uncle had done a whole formal routine the last time Aela had attached themselves to our minds. I bowed at the waist, trying to remember the words. "I consent to have you in—"

"Unnecessary," Aela said. Their faceplate popped open and the cloud streamed forth, flowing swiftly into my nostrils and mouth. For a moment, I tasted burned toast and electricity, and then—

I was on a beach. This spot was on Denza, the planet's three moons hanging like lanterns in the twilit sky. Behind me, I knew, was the craggy bowl of the crater that surrounded the capital city of Primclef. The air was salty and warm, the purplish waves gentle as they lapped at the shore.

"I remember this place," I said. "You brought me here during orientation."

"You remember," Aela said, almost sounding surprised. "Good."

The wisp stood at my side. Every time we did one of these mind-merges, I was always struck by the appearance they chose—like a humanoid-shaped streak of lightning. Aela was taller than me here, long-limbed, with broad shoulders and curving hips. In place of hair, a flowing comet's tail of swirling magenta rippled out from their head, like a wild streak of marker in a kid's drawing. Aela's expression was unreadable as they stared out across the water. I remembered how they smiled when they first brought me here, totally at ease, and excited to share this place with me.

"Of course I remember," I said, lightly touching their arm, a fizzy feeling on my fingertips. "This is one of your favorites, right?"

"Yes," Aela said. "It was."

I took a closer look at Aela. There were subtle changes to their form. Fine cracks as thin as a spider's webbing spread across their bare arms and legs. Last time, their eyes had looked like pools of quicksilver, but now seemed duller, like ash from a cigarette.

"Are you—?" Stepping around to get a closer look at my friend, the sand dug sharply into the bottoms of my feet. The beach looked completely normal, but every grain of sand felt like a tiny razor blade. "*Ow*, Aela, what the fuck?"

"It's not right," Aela said flatly. "Tell me what isn't right."

I stood still, trying not to even shift my weight, but no matter what I did it felt like I was standing atop a pile of thumbtacks. "Sand doesn't feel this way," I said, my voice shaking a bit with the pain. "This is like torture."

Aela blinked their eyes, and a bit of the iciness seemed to melt away. "I'm sorry, Syd. But I need you to remember. Remind me what this place felt like."

It wasn't easy to focus with hundreds of tiny needles digging into my heels, but I called to mind the sensations of the beach. The sand packed and soft, the way you could squeeze the grains between your toes, the soothing coolness of the muddy patches closer to the water . . .

"Yes," Aela said. "I remember now."

I exhaled as the stabbing sensation on my soles was replaced by normal-feeling sand. I checked the bottoms of my feet just to make sure they weren't gashed, but they were totally fine. The pain had been all in my head—no less real, though, for being imagined.

"Never realized you wisps could plug people into painful memories," I said.

"I'm sure your ancestors realized that."

I scratched the back of my neck. "You're probably right."

Looking around, I noticed other changes to the beach scene. When Aela first brought me here, there had been Denzans enjoying the view. Now the place was completely empty. There were supposed to be boats on the water, but those were gone, too. Instead, huge shadows swam beneath the waves, dark and foreboding, like leviathans. What had once been a pleasant memory now felt grim and foreboding, and that was without the broken glass digging into my feet.

"This is because of what happened on Ashfall?" I asked.

Aela nodded. "I've been corrupted. The experiences that I've accumulated have been damaged. In some cases, they're gone completely. I cannot remember when we met, Syd. In my stored memories, one day you are just on the *Eastwood* and we are friends.

But what came before is gone."

"That sucks," I said. "I made a lot of really good jokes when we first met."

Aela smiled sadly. "I'm sure."

I held open my arms. "I remember how we met, though. And I remember this place, too. Couldn't you just take those memories from me?"

"If you'd permit me, yes, I could use your memories to restore some of my experiences, like I already have with the sand," Aela said. "At least, that would work for our meeting. But for this place . . . it would be like a copy of a copy. Understand? The differences might seem subtle to you, but to me they are glaring."

I glanced over at my shoulder at the sea serpents prowling beyond the shore. "Not so subtle, actually . . ."

"The truest form of this memory is gone forever," Aela said quietly. Their comet tail of hair curled around their angular shoulders like a blanket. "What's worse is that this was not my experience to destroy. It belonged to the collective. All the experiences they lent to me when I was made into a wisp are now tarnished. They will never return to the Ossho. Just like me. I am experiencing sorrow, Syd. And something like loneliness. I have never experienced those emotions before. Normally, that would be cause for celebration, a unique experience. But I do not like this at all."

I thought of the wisps that Aela showed me back on Denza, the ones who had their chemistry damaged during their time away from the collective. They had opened a storefront called Remembrance and spent their days helping older Denzans relive pleasant memories from their past.

I started haltingly, not sure if anything I could say would make a difference to Aela. "Those wisps you showed me in Primclef, they didn't . . ."

"You are going to tell me that their life as exiles didn't seem so bad," Aela interrupted. "You cannot understand what it's like, Syd. To be a part of something bigger than yourself. To be awash in the accumulated experiences of millennia. I am not meant to be alone like this. I am not meant to be an *I*—not forever, at least. I am but a few sentences torn from a larger manuscript without the possibility of restoration. What meaning can I have?"

I frowned and stared out across the ocean with Aela. Slowly, details were being restored to the scene before us, probably from Aela tapping into my own memories. Eerie beasts still snaked through the water, but they were joined now by scattered fishing boats and some strangely still Denzans on the shore. It felt like the set of a movie before anyone said action.

"Is that why you want to go back?" I asked. "Are you hoping there will be a way to fix you?"

Aela shook their head. "No. I know it's impossible. I would only spread my contamination to the rest of the collective. I only want to share with them what information I've gathered. The Origin, as you think of it."

"You think they'll want to know that?"

"That we were once a messaging system that evolved sentience and has learned to take pleasure from our programmed purpose?" Aela tilted their head back as a breeze blew in off the ocean, salty and cold. "It's a good story, I think. One that the collective would be incomplete without. I think they will appreciate the information."

I thought about breaking the news of the Origin to my own species. I didn't think humans and Denzans would react with the same cold detachment as the Ossho.

"Yes," Aela said. "Cold detachment. That's a good way of putting it. Also, a good description of my future."

"Okay," I said with a sigh, "first, you're reading my mind too much."

"Sorry."

"Second, you won't be alone, Aela. I know we're no substitute for a . . ." I waved my hands in the air. ". . . a, uh, giant cloud of all the experiences in existence? But you have the crew of the *Eastwood*. You have me and . . ."

I trailed off, biting the inside of my cheek. I'd never been good in these situations—hell, I'd never *been* in one of these situations—one where I had to console someone. My mom and I moved too fast on Earth. I never had a friendship that deepened enough for me to be a shoulder to cry on. My friend was in mourning for a loss that I could barely comprehend. The words I had to offer didn't seem like much comfort by comparison. Like, *Yeah, you can never be restored to the collective consciousness that you've come from, and you'll never feel whole again, but at least you get to hang out with a bunch of arguing riffraff on a stolen spaceship as we knock the whole universe on its ass.* What could I say or do that would be worth shit? "Do you want a hug or something?"

"Yes," Aela said. "I do think that might help."

"Oh."

So I pulled Aela into my arms. Their skin crackled against mine, like pulling on a sweater fresh out of the dryer. I squeezed them and they squeezed back, the magenta streaks of their hair flowing around us. I exhaled deeply and squeezed my eyes shut when they started to well up. I know I was supposed to be comforting Aela, but it hadn't really hit me yet how badly I'd needed a minute like this, too.

"My first truly new experience since corruption," Aela said in my ear.

"Oh yeah?" I replied. "How is it?"

I felt their smile like a vibration against my neck. "It's a start."

6

Carefully, I pulled my consciousness back from the Vastness, sliding through the wormholes and their interconnected star systems. The information—endless and mazelike—throbbed at the front of my mind. I knew from experience that if I took in too much or released my grip too quickly, I could spiral out of control and set my brain on fire. Been there, done that.

When I was safely back inside my own head, I pressed the button on the chair's arm and raised the Wayscope's goggles. The lights on the *Eastwood*'s bridge felt penetratingly bright, and I had to squint until H'Jossu stepped in front of me, providing me with shade and also a squeeze bottle of fluids that I sucked greedily from.

"Well?" Zara asked. "Those of us with primitive brains are waiting."

I'd been using the Wayscope to map out a route from our current location to the Comorra system, where the Ossho Collective was located. Batzian and Melian sat in front of their own consoles, monitoring my progress, their faces both grim. I made eye contact with Melian, and she shook her head.

"I could try again," I said. "Maybe I missed a shortcut."

"You didn't," Batzian replied. "Your mapping was flawless."

"Eighteen wormholes," Melian said. "That's a lot of space to punch. Someone's bound to notice."

"How much time?" Zara asked, peeking at the route I'd charted over Batzian's shoulder.

Both Melian and Batzian looked to me, like they didn't want to be the ones to break the news. I leaned forward, elbows to knees, and massaged my temples, which were still tingling from the Wayscope.

"Twenty-six months," I said.

Zara barked a laugh. "Very funny."

"Um, that's a generous timeline," Batzian added. "It would mean finishing off what little remains of our sedatives. We could make it to the Comorra system and the Ossho Collective in twenty-six months, yes, but after that we'd only be able to travel at our present rate. By year three, our provisions would be running dangerously low and our fuel cells would be nearly drained."

When we'd gone off mission to fly to Ashfall, we'd been in high-speed-chase mode after Vanceval and his hired goons. Expending our sedatives to fly at unsurvivable velocities hadn't seemed like a big deal because we could just contact the institute for a pickup. There was also the chance that we'd find my father, and a cure for the Wasting, and be hailed as heroes. None of that had worked out, like, at all.

"You're talking about the time after we get there like that's the bad part," Zara growled. "Two years stuck on this boat? Most of it conscious? Haven't you heard the stories of exploration madness? When we finally get to a port, I'll be wearing your ears on a necklace."

H'Jossu scratched the top of his head. "That's a long time to go without real sunlight. I'm not sure I can do it. Sorry, Aela."

The wisp stood next to the captain's chair, which was still empty, while my uncle recovered in the med-bay. I kept my head down, not yet ready to look at them. After our journey to their disappearing beach, I couldn't bring myself to disappoint Aela again.

"Two years is a long time for organics," Aela said, no inflection in their tinny voice. I actually couldn't tell if that was a question or a statement.

"There have to be options," I said. "We can figure this out."

"Well, you charted a course using only new wormholes," Melian replied. "We could get there much faster via established routes."

"But that would mean passing through space monitored by the Serpo Institute," I said, shaking my head. "That'd be like willingly driving through a police checkpoint."

"We won't be able to outrun any pursuers," Melian said. "Not without significantly increasing our travel time afterward."

"We'll figure this out," I said, finally looking at Aela. The ink-streaked magenta cloud swirled behind their faceplate in a way I somehow interpreted as disappointed. "The captain should be coming around soon. He might have some ideas."

"I should go check on Hiram. His bio-tape probably needs changing," Melian said. "Should get his thoughts, too."

"Wow. We must really be desperate," Zara said.

"I wish you'd leave him alone," Batzian quietly said to his sister. "Hiram can take care of himself. It isn't safe."

"He's *not* taking care of himself, though," Melian replied. "Relax. He's not going to hurt anyone."

While the twins bickered, Zara bent to study Batzian's console. She tapped one of her claws against the screen. "Hey. What about this system here?"

Batzian must have felt Zara's fangs were a little too close to his ear, because he leaned away as he answered. "Jeuna? What about it?"

"How far are we from that?"

"Three jumps on the current route. About three months. But Syd didn't use the Wayscope to plot a path to Jeuna, so there might be a quicker way there." Batzian double-tapped the system and enlarged it. "But why do you ask? There's nothing out there."

I checked my own console to get a closer look. The Jeuna system contained five rocky planets, all locked in steady orbit around a white-hot sun. The Serpo Institute had already surveyed all these worlds and flagged them as rich in a variety of ores and minerals, but none of them were inhabitable, and none of them sustained even the most basic forms of life. A wormhole was maintained there, probably as a waystation between more interesting destinations, but otherwise the system was unmonitored. Our route to the Ossho Collective took us through Jeuna for only a couple weeks, and I'd made sure to keep us well clear of the existing wormhole to avoid any detection from Denza.

I looked to Zara, waiting for her to elaborate. The points of her ears twitched back and forth as she leaned up and away from Batzian.

"Never mind," she said. "It's the wrong system. I was thinking of Jonah."

"Not familiar with that one," Batzian said.

"You wouldn't be," Zara replied and swayed out of the room.

Batizian and Melian exchanged mystified looks. I had a pretty good read on Zara, though. She knew something. And she didn't want to say what it was in front of the others.

Sure enough, once I left the bridge to check on my uncle in the med-bay, Zara caught up with me. She slipped out of the doorway to the gym and fell into step with me in a way that would've made me jump during our cat-and-mouse games on Denza. I'd gotten used to the Vulpin's sudden lunges out of concealed spots, though, and greeted her with a raised eyebrow.

"Well, well, well. If it isn't Zara," I said, hamming it up. "I've been expecting you."

"You're stupid," she replied with a flash of her fangs. She held out a tablet in front of me, the planetary map of the Jeuna system once again spread out across the screen. "We should go here."

"Jeuna," I said. "I thought it was Jonah."

"I don't even know if Jonah exists," Zara said. "That was just a lie for the others."

"Wow," I said. "You're so slick."

"I should not even be telling you this," Zara continued. "In fact, if you prove to be an idiot and don't accept my plan, I may have to cut out your tongue to keep you from spreading what I'm about to tell you."

"Noted," I replied. "So what's in Jeuna?"

Zara pinched the screen and zoomed in on a gray swirl of rocks that it would've been generous to call a planet. I squinted at a churning blob of asteroids labeled on the star chart as Unstable-J3. The Denzans hadn't even bothered to give this conflagration a real name when they charted the system. I brushed Zara's hand aside and zoomed in closer to get a better look. Unstable-J3 had an unstable core, which led to constant tectonic activity across the surface. We weren't just talking earthquakes here; the planet was literally exploding. Chunks of the crust were tossed into space, only to be caught there by the body's gravity field and eventually sucked back down to the molten core. In effect, the planet was locked into a never-ending combustion.

"Okay," I said, "so you're picking out a place for us to kill ourselves?"

"No, dummy," Zara said. "Vulpin live there."

I raised my eyebrows. "No way."

Zara traced a finger across the edge of the swirling rock band. "On the edge of the Torrent. A space station. Well, an armada of mostly broken-down ships lashed together with some of the more stable asteroids. A *Vulpin* space station. Last I heard, it was den Stryke in charge."

"What are they doing out there?" I asked with a shake of my head.

She popped a shoulder into the air. "Oh, this and that. There are riches to be found in locations the Denzans have deemed too dangerous."

"So the institute doesn't know about this place?"

"Of course not," Zara said. "Which makes it perfect for us. There are always traders at the Torrent. Someone will have sedatives for sale. We can continue on your pointless errand to the Ossho without wasting two years of our lives."

I looked up from the craggy swirl to study Zara. "Do you have a hookup we can use?"

"My father brought me there years ago, back when he was a big man, before den Jetten fell to disgrace," she replied. I don't think Zara had said two words about her den since I'd known her. She must've seen the curiosity in my expression, because her ears twitched in annoyance. "Don't ask me any more questions, Syd. I know it's there, and I know they'll have what we need. The rest we will have to improvise."

I rubbed the back of my neck. "Okay, but what do we even have to trade?"

"Fuel cells? Reno's Battle-Anchor? One of the twins?" Zara shimmied her shelf of fur. "We'll have to see what they want on the Torrent. Good goes to bad, we have you and one-legged Hiram. We take what we need. Easy and dirty."

I exhaled through my nose. A Vulpin black market hidden on the edge of an unstable celestial body. Honestly, it seemed like a much better plan than an excruciating two years of mostly undrugged space travel.

"Can I take this?" I asked, and Zara let go of the tablet. "I'll show it to the captain."

She smirked. "Yes, show it to the captain. It is nice of you to let him pretend he's in charge. But I see it in your face. The decision has been made."

I started to walk away, but hesitated. Something else Zara had said was still bothering me.

"You really think it's pointless to go see the Ossho?" I asked.

"Have I not made that clear?" Zara asked. I waited for her to elaborate, and she rolled her eyes. "Look, I like Aela as much as you can like one of those wisps. I don't want them to suffer. But this is all just a distraction. A delay so you don't have to make any bigger decisions."

"Like what?" I asked. "What, exactly, am I putting off to help our friend?"

Zara's hand slipped into her fur and came back with a dagger, which she balanced precariously on her first two fingers. "Who to fight. Whose world to wreck. Yours, the Denzans', maybe both. You know it's coming, Syd. It's okay if you want to take a vacation first. But that doesn't change what's coming."

I shouldn't have asked. Zara always brought me too close to the truth.

7

Tycius had spent the last few days locked inside the hibernation pod. The coffin-shaped capsule held his body in a gravimetric field, stabilizing him and augmenting his body's own healing process. Honestly, I didn't really understand how it worked. Although it sometimes felt like a lifetime, I'd only been off Earth for about six months. So much of the technology on the *Eastwood* and Denza was still beyond my understanding. I mean, I could hit buttons and make stuff work, but I couldn't have explained the how or the why. It was all basically magic.

I'd been planning to hit the button that ended his hibernation, but he was already on his feet when I entered the med-bay. He stood with his hands clasped behind his back, studying a blown-up scan of his brain on the vid-wall.

"Captain, you're up," I said. "I was just coming to take you out of the oven. You're sure that brain of yours is fully baked?"

Like I said, I didn't quite understand the technology.

Tycius swiped away his scan and turned to me with a tired smile. "I ran a self-diagnostic from the inside. I'm fine. Close enough, anyway." He held up a hand. "And you can stow that Captain stuff. Ty is fine. Or Uncle."

"But you are the captain," I replied. Zara might have been ready to brush off my uncle's role as merely symbolic, but I wasn't. Because if my uncle wasn't the captain of the *Eastwood*, that meant someone else had to be in charge.

Okay, why dance around it? That meant *I* had to be in charge. And I didn't know what the hell I was doing.

"Captain of a stolen ISV, away without leave from the Serpo Institute," Tycius said. "It's my boyhood dream come true."

"Really?"

"No," Tycius replied. "Right, then. Bring me up to speed, Cadet."

I clicked my heels together like I'd seen soldiers do in movies. "We're a little more than three cycles removed from Ashfall, traveling at the maximum speed we can afford. We've kept all comms channels closed since Reno's last transmission. Staying in the dark."

"Good," Tycius said. "Where are we heading? Did you map a route to the Ossho Collective?"

"We're still trying to figure that out," I replied. "Check it . . ."

I called up the Ossho Collective's position on-screen and explained to my uncle the situation with Aela. I showed him the excruciating flight plan that I'd pulled from the Wayscope, then filled him in on the secret Vulpin outpost in Jeuna.

Tycius rubbed his chin as he studied the churning Torrent with the same disbelief I'd felt when Zara first told me. "Doesn't say much for my fellow spies that we had no idea this place existed."

"Yeah, well, no offense to the Denzan intelligence agency, but I think the Vulpin have you outfoxed."

My uncle winced. "Don't let Zara hear you use that term." He paused for a moment of thought, then nodded to himself. "This sounds like a solid plan. Solid in the sense that it exists and it's our only choice. You should refresh the Wayscope chart to bring us in closer to this Torrent, and then we'll get underway."

I breathed out through my nose and relaxed back against one of the med-bay cots. "I thought you might have reconsidered the trip during your hibernation. Like maybe you only agreed because you were concussed."

Tycius shook his head. "No. In fact, I think the Ossho could be valuable allies for whatever happens next."

I quickly picked up on his train of thought. "Aela was able to guide Hiram through the Origin without making him lose his mind. Maybe learning the truth doesn't have to mean war."

"The Ossho trapped on Ashfall, I think it was as disturbed as everyone else that had been stuck there," my uncle said. "Maybe we don't need to hide the truth . . ."

"We could just lightly edit it," I said, straightening up. "All right. I'll stick my head back out in the Vastness and get us a fresh course."

"Hold on," my uncle said. "Don't you think we should talk about him?"

"Him who?"

"Marcius," Ty said. "Your father."

"What is there to talk about?" I asked. "He's dead."

My uncle's mouth opened in a sad little O, but he didn't say anything. I hadn't meant for my words to come out so harshly. I guess I wasn't prepared for the question. Outside of my nightmares, I'd gotten pretty good at compartmentalizing. There were real in-the-now problems spiraling out of our trip to Ashfall. I wasn't going to expend my mental energy dwelling on the past when the future gave me enough to worry about.

"That's it?" Tycius asked finally.

I shrugged and looked down at the floor. The tiles gleamed bright enough to sting my eyes.

"Fine, I'll talk about him," Tycius said. "Your father was a good man. He was brave, and he cared about humanity and making the galaxy a better place. When he left you, I know he didn't think it would be forever."

"He sent a message to Vanceval," I said quietly. "But not to us."

"That's true," Tycius replied. "You saw what happened in that temple. How it changed us. I don't think your father and his crew were as lucky as we were. I doubt he was thinking clearly . . ."

I shook my head. "You wasted years of your life on Earth searching for me," I said. "And here you are again, trying to clean up his messes. You don't have to always defend him."

Tycius closed the distance between us and touched my chin. "It wasn't a waste, Syd. Not to me."

Unconsciously, I found that I was squeezing my ring finger, right where my dad's cosmological tether would've been. I took a deep breath and braced myself to talk about the shit I didn't want to talk about.

"After my mom told me what I was, I used to dream about coming out here, into the Vastness. Following in his footsteps. I used to dream about *him*, literally. I still do. Whenever my mom and I were hiding in some shithole rental, I'd fantasize about my dad coming back for me. He'd save me from Earth and we'd go on a big adventure. And then you found me and it became real—he *was* alive; there *was* an adventure." I rubbed my hands over my face. "Except he never wanted me to find him."

"He never wanted anyone to find him," Tycius said. "Every night while I was searching for you, I used to check on his cosmological tether. I'd go to sleep praying that his beacon would still be lit when I woke up."

I snorted. "Yeah, thanks for that. I did the same thing when you gave that to me."

"Turns out, while I was whispering for him to hold on, his worries were already at an end." Ty's jaw tightened. "I'm angry with him. I'm disappointed in the decisions he made. Try as I might, I don't know if I'll ever understand him. But I'm also grateful to him. Because without Marcius, I would not have gotten to know you."

I nodded my head and looked away. I'd known my uncle was working up to a line like that, and I'd thought I could steel myself against the sentimental crap and brush it off, but my eyes still stung with tears. Somebody wanted me. I wasn't abandoned.

Tycius squeezed my shoulder. "I know it's been hard. But I hope you don't regret leaving Earth. If I'd known I was pulling you out of your life there to chase a ghost . . ."

My uncle trailed off. "Hard" was an understatement. My quest to find my father had ended in heartbreak and death. On the way, I'd had an encounter with an extradimensional Etherazi who had made a pretty convincing case that I was destined to destroy Earth. I'd also been beaten up and kidnapped. I guess be careful what you wish for when it comes to childishly dreaming of space-faring adventures.

And yet, even considering all that, I *didn't* regret leaving the Earth behind. I missed my mom, but I didn't miss our lifestyle, traveling the country like fugitives and hiding from a government conspiracy. I felt more at home here, on the *Eastwood*, than I ever had on Earth. Yeah, the fate of the galaxy weighed heavy on my shoulders, but oddly enough I didn't mind. Maybe it was because my mom had raised me to feel constantly in danger, so I was used to it. In a weird way, it felt *right*. I'm not sure what that said about me, that I was almost glad to be at the center of all this chaos, like it belonged to me.

I'd hesitated too long, and my uncle was watching me close now. "I don't regret it, Uncle," I said. "Not at all."

His face filled with relief. "Your dad would be proud of you, Syd. I know it." He cleared his throat then and began to straighten the front of his uniform. "Right. Better get to work. How's the rest of the crew doing?"

As I finished bringing my uncle up to speed, I lingered on what he'd said about my dad. Would he be proud of me? My dad had sacrificed everything to keep Ashfall's secrets buried on the dead planet. He'd warned Vanceval of my existence and indirectly gotten a Vulpin assassin dispatched to Earth to get me. My dad had died with the belief that Tytons were once the scourge of the universe and that humanity couldn't be given the chance to follow in their footsteps. In a way, I'd undone pretty much everything my dad had worked for.

My uncle was wrong. I didn't think my dad would be proud of me.

I think he'd be afraid of me.

8

"Syd? Can I show you something?"

Melian stood in the doorway to my room, holding a tablet. I sat up from where I was sprawled on my bed, massaging my temples. I'd used the Wayscope earlier to map us out a new route to Unstable-J3 and the Torrent. I found a path that brought us close to the planet with only two wormholes to transit. It would take us about a month of flight time and only use half of our remaining sedatives, which was good, just in case the black market Zara was so confident in didn't actually pan out. The residual headache from thrusting my consciousness out into the Vastness was starting to fade.

"What's up?" I said.

"Um." Melian hesitated a moment before sitting down in the bed next to me. I thought I saw a flare of color in her cheeks, our shoulders touching as she leaned in to show me what was on her tablet. "I should probably show this to the captain, but I didn't want to get anyone in trouble . . ."

On-screen was a live schematic of the *Eastwood*. I recognized the Subspace Piercer that we'd soon use to punch a wormhole into the fabric of this galaxy, the ship's thrusters, and then all the other parts of the ship that I couldn't have labeled if my life depended on it. If I ever got back to the Serpo Institute, I should really sign up for an ISV maintenance and engineering course.

"I was going down the prep checklist for interdimensional jumps and noticed this," Melian said, highlighting a jutting antenna that extended perpendicular from the *Eastwood*'s inner spoke.

"Ah yes," I said. "Look at that."

Melian eyed me. "It's our communications relay."

"Of course it is."

"It's aimed," Melian said.

"Aimed at what?" I squinted at the schematic. "What does that mean?"

"We're flying dark with comms down," Melian patiently explained to my dumb ass. "That means the communications relay should be down. Literally. Like pinned against the hull of the ship. I thought maybe it was just an oversight—we could have depowered the relay without actually retracting the antenna and still be off the grid, but no. The maintenance logs show that the antenna was raised in the last twelve hours."

I took the tablet from her as if that would help me catch on quicker. "You're saying someone used the comms?"

"I can't say that for sure," Melian said. "There's no record of an outgoing message in the system. If someone *did* send out a message, they could have scrubbed the logs but not realized they also had to reset the position of the comms relay."

"Or this could just be a malfunction or an oversight," I said. "Right?"

Melian half shrugged. "Sure. Maybe I'm just being paranoid. But I thought it was strange enough to bring up."

Hopefully it was nothing, I thought. But what if it wasn't? Who would want to sneak a message off the *Eastwood*? It wasn't me, my uncle, or Melian. That kind of subterfuge didn't really seem like H'Jossu's style, and Batzian wasn't enough of a rule breaker to try something like that. Aela had no reason to make contact with the outside universe. Maybe Zara had sent some kind of heads-up to her people on the Torrent to let them know we were coming— covert communications were definitely right up her alley—but I couldn't see why she'd do it without telling me. That left only one person.

Hiram.

"For what it's worth, we're in unchartered deep space," Melian continued. "If a message was sent, we'll be long gone before anyone can trace it back to our location. Unless someone picks it up in the local star system. But we're alone out here."

"I hope you're right," I said.

After Melian left, I went down the hall to Hiram's room. He'd been keeping to himself since the day we fled Ashfall. He hadn't shown up on the bridge for any of our crew meetings and never came to any mealtimes. He was avoiding us. I heard him shuffling around the ship during off hours, when he'd go down to the galley to scavenge some leftovers. Otherwise, Hiram never left his room. To be perfectly honest, I was okay with that. I didn't know how to handle Hiram or what to say to him. Even after he'd broken down in my arms following his mind-meld with Acla, I was still a little afraid of him. It was a relief to have him in hiding. One less problem to deal with.

Hiram didn't answer when I knocked on his door, so I let myself in.

The stink almost knocked me back into the hall. Hiram's room was a wreck. The smell of sweat, vomit, and something like burned bacon hung in the air. His bed was unmade, the sheets stained with sweat and crusted blood. There were discarded wads of bio-tape littered across the floor, all of them discolored a rusty brown. How many times had he changed the wrapping on that wound of his? And why was it still not healing?

At some point, Hiram had also properly trashed the place. He'd punched a hole in his mirror and torn up all the plants from their wall-gardens, scattering dirt and uprooted greenery everywhere. His shower was clogged—I didn't want to know with what—and there was a puddle of standing water in there. I don't know how Hiram had stayed cooped up in this grunge.

But he wasn't there now.

"The hell is this . . . ?" I muttered to myself as I picked up a tool from Hiram's desk.

A welding torch taken from engineering. Why did he have that?

I'd stumbled into Hiram's fortress of depression. This room was a cry for help, and I felt a sudden surge of guilt at having left Hiram to his own devices for the last few days. On our very first meeting, I'd written Hiram off as a meathead. I guess I still thought of him that way—like he didn't have feelings, or, if he did, they didn't run that deep. The state of Hiram's room made it look like he was drowning.

I moved with some urgency, quickly checking all the common areas but not finding Hiram in any of them. Only after I'd checked the kitchen did I realize that I was still holding the blow-torch I'd found in Hiram's room. I headed to the engineering bay, but he wasn't there either.

He was in the airlock.

I almost walked right by him. Probably would've if not for his BO. Hiram stood in the same airlock where H'Jossu and I had trapped him just a few days ago. His uniform was unbuttoned and hanging off one muscular shoulder, his hair greasy, pimples popping up from the skin on the back of his neck. He still favored his leg, a fresh roll of bio-tape tied around his wound. His back was to me. He had the airlock's vid-screen tuned to the exterior cameras, and he was just staring out into the cold Vastness. The airlock's interior door—the one H'Jossu and I had hidden behind—was still open, but Hiram leaned against the wall on the other side, right next to the release button, which would seal the room and jettison the contents into space.

You didn't need to be a psychologist to know what he was thinking.

I cleared my throat and edged up behind him, close enough so that I'd be in the way of the ultonate doors if Hiram decided to trigger them.

"Uh, hey, buddy," I said. "You're up and about."

The muscles across Hiram's shoulders tensed. "*Buddy.* Are you my buddy, Syd?"

"Sure," I replied with as much sincerity as I could fake. "You want to hang out or something?"

"You don't even like me," Hiram said quietly. "You don't have to pretend."

"I mean, I don't dislike you," I said. "Anyway, come on. Got some jump prep I could use your help with . . ."

That was a total lie. I didn't need his help with anything. But I figured the best thing I could do in this situation would be to talk Hiram out of the airlock.

He snorted and finally turned to look at me. Hiram's face was startlingly pale, the color accentuated by the dark circles under his eyes.

"What do you actually want . . . ?" Hiram trailed off, noticing the blowtorch I still held in my hand. "Oh. You went in my room."

"I wanted to ask you if you'd tried sending a communication off the ship," I said. I glanced down at the torch, turning the tool over in my hand. "But then I saw how you've been living, man. A real cry for help. And you're apparently doing some welding?"

Hiram's eyes narrowed. "I didn't send out any messages. We're supposed to be running dark, aren't we?"

"Just wanted to check," I said, rubbing the back of my neck. I'd immediately jumped to being suspicious of Hiram, and now, getting a look at him, I saw that he was barely holding himself together. I felt guilty and so found myself uttering a lame justification. "You haven't been showing up on the bridge. I wasn't sure you knew about the comms blackout."

"Yeah." Hiram sniffed. "Sure."

"So, let's talk, dude," I said. "Want to tell me what's going on? What's up with the blowtorch? Maybe we can go chill in the lounge instead of the airlock."

Hiram glanced at the button on the wall that would've vented him into space. He shook his head. "I'm not going to do what you think I'm going to do, Syd. You don't have to worry. I wouldn't have bothered with the blowtorch if I was just going to off myself like a chump."

There was a flash of the old Hiram. Still, I didn't understand what he was saying. "What do you mean?"

With an annoyed sigh, Hiram peeled down the layer of bio-tape that covered his upper leg. I winced and took a surprised step back. If he'd wanted to get me out of the way of the airlock door, all he had to do was show me that wound. The hole in Hiram's leg had stopped bleeding, at least, but now it was just a twisted, ridged mess of burned flesh and scar tissue. The skin was bright red and oozing brownish pus in places, healing in a way that looked like it would forever painfully pull the rest of his skin, even with the bio-tape to help it along.

"Goddamn, dude," I whispered.

"I had to burn it closed," Hiram explained. "Whatever that shit was on the bullet, it wouldn't let me heal. Had to use the torch. You've probably been burned before, huh? Back on Earth? Toasted your little fingertips over the bonfire you were using to keep warm?"

I shook my head. "Not like that."

As if abruptly realizing how insane he looked, Hiram hurriedly rewrapped the bio-tape around his leg. "It feels better now that I've burned it out," he said sullenly. "Never hurt like that before, Syd. Didn't think it was possible. I can still feel that shit crawling around under my skin, I swear. Probably won't ever be normal."

"We don't know what was in that stuff," I said. "Maybe we could . . ." I hesitated. I was going to tell him we could run some tests, but that meant letting Hiram know that Zara was in possession of a small stockpile of the ooze-like substance that had harmed him. Didn't seem like the sort of information it'd be helpful to share.

Hiram didn't seem to care anyway. He waved me away and turned back to the vid-screen, gazing out into the endless Vastness beyond the airlock.

"Okay," I said cautiously. "So what are you doing down here?"

"Wanted to look out the window," he replied.

"There are vid-walls all over the ship," I said.

Hiram shrugged, and his shoulders stayed bunched afterward, like he was bracing for a blow. "It was smart of you to bring me in here. You didn't know how I'd react. Could've lost my shit like Reno."

"Are you losing your shit now?" I asked. "Is that why we're here?"

He ran a hand through his hair and made a face at how greasy his fingers came back. "Aela showed me . . . Reno got so mad. Pure psycho. Like the Denzans had been playing a trick on her all these years. And then a guy like Batzian—you've seen how squirrelly he is now. Afraid of me because of the Tytons. You're half-and-half, Syd. How did you feel when you saw where we came from?"

"I . . ." I honestly hadn't paused to consider that question. "I didn't feel rage," I said after a moment. "And I guess it wasn't fear either. Not exactly. It was like—I don't know. One time I tripped in a souvenir store and bumped into a rack of snow globes. They all went flying, and all I could do was watch. And in that moment, you know, before they all shattered, I remember thinking . . . well, how much trouble am I going to get in for this? That's how it felt to me. Like, this is going to suck, but it's an open question as to how much and for how long."

Hiram nodded as I spoke. He crossed his arms and tried to draw himself up straighter, but that wasn't as easy as it should've been with his bad leg. "I was supposed to be a protector of the universe," he said. "A hero of Denza, like my grandfather. What will they think of me when this comes out?"

I thought back to how Hiram stood watch over the market on Denza and harassed a group of young Vulpin for doing some light shoplifting. And then there were all the times he leaped from terrace to terrace on Primclef, frightening as many passersby as he impressed with his abrupt landings. His notion of being a champion for Denza included a lot of unnecessary swagger, but now didn't seem like the time to point that out.

"It doesn't have to come out," I said, knowing how unlikely that was. "We don't know what—"

"The secret's out, Syd," Hiram interrupted me. "You set it free when you left Reno alive. Darcy—she doesn't know which way is up—maybe she could've been talked around when things calmed down. But Reno? She's going to make a mess. And there's no telling what my grandfather will do once he finds out. Fucking Earth-obsessed old bastard. They should've never let any of you off that mud-ball."

"You came from that mud-ball too," I said. No matter how many times I heard the same anti-Earth lines from Hiram, no matter the situation, I still took the bait.

"Bullshit," he replied, thumping his chest. "I'm a Denzan. Not like you're a Denzan, not by blood. But that's my planet. My home. What do I care about some shithole on the other side of the universe?"

I started to reply, but Hiram was picking up steam now. The more pissed off he got, the more I saw the old Hiram come out. Maybe letting him vent was a good way to pull him back from the edge.

"My grandfather always talks about going back there and uplifting our people," Hiram continued. "He doesn't get it. Earth was a test. The Denzans plunked our ancestors down there to see if they could evolve into a less shitty version of themselves. And from everything I heard about your planet, those dumb-asses failed. Knowing what we know now? They should rot down there. Check back in a couple centuries, see if they've evolved enough to not be dickheads."

"Kind of harsh," I said.

"Man, I hope I can be there when my grandfather finds out the truth about his precious Earth," Hiram went on. "I'd love to see the look on his face. But you know that's not going to be the end of it, right? If he can't fix the Earth, he's going to want to take people off it. Unlock the prison. We can't let that happen, Syd."

I hadn't made up my mind about the future of Earth. I mean, according to my Etherazi stalker, I was destined to destroy it. In that future, apparently, I'd sided with Hiram. But there were a lot of good people on Earth, people like my mom. They hadn't failed some test. They didn't deserve to suffer.

"Maybe we should look at the Origin as an opportunity to do things differently. To make better choices," I said. "Not all humans are necessarily prone to evil. I mean, you're not talking about sending yourself back to Earth."

"Shit, if it means keeping the Tytons from making a comeback, I'll go," Hiram said. "I'll waste away down there just like my . . ." He paused, his bluster fading away. "Do you know about my parents, Syd? You got in tight with Gramps. Did he mention them?"

I tried to remember if the other Butlers had ever come up. Rafe liked to complain about how the institute kept the humans in space all the time so they couldn't settle down and make babies. I always assumed Hiram's parents were stationed on ISVs and rarely came back to Denza.

"They work for the institute, right? Out on survey missions?"

"My dad, yeah," Hiram replied, his voice getting quieter. "He's first mate on a boat where he bangs the captain. His Denzan girlfriend. I got a couple little hybrid half siblings I've never met, actually. My mom, though . . ."

Something on the vid-screen caught Hiram's attention. He hobbled forward to take a closer look. I didn't notice anything, and, to be honest, this was the most interested I'd ever been in something Hiram was saying.

"Hiram? What about your mom?"

"Nah, forget that," Hiram said. "Look at this."

I had to edge around Hiram's broad frame to even see what on the vid-wall had so captivated him. At first, all I saw was the Vastness—endless darkness dotted with distant stars. It wasn't until one of those stars flickered out of sight for a moment that I was able to focus on what Hiram had already seen. A sliver of movement in the darkness, cutting toward us.

"What the . . . ?" I muttered. "Can we zoom in?"

Hiram pressed his palms against the vid-wall and did a dramatic swiping motion. The *Eastwood*'s cams centered the object—it was blurry and pixelated from still being so far away, but there was no doubt what it was.

"You said someone was fucking with the comms, right?" Hiram asked.

I could barely nod a response. I felt frozen in place, not at all sure how Hiram could sound so calm.

"Well," he said, "now we got a missile chasing us."

9

"How long do we have?" I shouted.

Aela tilted their head, examining model trajectories on their console. "We—"

Zara interrupted, covering her ears. "Turn the damn siren off, already. We're all here."

"Ah, apologies," my uncle said. "Regulations."

From the captain's chair, he flicked a few buttons and muted the alarm that had summoned us all to the bridge. The last time that red alert had blared throughout the *Eastwood*, it had been because of the Etherazi I'd accidentally summoned during my virgin use of the Wayscope. This time, at least, someone else had called disaster down on us.

"If we maintain our current velocity, we have four hours until impact," Aela answered my question.

My initial panic at seeing a missile streaking toward us was at least a little overblown. Everything happened slower in space. Whatever. This was my first missile.

"And then how long until . . . ?"

"Presently, the ship is fifteen minutes behind the missile, but closing fast," Aela replied, anticipating what I was going to ask. "I project impact and boarding within a five-minute window."

Once we'd spotted the missile, it wasn't all that difficult to pinpoint the ship that it came from. Of course we all recognized it. There was only one other ship in this dead system and it was the Vulpin cruiser that belonged to Nyxie and her mercenaries. At least, it used to belong to them. There was no doubt in my mind Reno was captain of that ship now. The Vulpin craft reminded me of a piranha, cutting through the Vastness toward us.

"Shouldn't the *Eastwood* have warned us about this?" H'Jossu asked.

Zara chuckled. She stood right in front of the bridge's vid-wall, tail sashaying back-and-forth as she admired the missile. "Vulpin stealth technology isn't going to get made by this floating class-room's dinky censors," she said. "Dumb luck that we spotted it at all."

H'Jossu shambled up beside Hiram who was leaning against the back of a chair, trying not to favor his leg too much. The Panalax patted Hiram's shoulder. "Good thing we've got eagle eye here to protect us."

Hiram grimaced and nodded. At least this emergency had gotten him out of the airlock. "It's what I do," he said, although the usual bluster rang a bit hollow.

"What I don't get is how this bitch found us at all," Zara said, clicking her nails against her teeth. "We're flying dark. It's a big system. What did she do? Pick a direction and get lucky?"

Melian started to say something, but I cut her off with a quick glance. I wanted to phrase what happened in a particular way.

"We forgot to actually put the comm relay down," I said. "We thought we were dark, but she must have been able to ping us."

My gaze swept across the crew, gauging their reactions. Frustration, confusion, swirling cloud of magenta gas—and there, a twitchy frown barely concealed and a sidelong look to avoid my eyes. I knew that look. It was guilt.

It was Batzian.

"That's not what you said—," Hiram started, but I cut him off.

"It doesn't matter how she found us," I said. "All that matters now is how we get away."

"Right," Tycius agreed. "Zara, you seem familiar with the missile. What are we dealing with?"

Zara's ears twitched with delight at being able to talk about weapons. "It's a kneecapper," she said. "The good news is it probably won't kill us. Pirates use them when they want to take a crew alive. It's tracking our energy core. That's where it will hit. Magnetize our fuel cells, knock out our systems, maybe some light explosions. No big deal, really."

"No big deal," Batzian said. "What you just described will shut down life support."

Zara shrugged. "We've got space suits and plenty of time to put them on. I'd be more worried about the boarding if I were you."

"Can't we shoot it down?" I asked. "Doesn't the *Eastwood* have some kind of missile defense?"

It was a stupid question, and I knew it. The Denzans were pacifists. Of course they didn't outfit their training vessels with any anti-artillery measures.

My uncle shook his head. "We don't have anything like that, Syd. The Vulpin have their war games, yes, but until now the galaxy has been a peaceful place. I think we might be the first ISV to ever be fired upon."

"Cool," H'Jossu said. "New record."

"What if we shut down the core?" I asked. "If that's how the missile is tracking us . . ."

"It would spare us the impact, at least," Zara said. "But then we'd be a sitting duck for Reno. We could at least prepare to be boarded on our own terms."

"No way to outrun her," Tycius said, then glanced at Aela for confirmation.

"We could immediately go into hyperspeed and begin our course to Jeuna," Aela said. Their metallic fingers executed some quick projections. "However, sustaining the speed we'd need to outpace both the missile and the ship would take our sedatives below the level necessary to reach the Torrent."

"They can't have much more sedatives on board that ship than we do," Tycius said thoughtfully. "It's a gamble, but we could try to run and hope that she dries up first."

"I don't like it," Zara said. "Putting us under with an enemy at our back. Bad way to die."

"No one's going to die," Melian put in. "Captain Reno wouldn't kill us." She looked around for support. "Right?"

I thought back to our journey to this system, how I'd come awake at one point during the transit and saw Reno sending a transmission back to Rafe Butler. The veins popping out on her forehead, teeth gritted—she wasn't sedated then. She'd gutted it out.

"Reno won't slow down," I told the others. "Even if she runs out of juice, she'll keep coming until the speed breaks her."

Melian's frown grew. "We could open the comms and talk with her. I don't believe the captain, ah"—she glanced at my uncle— "the old captain would want to hurt us."

Batzian lowered his head like he was embarrassed by his sister. "You weren't there, Melian. It changed her."

"She fired a missile at us. I'm not inclined to talk," Tycius said. "But I don't see a better option than killing our core and then trying to prevent a boarding."

I shook my head and called up a map of the system on my console. We'd barely made any progress to the Ossho, barely even gotten out of the shadow of Ashfall. "There has to be a way," I said. "Isn't there, like, an asteroid field or something we could lose her in? You know, evasive maneuvers?"

Everyone was looking at me. H'Jossu patted my shoulder.

"We're not in an X-wing," he said. "This isn't that kind of movie."

"What about the Subspace Piercer?" I asked. "We could open

up a wormhole right in front of her. Send her into another dimension."

Tycius raised his eyebrows. "That would likely obliterate her. No, Syd. I won't condone it."

"Second we rotated the wormhole puncher in her direction, she'd probably fire hers up," Zara said. "Mutually assured destruction. It's what I would do."

I sank back in my seat. There was no way out. We were going to have to kill the engines and face Reno. Yeah, I was all about *Run, lie, fight*. But the "fight" part was supposed to be a last resort.

Hiram had been pretty quiet throughout the discussion, but he finally cleared his throat. "We do have one weapon on this ship that could stop her."

H'Jossu clapped his paws together. "Please say, *It's me*."

Hiram's brow furrowed. "What? No. Don't be such a dork."

"Would've been a dope one-liner," H'Jossu said quietly.

Ten minutes later, we were all in the *Eastwood*'s loading bay, standing in a semicircle around Reno's Battle-Anchor.

"It's *me*," Hiram declared. "In *that*."

H'Jossu pumped his fist.

The mechanized suit stood about ten feet tall, its central cockpit open as if inviting Hiram to climb inside. The armor weighed about half a ton—we'd probably have improved our travel speed if we dumped it—thanks to the carapace's ultonate lining. It was called a Battle-Anchor because the precious metal running through the suit resisted Etherazi temporal disruptions. That's what the suit was meant for—killing creatures like my buddy Goldy. Besides hydraulic legs and piston-powered fists, the Battle-Anchor also featured a laser cannon and an energy sword, all meant for slicing open an Etherazi and destroying its core.

"Just so we're clear, your plan isn't to hurl yourself in a mech-suit at Reno's ship and punch her into submission," I said.

"Guys, I sometimes have other ideas besides beating people up," Hiram said. "The Battle-Anchor has weapons. We could use them to take out the missile."

I patted the suit's arm where the laser was mounted. I turned to Aela, who had once walked me through an introduction to these armored behemoths. "What's the range on this thing?"

"The beam loses effectiveness at 215 meters." It was Zara who answered. When everyone looked at her, she ruffled her shelf of fur. "What? It's the only weapon the Denzans have ever built. You think I wouldn't study it?"

I spun up some rough calculations in my head. The laser had a range of more than two football fields, which seemed like a lot, but in the empty space of the Vastness and at the speeds we and the missile were traveling . . . "We're going to have to let them get close."

"A six-minute window," Melian said, apparently having done the math herself. "Between when the missile enters the Battle-Anchor's range and impact with the *Eastwood*."

Tycius was more focused on Hiram than on the Battle-Anchor. My uncle put a hand on the taller human's shoulder. "Have you had any training?"

Hiram hesitated. "Technically, that would be a no," he said, and Zara groaned in response. "But Reno let me take it out a few times. You know, for fun? I can shoot the laser. The suit does most of the work anyway."

"We'll have to open the cargo doors and drop you out of the ship," Tycius continued. "You'll be in zero gravity."

"I can handle it," Hiram said, adding, "Captain."

"Assuming Hiram can hit his target, that still leaves Reno's ship," Zara said. "She'll be close enough to ram us shortly after we take out the missile. Smart thing would be to carve her up with that laser until she stops chasing . . ."

Hiram shook his head. "I won't do that. Not with Darcy on board."

"Then we kick on the jets as soon as the missile is taken out," I said. "And hope we can outrun her."

While the rest of us were talking, Batzian had gone up on his tiptoes to inspect the Battle-Anchor's laser array. I'd been watching him out of the corner of my eye as he hurriedly punched information into his tablet, then returned to studying the laser.

"Actually," Batzian finally said, "I might have an idea. How do you humans say it? To hurt one bird with two stones?"

"Kill," I said. "And it's . . . never mind. What have you got, Batz?"

I used the shortened name that Batzian hated on purpose. Because he was the one who'd opened the comms, which meant he was the one who'd brought Reno down on us. He was so eager to explain his plan that he didn't even correct me. It was his fault we were in this jam, and now he was trying extra hard to get us out of it. The question of why he'd opened the comms—and who he'd contacted—gnawed at the back of my mind. Everything was happening so fast, and we all needed to work together, so I kept that to myself.

Batzian's idea was solid. The best we had.

I just hoped we could trust him.

10

In my space suit, I felt like a burrito about to be microwaved. The air inside my helmet felt damp from my heavy breathing, and the internal defoggers kept kicking on to make sure my vision stayed clear. With my gloved hands, I gave the metal cable attached to the Battle-Anchor one last tug to make sure it was hooked securely to the back of the mech-suit, then double-checked that there was enough slack leading back to the crank.

I'd be responsible for activating the pulley system that reeled Hiram back onto the *Eastwood*. I hadn't trained much for zero gravity, but my enhanced strength meant I was the best person to stay down here in case anything went wrong.

It was just Hiram and me in the cargo bay now. Most of the crew had spent the last few hours making sure everything in the hold was secured—our excess provisions, fuel cells, medical supplies—we didn't want anything flying off the ship when we opened the cargo doors. Meanwhile, Batzian and Melian worked on their part of the plan, while Captain Tycius made subtle alterations to the *Eastwood*'s course so that, when the bay doors popped open, Hiram would have a direct line of fire on the missile.

Aela's tinny voice came over the shared comms channel. "We're nearing the window. Are you ready?"

I double-checked the cable for probably the tenth time. "I'm good," I said. "What about Batzian?"

"The code has been uploaded to Hiram's laser," Batzian said. "Remember, you need to maintain a steady connection to the missile for three seconds."

"Three seconds," I repeated. "Got that, Hiram?"

He didn't respond. I couldn't see Hiram's face from my position, but I could see how the massive pincer hands of the Battle-Anchor clenched and unclenched, doing their best to replicate the motions of the suit's pilot.

"Two minutes to the window," Aela said.

I jogged around the Battle-Anchor to see where Hiram was sealed in the cockpit. Only his face and shoulders were visible behind the glass—it wasn't glass, exactly, but a clear substance of infinitely greater durability that was laced with a webwork of ultonate veins—his skin aglow with the reflection of readouts from his HUD. I hopped up on the knee joint of the exo-suit so we could be face-to-face, but Hiram's eyes were faraway, as if he could see the Vastness beyond the cargo bay doors.

I slapped the glass. "Hiram! Are you with us?"

Hiram flinched and finally focused on me. "I hear you."

I took a closer look at Hiram. Only a few hours had gone by since I'd caught him in the airlock, maybe thinking about hurting himself. I switched over to a private comms channel so only Hiram could hear me.

"This isn't going to be some blaze-of-glory shit, is it?" I asked.

"No," Hiram said firmly, meeting my eyes. "I'm good, Syd. I'm good."

"Thirty seconds," Aela announced.

"Remember," I said to Hiram. "You've got to hold the laser on the missile for a three count for the download to take."

"I know," Hiram replied.

"Three seconds," I repeated. "You can count that high, right?"

Hiram grinned. "I'm going to beat your ass, Syd."

I put my fist against the glass. "Shoot straight," I said.

"Always do," Hiram replied, and tapped his own fist against the other side of the cockpit.

I hopped down and scrambled back to my position at the crank. The apparatus was meant for loading heavy cargo onto the *Eastwood*. It was all mechanized. All I had to do was throw the switch to reel Hiram back in and supervise.

"Window opening in ten . . . ," Aela said, and continued the countdown.

Almost as an afterthought, I remembered to check the cable on my own space suit that secured me to the back wall of the cargo hold. Didn't want to go flying out into the Vastness after Hiram. Everything was where it should be.

"Five . . ."

Behind us, the airlock to the cargo bay slammed shut. Hiram raised the arm of the Battle-Anchor, aiming where he assumed the missile would be, ready to fire as soon as the doors opened.

"Entering distance window," Aela announced. "Opening cargo doors—"

I lost the rest of Aela's transmission as the cargo hatch sprang open and all the oxygen rushed into the vacuum. For a moment, it was incredibly loud, like a windstorm at my back. The heavy-duty crates we'd secured to the floor creaked and held where we'd lashed them. The corrugated metal floor made a high-pitched ringing as the temperature dropped.

And then everything was eerily silent. All I could hear was my own breathing in my ears. And Hiram's over the comm channel.

There was the missile and the Vulpin mercenary ship behind it. It was like staring down a giant bullet as it inched toward you in slow motion. At least, it felt slow. We were actually traveling incredibly fast. I felt the clip on the back of my space suit strain to hold me in place against the tug of the Vastness.

The cable at my feet whipped through the pulley mechanism. Hiram let himself go, floating clear of the cargo bay.

Watching everything unfold through the rectangular opening of the cargo bay, in the oppressive silence of the Vastness, it all appeared sort of fake. Hiram's Battle-Anchor looked like a toy against the silky black backdrop of space. The missile and Reno's intimidatingly pointy Vulpin ship right behind it—they looked like cutouts floating in a bad diorama. For a moment, my breath caught from the unreality of it all.

Hiram didn't have that same moment of awe. He immediately aimed the laser, fixing it on the missile within a heartbeat. If we hadn't made some adjustments to the Battle-Anchor's calibrations, he probably would've burned a hole straight through the explosive. But we had bigger ideas than that. All he had to do now was hold steady for three seconds so that the code Batzian and Zara had whipped up could download and—

I glanced down at the pulley rig. There was still a lot of slack in Hiram's line, the weight of his Battle-Anchor carrying him farther and farther from the *Eastwood*. He was making his pass with the laser too soon.

"Hiram!" I yelled over the comm. "Wait to stabilize!"

The line snapped taut. As it did, the Battle-Anchor jolted and Hiram lost his target. The mechanized suit begin to spin head over heels.

"Shit!" Hiram yelled.

"Upload unsuccessful," Aela reported.

"Get yourself lined up," I said, trying to keep Hiram calm and focused. I kept a wary eye on Reno's ship. Surely, she'd seen that we were trying to mess with her missile. I wondered if there would be a response.

The Battle-Anchor had thrusters in its heels. Hiram activated them, bursts of compressed air firing from his feet, narrowly preventing him from going into a complete spin and becoming tangled with the cable. A more skilled pilot—one with actual training—would've brought the Battle-Anchor around smoothly, but Hiram was wobbly, improvising. He tried to make another swipe with the laser, but this one was completely wild as he'd over-corrected with the thrusters. Hiram grunted with annoyance over the comm as he tried to level himself off.

Meanwhile, the missile and Reno's ship were getting closer.

"Two minutes until impact," Aela said.

Jesus. We'd already gone through a third of our window.

"Plenty of time," I said with a calmness I didn't actually feel. "Get stable and take another shot, Hiram."

"Yeah, yeah," he grunted.

Just as Hiram finally got pointed in the right direction, a white flash erupted from one of the fang-like appendages on Reno's ship. I squinted, seeing little specks of red in my vision.

Zara came on the mic. "She's shooting at you."

"Shooting at us?" I replied. "With what?"

"Bullets, dummy," Zara replied. "Much faster than the missile. You better get to cover."

Those weren't flash-induced floaters I was seeing. They were the red-hot tips of a swarm of projectiles, like buckshot from a shotgun blast, except this ammunition was roughly the size of my forearm. Zara wasn't kidding. The cloud of chaff had already passed by the missile and was streaking right for the *Eastwood*.

I stared out at the Battle-Anchor. "Hiram doesn't have any cover."

"I'm good," he said. "The suit can handle it."

As he said this, Hiram got the laser pointed at the missile again.

He kept steady, even with a volley of projectiles hurtling his way.

I did the count-off in my head as I pushed off from my position at the crank, diving for a stack of containers that I hoped could absorb ship-to-ship artillery.

One one-thousand, two one-thousand, three one-thousand . . .

That should be it. We should have it.

"Hold it there," Batzian came on. "Upload is slower than anticipated."

"How much—?" I started to say.

"Can't—!" Hiram yelled over me. He was interrupted by a sharp impact as one of the bullets smashed directly into his cockpit glass.

Reno's blast peppered the side of the *Eastwood*. Fist-size pimples popped up in the walls where the bullets struck the outside of the ship. The *Eastwood* might have been a floating schoolhouse, but it was still built to withstand the rigors of space. The outer armor held.

The interior of the ship wasn't so lucky. Sections of the floor and ceiling were sheared away as the bullets ripped through the hold. Crates broke apart, including the one I'd been hiding behind. I was knocked to the other side of the cargo bay, surrounded by hundreds of dried mushrooms that were rapidly icing over from the exposure. I hit the wall hard and bounced back, narrowly avoiding an explosion of a fuel canister, glob of shapeless flame briefly floating through the air before being snuffed out by the lack of oxygen.

I came through intact. I mean, all my limbs were still attached,

I could breathe, and I didn't feel any frostbite spreading from a tear in my suit. There wasn't time to do a more thorough inventory than that. I activated the thrusters in my own suit and swam back toward the pulley rig.

"Hiram!" I yelled. "You good?"

The Battle-Anchor had definitely absorbed some direct hits. One of its arms—luckily not the one with the laser array—was bent backward like the hinge had busted. A shower of sparks floated ceaselessly from one of the suit's thrusters, indicating that something was wrong internally.

I just hoped all that damage hadn't knocked out Hiram. Or worse. He was slow to answer.

"Don't shout, my head's already ringing," he said finally, his comm crackling more than before. "Took one to the dome over here. I got all kinds of warning lights going off. Don't know what they mean . . ."

I half expected another volley to fire from Reno's ship. Strangely, there was no follow-up to her first attack. Maybe the mercenary vessel was short on bullets, or maybe the old captain had a change of heart.

"Ninety seconds," Aela announced.

"Yeah," Hiram replied. "No shit."

The missile was much closer now. In another minute, it'd be close enough for Hiram to reach out and touch. Flashes of exhaust puffed from the missile's tail as its internal guidance system adjusted its course toward the *Eastwood*'s core.

"Now or never," I told Hiram.

"Even he can't miss at this range," Zara observed over the comm.

Hiram raised the Battle-Anchor's arm, the motion looking a bit janky from the damage the suit had sustained. He fixed the laser on the tip of the missile, but then his aim swung suddenly wide.

"Damn it," he snapped. "What the hell was that, Syd? Why am I moving?"

I glanced down. "Oh, shit   "

Hiram was moving because Reno's bullets had torn away a section of the floor right where the pulley system was attached. The steel plating was slowly peeling away, the cable that anchored Hiram to the *Eastwood* going with it.

And, as soon as I noticed it, the entire mechanism came loose.

I dove forward and grabbed the cable. An alarm blared in my ear as jagged metal from the ruined floor tore through the thigh of my suit. Luckily, the Denzans had built in an auto-patching system, but I would still be leaking oxygen.

The more important thing was Hiram. At the speed we were going, if I lost my grip on the cable, he'd got flying into the Vastness. We'd be hundreds of miles away from him in a few seconds. He'd be alone and afloat in a very empty galaxy, and our engines would be blown, with no way to search for him.

The cable dug into my palms through the space suit. I managed to swing my legs up and brace them against the freshly torn rend in the cargo bay floor and then leaned back, straining against the weight of the Battle-Anchor. The thing weighed half a ton and was straining against a vacuum. I'd never tested my human strength quite like this before. Searing pain lanced through my forearms, my shoulders, my chest. My muscles felt like shredded meat.

"Syd? What's wrong?" His voice sounded a little shaky, worried, probably because I was spitting and grunting into my comm.

I couldn't respond. My teeth were gritted so hard that I pictured them shattering in my mouth.

"The line broke and he's holding you," Tycius said. My uncle's voice was calm and cool, no doubt in his mind we were going to survive this. "You better make that shot, Cadet, then reverse your thrusters back on board."

The laser steadied. The upload began. Reno's ship edged closer, but no further artillery exploded forth.

Four seconds. Batzian had been off on his calculations by an entire second—I guess that's what happens when you rush through the math in a couple hours. Four seconds seem like an eternity when your joints are popping and your muscles are screaming bloody death as you drag a mech-suit behind a spaceship flying at hyperspeed.

But also? Not going to lie. My life was cool, and I did cool shit.

The upload completed. It was a pretty simple trick, really. With Zara's knowledge of Vulpin technology, Batzian had been able to recalibrate the laser in Hiram's Battle-Anchor to match the communications system on Reno's vessel.

We hacked her kneecapper. And we sent it back where it came from.

As soon as the missile spun around, Hiram kicked on his thrusters. The cable went slack and the weight eased off me and I threw up in my helmet from the exertion and collapsed.

I didn't see Reno's engines get magnetized and her ship lurch to a stop in our wake, but I'm told it was pretty satisfying.

11

You tasted blood leaking from the loose tooth in the back of your mouth, the one you couldn't stop wiggling with your tongue. A cloud of your own stale breath filled your helmet. That wasn't the worst part of living inside this space suit—a suit that was made for Vulpin and thus a little too small for you, so that you felt constantly hunched over. The worst part was your own filth. Letting go of your piss and shit and sitting in it, basically. The suit had a waste tank, a filtration unit, but you could still feel it down there.

Disgusting.

At least, since you hadn't had anything real to eat for days, the urge to go to the bathroom had died down. A small comfort in this misery.

Was it days? Weeks? You couldn't be sure anymore. Stranded in the perpetual night, there was no way for you to really keep track of time.

You were adrift. The *Eastwood* had blown out the Vulpin ship's core.

There was no way to repair it. The life support system had gone down shortly after that. You only had auxiliary power now, enough to keep the emergency lights on and the comms up. Batteries. At least the mercenary ship was provisioned for these kinds of desperate circumstances. There were rations and plenty of spare oxygen.

Especially since there were just the two of you.

Your old crew had left you behind again. Not that you could really blame them this time. Looking back on everything that had happened since Ashfall, you were pretty sure that you'd chosen the wrong side. Not that you would ever admit that. Too stubborn. But once you made it back to Denza, you were going to try to set things right.

If you made it back.

Your stomach murmured. It couldn't growl anymore—it was too empty for that, too long since you'd had anything solid to eat. At this point, your belly just made these sad little mewling sounds and twisted in on itself like a dry dishrag being wrung out. A pitiful reminder that it was time to clip another bag of feed into your suit.

The Vulpin ship was stocked with bags of preprocessed rations. Not the good stuff. You got the sense from the beat-up interior of the ship— the short circuits that went down even before you'd been struck by a missile, the layers of grime built up in every corner, the sloppy patch jobs across the hull—that Nyxie and her crew weren't really raking in the dough before Ashfall. Or maybe this was just the hard life that mercenaries chose when they took to the Vastness and you'd gotten too used to the comforts of the *Eastwood*.

Anyway, the rations. They were bags of rust-colored slurry that you sucked down through the straw built into your helmet. They didn't eat meat on Denza, so you'd only tasted it a few times in the little bits of round jerky that Rafe sometimes smuggled in for his pizzas. The slurry was definitely meat, gamey and rich, with an undercurrent of the smoky peppers that the Vulpin preferred. One bag a day claimed to provide all the nutrients a Vulpin needed and, as the sword-swinging mascot on the bag promised, would also make you "sharp as a den Acen blademaster."

The hours after mealtime were always the worst. The Vulpin meat-shake left you feeling keyed up, like you'd had ten cups of coffee. The best way to pass time on this dead ship was to doze off or enter a fugue state, staring out at the Vastness until your mind completely turned off. Those were literally the only things to do. Feeling like you wanted to bounce off the walls and wrestle somebody? That was almost as tor-turous as living in this space suit.

But you had to eat. You had to survive. So you pushed out of the cramped compartment that had become your quarters and floated down the hallway to the mess.

You tried not to look at the bodies on the way, but you always did.

The Vulpin mercenaries were lashed to the bunk beds in the bar-racks. You'd brought them in there during the first day of listless floating through the Vastness, back when you thought it made sense to keep busy. Better to keep them out of the way than have them float-ing around the bridge where they'd died.

Where they'd been *killed*. Because make no mistake, even if she hadn't done it with her own hands, Captain Reno had killed them.

You'd tried to talk her out of it.

It started as soon as the ship picked up the signal from the *East-wood*. They'd made a mistake and turned their comms on for long enough to get spotted. Nyxie herself had noticed the ping and eagerly reported the coordinates to Reno, probably hoping that would earn her some points. She should've kept her mouth shut.

There was a lot of space to cover. You'd been traveling in the wrong direction, based entirely on a guess of which way the *Eastwood* might go. Reno wanted to get to them as quickly as possible. Like the *East-wood*, the Vulpin ship was low on sedatives.

Reno didn't care. She went to the maximum speed endurable without sedatives. The maximum speed *she* could endure.

Days later, your bones still ached from the force of travel, but at least you were alive. Your half-human physiology kept you upright with only a few nosebleeds and the lingering soreness as punishment.

The Vulpin weren't so lucky. They were in their seats on the bridge, plugged in, ready for the sedatives to flow. But the drugs never came. By the time they realized that Reno intended to fly at this speed without juicing them, the pressure was too great and they couldn't get out of their chairs. Not that they would've stood a chance against her. The first Vulpin died of an aneurysm only a few hours in.

You tried to reason with her. "We'll overtake the *Eastwood* with plenty of juice to spare," you said. "Let them have some, Captain."

"We don't know what we can spare," Reno had replied, staring out into the dark of space like she could see the *Eastwood* sailing. "If they pick up speed, we'll have to match. This could be a long chase."

"But—"

"Those Vulpin would've killed you on Ashfall without a second thought," Reno replied. "Toughen up, Cadet."

Nyxie survived the longest. In the end, she'd wheezily begged you for the juice, as the pressure squeezed her chest like a vise.

"I'm sorry."

The words sounded hollow, even to you. The Vulpin had reached up then—drool matting the fur on the sides of her mouth, one of her eyes gone red with blood—and at first you thought she wanted to hold your hand. But she'd been trying to claw at your face. The force pressing down on her was too much, though, and her arm folded back and that's how she died, expending that last bit of energy in an act of complete futility.

And then you were alone with Reno.

Not for the first time, you wished that this Vulpin ship were laid out differently. You needed to pass through the bridge to get to the canteen. That meant you'd have to see her.

From the hallway, you could see the smashed command console. Two fist-size craters right in the center, spirals of jagged metal and severed wires curling away from the points of impact. The occasional spark still popped up from the wrecked controls.

You'd done that. Brought both your fists down as hard as you could, harder even than when Hiram really pissed you off in training. You would've punched through the whole ship if you could have.

Reno had been shooting at Hiram. At Syd. At anyone on the *Eastwood* that might be in the wrong place and caught astray.

"You're going to kill them!"

"Hiram can take it," Reno said dismissively. "Whatever they're planning, we can't let them—"

That's when you'd rushed forward and smashed the controls, stopped Reno from firing any more on your old crew. You caught her by surprise. You even caught *yourself* a little bit by surprise.

She backhanded you with such force that you flew across the bridge, banging your skull on the far wall. Between the blow and the trauma of high-speed travel, you were out. When you came to, the power was out and Reno was roughly shoving you into a space suit.

"You really fucked us, Cadet," she'd said.

In the present, you wiggled the tooth in the back of your mouth, a reminder of the damage Reno had done. The captain was capable of things you never imagined. You'd grown up after the invasion of the Etherazi, when the attacks were mostly an afterthought. Denza was a peaceful place. The most violence you'd encountered was judo class.

Were all humans capable of this? Were you?

You floated onto the bridge hoping that Reno would be asleep, but her eyes snapped to you immediately. Reno sprawled in one of the chairs on the bridge, angled up at the blank vid-wall like she was about to watch a movie. She's taken for herself the one space suit on board that was closer to human-size—the one the Vulpin probably intended for the late Professor Vanceval—but the suit still bulged at the shoulders and hips. You hoped that she was as uncomfortable as you. You also wondered about her leg. The cut that Zara had made across Reno's hamstring wasn't healing like it should've. She'd already exhausted the ship's supply of bio-tape. Was it wrong to wish that she would bleed to death?

"There she is," Reno remarked as you pushed on toward the connecting hallway. You could've turned off the comm-link between your two suits, but you worried that would've just agitated her. "Is it breakfast time already? Or is it dinner? I've lost track."

You ignored her.

"Still with the silent treatment?" Reno snorted. "That's fine, Cadet. It won't be long now."

She clicked a button on the chair's console and the vid-wall activated, the screen's brightness severely muted due to the auxiliary power. At first, you weren't sure why she would waste the batteries, but then you stopped, using a hand on the ceiling to arrest your float off the bridge.

Rafe Butler appeared on the screen.

Hiram's grandfather spoke from the familiar confines of his pizza shop on Denza. How you longed to be back there, to listen to one of his rambling anecdotes about the First Twelve and their brave battle against the Etherazi. Apparently, Rafe had stopped shaving since you'd been off planet, the stubble on his cheeks filling in gray, a sharp contrast to the dyed black of his slicked-back mane.

"I've listened to your message a hundred times now, Marie, and I still can't make sense of it," Rafe said in the recoding. You recognized his tone. It was the one he used on Hiram when he wanted to talk the boy out of doing something stupid without seeming to stand in his way. "If what you say is true, then . . . then we have a lot to work out with *our hosts, don't we? But until I know all the details, I'd appreciate if you could keep a lid on things. Don't do anything rash, okay? Honestly, you sound a little space-mad. We've seen that before, right? We know the signs. Try to focus on home, somewhere happy. And keep your comms on. I'm rerouting a ship to your location, but that in itself is a delicate matter. We don't want to show our hand too soon if—"*

Reno cut the message off there. You glared at her, nostrils flaring.

"When did he send that?"

"Oh, a while ago," she replied. "I forget."

"And you still went after them? He told you not to. He—"

"Rafe Butler is not my boss," Reno snapped. "Do you know how many of our people have trusted him over the years—over the decades? *Oh, Rafe, he'll lead us back to Earth. He'll cure the Wasting and rescue our friends and families.* But there *is* no Wasting. He's spent decades trying to figure out a way to put us all back in a prison."

"He . . ."

No. Forget it. You couldn't be bothered. Arguing with Reno was no way to pass the time. You pushed off again, gliding toward the mess.

"I'm eighty years old," Reno said to your back. "I had two sisters back on Earth. Did you know that? Older sisters. While I was fighting my way to fighter pilot status, they were marrying sad little men and leading sad little lives. They're dead now. I kept tabs on them. They died in slow motion, choking on years of exhaust fumes and coal dust. One of their sons—my nephew, I suppose—he died when some other boy randomly shot up his school. Have you ever heard of such a thing? Could you imagine—creatures like us, dying like that?"

In spite of yourself, you once again slowed your drift and turned to face Reno. She wasn't even looking at you, instead focused on the blank vid-wall.

Could you imagine casual brutality like she described? Of course you could.

"The Denzans selected us—the First Twelve and the ones who came after—for our psychological profiles. Our mental dexterity. Our knowledge of highly complex weapons systems. Our willingness to cut all ties. That's how they selected the ones who came after, too."

You were the child of one of those second-generation Institute initiates. He'd been seduced by your mom, a Denzan, who was part of the Merciful Rampart. They believed that humanity was too dangerous to let loose throughout the galaxy and that hybrids like you would be Denza's only chance to fight them off in the future. You used to think that your mom was a total nutjob, but now you were having second thoughts.

"The only man I ever loved, he *chose* to go back to Earth," Reno continued. "He had a family there. A wife and daughter and eventually a grandson. The Denzans wouldn't let his family off planet. They didn't pass the requirements. So the fool man went back and let himself fall apart on that awful world. A true romantic. But none of it—not him, not my sisters, none of them—should've been stuck there. Generations of our people, robbed of a chance to live like I have. What compensations should the Denzans pay for that? What do you think, Darcy?"

"I think nobody cares about your sob story, you old cunt."

Reno's eyes narrowed. "Some balls on you, Cadet."

Before anything else could be said, the ship rocked back and forth like a tidal wave had crashed against its side. A disturbance in the Vastness, the fabric of the entire star system rearranging itself around a new intrusion.

A wormhole.

Pale yellow light from the ISV's searchlights drenched the deck of your ship. The ship that Rafe had diverted to rescue you was once one of the Serpo Institute's own. At this distance, you couldn't make out the insignia that identified the vessel, but the model was a more rough-and-ready version of the *Eastwood*, a ship prepared to explore new galaxies and everything that entailed. There was no way that the Denzan Senate would've approved a mission like this so swiftly. That meant that Rafe had ships that he could call on at a moment's notice to do his bidding.

You'd have more time to think about what that meant later. For now, you finally disconnected your comms from Reno. You didn't want her to hear you crying. The tears came from relief and suppressed fear and the slow-boiling sense of anger you carried with you everywhere. They felt hot on your cheeks and they didn't last long because you were too dehydrated.

The two of you waited in silence for the ISV to connect a bridge between the ships. Reno stood in front of you, hands on her hips, pretending that her leg wasn't hurting her. You wondered what Rafe had told the crew of this ISV. How would they react to what Reno had to say? You were sure she'd start blabbing about Ashfall at the first opportunity. Would they believe her? Would they see that she'd lost her mind? Both?

You didn't have to wait long to find out. The first astronaut from the other ISV moved through the connecting tunnel with a surprising sense of purpose, striding directly for Reno. His magnetized boots sent thunderous vibrations through the ship. Reno's body language changed as he approached; she went back on her heels . . .

You flipped your comm on just in time to hear her say, "Calm down, she's fine."

And then the boarder flung her out of the way with a force that made you step back, too. Bouncing off the far wall wouldn't hurt Reno, especially not in zero gravity, but there was a certain disgust in the movement that made clear where things stood with the old captain.

The ISV wasn't here for *her*. It was here for *you*.

As you realized this, the man took you by the shoulders and brought his helmeted face close to yours. If you hadn't already expended your tears, more surely would've come then.

"Dad?"

PART TWO

THE MOST DANGEROUS PLACE IN THE UNIVERSE

12

The juice seeped out of my system gradually, full consciousness returning like warm sun on a cool morning. The best thing about the cocktail of sedatives the Denzans used for interdimensional hyperspeed travel was that I didn't really dream while I was under. Occasionally, bits of consciousness bubbled up to the surface, and I was distantly aware that I was sitting on the bridge of the *Eastwood*, zooming through a series of preprogrammed jumps, but mostly I just sank down into nothingness. No danger, no secrets, no lingering visions of my dead father, no Etherazi bellowing about annihilating planets.

The ultimate nap.

"Welcome to Jeuna," Aela announced, doing their best to keep their tinny voice mellow as the rest of the crew groaned their way back to wakefulness. "We are ten hours away from Unstable-J3 and the black-market base known as the Torrent. You have been asleep for approximately seventy-seven days."

Sitting in the circle of chairs on the bridge, everyone on the crew had a fresh-from-hibernation ritual. I massaged the tops of my thighs until the pins and needles started to fade and I was sure I could walk. H'Jossu checked over his splotches of mold, gently rubbing the spots where his fungal form connected to the cadaverous tissue of his host body. Hiram wolfed down a smushed protein bar he'd zippered into his pocket before we started out. Batzian tied back his ponytail and then checked on his sister.

Batzian. Our eyes met across the bridge. He looked away.

Seventy-seven days we'd been out, but it felt like just yesterday that I'd blocked his path in the hallway outside engineering. To me, it *was* just yesterday.

This was a few hours after Reno attacked us. The crew, except for me and Hiram, who were given time to recover in the med-bay, were working in shifts to patch the bullet holes in the *Eastwood*'s hull and make sure we were jump ready. My muscles still burned like hell, and I had a crazy strip of blisters across both my palms from where the cable had dug into me through my suit, but otherwise I felt good enough to move around again. Hiram snoring from the bed next to me was some extra motivation to get going.

I hadn't sought out Batzian for a confrontation, it had just happened. I'd caught him coming down the hallway in his space suit, helmet off, laboring with a crate of spare solar plates to replace the ones Reno had damaged. I got in his way.

"Sydney," he said. "You're up."

"I know you were the one who used the comms," I said.

Batzian's arms shook from the weight of the box. He carefully set it down between us, and I figured he was using those few seconds to concoct a plausible lie. It's what I would've done. But instead, Batzian straightened up and looked me right in the eyes.

"Yes," he said.

"You almost got us all killed."

"I underestimated the Vulpin ship's ability to track a signal at range," he said. "It was a calculated risk. I'm sorry."

I flexed my hands, the skin stinging and tight. "You don't seem all that sorry."

"It's not like you or Hiram have ever shied away from dangerous situations," Batzian said. "It all worked out in the end."

My eye twitched at that. Because Hiram and I enjoyed near invulnerability, we could be thrown into any clusterfuck imaginable? I mean, there was some truth to that—but I at least wanted to consent to risking my ass before hanging it out there. Suddenly, I had a better understanding of Reno's anger, feeling used by the Denzans for all those years. I swallowed that, though, keeping my tone level.

"Who did you message?" I asked.

"We're going to be off the grid for almost three months," Batzian replied. "And then, once we reach this Vulpin outpost, who knows what will happen. In that time, Reno could do anything. At least, that's what I thought when I sent the message, before we left her stranded . . ."

"Get to the point," I said.

"I didn't want hers to be the only version of the Origin out there," he replied. "Someone on Denza—*a Denzan*—should know what's happening. They should be prepared in case . . ."

"In case humanity turns against them," I finished the thought for him. Batzian was already preparing for the war that I was trying to prevent. I guess I couldn't blame him.

He tugged on his ponytail. "I hope that's not what happens, Syd. I . . . I'm not antihuman."

I knew that to be true. The twins had come from a chain of islands on Denza that was absolutely devastated by the Etherazi during the invasion. Melian had once told me that Batzian wished he could be *more* like humanity, meaning less bound to the Denzan code of nonviolence. But I think something changed in him when the Origin infiltrated his brain.

"I can't shake the way Reno looked at me," Batzian continued. "Like I was less than her. Like my existence was completely insignificant. It was the look of the Tytons."

"I get it," I replied. "You shouldn't have done it, but I get it. So who did you message? The institute? The Senate?"

Finally, Batzian looked away from me. "I thought about that, but I worried such traditional contacts would jeopardize our mission. So I went with someone who is used to working a bit out of bounds and who . . ."

I already knew where Batzian was going. "And who already thinks humanity is a menace."

"Yes," Batzian said. "I messaged Arkell."

Arkell. The same Arkell who had his entire arm bound in metal because he once tried to blow up the wormhole to the Milky Way and sever Denza's relationship to humanity. The former member of the Merciful Rampart, an organization devoted to keeping humanity chilling on Earth. The same Arkell who had called me a half-breed when I'd arrived on the *Eastwood* and tried to make my life as miserable as possible.

I'd thought Arkell was the one who sabotaged the Wayscope back when I almost burned out my brain. I'd even accused him and roughed him up a little. It had turned out to be Vanceval, though—the nice instructor, what a twist—and Arkell had even tried to help me when the Vulpin mercenaries had drugged and kidnapped me.

So I had conflicting feelings on the guy. And on the Merciful Rampart. Because, if Reno was any indication, maybe they were a little right about humanity.

I'd taken that conversation into hibernation with me. Now it was seventy-seven days later, and I hadn't reported Batzian's actions to the captain. I didn't know what good it would do. What was done was done. We were heading to a dangerous place, and we all needed to trust each other. Letting the rest of the crew know that Batzian had almost gotten us scooped by Reno didn't seem like such a hot idea.

Or maybe I was too used to secrets and lies.

"We've got approximately three days until we reach the Torrent," Tycius announced. "Get something to eat, get your med scans, and then get some actual rest."

After a seventy-seven-day coma, you'd think the last thing any of us would want would be more sleep. But sedated space travel wasn't actually restful. We weren't mentally aware of any of the rigors of near–light speed, but that didn't mean our bodies didn't still go through them. The aches would come on soon, followed by the fuzzy-headed drug hangover. I already felt like I wanted to pass out again.

I trudged to the mess hall with the rest of the crew. The only one of us that wasn't feeling like crap was Aela, who'd actually been conscious the whole time. The wisp made sure the autopilot did as programmed and that all our vitals remained stable.

"So, what did you get up to for the last couple months?" I asked Aela as they walked next to me.

"I started the self-analysis process to determine which of my experiences are damaged," Aela said, the smog-tinged cloud curling tentatively behind the faceplate. "But this task proved a bit . . . depressing? So I helped myself to some of H'Jossu's catalog of Earth kung fu movies."

Behind us, H'Jossu gasped dramatically and lumbered forward to grab Aela's narrow metallic shoulders. "Which ones did you watch?"

"All of them, I believe."

"This is the greatest news I've ever heard," H'Jossu said. "Tell me everything. Rank them. Rank them *immediately*."

In the mess hall, Hiram sat with his bad leg straight out in front of him, like it was too stiff to bend. Otherwise, he seemed more like himself, scarfing down protein bars at a pace that he'd probably regret later.

"So, Zara, what happens when we get to this Vulpin hideout?" Hiram asked, watching Zara with a wrinkled nose as she mixed some kind of concoction that looked like half bone marrow and half dried jalapeno. "Do we just park the *Eastwood* and say, *What's up*? Is there a password?"

"The Torrent will be hidden," Zara replied. "We'll have to make them believe we're worth talking to. Pique their interests."

Melian tilted her head. "What if they don't want to talk to us?" she asked. "What do we do, then?"

"I doubt that will be a problem," Zara said, flicking a glance in my direction. "But, if they decide to be coy, we have options. Perhaps we threaten to ram them. Or maybe we just shoot Hiram at them and enter by force."

Hiram grinned. "It's nice to be on the same page with you for once, Z. Pretty soon we're going to be besties."

"I'd sooner drink my own piss," Zara replied.

"Kinda sounds like you're warming up to him," I said to Zara, who scowled at me.

"Right?" Hiram exclaimed. "There are way worse things than drinking piss. Wait. That sounded wrong."

The next few days were filled with recuperation and double-checking that the *Eastwood*'s systems were still working correctly. When we were a few hours from Unstable-J3 and the Torrent, I stopped by Zara's room.

She opened the door with her uniform completely unbuttoned, in the process of taping a throwing star under one of her boobs. I immediately looked up at the ceiling out of politeness, which just made Zara snort.

"Ah, right, I forgot tits make your kind nervous." Zara sighed and stepped back, letting me stumble into her room. "What do you want?"

"I thought we should, uh . . ." I heard her uniform snap closed and finally looked down. Zara had turned her back on me and was now in the process of dragging an ornate brush through the styled shelf of fur that ran across her shoulders. I wondered how many different blades she had hidden on her right now. "You said we're going to have to trade with these people."

Zara brushed a little harder. "Anything else might get bloody."

"I wanted to go over how much you managed to steal from Ashfall. We . . ." I tilted my head, observing her. There was something about the way Zara moved her brush—quick, jittery passes across her coat—that made me realize I'd never seen her pay so much attention to her appearance. "Hold up. Are *you* nervous right now?"

"No, shut up," she replied sharply, then seemed to realize how aggressively she was attacking her hair. "It has been a while since I was in a Vulpin place. That's all."

I thought back to my introduction to Zara by way of her memories and Aela. "Right. Back when you stabbed that guy's eye out."

"Kungo called me out," Zara said defensively. "Den Jetten . . . my family. We are not as respected as we once were. On the Torrent, they'll know me. They might . . ."

"I thought you were den *Eastwood* now," I said. "If anyone fucks with you, I've got your back."

"I won't need it." Zara's eyes narrowed in a way that I could tell was pleased. "But thanks."

She picked up her chair, set it on top of her desk, and then nimbly hopped up. With her toe-claws hooked on the seat of the chair, Zara stretched until she could reach the ceiling. She had a knife in hand—as usual, I hadn't seen her draw it—and she ran the blade along a groove in the plating that I wouldn't have noticed from the floor. A rectangle of ceiling popped open and hung there as Zara rummaged around in the space above. I remembered my own goofy efforts to hide my dad's cosmological tether in one of my room's planters and rubbed the back of my neck in shame.

"Should I look away?" I asked. "You trust me to know where your stash is?"

"I trust you wouldn't be able to disarm the traps," Zara replied.

After some ominous clicking and hissing, Zara tossed down a vial of the black sludge onto her bed. Another followed. And then two more. And two more after that. Eventually, there were thirteen containers clinking around on her bedspread, each of them about as big as my index finger and filled with the viscous goo that had somehow injured Reno and Hiram. I'd expected Zara to have one or two.

"You swiped all of these from Ool'Vinn's stockpile," I said, impressed. "With Captain Reno in the room with you?"

"I had to leave some of my knives behind to make room," she said with a note of regret. "Reno wasn't paying attention to me. And I had one more, actually, but Captain Uncle asked for one to run some tests."

Tycius hadn't mentioned that to me. I wondered if he found any-thing interesting. Deciding to conduct my own analysis, I picked up one of the vials, unscrewed the top, and sniffed. The stuff was pun-gent. It smelled a bit like gasoline, but also the ocean—no, not the ocean, dead fish rotting in the sun on the shore—salty and dead. There was also a bit of rancid milk stink in there. That little inhale gave me a dull headache behind my eyes.

I thrust the vial away from me. "Smells like ass," I said.

"Don't play around with it, fool," Zara said. She bounded down from her perch and took the vial from me. "You don't want to get it on you. Sticks like tree sap. We'd have to burn it off."

I thought about the grisly cauterized wound on Hiram's leg and cringed. "How much of this did Ool'Vinn have?"

"Lots," Zara replied. "Look at this."

She held one of her knives out for me to examine, the blade flat against her forearm. It was the same one she'd used to carve up Reno's leg. I could tell because the edge was still coated in the black sludge, although it didn't appear to be the least bit liquid now. To demonstrate, Zara picked at the darkened edge with her nail, but nothing came off.

"Like it was forged that way," she said. Then she whisked the knife across the back of her hand, shearing a couple centimeters of fur, which she shook onto the floor. "Didn't dull the edge at all, though."

"Crazy," I said.

I reached out to touch the knife but stopped just short of touch-ing the blackened edge. I felt a tingling in my fingertips, almost like the coating was curling up from Zara's blade to reach for me. I yanked my hand back.

"Yeah." Zara nodded. "I wouldn't either."

"We can't just go giving this stuff to anyone," I said. "Not until we know exactly what it does."

"We know what it does," Zara replied. "It kills humans. You know what that's worth to a Vulpin? And nobody said anything about 'give.' You want enough supplies to make it to the Ossho? This is how we get there. Just one of these vials with the right broker could set all of us up for life."

"Zara . . . ," I said warningly, although I didn't know where I was going with the sentence. We were on a stolen ISV, about to trade a biological weapon of mysterious origin for a resupply. In my head, I could justify that when it was to help Aela, or when it was to keep our forward momentum going. But when Zara started talking about getting rich, the whole notion of necessary evil started to slip a bit.

"Don't worry, Syd," Zara said, patting my cheek. "I'll get us a good deal. One your conscience can handle."

Pretty soon after that, we all gathered on the bridge to get our first live look at Unstable-J3. Island-size chunks of rocks swirled around a glowing molten core, creating a strobe-light effect. The chaos of the rising and falling slabs reminded me of one of those video games where you had to jump your character from platform to platform. It was the kind of sight that a year ago would've completely broken my brain. The rest of the crew must have felt the same, because we all stared in silence at the space tornado.

"I would like to be in that," Aela said.

"Don't think your suit could handle it," Hiram replied.

"Not in my suit," Aela said. "To float on the edge of all that. To hear the sound of perpetual annihilation, to feel the warmth of a world in collapse. A truly unique experience."

Granted, all I had to go on was Aela's tinny robot-voice, but it was the first time they'd sounded excited about something since we'd left Ashfall. It made me happy to hear, even if their idea of a good time was swimming in a maelstrom.

"You'll have your chance," Tycius said. "But for now, let's make sure we don't get the ship too close."

Aela nodded and tapped out some instructions on her console. Meanwhile, Zara walked closer to the screen, her hands on her hips.

"So, how do we get your peeps to show themselves?" I asked.

"I assume we'll need to open the comms," my uncle said, glancing in Melian's direction. She set about bringing our comms back online. As long as we kept it short-range, the local Serpo wormhole shouldn't ping our location. It was still a slight risk, but hopefully we wouldn't be on the Torrent long enough for anyone to catch up with us.

"Huh." Zara's skeptical grunt sounded like someone had just tried to sell her some fake jewels. She swiped her hand across the screen, zooming in. "There they are."

The Torrent was a chain of asteroids on the outermost edge of Unstable-J3. They rose and fell with the others, but only slightly, like a sailboat floating atop the waves. A series of sleek structures linked the asteroids together, the buildings angular and sharp and somehow familiar. It took me a moment to realize why I recognized the makeshift space station—because it reminded me of Reno's ship. The entirety of the Torrent was constructed of broken down Vulpin spacecraft. Even looking at the place for too long left me feeling a little nauseous. The Vulpin had basically built an RV park on the edge of a volcano.

"Hell no," Hiram said. "People live in that mess?"

"You told us they were secretive," I said to Zara.

"They are," she replied.

"Comms are up," Melian interjected.

Tycius crossed his arms. "Well, let's try opening a chan—"

Before my uncle could even finish, a chime alerted us to a stored message. Apparently, the Torrent had already tried to reach us while we were still running dark. At a gesture from my uncle, the communiqué began to play. It was audio only, the gravelly snarl of a Vulpin that sounded like she'd smoked too many cigarettes.

"ISV *Eastwood*, this is Ezziah den One-Left, governor of the Torrent. Welcome to our little hideaway, yes? Very happy to have you. Docking instructions are attached. We have much to discuss."

The message stopped there.

I exchanged a look with Zara. "Den One-Left?"

"Never heard of them," she said. "Sometimes exiles take new names."

"Does anyone else find it disconcerting that they know who we are?" Batzian asked.

"Yes," Zara said. "Extremely."

We'd drained most of our sedatives to get here. There was no turning back. If there was a trap waiting on the Torrent, then we had no choice but to spring it.

13

The *Eastwood* was too large to dock at the Torrent, so we took the shuttle. H'Jossu and Batzian stayed behind. We didn't want to have everyone trapped on the Torrent in case something went down. The narrow confines of a Vulpin space station didn't seem like the best environment for my bulky Panalax buddy, and Batzian seemed nervous as usual. Maybe it wasn't smart to leave Batzian behind with access to the comms, but I didn't think he'd pull the same crap twice.

We loaded the instructions sent by this Ezziah den One-Left lady into our shuttle's piloting system. The course swept us in a curve through Unstable-J3's uppermost atmosphere. Once we got close enough to the undulating rock flow, we could feel the vibrations through the walls of the shuttle. There was a sharp jolt of turbulence that momentarily bucked us all out of our seats.

Sitting next to me, Melian put a hand on my arm. "This is exciting," she said. I think she was happy to be included in the away team rather than being stuck back on the ship with her brother.

"I agree," Aela said.

I looked across the aisle to my uncle. He'd had a distant expression ever since he played the transmission from the Vulpin.

"Zara," he said, "how common is the name Ezziah among your people?"

She shrugged. "Pretty common."

"Why?" I asked Tycius.

"There was just something familiar about that woman's voice," he said, shaking his head as if to dismiss a ridiculous idea. "I knew an Ezziah once, that's all. But she was Ezziah den Halla. And she died years ago."

"What the hell kind of name is den One-Left, anyway?" Hiram asked.

I stuck a pinkie in my ear. I often forgot that there was a universal translator stuck in there, I'd gotten so used to relying on it. "She was speaking Vulpin, right? Is it, like, one of those names that means something complicated in another language or . . . ?"

"Syd wants to know if it's an idiom," Melian finished for me.

"He is an *idiot*," Zara said. "One-Left means 'one left.' Like the last one. It's not a traditional 'den' name. Maybe this Ezziah was the sole survivor of a bloody battle. Or maybe her old den was entirely wiped out by assassins."

Hiram crossed his arms. "You can't give yourself a nickname."

"No," Zara agreed. "For her to take that as her den name, she must have earned it."

Our shuttle coasted into an open dock at one end of the Torrent. This section used to be a huge Vulpin freighter built for hauling smaller ships across long distances. Now it was lashed to a bobbing asteroid on the edge of calamity and connected like the last car on a train to dozens of other ships and their rocks.

The shuttle settled into its berth. Immediately, I could feel the movement of the asteroid beneath me. The constant up-and-down sway felt like being on the dock of a boat during a storm. Saliva filled my mouth, and I swallowed back a bit of nausea. This would take some getting used to.

There was no oxygen in the makeshift docking bay, so those of us who needed to breathe pulled on our helmets. We exited into the cavernous freighter, where the gravity was so weak that I had to concentrate on stepping lightly so as not to go floating up to the ceiling. There were dozens of other ships parked in here, all of them Vulpin in design, and all of them pocked with dents, dings, and bullet holes.

We descended a metal staircase down to the main level. A pair of Vulpin waited for us there.

"Welcome to the Torrent," the female Vulpin said over the comm channel. I couldn't see much of her through her suit's grease-smudged visor. "Your ship looks nice and clean."

That didn't sound like a compliment.

"Are you Ezziah?" Zara asked.

The Vulpin snorted. "No, little sister. Come on. We bring you."

Our escorts led us through the freighter to an airlock that connected to the next section of the Torrent. The chamber sealed behind us and then flooded with oxygen. We peeled back our helmets as the next door unlocked, revealing the station proper.

"Whoa," I said.

I didn't go out a lot back when I lived on Earth. I wasn't exactly a social butterfly. Didn't get to make a ton of friends with my mom dragging me around the country, running from what she thought were alien bounty hunters. In fact, the only party I ever really got to attend was during my last days on the planet, when those rookie ecoterrorists were camped out by our cabin. I remembered that night like it was yesterday—cheap beer in red plastic cups, thumping music, meat-substitute hot dogs roasting over a campfire. And there was even a girl that I almost hooked up with. A couple days later, my mom would point a gun at her. Good times.

Anyway, my memory of that party was basically exactly what the inside of the Torrent smelled and sounded like.

We'd entered the hollowed-out shell of what used to be a Vulpin cruiser. Crammed into that space were like fifty Vulpin, some of them behind kiosks piled with different wares, and some of them milling around haggling or smoking or drinking or all of the above. It was like the Vulpin bazaar I'd visited back on Denza, but squeezed into a room not much bigger than the *Eastwood*'s bridge. My eyes stung from the smoke that hung in the air, the beleaguered fans someone had welded to the ceiling not doing much for the circulation. The room smelled like musk, and fur, and pipe smoke, and bacon. My mouth watered and my palms sweated and

I felt suddenly light-headed.

"Oh man, there's too many of them," Hiram said quietly. "I should've stayed on the *Eastwood*."

Almost as one, the crowd of Vulpin stopped what they were doing and turned to size us up. They wore their fur in all sorts of different ways—dreadlocks, leopard print, spikes—but I noticed that almost all of the ones operating stands had one side of their heads completely shaved, with the long fur from the other side swept over. Now that their helmets were off, I saw that our two escorts wore their fur that way, too.

We stared at the Vulpin and the Vulpin stared back. And then Melian raised her right hand and waved.

"Hi," she said.

That broke the ice. All at once they started shouting at us, propositioning us, trying to hawk their wares. One Vulpin held a chunk of space rock studded with glittering diamonds in my face while another tried to sell me a jar containing what looked like a scorpion except it had a set of very human-looking teeth in its grinning mouth. Melian ended up with a string of polished beads around her neck, a different color eye painted on each one.

"I think I just bought this," she said to me.

I squinted at the necklace. "Are those knucklebones?"

"Keep your arms to your sides," Hiram said as he limped along next to me. "That way they won't be able to pickpocket you."

"I don't have anything for them to steal," I said.

"Still," he replied.

"Back up, you buzzards!" shouted the female who'd met us in

the hangar. "These are Ezziah's guests! Anyone messes with them, you'll have to answer to the One-Left!"

That got some of the merchants to back off, but there was still a press as we tried to move through the market. Our second guide—a mean-looking male who was missing an ear on the shaved side of his head—resorted to kicking and punching any Vulpin that got too close.

As our path cleared, I noticed that Aela had drifted over to an uncrowded stall manned by a chubby Vulpin with sleepy eyes. On his table were rows of capsules that reminded me of lava lamps. They appeared to be filled with concentrated energy—lightning streaked back and forth inside the tubes, occasionally calming down enough to reveal a flash of some purplish-gray substance. Mounted atop each of the strange containers was a hollow attachment that looked like it would fit perfectly over a Vulpin snout.

"What are these?" Aela asked the merchant as I stepped up next to them.

"You kidding?" The Vulpin glanced at me, then swallowed. "Look, I don't want any trouble."

I took a second look at the capsules. Each one was labeled with a phrase like *NIGHT WITH DEN BAYO QUEEN* or *BLOODY MOMENT OF GLORY.*

"Do we seem like trouble?" Aela asked, their robotic voice making it impossible to tell whether they were trying to be sarcastic or genuinely curious.

"Wait a second . . . ," I said. I leaned down to study the capsule labeled, simply, *OKAY LAP DANCE.* The proportions were much different than inside Aela's exo-suit—the ratio of crackling energy to magenta gas was way off—but I saw it now. "Those are wisps you're selling."

"Renting. Memories for rent only," the Vulpin replied. He leaned across the table, lowering his voice so that only I could hear. "If you're selling the wisp, I know a guy. I could get you a good price. My regulars are getting pretty sick of this selection."

I almost decked him. "Where did you get these?" I asked through gritted teeth. "Who makes them?"

The Vulpin shied away like that was an off-limits question. "Beats me, furless."

I thought of the wisp that had been trapped in Ashfall's temple for millennia, forced to relay its dire message until Aela freed it. *A message in a bottle*, that's how Vanceval had described the technology used to control the Ossho. This kiosk renting pervy memories didn't seem nearly as sophisticated as what we'd encountered on Ashfall, but there was still someone out there in the galaxy working on isolating and controlling Ossho.

"Come on, Syd," Aela said. "We're losing the others."

Aela walked away from the table like they'd completely lost interest. I shot the Vulpin one last dirty look and followed.

"Doesn't that bother you?" I asked.

"Should it?" Aela replied. "I honestly don't know."

"I mean, those are wisps he's got trapped over there," I said. "Using them to just replay the same memories over and over. It's gross."

"Are those wisps?" Aela replied. "Single memories. Exiled from the collective. Removed from all context and connection. No, Syd, those fragments are not like me."

I rubbed the back of my neck. "But they could be. If they were part of a bigger entity, like the Ossho cloud. Or you."

"Yes," Aela said. "But then they would only be a piece of me. Is that any more autonomy than they have now?"

My head was starting to hurt thinking about it, so I edged forward. Just ahead of us, Zara had struck up a conversation with the woman leading the way.

"I don't recognize your style, sister," Zara said.

The Vulpin dragged her claws across the stubble on her head. "Ah, pup, you can't understand den One-Left until you meet the boss lady."

"Last time I was here, den Zuzza ran the Torrent," Zara replied.

"Den Zuzza was three governors ago," the Vulpin said. "You been here before, eh? You're . . ." She gave Zara a once-over, noting the mantle of fur she wore across her shoulders. "Den Jetten, yeah? How's the whoremaster keeping these days?"

Zara's flashed her fangs. "Ask your mother."

The den One-Left woman chuckled. "Yeah, yeah. The boss is looking forward to seeing you, y'know?"

"Seeing me—?" Zara started to ask her question, but the other Vulpin waved her off.

"Not you, pup," she said. "*You.*"

She pointed one of her claws at my uncle.

I raised an eyebrow at Tycius. "You didn't tell us you knew den One-Left."

"I don't," Tycius said, looking as confused as me. His eyes widened a fraction. "There was an Ezziah at the institute, though. But that's not possible . . ."

Our guides led us through two more sections of market, the next ones more dedicated to food and drink. Although the loose gravity of the Torrent made me feel like I was constantly going to float off, the booze sticky floors at least helped me keep my footing. Each new section was as dirty and rusty as the last. There were multiple walls that had clearly been breached at some point and then resealed with scrap metal. I noted how every Vulpin we passed wore a space suit, like they were ready to lose atmosphere at any moment. It also quickly dawned on me that the only well-maintained area of each section were the airlocks. The Vulpin had made sure to keep them operational. That way, if there was a breach in one section, it could be sealed off.

We stopped in a quiet area where an empty elevator shaft led upward. The Vulpin coming from the opposite direction were covered in soot and rock dust and weren't so lively as the ones back at the market. The Vulpin trudged to the opening in the ceiling and jumped, floating upward, using rungs placed along the walls to propel themselves higher. I was looking up at a dozen or so Vulpin ships stacked on top of each other.

"This is the tower," our guide said. She jerked her thumb in the other direction. "Refinery is that way if you want to pick up a shift, pay for your rooms."

Zara snorted. "We're good."

"Then you're going all the way up," the Vulpin said. "Ezziah is waiting for you at the top."

As a group, we did big jumps into the air, and the weak gravity released us upward. Hiram winced when he pushed off. I was going to ask if he needed help, but his pissed-off look told me it was better to just let it drop. Anytime it started to feel like gravity was regaining its grip, I reached over to the wall and propelled myself on from one of the handholds.

"Kind of a fun way to get around," Melian said.

"It's a very interesting place," Aela replied. "Your people are resourceful, Zara."

"Resourceful?" Hiram exclaimed. "This place is a death trap."

"That's what makes it fun," Zara replied.

We passed by compartment after compartment. Down the bisecting hallways, Vulpin hung around or slipped into and out of their living quarters. As we neared the top, I looked to my uncle.

"You're quiet," I said.

"Yes, well," he replied, "I do believe I'm about to see a ghost."

"Cool," I replied. "Keep on being cryptic."

We floated through the final airlock and reached the uppermost ship in the stack of derelicts the Vulpin referred to as the Tower. This boat was different than all the others we'd passed through. Where the others had been rusty and dingy, this section gleamed like it had been freshly buffed. There were gold and wood flourishes throughout the walls, which featured planter boxes flowering under soft UV lights.

"Shit," Hiram said. "They've got a yacht."

I'd seen ships just like this one cruising around the skies of

Primclef and occasionally plunging down beneath the surface of Denza's endless ocean. The Denzans used them for exploration and tourism, the vessels coming equipped with pressure-resistant glass bottoms. The Vulpin had installed the yacht with the glass floor as the ceiling, so the room offered a disorienting view of the maelstrom outside.

"Total kingpin office," I said under my breath. "H'Jossu would love this."

"Ah, finally," said the scratchy voice I recognized from our invitation. "My honored guests have arrived."

Ezziah One-Left was the tallest Vulpin I'd ever seen. She could look Hiram right in the eye. But that achievement came with a huge asterisk. Her organic torso was mounted on a pair of intimidating cybernetic legs, the prosthetic limbs doglegged like all the Vulpin but larger and equipped with an array of pistons and compressors that suggested they were capable of serious force. Ezziah's right arm was cybernetic too, although this one was made to scale to match her fleshy left arm. The diamond-tipped claws on her robotic limb winked in the flashing lights of the detonating planet outside.

One-Left. As in, only one limb left. Or one left arm.

Aela got the dark humor at the same time I did. "How wonderfully literal," they observed.

I guessed that Ezziah was about as old as my uncle. It was hard for me to put an age on Vulpin and even harder with Ezziah as half her face and snout were covered with old, puckered burn scars. No fur grew on the ruined side of her head, leaving her with just a prickly half mane. The Vulpin of her den shaved their own heads to emulate her.

Tycius stepped in front of the rest of us in a way like he'd forgotten we were even there. "By the tides, Ezziah, it really is you."

"Small universe," the Vulpin rasped.

Ty closed the gap so he was right in front of Ezziah. For a second, I thought he might try to hug her. "I heard you were dead," Tycius said.

"I lived," she replied. "I heard you were out of the game. Out to pasture on the blue ball."

"I'm back," Tycius said.

He reached up and glided his hand over Ezziah's burns, not touching her, but pushing his fingers through where the rest of her mane should have been. I suddenly remembered a story my uncle told me back when I first came to Denza, about how he'd made the mistake of touching a Vulpin diplomat's hair and ended up tripping from the hallucinogens she kept hidden there.

"Oh, my dear," Tycius said, "what did they do to you?"

"You know me, Ty," Ezziah replied. "No favor goes unreturned."

Maybe it was because I'd spent so much time around Zara and always half expected her to stab me, but I was surprised when Ezziah tilted her head to gently rest against my uncle's palm. With her good hand, she cupped the back of his head, dragging her thumb claw behind his ear.

"Bro," Hiram whispered. "Your uncle totally hooked up with that Vulpin."

Melian made a face. "Don't be gross, Hiram."

Zara glanced at me then, and took an uncomfortable step away.

Finally, and maybe a little mercifully, Ezziah and Tycius remembered we were in the room with them. Tycius turned to us with a sheepish smile.

"Ah, right. Ezziah, these are my charges— "

"The crew of the *Eastwood*," One-Left said. I saw the switch go off in the Vulpin's eyes. From nostalgic to shrewd in a split second. Her gaze swept across us. "A few short, aren't you?"

Tycius blinked in surprise. It did seem strange that this Vulpin woman would know how many were in our crew.

I decided to speak up. "We left the others back on the ship," I said. "In case we ran into trouble."

Ezziah smirked at me. "Smart boy." She eyed Tycius. "Surprised Marie Reno didn't come in person."

She was fishing. If I knew that, then my uncle did, too. He moved on quickly.

"We took some unexpected detours during a training exercise and blew through our sedatives," Tycius said. "Zara here, she knew about this place, and said we could get a resupply."

"Zara den Jetten," Ezziah said, particularly savoring the name. "How's your father?"

People were always mentioning Zara's dad, and not in a particularly favorable light. She stepped forward with her chin high, though. "Haven't seen him in two years," she said. "But I imagine he's still stubborn and snake-bit, as always."

"You took a big risk coming here, exposing our place to

outsiders," Ezziah said, her tone more bemused than scolding. "All for a routine resupply? Surprised the institute wouldn't scramble a ship to your location. Had to be easier than coming all the way to Jeuna . . ."

"I don't hear any music," Zara replied. "So let's stop dancing."

"Fine," Ezziah said with a chuckle. She gave my uncle's shoulder a parting squeeze, then moved across the room to her desk, every footfall echoing sharply against the metal floor. Accessing her console, Ezziah activated a vid-screen on the far wall.

A message appeared on-screen. A bounty.

Attention: all Vulpin freelancers. A price of 10,000 Stonelea'n ducats will be paid on the capture and safe return of the ISV *Eastwood* and its crew. There will be no interference from the Serpo Institute in this matter. Please see attached job history for references.

Account holder: Butler, R.

"Truly, I hope you've come with something amazing to barter," Ezziah said. "Because the opening bid is already in."

14

"Ten thousand ducats?" I asked. "Is that even a lot? It doesn't sound that high."

"That's start-over money on Stonelea," Zara said, not looking at me but at Ezziah. "Enough to turn you from a nobody into a somebody. Buy yourself a castle and make your den respectable."

"Oh, okay," I said. "Castle money. Got it."

"Imagine what den Jetten could do with that money," Ezziah said with a flash of her fangs. "Bring your family back from the brink. You should've collected on yourself, Zara, instead of handing yourselves over to me."

Hiram shifted from foot to foot, but I couldn't tell if that was from nerves or because he was sore from standing too long. "My grandfather put a bounty out on us. Where did he get that kind of money?"

"He must have sold a lot of pizzas," Melian said.

"He emphasized safe return, at least," I said. "That's better than the deal we were getting from Reno."

My uncle put his hands on his hips. "Come on, Ezziah. You're not really going to collect on that. You've never been the type to sell out a friend."

"Oh, Ty, that's lovely of you to say, but I am and always have been exactly that type. Is that what you've got to trade? Friendship and good vibes? Because that's not worth shit to me." Ezziah's mechanical claws scratched at her wrinkled scalp. "My crew was salivating when your ship appeared on our sensors. I had to talk them out of sending a boarding party. Figured you'd come right to me. Make it easy."

"If you think we're going to make it easy," I said, "you're not as plugged in as you think."

"Your nephew's a spunky one," Ezziah said to Tycius. "I don't suppose you'd sell him? Always wanted a hybrid. The strength of a human and the brain of a Denzan. Now, there's something not easy to acquire."

"Uh, Syd's not that strong," Hiram said.

"Or that smart, honestly," Melian added.

"Thanks, guys," I said, narrowing my eyes at Ezziah.

"He's not for sale," Ty said, his voice hardening. "This doesn't have to get ugly."

Ezziah chuckled at that. "I guess you think having one and a half humans at your back makes you untouchable, but you don't know the Torrent. This is my station. Before you leave this room,

I'll have my people on the *Eastwood*."

I checked my comms, thinking I could warn H'Jossu and Batzian that there might be a boarding party on the way. They were jammed. Because of course they were.

"And unless you plan on butchering some five hundred Vulpin, you'll never make it off the station," Ezziah concluded. "I know you too, Ty. You're not the butchering type."

"You got one thing wrong, boss lady," Zara said. She leaned her elbow against Hiram's shoulder, which earned her a surprised look. "Our humans don't make us untouchable because they *aren't* untouchable. None of them are. Not anymore."

"Zara . . . ," Tycius said warningly.

Ezziah cocked her head. "What are you saying, pup?"

"Hiram," Zara said, "Take off your pants."

"Um, how about no?" Hiram replied.

In the space of a breath, Zara's knife was in her hand. She swept it smoothly down the front leg of Hiram's uniform, cutting easily through the fabric and bio-tape that covered his injury. It was done before Hiram even realized what was happening. When he did, he made an angry grunt and took a wobbling step toward Zara, but she'd already danced out of reach. Even so, I grabbed Hiram around the waist to restrain him.

"What the hell—!" he shouted.

"Easy," I said in his ear. "Take it easy."

Ezziah was clearly intrigued. The Vulpin came forward, her cybernetic joints creaking as she bent to examine Hiram. "How did this happen?"

"I got shot," Hiram said through his teeth.

"On Earth," Ezziah said. "You carried this injury to the Vastness with you."

"Lady, do I look like a fucking Earthling to you?" Hiram waved to the message still displayed on the vid-screen. "That's my grandfather's money you're trying to take. You know who we are. You know who I am."

Ezziah stroked her chin with the sharp tips of her metallic fingers. "It's impossible," she said to Zara. "I shot one of these hairless apes point-blank with a scatter-gun loaded with irradiated rounds, and all it gave the bastard was some pimples."

"Cool story," Hiram muttered.

"Yes," Aela agreed. "Cool story."

"It's a chemical," Zara continued. "Any weapon can be treated with it and a human will feel it, just like you and me."

"Now, hold on," Tycius said, glancing at me for support. "We aren't bartering with—*with that*. The implications of a biological agent like that getting out—"

"Oh, you haven't lost your touch," Ezziah interrupted, smiling at my uncle. "Dangle the treasure and then yank it back. You've really got me on the hook now."

My uncle wasn't trying to help Zara negotiate with Ezziah. He was serious. I could understand his hesitation with putting that Ashfall goop out into the universe, but it was pretty much the only card we had to play if we were going to make it to the Ossho Collective. When Ty again looked at me for some kind of support, I responded with a half shrug. He blinked, scowled, and fell silent.

"I know what you're thinking now," Zara said to Ezziah. She strolled farther into the room and flopped down on a couch across from Ezziah's desk, crossing her legs demurely. "You're thinking, since you've got us trapped, why don't you just steal what we've got and collect the bounty?"

Ezziah's ears twitched in Zara's direction, but she kept her eyes on Hiram. His jaw was set rigidly, and he'd gone completely still while the Vulpin examined him, his eyes on the ceiling. Delicately, Ezziah did her best to close the torn fabric on his pant leg, then straightened up and put her hand on his shoulder.

"I've seen worse injuries than that, kid, believe me," Ezziah quietly said to Hiram. "You let it define you, the bleeding will never stop. You understand?"

At first, I thought Hiram would flinch away from Ezziah. But, after a moment, he simply nodded.

Ezziah swung away from him then and stalked toward Zara. "You're right, pup," she said. "I was thinking you'd make for a nice double dip."

While she waited on the couch, Zara had begun making a show of cleaning under her claws with her dagger. "You try to rip us off and we'll tell Rafe Butler what you've got. He'll turn this place upside down and inside out looking for it. Big waste."

"Zara den Jetten," Ezziah said with an amused shake of her head. "Who would've thought it?" She settled in behind her desk—there was no chair there, but her intimidating legs folded in to put her at eye level with her guest. "I suppose the two of us have some negotiating to do."

151

* * *

Ezziah arranged for us to bunk in a set of adjoining rooms in one of the ships in the Tower. Mattresses with the stuffing hanging out of them, sheets that stank like smoke, and sinks coated with grime—honestly, there was something comfortingly familiar about the place. It was like every sleazy motel that my mom and I had stayed in back on Earth. The ship we were in had been remodeled for guests, but it definitely used to be some kind of prison transport. There were stumps of metal bars still sticking out of the ceiling, and someone had carved a few hundred hash marks into one of the walls. No doubt Ezziah had meant to send a message with our accommodations.

"Should we really have left Zara alone with her?" Melian asked. She'd attempted to tidy the rooms when we first got in, but quickly gave up and now sat on the very edge of one of the beds.

"Probably not," Tycius admitted.

"Zara knows what she's doing," I said.

"It's Vulpin tradition for important negotiations between two den leaders to happen face-to-face and one-on-one," Aela said.

"Oh, so Zara's our leader now?" Hiram asked. He'd managed to keep a lid on his anger back in Ezziah's office, but now he paced back and forth across the room, trying constantly to overcome the painful hitch in his gait. "That's just great."

My uncle stood in the doorway between our two rooms with his arms crossed, watching me closely. "We're in it now, so it appears there's no turning back. But I wish I'd been consulted."

"If we're going to keep going, we needed to trade something," I said. "You had to know the price would be high in a place like this."

It looked like my uncle had more to say, but Melian spoke up first. "Is there any chance the Vulpin could make more of that stuff? Reverse engineer it?"

Tycius shook his head. "I ran some tests on one of the samples Zara . . . collected. The substance appears to bond with certain surfaces through what I can only describe as smart particles or perhaps nanotechnology. I'm not sure Denzan or Vulpin society could replicate the effect. Not to mention, some of the chemical compounds contained in the ooze are native only to Earth."

"So it's just a little bit, then," Melian said. "It's not like the Vulpin will start mass-producing human poison."

"Why shouldn't they?" Hiram muttered. "They're probably going to need it."

"There's a bleak thought," I said, even though I agreed.

"I just don't know why she had to humiliate me like that," Hiram said, his ripped uniform still flapping. "Bunch of bullshit."

"As all of this is being done to return me to the Ossho, in a way, I am as responsible as Zara," Aela said. The exo-suit clasped its hands together and bowed at the waist. "Thank you, Hiram, for trading your dignity on my behalf."

Hiram barely stopped his pacing to give Aela a weird look. "Yeah. Sure. No problem."

"If there are no objections," Aela said, straightening up, "I would like to take this opportunity to explore the Torrent. I have never visited a Vulpin space station before and may never get another chance."

Aela turned to my uncle, waiting for his approval. "Oh, right," he said, looking at me instead of Aela. "I'm the captain. It's fine if you want to explore, Aela. I'd say be cautious around the Vulpin, but we're supposed to be under Ezziah's protection. I doubt you'll have any problems."

Melian looked from Tycius to me and back, probably picking up on the awkward vibes. She fingered the bone necklace that she hadn't taken off since we got here. "Maybe I'll go, too. That cool with you, Aela?"

"Of course. Your company is always welcome."

"How about it, Hiram?" Melian said as she stood up. "Want to go check out the station?"

"And be surrounded by a horde of those furballs?" He snorted. "No thanks."

Hiram was too in his own head to take a hint from Melian. With an apologetic glance in my direction, she left with Aela, leaving my uncle and me to stare at each other from opposite sides of the room, with Hiram ping-ponging across the intervening space.

"Look," I said, "I'm sorry I didn't consult you about the sludge. But it wasn't really my plan. Zara's the one who swiped all those samples. They're hers, and she can do what she wants with them. I even tried to talk her out of it, actually—"

Ty waved his hand like he was tired of listening. "What's done is done, Syd. But if our goal is to preserve the peace, I'm not sure trading a lethal biological weapon is for the greater good."

"I promised to get Aela home," I replied. "This is how we do that."

"Single-minded in pursuit of a goal, ignoring the consequences," my uncle said. "Where have I seen that behavior before . . . ?"

Tycius let his question hang out there. Meanwhile, Hiram had stopped pacing and finally realized that he was in the middle of an argument.

"Oh," he said, "I should've gone with the others, huh?"

"You're fine," I told Hiram while making a *come on* gesture to my uncle. "Finish what you were going to say."

My uncle sighed. "Your mother kept you hidden on Earth for years, beyond the point of reason. Your father, well, we all know what he did. Both of them were so certain they were right, they stopped considering the consequences of their actions. What if this trade with Ezziah . . ." My uncle paused, choosing his words carefully in front of Hiram. "What if this brings about exactly the chaos you're hoping to prevent?"

World killer.

"No," I said firmly, even as doubt curdled in my stomach. "No. You're wrong. I know what I'm doing."

"All right, Syd," Ty replied. "I hope so."

At that moment, Zara floated into the doorway. At least her arrival defused the conversation between my uncle and I, but I was immediately worried it might touch off something worse.

"You." Hiram aggressively limped toward Zara.

"Relax, big boy," she replied. "I brought you a peace offering."

Zara chucked a wadded-up ball of fabric at Hiram. He caught the bundle before it hit him in the face and let it unroll, revealing a pair of black pants.

"What's this shit?" Hiram grumbled, although he stopped advancing to examine the slacks. I noticed a glint of some kind of metallic lining running around the waistband and down the inside of each leg.

"Got those made special for you," Zara said. "Go try them on so we can all stop looking at your gross leg."

Hiram glowered at Zara and clutched the pants like he was strangling them, but after a stubborn second he limped into the next room to get changed.

"I hope you got more than some skinny jeans out of her," I said.

"Indeed," my uncle added. "How much of our souls do we have to sell here?"

Zara swished her tail back and forth like a bored feline. "Thought old Only-Torso made it clear she don't buy existential concepts, Captain." As my uncle's expression hardened, Zara held up her hands. "Damn, everyone's so tense. I got us a fair deal. Go ask her yourself. She wants to talk to you alone, probably make sure I'm not full of shit."

Tycius nodded and pushed his hands down the front of his uniform, brushing out some wrinkles. "Well, at least I can be of some use."

As soon as he was gone, Zara turned to me. "What's up his ass?"

I'd been trying to brush off what my uncle had said to me, but it had shaken me. Back on Earth, my mom had taught me to always trust my instincts. If we needed to steal a car, we stole it. If something looked off about a place, we booked. But how could I trust myself when I knew my decisions eventually led to me blowing up a planet? And, I reminded myself, I wasn't the only one Goldy had a prophecy for. He'd told my uncle that he always failed me. That was surely weighing on Ty, as well, both of us second-guessing ourselves, trying to prove the future wrong. Of course, I couldn't tell any of that to Zara.

"He's pissed we didn't loop him in," I said. "So, what kind of deal did you get?"

"Full resupply of our sedatives, plus some extra rations to keep us living in the Vastness for five more years."

It was exactly what we came here for. More, really. So why didn't Zara sound happy?

"And how much of our antihuman arsenal did you promise to Ezziah?"

"Half," Zara said.

"*Half?!*" I exclaimed. "Are you nuts?"

"Wasn't exactly bargaining from a position of strength."

As Zara said this, she pulled up the hood on her space suit and motioned for me to do the same. I raised an eyebrow but quickly got the point, tugging on my own helmet and opening up the local comm channel.

"She's probably got the room bugged." Zara's low voice crackled in my ear. "I traded her half a vial. She thinks we've only got the one."

"Oh, damn," I said. "Way to hustle."

She shrugged. "I had to throw something else into the bargain, but it's got nothing to do with the *Eastwood*."

Before I could press her further, Hiram bounded back into the room. He made a face when he noticed we both had our helmets up. "What the hell are you doing?"

"Never mind," Zara said, quickly removing her helmet. "How's your leg feel?"

"Good, actually," Hiram said, bouncing up and down on his toes. "Tingles a bit."

"There are a lot of accidents in the refinery here," Zara explained. "Vulpin arms and legs aren't impervious to crushing like humans'. So Ezziah invested in a tech-tailor. I saw him on the way in and got Ezziah to put in a rush order while we negotiated. The lining supplements your muscles and adjusts with your movements. Should help you rehab."

"Wow, Zara," I said. "That's actually really nice."

"Yeah," Hiram agreed, his expression as baffled as mine. "I'm kind of touched, honestly."

Zara made a snarling face. "Nice," she repeated. "What a terrible thing to call someone."

"Underneath all the stabbing and poisoning and lying, you're just a little sweetie," I said, relishing in the chance to make Zara uncomfortable for once. "And taking care of Hiram, of all people."

"Seriously," Hiram said. "I mean, you act like you hate me all the time, but now you show up with this really nice gift and I'm like—*Whoa, does Zara actually have a heart in there?*"

Zara's eyes narrowed and she hunkered low, in her knife-fighting position. "I think I've spilled enough blood to avoid these accusations of . . ." She glared at me. "What was it that you called me?"

"A little sweetie," I said. "And don't worry, your secret's safe with us. We're den *Eastwood*, right? We take care of each other."

Zara's tail swished with satisfaction, and she relaxed her shoulders, coming over to sit on the ratty couch across from me. Meanwhile, Hiram checked himself out in the smudged mirror on the wall.

"These really enhance my butt, I think," he said.

"I very much regret my gift," Zara replied, and I laughed. "I got something else, too."

From one of her many hidden pockets, Zara produced a handful of small objects wrapped in cloth. She tossed one to me and another to Hiram. I unwrapped mine, revealing something that looked and sort of smelled like a cinnamon stick, although it was vivid red in color and the aroma had a sort of fresh piney undercurrent.

"Cool," I said. "An air freshener. We can hang it from the *Eastwood*'s rearview mirror."

"I don't understand any of what you just said, but I assume it was dumb," Zara replied. She held up her own scented stick thingy. "This is *chakmaw*. It's only grown on Stonelea. Vulpin warriors eat it the night before embarking on a particularly dangerous task. It relaxes the muscles and eases the mind."

"Sweet. That's like every day for us," Hiram said, flopping down on the couch next to Zara. He immediately bit off the tip of his stick and chewed thoughtfully. "It's good. Tastes like spice cake."

"Don't eat it all," Zara said.

I took a bite, too. The *chakmaw* broke against my teeth like a candy cane and then melted on my tongue. The flavor was warm and earthy—almost like apple cider if you were to somehow suck it right out of a tree, which I realized didn't really make much sense, but that was how my brain processed the taste.

Zara chewed her own piece. "You might also have some light hallucinations."

"Oh, so we're getting high," I said. "That explains why I was just thinking about drinking from a tree like a milkshake."

Hiram's eyes widened and he stuck out his tongue, which was now tinted red from the melted *chakmaw*. "Zara, you should've led with that part!"

She shrugged. "Oops."

The stuff worked quickly. My brain felt like melted butter spreading across a piece of toast. I had to grip the rough comforter on the bed I lounged on to keep from floating up to the ceiling. The dangers that had seemed so present moments ago—like the fight with my uncle, the whole Etherazi prophecy about blowing up that planet—they didn't seem like such a big deal. Like, big whoop, what's one torched planet? In the life span of the universe, that must happen all the time. Even the crappy room we were staying in seemed suddenly clean and cozy.

I could tell Hiram was feeling it too, by the way he stretched his legs out in front of him, like his injury wasn't causing him any pain. He stared up at the ceiling. "Zara, how long does this last?"

"A couple hours," she replied.

"I was hoping you'd say forever," Hiram said.

I snorted.

Zara curled up on her side of the couch, tail wrapped around her, more chill than I'd ever seen her. "And you fools say I'm not nice."

"Hey, Zara, I've got a question for you," Hiram said dreamily, still staring into the space above him. "What's the deal with your dad?"

In a faraway part of my mind—the part that worried—I expected Zara to tense up like she always did when her family came up. But she barely reacted at all, busy lightly dragging her claws through the fur on her forearm. "What do you mean?"

"I mean everyone's always ragging on him," Hiram said. "Why do they call him the whoremaster?"

"Because he's the whoremaster," Zara replied. "Obviously."

"That's his job?" I asked.

"His appointment," Zara replied, then sighed. "My father is Stonelea's Minister of Sex."

"They make fun of him for *that*?" I asked, not really understanding.

"Yeah, for real," Hiram added. "I want to be the Minister of Sex."

"It isn't exciting as you perverts think. He oversees the brothels, makes sure that they pay their taxes and maintain certain standards, and interacts with the different courtesan unions," Zara explained. "Traditionally, it's a job for a woman. My father once worked in the Ministry of Finance. He discovered that a powerful den was siphoning money from their province that was meant for public works. Not exactly a rarity on Stonelea. He tried to expose them—the old man has too many scruples for a Vulpin; it would have been wiser to blackmail them. Anyway, this den had powerful friends in the government and they got my father reassigned."

I'd never heard Zara go into so much detail about something that wasn't a weapon. "They expected him to quit, right?"

"Right," Zara said. "But he refused. Instead, he continues in his role, not caring about the shame he brings on den Jetten."

"How is it shameful?" I asked. "It's just a job."

"A cool job," Hiram said.

Zara straightened the shelf of fur across her shoulders that signified her den. "There are certain expectations about the Minister of Sex, that they be part of the business they oversee. So, on Stonelea, all of den Jetten are expected to go into what is now the family business."

"But you don't have to, right?"

"No," Zara said. "But the rumors persist. The talk. It is why I escaped to the institute."

I remembered how she fought another Vulpin the day she left her planet. "Poking too many eyes out to stay, right?"

Zara grinned. "Right."

"Hey, seeing as we're doing backstories, Hiram, you never finished telling me about your parents," I said. The fact that he'd only started telling me about his parents when he was considering jumping out of the airlock didn't really register with me—or, if it did, my mellowed brain just sort of fluffed it off.

Hiram looked down from the ceiling and aimed his unfocused

gaze in my direction. "Oh yeah. My dad, he's the actual whore-master."

"Humans have those?" Zara asked.

"No, just talking shit," Hiram said. "Dad's got a new wife and a couple kids. She's Denzan. I told you that, right, Syd? He's settled down now, but for most of my childhood all he did was party. He got assigned to an interstellar survey ship, and they'd hunt down tropical planets to get drunk on. Grandpa says he screwed half the women in his division." Hiram shook his head. "Rafe can't stand his own son, which is probably why he never comes around. Says I'm growing up to be just like him, which is nuts because I barely know the guy."

"What about your mom?" I asked. "They get divorced or something?"

"Nah," Hiram said, looking up at the ceiling again. "She went back to Earth."

I blinked through the haze, not sure I'd understood. "Sorry, what?"

"Yeah. She was from there originally," Hiram said. "I was just a baby, so I don't know how it went down. I guess she got real depressed and missed home. She stowed away on an institute vessel, and by the time they found her on Earth, her body had already broken down to the point where they couldn't save her."

"Whoa," I said. "I didn't know."

"She left you," Zara said quietly. "That's fucked."

Hiram shrugged sleepily. "I don't really think it was about me. But yeah."

"I guess my grandpa did the same thing," I said. "He went back to Earth after the invasion to be with his family. It's how my parents met, actually. My dad was there trying to fix him."

"Yeah, I know, my grandpa talks about your grandpa all the time," Hiram said. "Says it was a noble sacrifice. To go back to a place you know will destroy you. I'm too stoned to think about it, but I don't see what's so noble about that."

"Me neither," Zara said.

We fell silent after that, all of us slipping into the peaceful haze of the *chakmaw*. I ended up lying back and staring up at the rusty ceiling, just like Hiram, imagining that I could see beyond the walls of this ship and into the cosmos, like I was hooked into a Wayscope. I imagined Earth out there—beautiful and blue, poisonous and ruined.

Eventually, I drifted off to sleep. But before I did, I swear I saw something else through the metallic grooves of the ceiling.

A faint gold glow.

15

We had a few days to kill on the Torrent. As part of the deal that Zara had reached with Ezziah, a team of Vulpin technicians were repairing the damage that Reno's cannon had done to the *Eastwood*'s hull. None of the Vulpin would actually be allowed to board the *Eastwood*—we weren't willing to take that risk, backstabbing being the Stonelea planetary pastime—but the exterior repairs would at least make our long voyage to the Ossho Collective safer. Ezziah had also stopped jamming our comms, so we got a nervous message from Batzian almost every hour, worried one of the Vulpin was trying to force their way onto our ship.

I spent most of the time on the Torrent either buzzed on whatever illicit substance Zara plundered from the market or else squeezed into one of the station's innumerable gambling parlors. Zara wouldn't let Hiram or me gamble after we burned through some credits she'd pickpocketed in less than an hour, but Melian, surprisingly, quickly acquired a reputation as a killer tailbite player. As I understood it, tailbite was a lot like dice poker, but with swingy odds that caused bets to randomly triple and quadruple, and cheating encouraged. Melian, playing the part of the innocent and dopey Denzan, swindled table after table with Zara's encouragement while Hiram and I got shit-faced in the background. When we weren't doing that, we were sleeping or hungover.

All in all, the cramped and dangerous Torrent quickly started to feel like a vacation. If my uncle minded all our goofing off, he didn't say anything. Tycius was too busy spending every night in private dinners with Ezziah, catching up on old times.

I was sweating out some spiced Vulpin brew when I made my first visit to the station's refinery. Here, the Vulpin hauled in huge chunks of stone they'd plucked from the chaos of Unstable-J3 and cracked them open with massive drills and white-hot industrial torches, revealing the nests of gems that hid inside. The brute-force work of breaking open the asteroids was then followed by the more delicate task of chiseling out the flashing jewels within. As I watched them work, I noticed how for every four gems that passed down a conveyor belt bound for the Torrent's vault, one was pocketed by a Vulpin. They were all doing it, and they weren't even being slick about it. Maybe that was how they got paid. Even with the stealing, a small fortune must have passed through the refinery every day.

"You here to pick up a shift, human?" A Vulpin had stepped away from the stone he was sawing apart to snarl the question at me. Grime coated his half-sheared den One-Left mane, sweat dampening the fur on his neck. "With your strength, we could all get off early."

I shook my head and felt dizzy. The heat from the melting stone made me feel a bit nauseated. "I'm just looking for my friend."

"Lazy and hairless," the Vulpin grumbled, scuttling around me. "Your wisp went that way."

The Vulpin pointed toward an airlock. Beyond that was the loading bay where teams of space miners wrestled with the meteors they'd managed to lasso from Unstable-J3. I spotted Aela's exo-suit buckled silently inside the airlock next to some jackhammers and other spare gear.

The faceplate was popped open. Empty. Aela had already gone out.

I joined a crew of Vulpin in the airlock. They gave me weird looks as I pulled up the helmet of my space suit, but none of them said anything. In my short time on the Torrent, I'd learned the Vulpin valued independence so much that they never gave you crap for nosing around where you didn't belong. They might stab you—true—but only if you got in the way.

The rock cutting was giving me a splitting headache, and my pits were soaked from the molten heat, so it was a relief when the airlock sealed behind us and the frozen silence of the Vastness rushed in. I let the crew of Vulpin float out ahead of me. There was an asteroid the size of a tank waiting for them in the loading dock, supported by chains hung from a team of drones. One side of the rock still glowed white-hot from its exposure to Unstable-J3.

The chunk must have been freshly shot loose.

I stuck to the handholds along the side to keep out of the way as the Vulpin guided the rock in. They didn't pay any attention to me as I edged all the way out to the opening. Unstable-J3 was right below my feet. I had to squint at the strobe-like effect of its constant explosions and implosions. I clenched the very last safety rung on the wall and hung out as far as I could.

"Amazing," I whispered to myself.

I'd come a long way from Earth, that was for sure. How many sets of human eyes would ever see something like this? Even in my wildest fantasies while my mom drove us across the US, I couldn't have imagined a more insane sight. Behind me, the Vulpin continued at their work, not at all impressed by the planet-size whirlpool of energy and rock that churned beneath our orbit. They'd gotten used to life in the Vastness, but I was having a moment.

And so was Aela.

It took me a moment to find them down there amid all the flashing and swirling, but eventually I was able to focus on a thin band of magenta cutting across the edge of Unstable-J3. Aela's gaseous form floated lazily along the tectonic ruptures, like they were out for a leisurely swim. Watching Aela somehow made the whole scene seem peaceful instead of chaotic.

I'm not sure how long I stood there staring. Long enough that the chime from my communicator made me jump in my suit.

"Captain Tycius? Syd?" Batzian's voice came across the comm. It sounded like there was an alarm going off in the background. "Do you read?"

"I'm here, Batzian," Tycius said. "I assure you, none of den One-Left are going to break into the ship."

I snickered. Even my uncle was losing patience with Batzian. "Go hang out with H'Jossu, man," I said. "Relax a bit. Last I talked to him, he was binge-watching *Friends*."

"This is not a time for relaxation," Batzian said. I realized that his nervousness was different than usual. There was a shakiness to his voice, like fear mixed with giddiness. "The *Eastwood*'s Etherazi warning system just went off."

My grip tightened on the handhold. "You're shitting me."

"Where did it breach?" Tycius asked. "At the system's wormhole?"

"Let me guess," I said to Batzian, "it's headed right for us."

"Well, not exactly," Batzian replied. "The readings I'm seeing don't make much sense. It looks like the Etherazi sliced into our reality in an empty part of the system—"

"They can't do that," Tycius said. "They can't create their own wormholes."

"The energy signature isn't staying together either," Batzian said. "It's spreading out and dissipating as it goes. Almost like the aftershocks of an earthquake or the fallout from an explosion."

"Downloading the data now . . . ," my uncle said. He went quiet for a moment as he reviewed the strange phenomenon Batzian had picked up on. "You're right. It matches an Etherazi energy signature, but it's not staying together. Usually, they coalesce around a core . . ."

I'd gotten a close look at Goldy's insides when he swallowed me up, a view that not many managed to survive. There was a big-ass eye in there, gross and floating and monstrous. I shuddered as I leaned a bit farther out of the docking bay, staring into the Vastness. "Is it going to reach us?" I asked.

"It's traveling at the speed of light, but weakening as it goes," Batzian said. "The *Eastwood's* projections have the phenomenon washing over us in less than a minute."

"Could've led with that, Batzian," I said.

"There's literally nothing to be done," he responded. "And it doesn't appear any more harmful than solar wind—"

"I'm going to warn Ezziah," my uncle said. "There might be precautions the station should take."

"Aela and I are spacewalking," I said. "I need to . . ."

I trailed off as a gold dot appeared in the Vastness, like a new star being born. In the space of a breath, that dot had expanded into a line. A rippling band of energy, cascading across the emptiness. Batzian was right. There would be no avoiding whatever this was. Better, at least, to see it coming and hope it didn't dissolve our molecules.

"Hell is that?" one of the Vulpin asked over the comm channel. Their work had stopped, the boulder bobbing serenely in the loading bay.

I glanced down to Unstable-J3. Aela had floated clear of the swirling rocks and now seemed to be watching the approaching glow.

I tightened my grip and took a deep breath.

The glow washed over the station. Lit us up. For a split second,

I was somewhere else. Some *when* else.

Leaning back on a bed, staring up at the ceiling, my body and mind light and weightless—

That was a couple of days ago, when I'd been tripping with Zara and Hiram. I thought I'd seen Goldy's otherworldly glow then, but written it off as a hallucination. I'd experienced an Etherazi's temporal displacement effects before. I'd also seen how twisted an Etherazi's energy could get when it interacted with organic matter. Back on Denza, Goldy had ripped through a team of Vulpin mercenaries, reducing them to bones with just a brush of his power.

This experience wasn't like that at all. It was weak, like mild déjà vu. An unsettled feeling that lasted only for a second, like wondering if you remembered to put your math homework in your backpack.

And then it was over. The wave of energy passed on, fading into the Vastness.

"Hey, anyone else just eat their breakfast for a second time?" one of the Vulpin asked on the comm channel.

"Shut up and get back to work," said another.

"Bad mojo to have these outsiders here. Ezziah gotta wake up to that," said a third, who then must have noticed me standing in their vicinity. "Go private, boys."

"*Eastwood* crew, report in," Tycius said over our channel. "The phenomenon seems to have passed. Everyone okay?"

"Feel like I just watched a rerun," H'Jossu said. "The *Eastwood* is good, though. All systems normal."

"I've got a splitting headache," Melian reported. "But otherwise, I'm okay."

"Same," Batzian said. "Doesn't seem to have done any harm otherwise."

"Indeed," Tycius replied somewhat skeptically. "Keep an eye on the sensors. Let us know if anything else pops up."

"What's everybody yelling on the comms for?" Hiram asked. "I just woke up."

I felt a bit of tension behind my eyes as well. It made sense that the Denzans all had headaches. They were more sensitive to the Etherazi's physics-defying forms than any of the other species. There was no doubt that what we just encountered was Etherazi-related, but it hadn't been one of the creatures itself. More like a shadow. Like going into an empty room and smelling perfume, so you knew someone just left.

"Has that kind of thing happened before?" I asked over the comm. "Like, a little Etherazi toot or whatever that was?"

"No, Syd," my uncle replied. "I'm not sure your scientific lingo is up to snuff, but regardless. That's a new one to me."

"I'm sure there's a rational explanation," Batzian said.

Why was Batzian, of all people, sure about that? And why did he seem so chill about this? When he first got on the comms, he'd almost sounded excited . . .

Just then, someone tapped me on the shoulder. I turned to find Aela, restored to their exo-suit, standing behind me. They must have floated back in while I was focused on the anomaly.

"That was strange," Aela said.

"You felt it, too?"

Aela shook their head. "An Etherazi's signature doesn't disrupt my molecules, but I was able to observe the temporal distortion from a distance. For a moment, that rock there was part of the planet again." The wisp pointed to the boulder that the Vulpin were finally hauling inside. "White-hot and raging."

"Seriously?"

"Yes, look." Aela pointed to some very real scorch marks on the inside of the loading dock that hadn't been there before. "All of you winked out of existence for a moment or you surely would have been incinerated."

I blinked. I guess the whole thing was a bit more serious than some mild déjà vu. "Well, thanks for telling me that. I'm not freaked out at all."

"Oh," Aela said. "I thought you would be."

"I was being sarcastic, Aela."

"Whatever that was, it certainly was not a coincidence," Aela continued. "Just like it was not a coincidence that we came to this place and found an old friend of your uncle's prepared to help us. What are the odds of that, Syd? Astronomical. I have heard it said—*small universe*—when something odd occurs. The universe is actually enormous. Impossible to comprehend. Random, but not where you are concerned."

I held up a hand. "Okay, Aela. You did it. You're freaking me out."

"Think about it, Syd. A previously undocumented phenomenon clearly related to the Etherazi just happens to take place in your immediate vicinity? We Ossho have an intuition for events of intergalactic importance. I told you that I had that feeling about you. And it seems I was more correct than I even realized. The universe bends around you."

The first time Aela brought that up, back on Denza, as a reason to stay close and observe me, they'd wanted to get in my head to see what it was like when I bonded with Goldy. At the time, I was pretty freaked out by my vision of planetary destruction, but—I can't lie—I thought it was pretty cool to have some great destiny. I'd come to the Vastness to look for my dad, but I'd also come in pursuit of something bigger than my transient life on Earth. But now that I understood what it was actually like to have the fate of the universe hang on you, I felt like I could crumble at any moment.

I looked past Aela at the endless darkness beyond the loading dock. "I didn't ask for that," I said quietly.

"No," Aela agreed, resting a hand on my shoulder like I'm sure the wisp had seen other organics do. "But here we are."

"What if the universe doesn't just *bend* around me?" I asked Aela. "What if it *breaks* because of me?"

"Normally, I would write that off as organic hubris," Aela replied. "But you are thinking of the vision the Etherazi shared with you."

I nodded. "What if I can't stop it? What if I become that version of myself?"

Aela was quiet for a moment. "We Ossho live in the present and catalog the past. These experiences are measurable. Quantifiable.

The future is but a dream, Syd. It is not real until we make it so. I have seen your past and I know your present and I have observed nothing that would make you capable of such a malevolent act."

I breathed out slowly. "Thanks, Aela. I hope you're right."

Apparently, Aela wasn't the only one who'd realized that trouble followed me around, because an hour after the gold wave passed over the station, Ezziah summoned all of us to her office. She sat perched on her cybernetic legs, her one remaining hand thoughtfully pulling at the fur on her chin. On the vid-wall were station security images of that day's cosmic event playing out in super slow motion, so we could all witness the time-space continuum pulling itself apart and then fitting back together. If you looked really close, for a moment as the wave crested over it, Unstable-J3 seemed to be a whole planet, a perfect marble of undisturbed stone.

"Our business is done," Ezziah said. "It's time for you to return to your ship and forget this place exists."

My uncle stepped forward. "If this is about today's . . . event, Ezziah, I assure you, we have no idea what that was. We'd never knowingly put your station in any kind of danger."

Ezziah's eyes flicked across us one by one. I tried to see our crew from her perspective. A Denzan spy who'd stolen an institute ship, his hybrid nephew with hair tinted suspiciously close to the cosmic shock wave that had everyone freaked out, an injured human, a corrupted Ossho wisp, a Vulpin outcast, and Melian. Well, she was pretty normal, anyway. I could tell by the way the claws on Ezziah's mechanical hand flexed and unflexed that she'd come to feel like her denmates down on the loading dock. We were a bad omen. Or, at best, a bet that wasn't worth taking.

"Forget it, Captain," I said to Tycius. "We should be moving on anyway. We all got what we wanted out of this little stop, didn't we?"

Ezziah cocked her head. "Actually, I'm still waiting on my payment."

"Right, right," Zara said. "Almost forgot."

"I'm sure you did, den Jetten," Ezziah replied with amusement.

With a flick of her wrist, Zara sent a half-full vial of the anti-human toxin straight at Ezziah's head. One-Left didn't even blink as her cybernetic hand plucked it precisely out of the air, the claws ticking sharply on the glass. She held the container up to the light for a moment, then stashed it in a compartment on her robotic forearm. Finally, her gaze slid back to Tycius.

"I should tell you that shortly after that *event*, as you called it, our scanners picked up a Denzan vessel heading in this direction." Nice of her to withhold that bit of information until after we'd paid her. I opened my mouth but shut it when Ezziah glanced in my direction, anticipating my complaint. "No, I didn't sell you out. But unless you intend to cross paths with your friends from the institute, I suggest you return to your ship. I'm planning to roll the Torrent at the top of the hour, hiding us from whatever prying eyes you've attracted. You should be gone by then."

Tycius nodded slowly, then bowed at the waist. "It was good to see you, Ezziah."

"It was a pleasure, Ty." Ezziah's smile was sincere, but quickly hardened. "But next time you need a place to hide, don't darken my docks."

"Understood."

"Hold up," I said. "It was a Denzan ship that popped up on your scanners? Not, like, a Vulpin mercenary ship that looks like it got hit by a missile?"

"Now, that sounds like a hell of a story," Ezziah said. "But no. It's a Denzan SDV-class. Not sure what it's doing out here. Don't care to find out."

"SDV?" I asked.

"Science and discovery vessel," Melian said. She elbowed me. "The top of the hour is in like ten minutes, Syd. We need to get back to our shuttle."

Ezziah flashed her fangs. "Nice to see one of you learned to tell time at that fancy institute of yours."

With that, we were given the boot. Ezziah planned to spin her station beneath the rocks on Unstable-J3's outer orbit, which would make it impossible to access without an extremely skilled and suicidal pilot. None of us felt particularly inclined to test her willingness to do that before we got clear, so we speed-walked from her office back to the docks.

"I actually kind of liked this place," Hiram said wistfully.

"You liked getting wasted with Zara three nights in a row," Melian said.

"I guess I did, yeah," Hiram replied. "Just a human and a Vulpin having a blast on their semester break. Sounds like a comedy-vid."

"Sounds like a horror-vid," Zara replied.

While the others bantered, something nagged at me. I moved next to my uncle.

"If the Torrent picked up this Denzan ship, shouldn't it have popped up on the *Eastwood*'s scanners, too?" I asked.

My uncle narrowed one of his eyes, then immediately got on the comm. "Batzian? Do you read?"

"Yes, Captain?" The voice came back a half second later, like Batzian had been waiting with his finger on the receiver.

"Has the *Eastwood* picked up any ship traffic in the area?" Tycius asked.

"Yes, Captain," Batzian replied. "And before you get angry or take us on the run, I really think we should hear him out."

In the message, Arkell sat in a captain's chair with his wiry legs stretched out in front of him. His light blue hair was still thinning across his scalp, and the one side of his face still drooped like melted butter from his days as a bomb maker, but the *Eastwood*'s old chief engineer somehow looked more invigorated than I'd ever seen him before. There was a surprising brightness to his dark eyes. He wore a sleeveless uniform patterned in black and red and emblazoned with the brick-wall logo of the Merciful Rampart. Arkell's dorky old-man-summer look definitely wasn't meant to show off the guns. It was meant to call to attention to his right arm, which had once been entirely bound in the obsidian metal the Denzans used to signify their shame. Now it was pale, wrinkled, and free.

"Greetings, Tycius," Arkell said in the recording. "Or is it

Captain Tycius now? And first mate Sydney Chambers, yes? This is Captain Arkell of the SDV *Cavern*." He grimaced—or no, wait, that was an attempt at a smile. "It seems here, at the end of an era, all of our stations have risen. I know that you are on some kind of foolish errand to the Ossho Collective, and I have no intention of stopping you. But I would request that you give me the courtesy of a meeting. I believe we can help each other. And Sydney . . ."

Arkell leaned forward, getting uncomfortably close to the camera.

"We have an old friend of yours on board."

16

How could we resist an invitation like that?

Back on Earth, there were occasions when my mom had to deal with shady characters, usually to score us some new identities. We'd roll up to a dead part of some city underneath an overpass or take winding roads out into the country, where there were more abandoned barns than people. Out in the middle of nowhere, we'd find our contact—usually some creep in a truck with tinted windows.

Our meeting with Arkell felt like the space version of that. It was three days' journey into an empty part of this largely empty system. No planets, no wormholes, not even any space junk. Just our two ships floating in all that nothing.

Based on its lusterless hull, dented plating, and propulsion system that Hiram had said looked retro, the SDV *Cavern* was an older model than the *Eastwood*. Not that our ship looked all that spectacular after getting shot up by Reno and then half-assedly patched by the Vulpin. Structurally, the two ships looked pretty much identical to me, with one major exception. A bulb-shaped attachment that was half as big as the main ship sat atop the *Cavern*. It reminded me a bit of a cement mixer or a hot air balloon. That was the only part of the *Cavern* that looked recently updated.

"Any idea what that thing does?" I asked Tycius.

He shook his head. "SDV-class ships are built to the specifications of the research they're conducting. I don't know what sort of mission the *Cavern* was on. Looks like the ship was sitting in dry dock for a while before now. Never seen anything like that contraption on top, but I'm sure Arkell will delight in telling us."

Tycius and I were seated next to each other in the shuttle on our way to meet the *Cavern*. Batzian and Melian sat across from us. We'd decided to keep this visit strictly Denzans. Well, the Denzans and me. I don't think Batzian would've let us leave him behind, anyway. He'd showed up at the shuttle with a bag slung over his shoulder and his sister in tow, even though we hadn't actually invited either of them. My uncle raised an eyebrow but wasn't inclined to waste energy debating the matter. This wasn't like when Reno was running the ship for the institute. Rules and chain of command were more like suggestions now, and everyone, including Tycius, understood that.

"What's with the bag?" I asked Batzian. "We aren't going to a sleepover."

"It contains our personal effects," he replied. Batzian was

making a big show of keeping his voice level, but he couldn't stop his leg from bumping up and down as he turned to Tycius. "I should tell you now, Captain Tycius, that we plan to stay on the *Cavern* with Arkell."

"Seriously?" I replied, leaning forward. "Arkell always treated you like dirt."

"He treated me like *a student*," Batzian countered. "He didn't—he didn't consistently put my life in jeopardy."

I felt my face getting hot. "So what? You're buying into his Merciful Rampart shit now? Want to send all the humans back to Earth?"

"I don't know what I believe," Batzian said. "But I do think their ideas might have earned a second look after—after everything we've seen."

"Oh, come on," I replied. "You're just being a pu—"

My uncle put a hand on my leg to cut me off. "We're operating outside the jurisdiction of the Serpo Institute, so I've got no real authority to stop you," he said to Batzian. "You're both valuable members of the crew, and I hope you'll reconsider."

Tycius was being way more diplomatic about this than me. Not that I really blamed Batzian for wanting to get the hell away from us. *From me.* It was the smart thing to do, even if the alternative sucked. I'd been so focused on Batzian, though, I hadn't seen the storm clouds gathering in Melian's eyes.

"My brother doesn't speak for me, Captain," she said sharply. "I'm not leaving the *Eastwood*."

Batzian turned like his sister had slapped him, which I kind of wish she had. "Melian—"

"Don't you think this is something you should've talked about with me first?" Melian asked, her eyes going wide and staying that way. She kicked the bag at Batzian's feet. "Before you stuffed my things into a duffel? Did you sneak into my room to do that?"

"I would've talked to you, but first you were on the Torrent and then . . . This is a good opportunity for us. We've probably been expelled from the institute, but Arkell has connections. And it'll be safer with him than on the *Eastwood*." Batzian tugged his ponytail as he floundered for the right words, which I knew he wouldn't find. "You haven't been thinking straight, Mel. None of us have."

"Oh, so I'm out of my mind now? You have to lead me around like a pet so I don't get myself into trouble? Is that what you're saying?"

"Please, calm down," Batzian replied quietly, looking down at the floor.

"Did you really just tell me to calm down? Are you serious right now?"

"Can we discuss this in private?" Batzian said, hazarding a glance over at me. I did a terrible job of hiding my smirk. "Later?"

"We could've discussed it in private back on the *Eastwood*," Melian shouted. "But now there's nothing left to say!"

I think we were all pretty relieved when the shuttle docked with the *Cavern* and we could escape the postargument awkward silence.

I'd expected the interior of the *Cavern* to be similar to the

Eastwood, considering that both ships were of Denzan origin. However, where the *Eastwood* was like a floating hotel, with its mellow lightning and curated plant life, the *Cavern* was like a state-of-the-art hospital. The lights were bright enough that I needed to squint coming out of the shuttle, and the air was so antiseptic clean that it stung my nostrils to breathe. The whole place buzzed with ozone, the little hairs on the backs of my hands standing up.

The last time I'd boarded a spaceship with Arkell waiting to greet me, he'd been stooped and grumpy, called me a mutt to my face, and rudely jammed my universal translator into my ear. This time, Arkell stood tall, like a weight had come off his shoulders—which, with his arm unbound, it literally had. At one of the schools I'd briefly attended on Earth, there was a biology teacher who everyone made fun of because he'd gotten divorced over summer vacation, come back to school with a Ferrari, and started always trying to high-five the students. This remodeled Arkell reminded me a lot of that guy. It was disconcerting to see his scarred face rearrange itself into a smile.

"Tycius, Sydney, I am glad you decided to come," Arkell said. He strode forward confidently with his hand extended to my uncle.

Ty had bickered constantly with Arkell aboard the *Eastwood*. Arkell had served on our vessel as part of his rehabilitation for trying to blow up the wormhole to Earth, and Ty never believed that he was even close to reformed. Ironically, only now did Arkell actually look rehabilitated. I wondered if this was what the old version of Arkell was like, before he'd become the Denzan version of a felon.

"Arkell," Ty said, clasping his old colleague's hand for the briefest of moments. "We're here. Now, what is this about?"

Arkell ignored the question and stuck his hand out to me next. "Sydney. I am relieved to see you are well after our last encounter."

"Yeah. You tried to help me with those Vulpin," I said, limply shaking his hand since it was just hanging out there. "Thanks, I guess."

"I should be the one thanking you," Arkell replied. "You have done a great service for our people by clarifying the relationship between Denzans and humanity. I hope we can put our differences behind us and work together going forward."

Oh, so it was *our* people now. I kept my mouth shut, but I hadn't forgotten how Arkell treated both me and Darcy like we were wild animals. Some of the Merciful Rampart—like Darcy's mom, apparently—believed that hybrids like me were a necessary tool to keep humanity in check. Arkell never seemed to subscribe to that line of thinking, but maybe whatever he'd been up to out here had changed his mind.

"Batzian, Melian, I hope you're finding time to continue with your studies." Arkell barely even looked at the twins. He waved forward a young Denzan who was standing a respectful distance behind Arkell. "Jamdora? Please show them to their quarters. Tycius, I was wondering if you still had any contacts in the intelligence bureau . . ."

Arkell led my uncle down the corridor while this Jamdora

guy stepped forward to welcome us. As he approached, I noticed Melian casually fix her hair. There was no other way to put it—the guy was pretty. Jamdora wore his aquamarine hair in braids that were laced with colorful patches of fabric. His eyes looked like they were lined with charcoal. He wore a Merciful Rampart uniform like Arkell, but it was wrinkled like he'd just rolled out of bed and decorated with pins and buttons featuring a bunch of cartoon characters I vaguely recognized from Denzan entertainment-vids. This sloppy uniform didn't hide his strong forearms and broad—

Wait a second. He wasn't a Denzan.

He was a hybrid. Like me.

"Wow," Jamdora said, smiling at us. "Can't tell you how cool it's going to be to have some people my own age around."

"You're—," I started to say.

"Very handsome, but I'm not staying," Melian finished, then clapped a hand over her mouth. "Oops. I only meant to say the second part out loud. Stressful day."

Batzian grimaced, tugging on his ponytail. "I believe you were going to show us to our quarters?"

"Right, right," Jamdora said with an easy smile. "Come on."

Jamdora led us down the hallway at a slow lope so that we wouldn't catch up to Tycius and Arkell. Although his demeanor was laid-back, he still looked at me with interest.

"I think you were going to say that I'm a hybrid," he said.

"Yeah," I said, shoving my hands into my pockets. "I am too."

"I know," he replied with a friendly laugh. "I've heard all about you from Arkell. You're from Earth. Your father was a theoretician and a great hero to the cause."

I don't think Jamdora meant anything by it, but hearing Arkell's version of my family history put a bad taste in my mouth. The story of Darcy's mom and dad popped into my head as I responded. "I've heard about you Rampart guys, too. Pretty grim stuff."

"Ah, that's right, you're on a crew with Darcy Ward," Jamdora said, completely unruffled by my tone.

"We *were* on a crew with her," Batzian corrected. "She betrayed us."

"That's a bit harsh," Melian said, obviously ready to contradict anything her brother said.

"I've heard about the situation with her parents," Jamdora said. "You're right, Syd. It is grim. I don't really get down with some of the Merciful Rampart's more radical ideas. My mom didn't trick a human so she could have me. She used a sample."

I raised an eyebrow. "A sample?"

"A sperm donation," Jamdora said with a shrug. He held up a hand with two fingers spread apart. "My dad's a test tube."

"I mean, there's still a human involved at some point," I said.

Batzian moved ahead of me to get a closer look at Jamdora's hand. I'd noticed it, too. His knuckles were wrapped in the obsidian metal that the Denzans used to denote their shame, but Jamdora's was slightly different. A silver filigree ran across the dark metal, the whorls like decoration.

"Are you wearing a *kenfa*?" Batzian asked.

"Ah yes." Jamdora nodded, hiding the knuckles inside his other hand. "Good eye, Batzian."

"I thought *kenfavism* was outlawed," Batzian said, sounding way too excited.

"Not so much outlawed as frowned upon," Jamdora said. "We actually have one of the last practicing masters on board."

"Sorry," I said, raising my hand. "What are you guys talking about?"

"*Kenfavism* is a Denzan self-defense technique," Melian explained. "Most of our people believe that training to inflict harm is a poor use of one's life span. It's something of a cultural gray area, I guess."

Jamdora bent his knees and extended his hand like a knife's edge. "I wear the *kenfa* to remind me of the harm I might one day inflict should all other choices escape me. With the ocean's blessing, may the waves be tranquil."

I snorted. Jamdora sounded like some strip-mall karate teacher. I glanced at Batzian and Melian, though, and they were both looking at him starry-eyed.

"Here we are," Jamdora said, stopping at a corridor that led to the sleeping quarters. "I'm supposed to pitch you on staying with us," he continued, patting my shoulder. "Especially you, Syd. But, honestly, the amenities kind of suck and the scientists on board barely stop working to eat. It's pretty boring. I'd much rather be out there with you on an ISV."

"A stolen ISV," Batzian said.

"Even better," Jamdora replied. "Anyway, now that my mother's work is finished, we're hopefully going to be headed back to Denza."

I tilted my head. "Your mother's work . . . ?"

Before Jamdora could answer, Arkell shouted at us from farther down the walkway. "Enough socializing. Sydney, come. There's someone I'd like you to meet."

"The captain's calling. Better go," Jamdora said with a lopsided smile. He slung an arm around Batzian's shoulders. "Let's get you settled in, new friend."

"I'm going to say good-bye to my brother," Melian said to me, her tone indicating that she might also strangle her twin. The three of them continued down the residential wing while I went to catch up with Tycius and Arkell.

They stood with a short Denzan woman who seemed to be about a hundred years old, curved like an apostrophe, a cane clasped in her gnarled hands. Both of her eyes were milky white. She was clearly blind.

"It is my honor to present Theoretician Ayadora," Arkell said with reverence.

My brow furrowed. Based on the name, this old lady was obviously related to Jamdora. Could it really be his mother? He was about my age and she was absolutely ancient.

"Theoretician Ayadora." My uncle repeated the name, almost like he was trying to remember where he'd heard it before. "I'm not familiar with your work."

Ayadora tipped her head in our direction in something that might have generously been interpreted as a hello. "No," she said to Tycius. "You would not be." She tapped her cane on the floor impatiently and angled herself toward Arkell. "I have participated in your meet-and-greet, Arkell. May I return to my analysis?"

"Of course, Ayadora," Arkell replied. "I didn't mean to keep you."

With a grunt, the old lady turned and ambled down the hallway, seeming to know the way without the use of her cane.

"Cool that you found someone ruder than you, Arkell," I said.

"Theoreticians can be of a single focus when it comes to their work," he replied. "I am sure you, of all people, can understand that."

My father. Vanceval. Both theoreticians whose obsessions had sent cracks shooting through my whole life. I'd walked right into that one and didn't have a snappy comeback ready for Arkell. It warmed my heart when Tycius took a sharp step toward Arkell.

"I'm getting tired of this cryptic victory lap you're forcing us to endure," Tycius said, squeezing Arkell's bare shoulder in a way that wasn't at all friendly. "Get to the point. What did your message mean, Arkell? What is Ayadora's work?"

Arkell shook off my uncle's hand with a cold stare. "Better that you see him for yourself," he said.

"Who?" I asked. "See who?"

"I believe you call him Goldy."

17

Arkell led us down a corridor where the walls were huge windows looking into busy research stations. There had to be at least fifty Denzans working in the two rooms, leaning over terminals to scroll through data or plugged into VR headsets while their hands swiped at invisible patterns. There were a lot of numbers, a lot of measurements, a lot of patterns. Something in the Denzan part of my mind latched on to the idea of energy fields, light waves, ripples in a pond when you skipped a stone.

Goldy. It seemed impossible, but somehow I knew that it wasn't.

"Young Batzian told me everything about your journey to Ashfall," Arkell said conversationally, like he hadn't just dropped a bomb on us. "The origin of our so-called shame. The true nature of humanity. The fact that there's no cure for the Wasting."

I figured that Batizan had told Arkell a lot, but I didn't expect him to have so many details. "He shouldn't have done that," I said. "It's more complicated than—"

"Did you expect you could keep it all a secret, Sydney?" Arkell asked, interrupting me. "If that was the case, you should have stayed on Ashfall like your father. Information is the galaxy's most powerful virus. What you've released will spread, whether you want it to or not. Perhaps the version I received from Batzian was colored by his mental weakness and cowardice, but I don't hear you disputing the core truths. I imagine the version Rafe Butler received is similarly colored, yet that hasn't stopped him from taking action. And we must be prepared to respond."

"Wait. What did Rafe Butler do?" Tycius asked. "What's happening on Denza?"

Arkell handed a tablet to my uncle. "I assumed being off the grid, you wouldn't be plugged into the newsfeed. Rafe's mysterious protest is all anyone on Denza can talk about."

The frozen image on the screen showed four ISVs hovering low over an island on Denza that I immediately recognized. The rows of Earth flags flying over the main thoroughfare made it pretty obvious.

"That's Little Earth," I said. "What are those ships doing?"

"So far, nothing," Arkell replied. "The humans on board commandeered the vessels and kicked off their nonhuman crew. Since then, they've just been hanging over Little Earth. Everyone assumes Butler is behind this little coup, but he hasn't made any demands yet."

"He's waiting until he can get to us," I said, more to my uncle than Arkell. Even rumors of the Origin were enough to cause major unrest on Denza. It was starting to feel like keeping peace between the species would be impossible.

"Indeed." It was Arkell who answered, almost like he agreed with my thoughts. "Last I heard, the institute had lost contact with a number of other ships on missions throughout the galaxy. They're assumed to have fallen under human control as well. I noticed the *Eastwood* was on the list."

"So the institute thinks we've defected with Rafe," my uncle said, "while in actuality, those ships are probably hunting us."

"An interesting predicament," Arkell said.

"And I suppose this is when you offer us a solution, right?" I asked.

"For your specific problem? No. I can't help you avoid Butler or the institute. But with our research, I believe we have discovered a way to rid Denza of humanity before they further indulge their fascistic urges."

"With an Etherazi," I said dryly. "You know humanity already won a war against them once, right?"

"The human part of your brain thinks in terms of war," Arkell replied. "But you should think in terms of peace."

"You wouldn't understand half the shit I think about," I muttered.

Ignoring my weak comeback, Arkell led us to an elevator, and the three of us squeezed inside. Based on the design of the ship, I had no doubt we were ascending into the large domed section atop the vessel.

"Less philosophizing, more answers," Tycius said. "Our kind can't even look at an Etherazi without unraveling. And you expect us to believe that you captured one?"

My uncle was right. The physics-defying forms of the Etherazi wreaked havoc on Denzan brains that had evolved highly sensitive pattern recognition. They literally couldn't make sense of what they were seeing—although, if an Etherazi was close enough to stare at, you were probably in big trouble already. Even so, I believed Arkell. There was no doubt in my mind that the wave of energy that had passed through the Torrent had emanated from the *Cavern*. I tasted bile in my throat. It wasn't Arkell's experiment that made me uneasy. It was a memory of something Goldy had told me the last time we met, when he was barfing out prophecies.

"Theoretician Ayadora's work has long been of interest to the Merciful Rampart," Arkell continued, earning a glare from my uncle for another nonanswer. Arkell held up a finger like he was getting to the point. "She's a brilliant woman, singularly devoted to her research, even after she lost her vision and her youth during an early trial."

So that explained why Ayadora was so much older than Jamdora. I shook my head. "This all sounds insane."

Arkell sighed. "Sometimes madness and genius are indistinguishable," he said. "Ayadora's work focuses on the temporal energy fields generated by Etherazi. Understanding them, harnessing them, stripping them. Unfortunately, the Denzan Senate viewed her efforts as too dangerous and pulled her funding decades ago. She has continued on in secret ever since and, thus, was prepared to move quickly when recent events required radical thinking."

The elevator doors opened into a massive dome-like chamber. It was like stepping into an airplane hangar, our feet echoing on the metal floor. There were stations fanned out across the room's perimeter, all of them walled off behind glass that I noted was laced with ultonate filaments. All of the terminals were occupied by Denzan scientists who stopped what they were doing to watch us as we entered.

No, not us. They were watching *me*.

"What the hell is that thing, Arkell?" Tycius asked.

My uncle was pointing at the huge hourglass-shaped structure that ran from floor to ceiling. The upper bowl appeared empty at first glance, but as we drew closer I made out flitting sparks of gold floating there, almost like fireflies. Whenever one of these flare-ups occurred, a nearly imperceptible streak of lightning lanced out from the glass wall and eradicated it. The effect kind of reminded me of one of those plasma balls sold in corny mall gift shops on Earth.

"Before we began punching wormholes throughout the universe, the Etherazi were trapped in the negative space between galaxies," Arkell explained. "They were unable to break loose on their own. We've long theorized that their temporal disruptions are also rendered ineffective while in that state due to a lack of matter, a lack of even *time*. Ayadora sought to re-create those conditions in a controlled environment."

While Arkell lectured, my gaze shifted to the lower bowl of the hourglass. Looking at it made my frontal lobe throb in way that reminded me of jacking into the Wayscope. Suspended in the lower half of the containment unit was what I could only describe as a slice of the Vastness itself. A disc of pure emptiness, like a miniature black hole. The glass around it pulsed from the vacuum contained within. They'd basically punched a wormhole inside their own ship and were somehow keeping it stable.

"To put it in terms you can understand, the *Cavern* functions as a sort of magnet, attracting Etherazi by breaching their negative space," Arkell continued. He clasped his hands behind his back as we reached the base of the hourglass. "Once they're reeled in, the mechanism creates a negatively charged environment that literally shears the Etherazi of their temporal coating."

"That's what we encountered a few days ago," Tycius said. "Your machine's . . . exhaust?"

"Indeed," Arkell replied. "All that energy has to go somewhere. We're still measuring the ramifications, but they seem mostly harmless."

"Mostly harmless," Tycius said with a shake of his head. "By the tides, you could've destroyed yourselves, turning this machine on."

"The only way to test it was *to test it*," Arkell said. "The risk has proved worth the reward."

We stopped at the bottom of the metal staircase that led up to the middle section of the hourglass, the narrow piece where sand would tumble down. Arkell kept going, and I followed.

"Madness," Tycius said. "You're meddling with forces beyond our comprehension."

Arkell turned to look back at my uncle. "If it hadn't worked, I would agree with you," he said. "Well, I would be dead if it had not worked, but you take my point. It is not madness, Tycius. And these forces are very much within our comprehension. As you can plainly see."

I continued on up the stairs, past Arkell, drawn to the object suspended in the narrow section of the hourglass.

Not suspended. Trapped.

Like a wrinkled asteroid. An enormous peach pit. A chestnut the size of a car.

An Etherazi's core.

The carapace peeled back, revealing the eye within. I'd seen that before, up close and personal. Fresh flares of gold fired from the searing pupil, crackled upward through the hourglass, and were swiftly disintegrated by the negative energy current.

In that giant golden eye, I saw nothing but rage.

"It's him," I said. "It's really him."

The last time I met Goldy had been back on Denza. He had just stopped Vanceval and that Vulpin mercenary Nyxie from killing Tycius and me. He'd shown up in the guise of an Ossho wisp, his inconceivable shape somehow squeezed into a dented exo-suit. The Etherazi had wiped out half a team of Vulpin mercenaries with ease, but he'd let the others escape with Vanceval. That was on purpose. He needed me to chase them.

He wanted me to go to Ashfall.

He had plans for me. And I kept walking right into them.

"I have saved your life twice, Sydney Chambers," Goldy had

said in that abandoned Denzan warehouse. Outside, a beach that he'd partly turned to glass shone in the sun. "The next time we meet, you must save mine."

"Don't—," I started.

"—count on it, Goldy," the Etherazi finished. "Predictable as ever."

I put my hand on the glass that separated me from the Etherazi. Vibrations like a heartbeat thrummed through my fingertips. The disturbingly huge floating eyeball—the core of an Etherazi, something seen this close by only the First Twelve when they penetrated their temporal carapaces and killed the monsters during the invasion—fixed on me, unblinking. Curls of gold energy floated up from the eye but were quickly sucked into the upper chamber of the hourglass and vaporized.

This was the moment, then. I was supposed to return the favor. Up close, I could see how the glass prison was studded with millions of ultonate filaments. Still, I applied a little more pressure and felt the wall give a bit under my palm. How hard would I have to hit this thing to break it open? And what would happen if I did?

I sensed a buzzing around the edges of the room. The team of Denzan scientists monitoring the Etherazi were huddled around their terminals, conferring in hushed but excited tones. I caught snatches of their conversation.

". . . an uptick in energy production . . ."

". . . what does it mean?"

". . . the environment remains stable . . ."

I dropped my hand away from the glass and stepped back,

bumping into Arkell, who had sidled up right behind me.

"Fascinating, isn't it?" he said. "I never thought I'd be able to look at one of the beasts, much less study it up close. It's almost intimate to see it exposed like this."

"What are you going to do with him?" I asked.

"Study it, of course," Arkell replied. "We've barely scratched the surface of the tests we want to run. The more data we gather, the more we can optimize the *Cavern* for a second use. You've already helped us a great deal, Sydney. Until now, we weren't sure if the creature was aware or if stripping away its energy field rendered it comatose. The eye only opened when you entered."

The fiery pupil remained locked on me. I couldn't help but stare back. "Oh, he's aware," I said. "He's pissed."

"Yes, we can see that now, based on the increased attempts at energy production," Arkell said. "It recognizes you, Sydney. I wondered if it would. I thought it might even try to communicate with you."

"It can't talk," I said flippantly. "Maybe you could teach it to blink once for yes and twice for no."

I tried to make a joke of it, but Goldy was absolutely communicating with me. The message was clear in the piercing stare. *You owe me.*

"Simplistic," Arkell said, stroking his chin. He'd taken me seriously. "But it might work if we can force the creature to cooperate."

"You've done the unthinkable, Arkell," Tycius said, standing a few steps down from the landing. He tilted his head away from Goldy, like even though it was trapped my uncle didn't want to risk exposing himself to its mind-bending appearance. "But what now?"

"Now we will learn as much as we can about these beasts that killed hundreds of thousands of our people and hopefully determine how to dispose of them," Arkell replied. "And then, more important, there are the more immediate implications for our relationship with the humans."

"How do you mean?" Tycius asked.

"Ayadora's technology works," Arkell said. "We can replicate the *Cavern*. Position them in orbit around Denza and outside every wormhole. We can trap the Etherazi. Contain them. Stop living in fear of their very approach. And if we can do that all ourselves, then what need does Denza have for humans? We can thank them for their service and send them back to Earth."

"Yeah," Tycius replied. "I'm sure it will be that simple."

"No, it will be ugly, and there will likely be blood," Arkell said. "But your voyage to Ashfall has caused Rafe Butler to expose humanity's true nature. When we bring them this solution, the Denzan Senate will at last acknowledge the rightness of the Merciful Rampart." He patted my shoulder. "In a way, this is all thanks to you, Sydney."

I jerked away from Arkell's touch and again approached the containment tank, staring down Goldy's unblinking eye. "You saw this coming, huh?"

"Saw what coming, exactly?" Arkell asked.

"He's not talking to you," Tycius said. He took a cautious step up as I pressed both my hands against the glass. "Syd? You good?"

My uncle had been there when Goldy told me I would save his life the next time we met. Goldy had some choice prophecies for Tycius, too—that he would fail me, and that he would die, in that order. The Etherazi was so certain about everything. Forcing all of us to play his game. And so far, I'd given him everything he'd wanted. I'd gone to Ashfall, I'd uncovered the truth about my father, and I'd given the galaxy a nudge toward chaos. I'd played my role to perfection.

World killer.

I still vividly remembered what it felt like to be that grizzled, older version of myself from the vision that Goldy had inflicted on me. The future he was grooming me for. As if staring down at a burning Earth, knowing that I'd caused its destruction wasn't disturbing enough, I could recall exactly what the older me thought about the whole apocalypse.

Righteous. Justified.

I'd lived that part of my life for only a few seconds, but I couldn't imagine what could bring me to that point. I didn't want to find out.

Staring at the Etherazi—captured, stripped of his temporal armor, booming voice muted—I realized this was my chance. Like Aela said, the future wasn't real until we made it so.

I could prove him wrong.

The sweat on my palms had stuck them to the glass between Goldy and me. I slowly peeled them back, my gaze lingering on that enormous pupil and the short-lived bursts of ferocious energy that erupted from within. I smiled at him. All teeth.

"Hope you have a backup plan," I said, and I gave Goldy a wave good-bye.

Arkell glanced down at his handheld. "Some fascinating readings here, multiple spikes in the creature's energy levels—"

I clapped him hard on the shoulder and he stumbled a step to the side, nearly dropping his tablet. "Cool, cool, cool," I said. "Good luck with everything."

His eyebrows knitted together, and he gave me one of those old down-the-nose Arkell glares. "That's it? You're witnessing scientific history here, Sydney. Given your connection to the creature, I had thought you might wish to aid in our testing—"

"Nope," I interrupted. "I'm good." I turned to Tycius. "Ready to go back to the ship?"

My uncle smiled. "Ready if you are."

I didn't look back at the giant hourglass with Goldy in the middle, frozen in time. I felt heat on my shoulders, like his enraged stare could penetrate the glass and ultonate architecture, but that was probably just my imagination. The Etherazi and the Merciful Rampart—I left them all behind. They deserved each other.

I would choose my own future.

18

Once you were old enough to know that he wasn't the strongest and smartest man in the universe, you felt nothing for your father but secondhand embarrassment. He was a skinny man, with a horseshoe of unkempt hair, and watery eyes so that it looked like he might cry at any second. A weak man. He was from a place on Earth called Paris, and the only things he brought when the Serpo Institute recruited him were these hardcover paper tomes filled with reprints of paintings. Your parents had bonded over those books. Your mom had visited Earth a few times, ostensibly to study the artwork of humanity, but really to find a sperm donor. She was aligned with the Merciful Rampart, who believed that hybrids like you were Denza's only hope to stop an eventual takeover of the planet by humanity.

You remembered how he cried when she confessed the truth and exiled herself to Denza's northern islands in shame. *Pathetic*, you thought. Your family's whole life was a lie, your father a sucker, you an experiment—and yet, he never dissolved their union. In fact, once, you hacked his messages and found that he was writing your mom long, flowery missives about how much he missed her. She never even responded.

"Not all humans are as strong as us," Rafe told you once when you'd been complaining to him about your depressing father. "We should be gentle with the broken ones, Darcy. Don't forget that."

You didn't really listen to that second part. Instead, you thrilled at Rafe referring to you as human, including you as part of his group.

It was a relief when your father signed up for a monthslong exploration of a distant galaxy. He entrusted you to the care of the Serpo Institute and Rafe Butler. You could forget about his sad eyes and broken heart.

And yet, you ran into your father's arms when he rescued you from that Vulpin cruiser. You crawled into his lap and cried like a little girl, not caring at all if Reno was around to see. He rubbed your back and whispered gentle words and you told him everything—about Ashfall, the *Eastwood*, the dead Vulpin.

"You're safe now," he said. "I've got you."

Funny. You actually believed him.

The name of your father's ship was the ISV *Greenleaf*. It was a ship just like the *Eastwood*. Malnourished and exhausted, you spent a few days recovering in the med-bay. You'd wake up and, for a brief moment, feel like you were home again, like the worst of your problems were dirty looks from Denzan cadets who didn't like the color of your hair.

It took you some time to realize how strangely quiet the ISV *Greenleaf* was. Your father, it turned out, was more alone than you'd been.

When you were well enough, you took a walk around the ship. The canteen, the gym, the theater—all empty. You didn't see another soul until you walked onto the bridge.

Six Denzan adults and a squat Panalax that had infested the form of a creature shaped like a giant caterpillar. Your father's entire crew. All of them safely buckled into their seats, all of them dosed like the *Greenleaf* was traveling at hyperspeed, even though you were barely crawling through the system. When you entered, your father was in the process of checking the vitals on the Denzan woman who was the *Greenleaf*'s actual captain.

"Ah," your dad said, seeing you. "Feeling better?"

You nodded, more interested in the comatose crew. "You're keeping them drugged."

"Better this way, don't you think?" he said. "Avoid any unpleasant confrontations."

On instinct, you accessed the terminal at your old spot on the *Eastwood*, checking the ship's systems. Everything read as normal, but you knew there were supposed to be fail-safes built into the ship's AI to prevent overdoses and prolonged catatonia.

"How?" you asked. "I don't understand."

Your father's mouth compressed. "One of Rafe's solutions. A bit of code delivered to the ship's computer. Not sure when he developed it, but he had it ready."

"Rafe's solutions," you repeated.

Reno's voice came from behind you, causing your shoulders to bunch up like you might be struck. "Oh, our Rafe's got *solutions* for every species, so he says," Reno said. "Just in case a situation like this one should ever arise. Say what you will about the man, but he's got foresight."

Since you last saw her, Reno had cleaned herself up. She'd found a uniform that fit her, washed off the blood and grime, and slicked back her white-blond hair. She still favored her leg, though, and you could see the bulge of bio-tape wrapped around it.

"Good to see you back on your feet, Cadet," Reno said. "Now that you're out, I can finally use the med-bay. Damn wound isn't healing right, but your daddy here wouldn't let me go near you while you were recovering."

"You're lucky I don't have you confined, Marie," your dad said. His usually teary eyes were surprisingly clear when he glared at Reno. You'd actually never seen him like that and hadn't thought your father capable of even attempting to come off as tough.

"Oh, honey, I respect that this is your ship now, but let's not get carried away with talk like that," Reno replied. "What generation are you, Alain? Fifth? Sixth? That's when the Denzans started selecting humans who were docile. Me? I was chosen because I'm a warrior."

"I've had enough of your mythologizing," your dad said with a dismissive sniff. "First Twelve or not, you'll answer for the things you've done when we're back on Denza. Until then, keep your distance from my daughter."

"Aye-aye, Captain."

Reno snapped off a sloppy salute and limped off the bridge. As soon as she was gone, your father visibly deflated, and his eyes took on that glassy quality, like he was capable of puffing himself up for only a few moments in your defense. He put his hand on the back of the nearest chair like he needed to keep himself from falling over. This was more like the man you knew.

"You did good, Dad," you said quietly. "But be careful. She's lost it."

He smiled, perhaps brighter than was appropriate, at your compliment. You tried to remember the last time you said something nice to the man and couldn't. It had all been shouting and sulking after your mom left. And then he'd left, too.

"I knew that the second I saw her. What she did to those Vulpin . . ." He trailed off, looking around at his own sedated crew. These were his colleagues and probably his friends. A shadow passed over his face, but he shook it off. "Your mom worried something like this could happen. She—"

"I don't want to talk about her," you said sharply. Your dad snapped his mouth closed, that faraway look in his eyes again. You quickly changed the subject. "Are we going back to Denza?"

"Not yet," he replied. "First, Rafe has asked us to look for your old ship. He wants the *Eastwood* brought in safely. No more shooting at each other."

"I never knew you worked with Rafe."

"Every human works for Rafe," your dad said. "Nearly every ISV with a human on board is under his control now. I heard about a few holdouts who wouldn't betray their nonhuman crews. The ISV *Feather*, ironically enough . . ."

It took you a moment to place how you knew the ISV *Feather*. That was Hiram's dad's ship. You wondered how Hiram was doing, back on the *Eastwood*. The last you'd seen him, he'd been piloting Reno's Battle-Anchor and turning Reno's own missiles against her. It wasn't the side you'd expected him to take, just like Rafe probably didn't expect his former son-in-law to refuse to join his uprising.

"I'm surprised you joined in," you said.

"I probably wouldn't have, not if you hadn't been involved," your father admitted. He stood over his Panalax crewmate, brushing his fingers across a fuzzy patch on the creature's head. He didn't seem pleased with the mold growth, because he produced a handheld UV light and held it up to the Panalax while he spoke. "I don't pretend to know what Rafe's endgame is, but things will never go back to the way things were. My hope is that by finding the *Eastwood* we might stabilize things. Do you have any idea where they might be headed?"

For a moment, you wondered if it might not be better to let the *Eastwood* disappear. Rafe had some dozen ships searching for them, spread across some hundred million galaxies—if your old crew was smart, they could stay hidden forever. But Rafe had always been honest with you. He'd taken care of you when your own parents were too broken to do it themselves. He'd treated you like a whole human, even though you weren't. If he was making a move now, and if he needed the *Eastwood* found, then you would help him.

You'd heard Syd promise Aela to bring the wisp home. He wouldn't deviate from that. Spinning the *Eastwood* out to the farthest reaches of the galaxy would be exactly his move.

"The Ossho Collective," you said. "Where is it now?"

In the days that followed, you logged a lot of hours in the Wayscope, stretching your mind like Tycius had taught you in the basement of Rafe's pizzeria. You'd been a slower learner than Syd during those covert classes. You weren't as comfortable letting your mind go free, exposing it to the endless openness of the Vastness. But you kept trying, squinting through the pain in your temples, ignoring the burned taste in your mouth.

You mapped hundreds of possible routes to the Comorra system, where the Ossho Collective was currently located. Your father sent these out to the other ships in Rafe's search party. They started sweeping those galaxies, but it was still like looking for a needle in a haystack. Without knowing exactly what system the *Eastwood* was coming from, there was no real way to predict their path. And you knew they had to stop somewhere to resupply their sedatives if they were truly making the voyage to Comorra.

"I didn't realize you'd gotten so good at this," your father said to you one day as you pushed the Wayscope's visor off and bent forward in the seat, feeling like you might throw up.

"I'm not that good," you grumbled. "My head feels like it's going to explode."

"Darcy, do you not realize that Rafe's entire fleet is taking directions from you?" Your dad reached down and touched your cheek, lifting your head. "You're the only person he has capable of using the

Wayscope. Never forget how valuable you are to them."

By "them," he meant the humans. You found it odd that your father would hold himself separate from the rest of his species, but you didn't comment.

"I don't understand the point of all this," Reno said from where she leaned in the bridge's entrance with her arms crossed. "If we know where they're going, why not just meet them there? Set a trap in Comorra and be done with it."

"How would that trap function, exactly?" your father asked. "Would we ram them? Forcibly board them? What would prevent the *Eastwood* from simply turning and running, disappearing to a place we'd never find?"

"These ISVs don't have guns for you to shoot at them," you added.

"Rafe's solution works best if we can catch them during their transit," you father said. "Preferably when they're moving at high speed. It's the best chance we have to peacefully bring them in."

"Rafe's solution," Reno repeated. "God, I'm already tired of hearing that."

Later, you pored over reports from the monitored systems, hoping that one of the permanent Denzan wormholes had caught sight of the *Eastwood*. They hadn't left a trace. But you did come across one strange report.

A potential Etherazi sighting in some backwater system called Jeuna. There were no known ships in the area. The galaxy was basically abandoned. But there had been an unexplained flare of Etherazi activity, and it didn't even emanate from the system's wormhole. Based on the intelligence intercepted from the Serpo Institute, the scientists were baffled by the readings.

Goldy. That was the name Syd used. Like a pet.

Based on a hunch, you mapped a course from Jeuna to Comorra. Then you mapped it again. And again. Until you were certain that you'd found the most efficient course, the one that Syd would take. When you were done, your nose bled and you had a splitting headache. But you also had a deep, satisfying feeling of certainty.

Your old crew was resourceful, so you assumed that the *Eastwood* had somehow resupplied their sedatives. They would be traveling at maximum burn, knowing they needed to get where they wanted to go before the net closed. Assuming they left Jeuna within a few days of the strange incident with the Etherazi . . .

You knew where to catch them.

Rafe Butler wasn't like Reno or your father. He knew what was best for the galaxy. And he thought you were valuable. If he wanted the *Eastwood* captured, then you would make that happen for him.

Three weeks later, the *Greenleaf* passed through a wormhole in a fly-through system that had been punched only a few days earlier.

You were right.

The trail was easy to follow from there. Soon, the *Eastwood* appeared on the vid-screen.

"Now what?" Reno asked, her eyes aglow with the reflected light from the *Eastwood's* flaring thrusters.

"It's already done," your father replied. "We just have to wait for the program to bring them to a stop."

Rafe's solution. A simple bit of code sent from the *Greenleaf* to the *Eastwood*. Even a ship running dark with its communication array down–like the *Eastwood*–needed to have its navigation sensors online during high-speed travel to make sure the vessel didn't crash into any stray asteroids. The virus Rafe had supplied entered there and, once uploaded, completely supplanted the *Eastwood*'s control systems. Much like your father had done to his crewmates, you could now keep the *Eastwood*'s crew in peaceful hibernation while slowing and boarding their ship.

"And look," your father said with a glance at Reno. "Not a single missile fired."

"Thank you, Alain," Reno said. "For getting my ship back."

How long, you wondered, had Rafe had this virus in his back pocket? He could control any ship in the Denzan fleet with just a simple upload. And the Denzans seemed woefully unprepared for such a maneuver. The pacifists couldn't imagine a universe where someone might want to do them harm.

While Reno prepared to board the *Eastwood*, your father took you aside.

"I want you to know that you can stay with me aboard the *Greenleaf*," he said. "Now that we've secured the *Eastwood*, we're bound for home. For Denza."

"But . . . ?"

"But I think you should go with Reno. Keep an eye on her. Your crewmates might need someone to watch over them."

"They didn't watch over me back on Ashfall," you said. "They left me with her."

"I know." He accessed a terminal, pulling up a list of audio files from a directory you didn't recognize. "I downloaded the logs from that Vulpin ship and found this . . ."

"It's over, Reno, enough is enough . . ." You recognized Tycius's voice crackling over a comm channel. When had this conversation taken place? It must have been when she'd knocked you unconscious. "I don't want to leave you stranded out here, but I don't trust that you can control yourself."

"Give me back my ship, you Denzan worm." Reno's voice was raw with rage.

"Oh yeah, sure, since you asked so nicely," Syd said in the background.

"You've forgotten your oaths, Reno. Your responsibility to protect these cadets. To safeguard Denza and the Vastness," Tycius said.

"Oaths I swore based on a lie," Reno replied. "I won't be used by your people again, Tycius. Never again."

"Holy shit, this is a waste of time," Syd said, then raised his voice. "Darcy, are you there? You can't be buying into this! Are you okay? Where's Darcy, Reno?"

"At least let us send a shuttle over for—"

The transmission ended there. Reno cut them off.

"I'll go," you said.

Outside the shuttle, with Reno impatiently waiting inside, your father hugged you good-bye.

"You have goodness in you," he said into your ear. "Don't let anyone convince you that you're something that you're not. I love you. Your mom loves you."

You tensed up at the mention of your mother and probably would've shoved your father away if he hadn't squeezed you tighter. There was human strength hidden in those scrawny arms. You sometimes forgot that.

"Okay, Dad," you said. "Let me go."

A short shuttle ride later and you were back on the *Eastwood*. It was that easy. Reno tilted her head back and sucked in a deep lungful of air that wasn't any different from the air aboard the *Greenleaf*.

"Ah," she declared. "Home sweet home."

You trotted ahead of her, wanting to make it to the bridge first. There was one issue with Rafe's solution, taking over the vessel by keeping the crew in a hyperspeed stupor.

Aela didn't sleep.

When you entered, the wisp was bent over Syd, shaking him by the shoulders. The others were all where they should be, sound asleep, except that Batzian's usual seat was empty. Aela had forcibly removed the sedative IV from the back of Syd's neck and pulled him to the edge of his seat. It wasn't a pleasant experience to come off the drugs suddenly. Syd had thrown up in his lap, and his head lolled back and forth, not fully conscious.

"Aela," you said. "Please. Don't resist."

"Darcy?" You detected incredulity in the wisp's tinny voice. "How?"

And then Reno shouldered by you, charging at Aela. She closed the distance quickly, pouncing on the wisp before Aela could react. Reno grabbed her by either side of the faceplate, thumbs pressed down tightly against the glass to keep the exo-suit from opening. Aela swung their arms and kicked at Reno, but the captain barely noticed.

"Hello, little wisp," Reno said. "What a story you must have to tell. Darcy, get me the blowtorch from engineering. We don't want Aela floating around loose, do we?"

You did as you were told.

PART THREE

WHOSE PLANET IS THIS?

19

I had a terrible dream when I was under. Something had gone wrong and Aela was trying desperately to wake me up. My head felt like it weighed a thousand pounds. I couldn't keep my eyes open or get my legs under me.

My ears felt packed with cotton, but I swore I heard Reno's booming voice.

And then the darkness came again. My body skipping across star systems, my mind a void. A dreamless sleep where I wasn't visited by my dead father or frightening future versions of myself.

It ruled.

Until the sedatives slowly receded from my system and I immediately sensed that something wasn't quite right. I was a veteran of drugged-up hyperspeed travel at this point. I knew the fuzzy-headed hangover feeling and the pins and needles in my extremities. I was getting used to the weird hungry/nauseous backflips that my stomach did as my digestive tract kicked back into gear. All of that was as it should be.

But, in the seats around me, only Hiram was also stirring.

And on the vid-wall, our destination was a familiar blue planet speckled with thousands of islands.

That was Denza.

"Try not to freak out," Darcy said.

Of course I didn't listen.

I lunged out of my seat at the sight of Darcy in her old spot next to me, her hands shoved in the pocket of the worn-out hoodie she'd left behind on the *Eastwood*. At least, my brain told my body to lunge. In reality, my opening maneuver was more like a messy roll onto the floor as my jelly legs refused to support me.

Darcy, who had clearly been awake for some time, lazily got to her feet and picked me up from the floor. "Please don't make me beat you up again, Syd."

"I won that fight," I replied as she held me around the waist like she was leading a slow dance, then flung me back into my seat.

"Whoa, it's Darcy," Hiram chimed in, groggily leaning forward. "Did we time travel?"

"Hi, Hiram," she said, a flicker of a smile threatening to break through Darcy's cool façade. "How's your leg?"

Hiram reached down to massage feeling back into his upper thigh. "Honestly, it sucks. How are you?"

"Had a rough time for a while, but I'm better now," Darcy said.

I looked around to see if anyone else thought it was unbelievable that these two were just engaged in a casual catch-up, but the rest of the crew were all still under. Tycius, Zara, H'Jossu, Melian—all slumbering soundly like nothing had changed and we were still on our way to the Comorra system.

"How did this happen?" I asked. "Where's Aela?"

Darcy winced at my second question, choosing instead to focus on the first. "I figured out where you were going and how you were getting there," she said, unable to keep a bit of pride from sneaking into her voice. "Rafe has a virus that we uploaded via your navigation system that allowed us to take over. We kept you under while we took back the ship."

"Gramps has an answer for everything," Hiram said. He reached into his pocket and pulled out a protein bar, our situation not deterring him from his usual posthibernation scarfing.

"And what about Aela?"

"Reno took them," Darcy replied.

"What? Took them where?"

Darcy shook her head. "I don't know. That wasn't part of the plan. We were supposed to bring you all down to Little Earth to meet with Rafe. As soon as we got within range of Denza's atmosphere, she grabbed Aela and took the shuttle down. I couldn't stop her."

"Did you try?" I asked.

Darcy frowned at me, then looked away. "No."

"She's really lost her shit, huh?" Hiram said. "What does she want with Aela, anyway?"

"Aela's the only hard evidence of the Origin in existence. Reno probably wants to control that," I said, pushing up from the chair. This time, I was able to get my legs under me, staring at Darcy the whole time. "We were trying to help Aela, but you just had to jack our ship. Now who knows what Reno will do to them."

When Darcy refused to look at me, Hiram spoke up. "Relax, Syd. It's not like Aela is going to just start showing people the Origin because Reno asks them to. We'll get them back and get them home."

"Hold on," Darcy said, focusing on Hiram. "They showed you the Origin?"

"Yeah," Hiram replied. "I've been having a, uh, tough time coming to terms with it."

"But he kept it together," I said sharply. "Unlike Reno."

"She's angry," Darcy said, her eyes seeking out the vid-screen where Denza was getting bigger and bigger as we approached. "I think that anger has been in her for a long time and we never realized it. Maybe she didn't even realize it."

"You took her side," I said.

Maybe I was being stubborn, but I wasn't ready to let Ashfall go. I could still remember Darcy driving her elbows into my back while, just a few feet away, the remnants of my father's head blew away like broken leaves.

Darcy finally met my eyes, her gaze unblinking and unreadable. "You've never done anything you regret, Syd?"

Not in the present, no. But in the future . . .

"I regret letting you catch me," I said.

With a groan, I stumbled over to the control terminal where Aela usually stood. Darcy watched my every fumbling move, making no effort to stop me. I tried to access the sedative controls but found myself locked out.

"What the hell?" I asked, slapping the console. "How do I wake up the others?"

"You don't," Darcy replied.

"So what? They're prisoners?"

"Calm down," Darcy said. "We'll bring them around once we're on Denza."

"I'm not in the mood for shitty pizza, so what if I don't want to go see Rafe?" I asked.

Darcy tossed up her hands in frustration. "I guess you can just stay on the *Eastwood* and sulk until he comes to see you. We'll be in the atmosphere within the hour. I don't really care what you do once we're there."

Hiram stood up, did a couple dramatic stretches, and then limped toward the door. He took me under his arm on the way. "Come on, Syd," he said. "It's like we told you last time. Everybody's got to see the mayor."

Squeezing me around the shoulders, Hiram led me to the canteen. The *Eastwood* felt eerily quiet and also like it had been invaded. Back on Earth, there had been times when my mom had forced us to bail on a ratty motel room because she was sure someone had been snooping around inside while we were out. The *Eastwood* felt like that now.

Hiram got himself a packet of fluids and tossed me one. "You know," he said, and paused to slurp greedily, "you could take it a little easier on Darcy."

"She didn't take it easy on me when she was beating my ass," I replied.

"Oh, get over it," Hiram said. "Darcy's always been a little confused. Between her parents and my grandpa, she doesn't know where her head's at half the time. She's a lot like you with all your . . ." Hiram waved his hand. "Whatever's always eating at you that you refuse to talk about. All your shit."

"I don't . . ." I started to protest but trailed off, taking a deep drink of nutrient-infused water instead. Hiram was probably right, not that I'd ever admit that.

"Anyway, I know she messed up siding with Reno, but Darcy's still one of us," Hiram said. He squeezed the last drops out of his bag, chucked it in the bin, and started another. "We need to stick together. Especially you two, since you're both—oops, gotta piss."

Hiram bounced up from the table, leaving me to finish his thought. Darcy and I were both hybrids. There weren't many of us in the universe. And I had a feeling that pretty soon we were going to be in high demand. For the Denzans, we were the only species capable of matching the strength of humanity. And unlike humans, we could use the Wayscopes. We could be a bridge between the species or a resource for either side to exploit against the other. By lavishing attention on first Darcy and then me, Rafe Butler was ahead of the game, but soon there would be others trying to win our support. Hiram was right. I didn't want to navigate that alone.

An hour later, I stepped out from the shuttle on legs that were still rubbery from space travel and immediately had one of those full-body spasms at how great it felt to actually be back on a habitable planet. The salt tang of the Denzan air, the heat of the sun on my cheeks, a breeze tousling my hair like an old buddy. I'd spent months aboard the *Eastwood* breathing recycled air and soaking in vitamin D from artificial light sources. In that time, I hadn't realized how much I missed actual gravity, the feeling of solid ground under my feet.

I could tell Hiram and Darcy felt the same because we all took a moment to just stand there and breathe.

But then reality sunk in.

I tilted my head back to look up at the sky and saw the collection of ISVs floating there, blocking out the three Denzan moons. That was Rafe's armada up there. All of those ships had been commandeered by the humans on board and brought here.

Meanwhile, a different kind of fleet had formed out on the water.

Our shuttle had put us down on a small landing pad at Little Earth's docks. There were more than a hundred boats of various shapes and sizes anchored off the coast. Fishing boats, rafts, yachts like the one Ezziah den One-Left had turned into an office on the Torrent, pretty much every kind of floating vessel the Denzans had at their disposal. I wouldn't say they formed an actual blockade—they were loosely organized, if at all, so much so that you could sail a barge right through the gaps between them.

The one thing all the boats had in common were the signs.

Some were your classic posters mounted on sticks, others had messages that were painted across canvas sails, and some splashed across the air emanating from holographic projectors.

DENZA + HUMANITY = PEACE
TALK TO US LITTLE EARTH
HUMANS ARE OUR BROTHERS AND SISTERS

There was some poetry, too, and photos of humans doing heroically human things like protecting crowds in their Battle-Anchors or pulling Denzan children from beneath piles of rubble. A holographic image of the First Twelve hovered above all of that—the same image of Rafe, Reno, my grandfather, and the others that existed in statue form here on Little Earth—showered by a perpetual fall of rose petals.

"I guess Rafe got their attention," I said.

Hiram grinned and waved at the demonstrators. Darcy pulled her hood up and yanked the strings tight.

I hadn't noticed them at first—they were only a few boats darting around the others—but not all the Denzans on the water were here to show humanity love. There were vessels operated by Denzans wearing the Merciful Rampart uniform I recognized from Arkell's ship. They kept their backs turned from Little Earth, instead focused on shouting down their fellow Denzans.

The wind picked up and one particularly loud Rampart voice carried to the docks. ". . . feeding yourselves to the beasts!"

The three of us started up the main boulevard of Little Earth.

The last time I'd been here, the island had been a ghost town. Now, however, there were dozens of humans hanging around on the sidewalks outside the quaint '50s-era Main Street that Rafe had constructed. They chatted in small groups and sipped iced tea in the sun, and a few even kicked around a hacky-sack as if to prove that humanity was indeed a hopeless cause.

I'd always thought that Rafe's attempt at re-creating a small town on Denza was phony as hell, but it somehow looked even weirder with actual people around. They were like actors on a set waiting for a scene to start. From the looks of things, Rafe's rebellious humans didn't really know what to do with themselves.

Of course, we became the main attraction as we made our way up the road to Rafe's pizzeria. It was like walking into a party late, where everyone had already been hanging out for a while. Some of the humans nodded or waved, but most of them just stared. A few of them even came together to exchange quiet words.

"Yeah," Hiram barked. "Get a good look."

Until the moment he spoke, I hadn't realized that the humans were paying more attention to Hiram than to Darcy and me.

They noticed the hitch in his step. The limp.

Since leaving Earth, they'd probably never seen an injured human.

"Ignore them," I said quietly. Hiram gritted his teeth and kept going.

Rafe Butler met us in the street outside his restaurant. Despite leading a revolt that threatened to upend life on the entire planet, Rafe didn't look all that changed. The hairy little dude was still dressed like an overworked pizza maker, his flour-crusted apron slung under his belly. I guess with all these humans hanging around, Rafe probably had more customers than he's seen in a long time. He grinned when he saw us and spread his arms wide.

"There they are!" Rafe bellowed, loud enough so the others could hear. "The heroes of the human race! The brave cadets who traveled to the edge of the galaxy in the name of enlightenment!"

So that's how Rafe was framing our trip to Ashfall. Noticeably, he didn't mention that we'd gone on the run and he had to pull out all the stops to bring us back home.

Darcy, of course, went straight into Rafe's arms for a bear hug. While that was going on, I cut to the chase.

"Where's Marie Reno?" I asked, making like Rafe and pitching my voice loud enough for the bystanders. "Where's Aela?"

Rafe's jovial act slipped for a moment as he shot me a look and raised a hand to indicate I should shut up.

"There aren't many places on this planet for a woman like Marie to hide," Rafe said quietly. "We'll find her and your lost crewmate. That's my promise."

"So you don't know," I replied.

"My people located her shuttle an hour ago, but she was gone," Rafe said. "Is that enough of a status report for you, Sydney?"

I glanced over my shoulder at all the humans, most of who were still watching us. "Why don't you send some of them out to look?"

"There are only some of our people that I trust with a difficult matter like Marie," Rafe replied. I could see he was making an effort to keep his tone even. "Believe it or not, I know what I'm doing. I . . ." He trailed off as his gaze shifted to Hiram for the first time. "What's wrong with you? Why are you standing like that?"

Hiram had been standing hunched, with his bad leg slightly cocked. He'd opted to wear one of his institute uniforms down to Denza, which means he wasn't rocking the special pants Zara had scored him back on the Torrent.

"Don't worry about me, Gramps," Hiram responded. "I'm good."

Rafe took Hiram roughly by the jaw, turned his face from side to side, and then shoved him backward a bit. Hiram winced in pain. "You don't look good, boy."

"Rafe, come on," Darcy said. "He got hurt."

"*Hurt*," Rafe repeated the word like it was in a foreign language. "You can't be hurt."

Hiram looked down at his feet. "Thanks for the concern and shit."

Rafe's lips curled back in an expression of utter digust. He looked from me to Darcy, like we were to blame. Which, well, I guess I kind of was. Hiram had taken a bullet intended for me.

"And you paraded him up here with no thought of how that might look?" Rafe asked. "Leave it to you, Hiram, to be the first human crippled since the invasion."

"Hey, we didn't ask to be brought here," I said, stepping between Hiram and Rafe. "You hijacked our ship, and now you're forcing us to participate in whatever this is—your invasion of Denza."

"Invasion . . . ?" Rafe glanced up at the ships hovering in the sky and chuckled. "I suppose it might look like that, but I'm not invading anywhere. Our plans to retake the Earth died with your father, and I would never presume to challenge our gracious hosts. No, I don't want this world, Sydney. They might not know it yet, but the Denzans are going to give us a new one."

20

The four of us squeezed into a booth at Rafe's empty pizzeria, a cooling cheese pie that not even Hiram would touch on the table. What a dorky place to potentially start a war from. Above us, a projector attached to the restaurant's ceiling produced a rotating hologram of a planet.

"Illaria," Rafe said, naming the world as he smiled up at its image, his eyes shining. "Discovered by the Serpo Institute twenty-three years ago. A garden world. A unicorn."

Rafe ran us through the rest of the details. Illaria was slightly larger than Earth, with three jagged landmasses separated by sprawling oceans. According to the institute's report, an ice age had loosed its grip on Illaria an estimated five hundred years prior, and so far life had only advanced to the low primate stage. The atmosphere was perfect for humanity. A single moon kept the tides in check.

I was sort of amazed how quickly Rafe had moved on from his scheme to save Earth from itself with an army of enhanced humans cured of the Wasting. My mom had told me about that one before I even left for Denza, which meant Rafe had been working on it for decades. Years of planning were down the toilet, but Rafe didn't seem at all unsettled. In fact, he looked hyped. He must have had this planet—Illaria—in his back pocket the whole time.

"You think the Denzans are just going to give you this planet?" I asked when Rafe finally finished running down all of Illaria's features. "It's that easy?"

"Well, Sydney, I suppose that depends on our negotiating position," Rafe replied. "Which is why I need the three of you to tell me everything that happened on Ashfall."

I crossed my arms and leaned back. This dude had put a bounty out on us and brought us back to Denza against our will. And now he wanted our help? I was about to tell him to kick rocks, but then the non-idiot part of my brain took over. Even if I held out, Darcy would tell Rafe everything. But if I played ball, maybe I could learn what Rafe's plans were. Sticking close to him might be the best place for me to be if I wanted to head off conflict between humanity and Denzans. Plus, I wanted to make sure he was serious about shutting down Reno and getting Aela back safe.

Still, I couldn't just roll over. Wouldn't have been in character.

"I'm not telling you shit until you let the rest of our crew go," I said. "That's my negotiating position."

"I'm not holding anyone prisoner, Syd," Rafe said with a hand draped across his heart. "I'll have them woken up immediately and returned to the institute. You have my word."

Well, it was better than nothing. Rafe peppered the three of us with questions, beginning with our arrival on Ashfall. I kept my answers short and to the point and sometimes missed details that Darcy or Hiram had to fill in. I honestly wasn't trying to hold out on Rafe—although that's probably what he thought. I was distracted by the rotating hologram of Illaria. The blue planet tickled something in the back of my mind, like I'd seen it before. Maybe my consciousness had zipped by it during one of my runs in the Wayscope.

"You were shot before you even made it into the temple," Rafe said, staring hard at Hiram. "Goofing around, I bet. Not taking the search and recovery seriously."

"I was taking it seriously," Hiram replied. "What are you giving me shit for? I didn't even know I *could* be shot."

"I raised you too soft," Rafe said, shaking his head. "Like your father, you have no concept of consequences."

I glanced at Darcy to see if she was going to say anything, but she was too busy studying the piece of congealing pizza in front of her. When it came to Hiram getting ragged on by Rafe, she stayed out of it.

"I was lucky to have Hiram with me," I said. "When Reno attacked the *Eastwood* . . ."

Rafe waved me off. "What are we supposed to do with you now, boy?" He leaned across the table to try to look in Hiram's eyes, but Hiram kept his chin down. "At a time when we should all be unified, the very sight of you sends fear and uncertainty through the entire population. My own grandson. Pathetic."

"I don't have to listen to this crap," Hiram said and stood up. "I'm going home."

Before Hiram could storm off, Rafe grabbed his wrist. Hiram tried to yank it away, but Rafe held firm, veins popping out in his forearm as he squeezed. The two of them stared at each other for a moment before Rafe finally let go.

"Go out the back way," he said. "Don't want the others to see you limping."

Hiram made a noise in his throat like he was stifling a scream. He did as he was told, though, the swinging door to the kitchen banging against the wall as he exited.

"You could be kinder to him," Darcy said quietly.

"I think maybe I've been too kind," Rafe replied.

I snorted. "If that's your version of kindness, I can see why his mom went back to Earth."

Yeah.

So, I regretted the words as soon as they were out of my mouth. The first thing to break the silence that followed was the sharp snap caused by Rafe squeezing the edge of the table hard enough that the Formica cracked.

"By the tides, Syd," Darcy murmured.

"I'm sorry," I said. "That was low."

Rafe just stared at me. His face was a blank mask—not furious, which made it more frightening. Slowly, very slowly, like controlling the muscles in his face required a greater effort than he'd expended damaging the table, he managed to plaster on a patient smile.

"This substance that was capable of injuring my grandson, you said there was a stockpile on Ashfall," Rafe said, like nothing had happened.

Part of me was relieved that Rafe let my thoughtless remark slide. But another part of me sort of enjoyed knowing that he wasn't unflappable. He had weak spots like the rest of us. He wasn't always in control.

"Yeah, my father . . ." I paused. "The Panalax Ool'Vinn, I mean, he was protecting it."

"Did you bring back any samples?"

Here was something that I didn't want to be completely honest about. "No."

"Zara stole at least some of the stuff," Darcy said. "She used it against Reno."

Of course, Darcy had snitched like I expected, so I filled in the rest of the story. "We ran out of sedatives after Ashfall. We needed a resupply, so we traded what Zara had taken."

"Traded it? With who?" Even as he was asking these questions, I saw a chuckle bubble up from Rafe's belly. "Don't answer that. You were in the Jeuna system. You visited the Torrent."

"Wait," I said. "You know about that place?"

"Of course," Rafe replied. "Those Vulpin have been good trading partners for me over the years. Helped me to acquire technology that the Denzans weren't necessarily forthcoming with. Who's in charge there these days? Has Ezziah been assassinated yet?"

"Nope, she's still the boss," I said. Now that Rafe mentioned it, I realized how similar the build of Ezziah's mech body was to a Battle-Anchor. It seemed like both of them had benefited from their trades over the years.

"And Darcy, you were able to track the *Eastwood* based on an assumption about an Etherazi sighting," Rafe said. "What else happened in Jeuna, Syd? Did you have another encounter with one of those beasts?"

I hesitated for a moment, not sure how much I should divulge of what Arkell and the Merciful Rampart were doing in the far reaches of space. Of course, with that little hitch, I gave myself away. And whatever—Arkell was far from a pal; I wasn't going to keep his secrets.

"Not exactly," I said. "We bumped into a ship called the *Cavern*. They—"

"Wait . . ." Rafe squinted like he was trying to remember something. "Theoretician Ayadora, right?"

I shook my head. "Goddamn, is there anyone in the universe you don't know?"

Rafe flashed a smile that was genuinely pleased, which, after the dead stare I'd gotten a few seconds ago, actually made me feel pretty good. I didn't entirely trust Rafe, but even when he was a prick it wasn't easy to dislike him. I remembered the lecture I'd taken last semester where he'd hypnotized the entire room with his war stories. He was magnetic, and his approval could feel like sunshine. I needed to be careful or else I'd get as sucked in by him as Darcy.

"She's one of my favorite crackpots," Rafe said. "Blinded herself. Aged herself thirty years. All in the name of some cockamamie project."

"Yeah, well, it worked," I replied. "They captured an Etherazi."

"Are you serious?!" Darcy exclaimed. "They can . . . they can be captured?"

"Now, that is an interesting wrinkle," Rafe said, leaning back and crossing his arms. "I suppose the Merciful Rampart believes that renders our presence on Denza superfluous."

"You got it," I replied.

At last, Rafe breathed out a sigh and picked up a slice of his own pizza. I assumed that meant the interrogation was over.

"The Denzan Senate wants to talk to you," he said to me. "I'll arrange a meeting in a couple days, once you've had a chance to rest."

"To me?" I asked. "What am I supposed to tell them?"

Rafe shrugged. "Exactly what you told me. There's no reason not to be honest with them, Sydney. We shouldn't have any secrets between our species."

After all that, Rafe put me up in a one-bedroom cottage on the edge of the town. It was a distinctly Earth-ish place, somebody's little woodsy getaway—a living room with a checker-print couch, a simple kitchen, a fireplace. The back porch of the house looked out on the forest that filled the center of the island, and, at night, through the trees, I could see the glow of the monument to the First Twelve, which was always kept lit.

The house was freshly cleaned, the sheets on the bed recently changed, but it still had that lingering, dusty smell like no one had been inside for a long time. I quickly discovered why.

There were pictures of my mom on the mantel.

This had been my grandfather's house.

I was still coming off the hyperspeed sedatives and felt pretty foggy, so I must have stood dumbfounded in front of the fireplace for a solid hour, like a caveman discovering his first art gallery. There was a photo of my grandfather as a young man—handsome, an easy smile—posing in his NASA jumpsuit. In another, he tipped his head back to laugh while holding a wailing baby that had to be my mom. There was a shot of my mom at around age eight, peeking into a telescope.

And—yikes—there was a picture of young Marie Reno in a bikini, stretched out across a towel on a Denzan beach, fingering down her sunglasses and blowing a kiss to my grandfather, the photographer.

I tipped that one down.

All those photos of my grandfather's life on Earth, his wife and daughter, and yet he'd still come to Denza. He'd spent a good chunk of his life here before deciding to finally go home, where he let himself die from the Wasting. In all the pictures, he looked so happy, so perfectly happy. But there must have been something off inside of him, right? To leave his family on Earth, to go back there only to die. What drove someone to make decisions like that?

There were a few other relics of my grandfather's left in the cottage. A half-empty glass bottle of cologne from the '80s. A shelf filled with boring old-man books about navy battles. A collection of medals from the US Air Force and NASA mounted in a glass case. I wondered why he hadn't bothered to bring those back to Earth with him. Maybe, at the end, he'd grown to resent the life trajectory that had brought him to Denza. Or maybe after fending off an invasion from extradimensional monsters, some little chunks of tin and ribbon didn't seem so important anymore.

I spent a couple days recovering from space travel, tossing and turning in my grandfather's bed. Of course, I dreamed. My subconscious had no chill. In the one I remembered, we were all out to dinner at a fancy restaurant—my grandfather, young and vibrant like in the photographs; my dad, wearing an overlarge pair of sunglasses to hide the patches of white mold growing around his eyes; my mom, constantly looking over her shoulder and nearly lunging out of her seat anytime a waiter passed by. As the courses arrived, one by one, my family made some excuse, got up from the table, and left. Pretty soon, I was alone at the table with a bunch of plates of cold food.

Didn't exactly need to be Freud to unpack that one.

By the second afternoon in the cottage, I was starting to get antsy. Conveniently, the communicator was malfunctioning, so I had no way of checking in with the institute to see if Rafe had made good on his promise to release the rest of my crew. The cottage didn't feel like a prison, but I wasn't sure if I was allowed to leave.

I took one of my grandfather's books out on the porch and pretended to read. I was actually looking for patterns, something I'd picked up from mom during our travels. Sure enough, a pair of humans walked by every hour. They smiled and waved like they were just out for a stroll, but I knew that they were Rafe's people sent to check on me.

At hour four, when one of the couples repeated, I set my book aside and waved them down.

"You guys sure like wandering around," I said.

"And you sure like pretending to read," replied the man, a middle-aged guy wearing the uniform of one of the stolen ships hanging overhead.

"So, what's the deal?" I asked. "What are you supposed to do if I'm not here? If I decide to run?"

"We're to encourage you to stay," answered the woman. She was probably in her twenties and had that distinct glow of a human that had grown up on Denza and thus never known anything but strength. "He said you're industrious and a troublemaker and that it's important you stay on our side."

"Aw, that's sweet," I said. "Well, he doesn't have to worry. I'll stick around until my meeting with the Senate."

I also wanted to stay put to get a better idea of Rafe's plans and keep them from plunging the universe into war, if that's the direction this was going. But I didn't need to share that with these two randos.

"Hey," I said, as the two sentries started to walk away, "I was on the *Eastwood*. Did they let the rest of my crew off?"

The man nodded. "All the ISVs are clear except for human personnel."

So Rafe had kept his word, at least. "And what about Marie

Reno? Any news about her?"

The woman raised an eyebrow. "Marie? What do you mean? I assumed she was still on the *Eastwood*."

"Oh yeah," I said, hitting my forehead with my palm. "Duh."

Rafe was keeping Reno's defection a secret, at least from the humans who had the all-important job of peeking in my cabin's windows every hour. I wondered if he was as worried as me about what she might do with Aela and the Origin. Or was it just a bad look for his whole unified-humanity thing to have one of the First Twelve gone rogue?

Not long after the patrol strolled on, Darcy showed up. It was starting to get dark when she came stalking up the path with her hood pulled up like a little grim reaper.

"Hey," she said.

I stood up. "Let me guess. Rafe wants to see me."

She motioned for me to sit back down. "No. I'm here on my own."

"Oh," I said, surprised. "What's up?"

Darcy sat down on the bottom step so that her back was to me. She didn't say anything for a few long seconds, the silence hanging between us.

"I'm sorry," she said at last.

"For what?"

She shrugged. "Everything that happened on Ashfall. Your dad. That couldn't have been easy. Fighting against you guys."

I took a moment to bite back my usual sarcastic reply. I knew Darcy and so understood that hadn't been easy for her to say. "I'm sorry, too. We shouldn't have left you there. Everything just happened so fast, and I really thought Reno might kill us."

"You were right," Darcy replied. "She was our captain, so I stood up for her. It wasn't until after that I realized what she was. She killed all those Vulpin. The speed we traveled at to chase you down, she let it crush them. All I could do was watch."

"You did what you had to do to survive," I said, realizing how much I sounded like my mom. "Reno won't get away with what she's done."

"She's a supremacist," Darcy said. "I think it was always inside her. That feeling of superiority. The Origin just brought it to the front. Justified everything."

"Seeing that messed with all our heads," I said.

"I've always wished I was fully human," Darcy continued, her voice quiet enough that I had to lean forward in my chair to hear. "Especially once I found out the reason why my mom had me. You came to Denza as an outsider. You got to discover your roots, not have them tie you down. I guess I've been jealous of that, Syd. How you're so sure about who you are."

I chuckled. If only Darcy could hear my messed-up internal monologue.

"What's funny?"

"Darcy," I said. "I don't have a fucking clue who I am."

She glanced back at me, half smiled, then turned away again. "They're using us, you know."

"Who is?"

"The humans, the Denzans, our parents." She raised her hands as if to encompass the entire galaxy and beyond. "Everyone has an agenda for us hybrids, and we're just forced to play along."

"You talking about Rafe now? I thought you guys were tight."

"Rafe has always been good to me," Darcy said, a bit of that usual sharpness creeping into her words. "He practically raised me. But I saw my dad. He was the one that rescued me and Reno. And after talking to him, I don't think things are so black-and-white anymore. I want to believe Rafe's got good intentions, but after everything that's happened . . ."

"There's a saying on Earth," I said. "'The road to hell is paved with good intentions.'"

She nodded. "What happens if everything comes out and the Denzans still don't give him what he wants?"

"I don't know," I said. "But he thinks of you like a daughter, Darcy. You need to get in his ear. Make sure he doesn't do anything nuts. I don't think Rafe will become like Reno, but . . ."

"We're just cadets," Darcy said. "How is anything we do going to make a difference to Rafe or the Senate or anyone else?"

"Well, Acla did say that the universe bends around me, so there's that."

Darcy snorted. "That's dumb. And arrogant." She fell silent for a moment. "You think we could stop them? The humans, I mean. If we had to."

A chill went through me as the burning world flashed in my memory. I don't think Darcy noticed.

"I wouldn't want to have to try," I said.

Darcy's lips pursed, troubled by the thought. She stood up,

brushing off the butt of her jeans.

"Don't leave me behind again," she said.

"Don't beat the shit out of me again," I replied.

"No promises." She started down the path, then half turned back in my direction, her face hidden by her hood. "I hope we can talk like this again, Syd. I've never . . . I've never really known anybody like me."

"Yeah," I said. "Me too."

I wished that I had more answers for her. Or better answers. Or any answers. But Darcy was right: it was comforting to have someone like me out there, asking similar questions about their place in the universe. Hiram was right. I'd been too shitty to Darcy in the past. She was the kind of friend I was going to need out here in the Vastness.

Darcy wasn't the only visitor I had that night, though.

I was getting ready for bed when I heard a scratching at my bedroom window. At first, I thought it was just a tree branch brushing against the glass.

But then a dagger blade wedged underneath the pane and leveraged the window open. A furry shadow tumbled gracefully through the gap. I had a flashback to when a Vulpin assassin invaded my childhood home and cocked my fist back to throw a punch, but then Zara popped to her feet in front of me, the point of her dagger right under my chin.

"Boo," she said.

"Jesus, Zara," I replied, taking a breath as I dropped my fist and she lowered her knife. "What the hell are you doing here?"

"We're busting you loose, obviously," she said.

"We?"

H'Jossu's fluffy head poked over the window sill. "Um, hey, Syd, are there any wider ways into your house?"

My eyes lit up at the sight of the big Panalax, and I went over the window to give him a fist bump. "I'm glad to see you guys, but how did you manage to sneak all the way here?"

Zara flicked her tail back and forth. "I'm very good at it. And the big oaf is surprisingly nimble."

"Yeah, I am," H'Jossu added. He crouched down into a ball in the plants outside the cottage. "Check it out. I'm a bush."

"Come around to the back door before someone sees you," I said.

I led Zara out of my room and into the kitchen to let H'Jossu inside. Once he was in, I turned off the rest of the lights just in case one of Rafe's patrols passed by and caught sight of extra shadows moving around.

"Are you guys good?" I asked. "Rafe's people weren't rough with you when they kicked you off the *Eastwood*?"

"It was a big rush, but they didn't hurt us," H'Jossu said. "I had to leave some DVDs behind. Physical media from Earth, Syd. Do you know how rare that is?"

I glanced at Zara. "What about—?"

"Mm," she replied, cutting me off. "I also barely had enough time to collect all my things. But I got the important stuff."

I breathed a sigh of relief. H'Jossu's DVDs were a loss, sure, but nothing compared to Zara's stash of black sludge.

"What about the others?" I asked. "Tycius and Melian?"

"Melian's back in the dorms, probably mad I didn't invite her to sneak onto Little Earth," Zara replied. "Your uncle checked in on us briefly, but he's been pretty busy getting interviewed by the institute and the Senate. I don't think his people are very happy with him."

"No one will tell us what happened," H'Jossu said. "They just stuck us back in the dorms and said we're on probation pending a hearing."

"Reno and Darcy caught up with us," I explained. "Darcy's here on Little Earth, but Reno took off with Aela."

"Bitch," Zara said, flashing her fangs. "We were so close. And now we've lost our freedom and our *suqatal*. This cannot go unanswered. Den *Eastwood* must get back in the game."

"It's why we came to break you out," H'Jossu said, ambling over to open up the fridge. "This looks kind of empty, Syd." He came to stand in front of me, squeezing my ribs with his paws. "Are they starving you?"

"Stop tickling me, I'm fine," I said. "I wouldn't say I'm being held prisoner, exactly. I'm supposed to meet with the Senate too, and Rafe is letting me chill here under his supervision until that happens. He says he's got people out looking for Reno and Aela . . ."

"And you believe him?" Zara asked with a snort. "They were First Twelve together. She delivered us right to him."

"It was more like Darcy and her dad delivered us," I replied. "And I think they were trying to deliver Reno, too, but she bailed.

Darcy told Rafe all the fucked-up stuff Reno did. I think he's trying to keep it on the DL, but I don't believe they're working together. Either way, the best thing I can do is stick close to Rafe and see what his plans are."

H'Jossu's shoulders slumped. "Oh, so you don't need rescuing."

I patted his shoulder. "Appreciate the effort, big guy."

"Behind enemy lines," Zara said with a nod. "Good. Meanwhile, we will start our own hunt for Reno."

H'Jossu held up one of his paws. "Do you have a tracking device on her, too?"

Zara shook her head. "Unfortunately not."

"I'm sorry," I said. "Tracking device?"

"How do you think we found you so easily?" Zara asked, tapping her claw on her wrist console. "I put a tracker in your sneakers. All your sneakers."

I blinked. "What? When?"

"Back when you took my class," Zara said. She smirked at me. "Guess I forgot to deactivate them."

"Zara's like Bruce Wayne, dude," H'Jossu said. "Or Barbara Gordon. But with way more stabbing."

"An appropriate amount of stabbing," Zara said.

"Look, I was the one who promised to get Aela home, not you guys. I couldn't handle it if you guys got hurt trying to take Reno on alone."

Zara gripped my shoulder. "A promise from one is a promise from all. I can handle the old lady. Bringing an insane human to justice. If we do that, the institute won't dream of kicking us out."

"We'll be careful, Syd," H'Jossu rumbled. "You stay here and make sure Rafe Butler doesn't take over the planet."

"Or, if he does, try to get us good positions in the administration," Zara added.

"He says he's not interested in world domination," I replied. "Not this world, any—"

Through the window, a flash of orange light and a boom like a firework going off. All three of us ducked for cover. The floorboards vibrated and the glasses in the cupboards rattled. As I poked my head up, I could see a steady, flickering orange glow through the trees and smelled smoke in the air.

That was an explosion. Deeper into the woods, but not that far.

I shot Zara a look. "You didn't set some kind of bomb as a diversion, did you?"

Zara laughed like I'd offended her. "Please. I would've timed it better."

"If we want to find Reno," H'Jossu said, "I have the sinking feeling we should start at the mysterious explosion."

21

Running toward an explosion. My mom never would have approved.

The three of us took off into the woods toward the steadily growing fire. The reek of burning fuel hung in the air, smoke curling into the night sky. I tried to visualize Little Earth as I'd seen it from above. There was nothing out this way except for more woods. At least, nothing that I'd noticed from the air.

To my right, H'Jossu barreled forward on all fours like a bear. Zara kept pace on my left, barely making a sound as she dipped and ducked through the trees. These two had come to rescue me, and instead I now had them running toward obvious danger. I felt a little guilty about that, but I was also glad they had my back. Whatever was out there—Reno, impending war, the universe in shambles—it felt good to not go it alone.

"Hold," Zara hissed, suddenly at my side. "Something's coming."

We skidded to a stop. I stilled my breathing to listen and heard the sound of branches breaking. The noise wasn't coming from ahead of us, though.

It was coming from above.

Zara and H'Jossu both lunged for cover as a dark shape plummeted toward us through the trees. I started to go with them, but at the last second realized that was no chunk of debris dropping out of the sky.

That was a body.

I caught the shape in my arms, stumbling back a few steps, heels digging into the soft earth. To my surprise, I realized it was the young woman who I'd spoken to from my porch just a few hours ago. There were twigs and leaves stuck in her hair from her descent, but her unbreakable skin was otherwise undamaged from crashing through the trees. She was wheezing like crazy, though, and tried to curl into a ball as soon as I set her in the grass.

"Punched me . . . ," she said through gasps. "Threw me . . ."

"Who?" I asked. "What happened out there?"

In answer, she rolled over and threw up.

"That is the look of someone who just lost a fight," Zara said from over my shoulder.

H'Jossu made an uncertain rumbling noise. "Are we sure we should keep going?"

"You should not," a gruff voice said. "The fight is already over. They're gone."

250

We turned to see Rafe, Hiram, and two other humans emerging through the trees. The pizza maker wore jeans and an untucked flannel shirt, half-unbuttoned over his hairy chest, like he'd gotten dressed in a hurry. Hiram stood a few paces off from his grandfather with his shoulders cocked away from the older man, like he didn't want to be there. He threw up a weak wave in our direction.

"See to Chelsea," Rafe said to the others with him, "Get her to the infirmary And not a word of this to anyone."

Rafe's two helpers went to the woman—Chelsea, I guess—helping her to stand and leading her back the way we had come from. Meanwhile, I sensed a familiar ruffling of fur and turned my head, noticing that Zara had manifested a black-coated dagger. Rafe's eyes twinkled in the moonlight, not faltering in the slightest as he swaggered toward us.

"Zara den Jetten, you do me a great honor by baring your blades for me, but I'm not your enemy," Rafe said. "In fact, I'd love to have a closer look at your weapon."

"Be careful what you wish for, old man," Zara whispered. She glanced at me, and I responded with a quick head shake. Zara slipped her knife back into her fur.

"I always am," Rafe said with a laugh. He stopped in front of us and extended a hand. "H'Jossu of the Panalax. It's good to meet you. May the sun always find you, fledgling."

H'Jossu took Rafe's hand in his furry paw and shook vigorously. "Wow. You're one of the First Twelve and you know my name."

"Of course I do," Rafe said. "I know everyone worth knowing on Denza and beyond. Right, Sydney?"

When Zara snorted, H'Jossu hunched his shoulders sheepishly and stepped back. "I mean—uh, pretend I said something menacing and cool."

"What happened out there, Rafe?" I asked. "You know you've got a fire on your island, right? People falling out of the sky?"

"We've had an incident. Thank you all for springing into action, but it's under control," Rafe replied evenly. "I'm glad the two of you were able to pay Syd a visit, but we're temporarily locking down the island. Hiram here will escort you to a boat that will take you back to Primclef."

Zara's legs bent in a way that I knew meant she could spring deeper into the woods in a heartbeat. "What if we don't want to go?"

"Well," Rafe said, "I suppose we could have some cabins made up, but I'm sure the institute might soon miss you two."

"Just come with me and save yourself the aggravation of Gramps talking you to death," Hiram said from over Rafe's shoulder. "It sucks ass here anyway."

Rafe's brow knitted together at Hiram's tone, and I thought he might rebuke his grandson, but he swallowed any reply in order to keep up the folksy charm for the nonhumans. Zara looked to me again and I gave her a subtle nod. Whatever had happened, Rafe wasn't going to talk about it in front of outsiders. If they left, I might have better luck finding out what had caused the explosion.

"Thanks for coming, guys," I said. "Sorry about the fireworks."

"I love a good show, even if I miss the ending," Zara replied. To my surprise, she snatched me into a hug. The fur on top of her head tickled the bottom of my chin, her claws skitching across the back of my shirt. "See you soon," she said.

"Oh, cool, we're hugging," H'Jossu said and enveloped me in his massive arms, pressing my face into his earthy-smelling chest. "Topic for next time. Top five prison break movies."

I laughed. "I'll give it some thought, man."

"Are you going to hug me, too?" I heard Hiram ask Zara as he led the two intruders back through the woods.

"Eat shit," she replied.

When they were gone, Rafe and I stood side by side to watch the fire flickering through the trees. There were shouts in the distance, but not the *oh God, we're going to die* kind—more like the barked orders of an organized group trying to put out the blaze.

"You've got some loyal friends," Rafe remarked. "That will serve you well."

"Are you going to tell me what happened or not?" I asked impatiently.

Rafe took a handheld out of his back pocket and glanced at the screen. A stream of text flew by, faster than I could read. Reports coming in from his people around the island.

"One of my vaults was hit tonight," he said.

"You have vaults? Filled with what? Gold coins?"

"Not exactly gold coins, but yes, I've managed to amass a fair bit of every culture's currency. More important, I've been storing technology that I've collected over the years. Items that the

Denzans don't want us to have. Or don't know about." Rafe put his handheld away and reached into his other pocket, producing a small packet with what I soon realized was an antacid. He spoke while chewing the pill. "Only my most trusted lieutenants know about my stashes."

"Most trusted like Reno," I said.

"Unfortunately, yes," Rafe said. "A few of our people are also missing. Unsurprisingly, they're ones who served on ships with Reno at one point or another. I don't know if Reno came in person or put her allies to the task."

I put my palm to my forehead. "So she's not alone now," I said. "Do you know what technology she stole?"

Rafe shook his head. "We may never know. What they didn't take, they burned."

"Goddamn, Rafe, I thought you had this under control," I said. "What the hell have you been doing? Stuffing calzones?"

In the shadows, Rafe's fists clenched. Slowly, though, his fingers relaxed and he nodded. "I deserve that," he said. "You're right. Perhaps I've underestimated Reno and overestimated my own powers of persuasion. Given a chance to cool down, I thought she would find her way back to us peacefully. That she would see reason and face justice with the nobility befitting the First Twelve."

"Well, she found her way back, at least. Pretty sure she punched one of your people into the sky tonight," I said. "She's lost it, Rafe. We have to bring her in and get Aela back, before Reno does something worse than blow up one of your vaults."

"You have my word, Sydney," Rafe said. "She won't evade us for long."

The two of us walked back to the cabin in silence. I wanted to believe that tonight's incident would spur Rafe on to do something about Reno, but I wasn't so sure. He was playing the angles—trying to negotiate with the Denzans while presenting a unified front for humanity. I'm not sure where Reno fit into his plans. It didn't seem like Rafe to let loose ends dangle out there. If the way he was gobbling those antacids was any indication, though, Rafe was more stressed than he was letting on. Maybe that was a good thing.

"So, what now?" I asked once we were in my cabin's backyard. "You know, if you need me to join one of our Reno search parties, I'm happy to do it."

"You have other business, I'm afraid," Rafe replied. "The Denzan Senate will see you tomorrow. And the day after that, the people of Little Earth will march on Primclef to deliver our demands." He patted me roughly on the shoulder. "Get some rest, Syd. Your people will need you sharp."

Rafe left me there to watch the fire die out through the trees. *My people.* He meant humanity, but that's not how I took it. My people were Zara and H'Jossu. Hiram and Darcy. Tycius and Melian. We were all in danger. Things were escalating now, I could feel it. I wanted to believe that I'd changed my future by leaving Goldy trapped on the *Cavern*, but the universe still felt balanced on the edge of chaos and war. I needed to make sure I was in the right place at the right time to keep that from happening.

It wasn't until I started back to the house that I felt a scraping at the small of my back. I reached around, feeling like a particularly nasty bug was crawling on me.

Shoved into the back of my pants, I found a knife. Small, shaped like an arrowhead, with a grip that fit over the knuckles. "Push dagger," I think, was the technical term. I slipped the business end out of its leather sheath and found the blade was coated with black-sludge.

"Thanks, Zara," I said, and went inside.

The next morning, an empty train was waiting to zip me across the water from Little Earth to Primclef. Rafe or one of his people had taken the liberty of retrieving one of my uniforms from the *Eastwood*, pressing it, and hanging it in my closet. It felt a little strange to be wearing the crossed-pistols insignia of Reno's ship given the circumstances, but the *Eastwood* had been stolen twice since Reno was her captain, so I justified it as the ship being as much mine as hers.

The train hadn't been running between Primclef and Little Earth since Rafe commandeered every ISV he could. I guess that was as close as the Denzan Senate had come to sanctioning Rafe. They'd restored service specifically for my journey, so I was all alone in the air-conditioned car with nothing to do but stare out at the shimmering ocean and then, a short ride later, the perfectly organized grid of the bustling Denzan capitol. The sight of the city—nestled within the walls of a massive crater, its architecture gleaming and clean, the air buzzing with antigravity skiffs—it still took my breath away.

I spotted Keyhole Cove, where the walled city opened up to the beach, the boardwalk lined with stands where I knew for a fact you could score some truly strong Vulpin booze. In the distance, I recognized the towering spire of the Serpo Institute, its walls part of the mountain itself, spiraling walkways carved into the building. For a moment, I actually missed the sanctuary of my dorm room there. I'd only stayed for a few months before jetting off to Ashfall, but after years of living on the run, that little room had felt like the first place that was really mine.

That hadn't lasted long, huh?

Like the institute, the Senate was built directly into the mountainside. At first, I thought it lacked the pomp of like every capitol building on Earth, but as the train zoomed closer what I at first thought were natural creases in the stone façade revealed themselves to be carvings. Shining with the silver glean of ultonate, the carvings depicted hundreds—maybe thousands—of long-fingered Denzan hands, all linked together in an endless chain that encompassed the entire front of the Senate. That must have taken years to chisel into the stone.

My train zipped into a tunnel and stopped at a private station reserved for Senate personnel. I exited into an empty chamber, naturally chilled from being within the cavern, the stone ceiling above polished smooth and painted with a dazzling map of Denza's constellations that reminded me of peering through a Wayscope.

Concerned shouts reached me from below, so I edged over to

the railing and looked down at the landing underneath mine. It appeared to be a public platform with multiple trains coming into the mountain from different directions and Denzans—only Denzans here; there were no longer any humans interspersed throughout their ranks—milling about waiting for their rides. Something was causing a delay.

As I watched, a group of Denzans carried an exo-suit off the train. I flinched and nearly jumped over the railing before I realized that wasn't Aela down there. The suit was shiny and sleek, a newer model than what my friend walked around in.

Strangely, the exo-suit was empty. The faceplate clattered on its hinges as the Denzans lowered the empty metal shell on the platform, looking totally bewildered.

"Sydney!"

I turned to see my uncle striding toward me. Tycius grabbed me by the shoulders, looked me over to check that I was still in one piece, then pulled me into a hug.

"I am beyond relieved to see you," he said. "No one here has any idea what's going on inside Little Earth. Have they been treating you okay?"

"Besides all the crappy pizza, I'm fine," I replied. Reaching out, I squeezed my uncle's shoulder. I'd noticed that it felt like he was wearing armor when I hugged him. There was a new carapace of metal binding his shoulder and upper arm. "Ty? What's with that?"

Tycius swung his arm in a circle like he was trying to work some feeling back into it, looking away from me as he did. "The way things have gone since taking you off Earth, that's mine to carry, Syd."

"You don't have anything to be ashamed of," I replied. "I mean, what would you have done differently? Not brought me to Ashfall? Not looked for Dad?"

"When I can understand what I might have changed and once I've come to terms with the fact that those paths are forever closed to me, then I can take this off," Ty said with a sad smile. "Now, come on. Senator Formachus is waiting to meet you."

We entered into what turned out to be the upper tier of the Senate chamber. It was like walking into a basketball arena. Rows upon rows of tiered benches looked down on the floor, which was painted with a map of the Denzan islands. Each archipelago had a hard-backed chair stationed atop it, presumably where the senators for each area sat. The chairs were all angled toward a central upraised lectern that looked like a raft afloat on the painted ocean.

"Wow," I said. "Pretty intense."

"Senate meetings are open to the public here," Tycius explained. "It's arranged this way so that our representatives don't forget that they are not above the people."

Tycius led me down the stairs toward where a thin Denzan woman waited in an empty section. My frame of reference for senators was the collection of angry old men that ran the US, so I was surprised that Formachus looked to be in her early thirties. She stood up to meet me, wearing a formfitting dress patterned with swooping birds, her aquamarine hair tied up in a sloppy bun. She studied me through a pair of wide-rimmed glasses, one of the lenses constantly scrolling what appeared to be a newsfeed. I'd been expecting this Senate interrogation to involve a dark room with a bunch of judgy Denzans, not a stylish lady who resembled an alien version of every teacher I'd ever had a crush on.

"Sydney Chambers," Formachus said, shaking my hand. "Or do you prefer Sydneycius?"

"Um, Syd is fine, Senator," I replied.

"You can call me Forma," she said with an easy smile, then patted a spot on the bench next to her. I sat and Tycius slid into the row behind us. "I represent the island of Primclef, including the Serpo Institute, where you technically reside, which means I'm in your service. Thank you for meeting with me."

"Sure. I actually thought there would be more of you." I gestured at the Senate seats below us. "Thought everyone would want to hear about Ashfall."

"Ah, we've just concluded fifteen hours of closed testimony with your uncle," Forma said with a tired smile. "Unless there's something you think Tycius might have left out, I think we have a pretty clear picture of what transpired. In which case, I could reconvene the entire body . . ."

I glanced back at Tycius for help.

"I told them everything, Syd," he said. "Everything they *need* to know."

I'd been around my uncle enough to catch the implication there. He'd told the Denzans about the Origin, about my father and Reno, the secrets we'd uncovered that currently had the whole planet on a razor's edge without even fully coming to light. But I figured he had left out the juicy bits about my relationship with a certain Etherazi and my destiny to blow up a planet.

"Yeah, uh, I don't have anything to add," I said.

"I'll admit, it's a difficult story to wrap one's head around," Forma said. "Some of my colleagues are skeptical, not having experienced the Ossho's recordings for themselves. Others believe the Origin but think the information is too destabilizing to share with the planet at large. What do you think, Syd?"

I blinked. "What do I think about what?"

"The Origin and its consequences," Forma said. "The effects it might have on society."

"Nice of you to open with an easy question," I said, trying to make a joke.

Forma smiled. "I'm genuinely curious. There are no wrong answers here. We're just chatting."

I'd had a lot of time to dwell on the Origin, but I'd never really attempted to put my feelings on it into words. I cleared my throat to buy myself a second to think.

"I mean—I'm sure my uncle told you what the Origin did to Marie Reno. But, since then, I've seen other humans handle it without unlocking their inner fascist. I've seen them come to terms with it. Knowing the truth about yourself . . . I guess it can be an excuse to really let the monster go, if that's who you are. Or it can be an opportunity to try to be better."

I wasn't sure what I said made total sense, but Forma smiled at me like it was exactly what she wanted to hear.

"Yes, I agree," the senator said. "For Denzans, too, this might be a painful reckoning. Our culture grew from the knowledge that our ancestors once did something unspeakable, an act so heinous that it was purged from our history. We have ever since been a people of peace and pacifism. But what if—knowing what we do now of the Origin—some Denzans found our ancestors' actions not shameful, but justified? Might some of us not be drawn to dark waters, much like Marie Reno?"

I thought of Arkell strutting around without his bindings on his science ship and figured that my uncle must have told the Senate about that. Hell, they probably already knew, since Arkell had said there was interest in Ayadora's research ever since the humans of Little Earth started getting restless.

"But, so . . ." I pinched the bridge of my nose as I tried to sort things through, glancing back at my uncle. "What are you guys saying we should do? Tell everyone the Origin or keep it a secret?"

"I fear that might not be entirely under our control," Forma replied. "Personally, and I think Tycius agrees with me, I believe that honesty and openness are the way forward here. We are tilting toward a reordering of society that hasn't been seen for generations. Our goal can't be to keep people in the dark. Instead, we have to lead. To make sure that when the Origin comes to light, as it inevitably will, that our reaction isn't fear but acceptance and understanding. We cannot let ancient history dictate our present."

I whistled. "That's pretty good. I can see why you're a senator."

Forma smiled wryly. "Thank you. Don't tell anyone, but I've been practicing that speech in the mirror."

I looked around the cavernous Senate chamber—empty now,

but soon to be filled with Denzans and humans. "So why did you bring me here?"

"Well," Forma said, "your uncle told me you were an impressive young man . . ."

I snorted. "Not really."

"As someone of both human and Denzan heritage, you're uniquely positioned, Sydney," Forma continued. "A protector of the interests of both species. A symbol of unity."

I bit the inside of my cheek. It always came down to being a hybrid. "I'm not sure I'm crazy about being a symbol."

Tycius interjected. "Personally, I knew a meeting with the Senate was a request Rafe wouldn't say no to. I thought if you were being held against your will . . ."

"I'm not a prisoner on Little Earth," I said. "I mean, not really. I don't think."

"No, I imagine Rafe Butler is doing everything he can to make you feel at home there," Forma said.

"The Senate is in the dark here," Tycius said. "We all know Rafe's penchant for grandeur. We know they're planning to march here and make a request to the Senate. But we don't know what he's after, what his endgame is . . ."

"Oh, that's easy," I said. "He wants a planet."

Forma blinked. "A planet."

"A new home for the, uh—the Earthlings?" I said. "It's a place called Illaria. That's going to be his demand, Senator. You think you can swing that? Or find a way to say no that doesn't end with everyone trying to kill each other?"

"It appears I have much to discuss with my colleagues," Forma said. She patted my knee and stood up. "Thank you, Syd. This has been very illuminating. There is one other request we have for you before you return to Little Earth."

"Oh? What?"

Tycius reached over my shoulder and handed me a tablet.

"Call your mother."

22

I'd been gone for months.

It didn't feel that way to me as most of that time had been spent asleep as my body rocketed through the Vastness. But it was a long time to go without checking in.

My mom knew I was going away on an expedition that would put me off the grid for a while. But when the timetable I'd given her for my return came and went, she started trying to get answers from the Consulate and the institute. They'd put her off—because the *Eastwood* had never gone on its assigned mission and they had no clue where we were.

I can only imagine what that was like, how much it must have reminded her of what happened with my dad. No one telling her anything. Another mysterious disappearance.

Then Rafe had pulled his stunt with the ships. In response,

they'd shut down the Consulate in Sydney, sending all the human workers there home without explanation. The Denzans weren't sure what was going on with humanity and wanted to play it safe.

Apparently, my mom had tried breaking in three times. Each time, she was rebuffed by Denzan security.

On the fourth time, however, she'd taken a hostage. That was six days ago.

I could picture it, honestly. My mom snatching up some Denzan paper pusher when he stepped outside the sanctuary of the Consulate for some fresh air. Stuffing him in the trunk of her car and driving out to an abandoned ranch on the edge of the outback that she'd spent days booby-trapping. Hunkering down with her jugs of water and her dehydrated noodles and her guns and telling the Denzans that she would expose their whole operation on Earth and kill their agent if they didn't give her the answers she was after.

That was so Mom.

The Denzans handled the situation delicately. They were reluctant to involve local authorities because that meant depending on humanity, who they were no longer sure they could trust. They didn't want to risk anyone getting hurt by laying siege to my mom's ranch. And, pretty soon, word reached them that I'd been returned to Denza, anyway.

So now I needed to fix things.

The last time I saw my mom—via wormhole-transmitted light-speed satellite—it looked like she'd really gotten her life together. I remember her sitting in a sleek Consulate office, dressed in a suit, looking like she'd actually gained a bit of weight.

All that had been reversed over the last few months. Even during our more desperate times on the run, my mom hadn't looked this strung out. Her face was gaunt, hair tied back and greasy, dark circles like craters around her eyes. There was a big scab in the middle of her upper lip where it looked like someone had punched her. She wore a sweat-stained tank top and was vibrating when she first came on-screen, nervous energy like she was ready to fly into action at the first sign of a trap. A shotgun that she was holding across her lap occasionally appeared in the frame as she moved. Behind her were boarded-up windows, yellow slashes of sun highlighting the dust hanging in the air.

"Mom," I said. "Hi. I'm okay. Everything is okay."

I didn't like opening with a lie, but that seemed like the right angle to take.

"Sydney, you're . . ." She clapped a hand over her mouth, relieved tears filling her eyes. However, just as quickly as they appeared, those tears froze over as my mom squinted into the camera. "No. This is some kind of trick. A simulation."

I sighed. "No, Mom, it's me."

"Tell me something only my son would know," she barked at me. "Tell me—tell me how we spent your ninth birthday."

"My ninth . . . ? Jesus Christ, Mom, I don't remember that."

She cocked the shotgun. "Stop playing games with me, Denza."

"Wait, wait," I said, squeezing my eyes closed like that would help me remember. "Ninth birthday? Was that Utah? I was Darren Drake, right? That was my alias. We went camping in the Red

Rocks. You told me that I couldn't get my present until I found water on my own and I had to climb down into that cave for it and I'm pretty sure I ended up drinking bat piss. And then, after all that, you said my present was a sense of accomplishment and self-sufficiency. Is that the right birthday?"

I opened my eyes and found that my mom's expression had softened. She had two fingers on the screen of her own tablet now, as if she could touch my cheek across the galaxies.

"Oh, Syd, it is you," she said. "You just look so much older. I thought . . . And I had a real present for you that year, too. A knife, I think."

"Everyone's always giving me knives," I muttered.

"Where have you been?" My mom's voice cracked. "You were gone so long and no one would tell me anything."

My mouth opened and closed. I hadn't exactly had time to prepare for this conversation. Considering my mom's fragile state, and with the certainty that our call was being monitored by more people than just my uncle sitting nearby, I decided to go with a slightly tweaked version of the truth.

"I'm sorry about that. Our ship's comms went down and we lost contact with the institute," I said. And then I just came out with it. "I found Dad. Or I found his remains. He's gone, Mom. He's been gone for a long time."

My mom's narrow shoulders trembled. "But the signal? From the cosmological tether?"

"It was a glitch, basically. A, uh, phenomenon on the planet was keeping it active, even after Dad died. I can't really explain it." Actually, I didn't *want* to explain it. She didn't need to know about Ool'Vinn or my dad's shambling corpse or his head getting pulverized into dust by Reno. "He'd been dead for a long time, Mom."

"Oh, my dear, I'm so sorry you had to find that out," my mom said. She shook her head, red-rimmed eyes looking down at the floor. "I always knew he wouldn't just abandon us. Not if he had a choice. It's good—it's good that we finally know the truth."

My throat tightened. My dad did have a choice and had decided to stay on Ashfall, to die there, in order to hide the Origin from the rest of the universe. Another thing that my mom didn't need to know. Let her hold on to her idea that Marcius was a caring partner and father.

"Yeah," I said weakly. "Now we know."

My mom's eyes sharpened, like she could tell that I was holding something back. "What about his research? What is going on up there? Why did they kick all of us out of the Consulate?"

I wanted to glance to my uncle for help, but I knew that if I looked off-screen my mom might jump to the conclusion that someone was holding a gun to my head or something. I kept my gaze steady.

"There's no cure for the Wasting," I said, choosing my words carefully. "Word about that got around on Denza, and some of the humans . . . aren't taking the news well. I guess that's why they shut you guys out of the Consulate. Probably only until things get sorted out here, which I think will be soon."

I'd turned into a real optimist all of a sudden. Guess that was what happened when your mom went full terrorist. You tried to keep things light.

"Your father was always so sure that he could fix things," she said, a note of bitterness creeping into her voice. "Your grandfather. Rafe Butler. Those others like them. Always so sure a new dawn for humanity was on the horizon."

"Well . . ." Out of the corner of my eye, I noticed Tycius shift uncomfortably. "I mean, something like that could still happen, Mom. You've got to have hope. What would you think . . . what would you think of leaving Earth? Of coming up here to be with me?"

My mom scoffed at the notion. "They'll never let me up, Syd. Especially not after . . ." She pinched the bridge of her nose. "I'm sure they told you what happened."

"You mean the guy you kidnapped? Yeah. You should probably cut him loose, Mom. I'm alive. The Denzans weren't trying to hide anything from you. It was all a big misunderstanding."

"Do you hear that?" My mom looked at someone off-screen, her lips curled back over her teeth. "My son is kindhearted. He's sticking up for you."

In response, I heard muffled pleading. Her captive was trying to communicate through a gag.

"Listen, Mom, you have to stop," I said. "You were upset that the Denzans were keeping you in the dark. But I'm back now. I'll call you on the regular. You won't have to worry about me like that again. And, since you haven't hurt anyone too badly and since I'm such a valued student at the Serpo Institute," I added for the people I'm sure were listening, "I bet the Denzans will let this all blow over."

"Stop talking to me like I've lost my mind," my mom snapped. "I'm not crazy."

"No," I said. "Of course not."

But I had a sudden vision of my mom grabbing me by the shoulders and shoving me underwater in order to prove that I was part extraterrestrial. She'd felt she was justified then, just like she thought she was justified now. Something of that memory must have shown in my face, my eyes, because the hardness in my mom's glare shattered and she put her face in her hands. The shotgun on her lap clattered to the floor.

"Oh God, Syd, I'm sorry . . . ," she said, shoulders shaking. "I lost control. Sometimes I feel like I'm living in a nightmare and I don't know how to wake up."

"It's okay, Mom, it's over now," I said, feeling like words from light-years away just weren't enough. "I love you. You're okay."

We watched on livestream as my mom released her hostage, then sat in the harsh sun of the ranch's front porch and waited for authorities from the Consulate to move closer to the house. She walked them through disarming the booby traps on the road. We said our good-byes before they took her into custody.

I felt completely drained. Tycius and I walked slowly along the Senate chamber's upper level, heading back toward the train platform.

"You did good," Tycius said, resting his hand on my shoulder.

"Did I?" I replied, shaking my head. "I just don't know with her. She wasn't always like that, you know? Or . . . maybe she was and I just couldn't see it. I know it's fucked up, but all I kept thinking while we were talking is how lucky I am to have gotten away."

My uncle squeezed my shoulder. "Families are complicated, Syd. I don't have to tell you that. But she loves you. She always did what she thought was best, which is all any of us can do."

"What do you think is going to happen to her?" I asked.

"I'm speaking with the Consulate's director of personnel today," Tycius said as we reached the train platform. "I doubt I'll be able to get her old job back, but hopefully they can find some way to make use of her. I won't let them cut her off completely. She knows too much for that to happen, anyway. And given your cooperation with Senator Forma, you being our only eyes and ears on Little Earth—I think that's worth some special consideration."

"Well, if you're pulling strings, I don't want any of the *Eastwood*'s crew to be kicked out of the institute," I said. "Not even Batzian, if he decides he wants to come back."

"I'll see what I can do," Tycius said with a nod. "You're sure you want to return to Little Earth?"

"I think that's the best place for me to be right now," I replied. "Rafe's planning to march on Primclef tomorrow. I should be close to him when he does."

My uncle left me on the platform, where an empty train waited to take me back to Little Earth. I didn't get on right away. Instead, I went to the overlook to check on the platform below, where earlier I'd seen the empty exo-suit being removed from the train.

Things had returned to normal. Still, something bothered me about that scene. My mom's words repeated in my head.

Sometimes I feel like I'm living in a nightmare and I don't know how to wake up.

I was lost in thought so at first I didn't notice Melian down there. She was waving her arms back and forth to get my attention, earning annoyed looks from the commuting Denzans who needed to get around her. I blinked, smiled, and waved back. Looking over my shoulder, I figured there was probably a simple enough way down from my private platform to the public one below, but I didn't want to bump into any senators or security personnel, and I assumed I was probably being watched.

So I pulled a Hiram.

I waited for a break in the passersby below and then vaulted over the railing. It was a twenty-five-foot drop, but I landed softly with my knees bent, barely feeling the shock in my heels. Some nearby Denzans gasped and shouted as I dropped out of the sky and, so as not to make a bigger scene, I put my arm around Melian and led her onto a train just as its doors were closing.

"Wow," she said, her cheeks flushing a light shade of purple, "the stairs were, like, right there."

"Sorry," I said, dropping my arm away as we stood in the train's entrance, leaning against the closed doors. "I'm not sure I'm supposed to be free-roaming around Primclef, so I thought I should go ninja mode. What are you doing here, Mel?"

"Trying to see you, obviously," she replied. "I heard you were visiting the Senate today and wanted to talk to you, but they

273

wouldn't let me up. My sneaking-in skills aren't quite Zara-level."

"No one's are," I replied.

Melian leaned into the walkway to check the digital map projected from the train's ceiling. "Jeez, where are we going, anyway?"

I didn't have a destination in mind when we boarded the train, but things clicked together in my brain and I suddenly had an answer. "Have you ever heard of a place called Remembrance?"

"No," Melian replied, then looked the place up on her wrist-console before I could explain. She glanced back at the map. "We're going to have to transfer to a different train. Why do you want to go there? Do you think Aela might be . . . ?"

I shook my head. "It's a hunch, honestly. Something I hope that I'm wrong about." I awkwardly pushed a hand through my hair, realizing that I'd just dragged Melian onto a train without even saying hi. "So, uh, what's up with you?"

"Oh, not much," she replied, rocking back on her heels and smiling up at me. "Happy to be included on an adventure for once."

"I mean, hopefully this isn't an adventure and just a waste of our time," I said.

"Either way," she replied cheerily. "I also thought you'd want to see this." Melian leaned close so we could both look at her wrist-console. She called up an encrypted message that had been sent to her private account early that morning.

Batzian appeared on-screen, looking more repressed than ever—his ponytail had somehow achieved a new level of tightness, not a single white strand out of place. He'd also donned one of those Merciful Rampart uniforms, the black-and-red fabric drawn up all the way to his chin.

"Hello, sister," Batzian said into the camera. *"I noticed that the Eastwood was among the ISVs stationed above Little Earth, which means that the waves have brought us both back to Denza. I hope you're safe. Things are . . . different with this crew. My life doesn't feel constantly in danger, that's true. I suppose that's what I wanted. But they are afraid. Always so afraid of the humans. And that fear, it makes them . . ."* Batzian glanced over his shoulder, like he was worried someone might walk in on him. He wrapped the message up quickly. *"I regret how we left things. I hope we can meet in Primclef."*

"Great," I said as the message ended. "So the Merciful Rampart are here, too."

"Do you think they're going to crash the Senate meeting?" Melian asked.

"Of course they are," I said. "It'll be perfect. Rafe, Arkell, probably Reno, too—everyone can get together and talk out their differences." I shook my head. "Forget all that, though. What are you going to do about that message? Are you going to, like, meet Batzian for lunch or something?"

"I don't know," Melian replied. "I've never been apart from my brother for this long before. I do miss him."

"I sense a 'but' coming," I said.

"But . . ." Melian wormed her finger under her collar, twisting it around her necklace. She still wore the morbid knucklebones that she'd been given on the Torrent. "Have you ever spent so much time around a person that, without even realizing it, you kind of let them shape who you are? And then, when you're apart, it's like you can finally be yourself?"

I thought about my mom, sweaty and wild-eyed, holding some Denzan bureaucrat at gunpoint. "I know exactly what you're talking about. It's how I felt when I first came to the *Eastwood*."

Melian flashed a relieved smile. "He's my brother. Of course I'll see him. But . . . I don't know. I kind of like who I am more when Batzian isn't around. Is that horrible?"

"Not at all," I said, shaking my head. "You know, he didn't look too happy in that message. I bet Batzian is feeling the same thing as you, except he likes himself *less* when you aren't there to balance him out. I don't think your brother really understands himself—I know what that's like, too. Maybe seeing you will help him realize that. Especially since you're totally thriving."

I winced at how much I sounded like a bad advice column, but Melian didn't seem to notice. She pushed a strand of loose hair behind her ear. "Indefinite suspension from the institute, afraid to call home, weirdly attached to wearing bones—you think I'm thriving?"

"Totally," I said with a grin. "Your whole vibe is like—*Come at me, world. I'm the cool twin.*"

Melian rolled her eyes, but there was a new flush of purple in her cheeks. She glanced at the map. "We've got to transfer at the next stop."

With Melian navigating, we reached Remembrance's sector in about thirty minutes. I caught some weird looks from the Denzans on the way—pretty much every human was sequestered on Little Earth, so I was truly an oddity—but those side-eyes turned to nods of recognition and relief once they realized I was a hybrid. Suddenly, everyone loved a hybrid.

"How did you know about this place?" Melian asked as we rounded the corner.

"Aela brought me here," I said. "They wanted to show me what happened to contaminated Ossho."

Remembrance was in a quiet, residential neighborhood in one of Primclef's southern sectors. I felt like something was off right away. When I'd last visited Remembrance, there had been a line around the block—the neighborhood's older Denzans waiting their turn for the exiled Ossho to let them relive their cherished memories.

There was no line. The blinds were drawn on the storefront's big windows, and the front door swung ajar, its hinges broken. There was no one at all on the street. The windows on the surrounding buildings even had their shades drawn, like the whole block had gone into hiding.

Like I'm living in a nightmare.

The empty exo-suit I'd seen on the train platform.

The raid on Rafe's stash.

"The Vulpin have been a good trading partner for me over the years," Rafe had said.

That merchant on the Torrent, selling memories.

The pattern fit together.

"Shit," I said. "I'm right."

"What do you mean?" Melian asked. "About what?"

"I think I know what Reno is planning to do with Aela," I said.

As we approached the front door of Remembrance, an old Denzan woman emerged from the doorway of the neighboring building. Her hands were nervously shoved into the sleeves of her sweater.

"I wouldn't," she said, indicating the door I was about to open. "I think he's still in there. I thought about calling the authorities, but who would they send?"

"What do you mean?" I asked. "Who's in there?"

"The human."

23

Obviously, I wasn't going to listen to some old lady. I went inside.

And obviously, Melian wasn't going to listen to me when I told her it was dangerous and she should wait for me in the street.

The first thing I noticed were the empty exo-suits. They were sprawled on the floor of Remembrance like dead bodies. Three of them in total, each with their faceplates forcibly torn off. One of them also had a torn-off arm—someone with extraordinary strength had crumpled the limb like tinfoil and chucked it across the room.

The grim scene was at odds with the serene interior. The room smelled like spiced vanilla. A track of chirping birds played from the vid-wall, which depicted a slowly morphing painting of a shadow staring into a sunset. And then there were the rows of empty recliners, each equipped with a machine that reminded me of an anesthesia mask but that I knew allowed the wisps who worked here to safely connect with their Denzan clients. All in all, a pretty chill place to catch a nap or revisit some cherished memory.

Except, a human man had an exo-suit pinned down in the last chair.

He had wrenched the exo-suit's faceplate open and held a glass capsule roughly the size of a football over the opening. At the bottom of the capsule was a crackling ball of energy that seemed to attract the wisp, drawing them out from their shell. The current didn't seem all that dissimilar from the flashes of lightning that I'd seen running through Aela and other wisps. Unlike the electric streaks that ran through healthy wisps, the energy in the capsule seemed to be clawing at the Ossho, tangling up its form rather than mingling with it. It wasn't easy to assign emotion or motivation to a gaseous cloud of memories, but the Ossho definitely seemed like it was trying to cling to its exo-suit.

"Stop!" I yelled. "Let them go!"

The man turned his head to look at me but otherwise didn't stop what he was doing. He was in his thirties with short-cropped dark hair and a lean swimmer's frame. He was a totally unremarkable dude. Even back on Earth, in full paranoia mode, I probably wouldn't have given this guy a second glance.

But here? He could probably rip my head clean off.

"I know you," he said to me.

I squinted. If I'd seen this guy among the humans hanging around Little Earth, I hadn't noticed.

"I don't think so," I replied.

"Sure," he said. "You're one of Butler's little pets."

"I'm nobody's pet."

He shrugged. "If you say so."

The capsule in the man's hand made a satisfied hissing sound, and an automatic lid snapped closed, trapping the wisp inside. Through the glass, the compressed cloud seemed to writhe, shot through with voltage from the capsule's core. The man straightened up and shoved the capsule into a messenger bag slung over his shoulder, where it clinked against others.

"Where's Reno hiding?" I asked. "Where's Aela?"

The man raised an eyebrow. "Who's Aela?"

"The wisp Reno kidnapped," I said.

"They aren't people, kid," the man said, sounding bored. "You can't kidnap information. Whatever you called Aela, that's gone now."

My fist clenched, but Melian spoke before I could do anything.

"What you're doing here is wrong," she said. "It's in violation of your oath to Denza and the Serpo Institute. You should be ashamed."

"You should kneel," he replied.

"Excuse me?"

"You and all your kind should learn how to kneel," he said. "Beg us for forgiveness."

I took a protective step in front of Melian. The man's voice didn't have any malice in it. There wasn't any feeling at all, and that somehow made it worse. Clearly, Reno had exposed him to the Origin and the result was an aloof freak. The way he talked to us, it was like we were beneath his notice.

"Look, man, I've seen what you've seen." I had a feeling it was pointless to try reasoning with this guy—he'd been picked by Reno for a reason—but I had to try. "It's got your head all spun around. Whatever you're doing, it's not too late to walk it back. Come to Little Earth with me. Tell us how to find Reno before she hurts more people."

The man waited patiently for me to finish, then shook his head. "No. I'm leaving now."

He tried to walk by us—through us, really. I stepped to the side and Melian did the same, but as I did I grabbed the strap of his bag. "Hold up—"

First, I heard the squeak of the man's heel twisting on the floor as he planted his back foot, then I felt his fist like a cannonball strike me right in the sternum. The air rushed out of my lungs and my fingers lost their grip on the bag just like my feet lost touch with the floor. I flew backward, crashed into Remembrance's window, and kept right on going. I rolled to a stop in the middle of the street, broken glass stuck in my hair.

I saw spots and couldn't suck in a good breath. Still, I managed to clamber to one knee, the knife that Zara had given me looped around my knuckles.

"Syd!" Melian shouted, running over to me. "By the tides, are you okay?"

The man was already gone. I wasn't worth more than a single punch.

Guess that made me lucky.

A few hours later, I was staring at my attacker's face again. His institute-issued digital ID was projected on the vid-screen in Rafe's pizzeria alongside Marie Reno and two other humans. They were the trio who had disappeared from Little Earth the night of the fire. Apparently, the guy I'd faced off with was named Hiro Takagi.

"Yeah, that's him," I said, adjusting the ice pack that I held against my sternum. Hiro hadn't broken any ribs, but I was already developing one hell of a bruise. "Guy caught me with a cheap shot."

"At least we know you can take a punch," Darcy said with a smirk, sitting in the booth across from me with her legs up on the bench.

"Hiro's always been an asshole," Hiram said. He stood behind the pizzeria counter, peering in at the selection of pies, trying to make a decision. "Ever since his dad—"

"That's enough," Rafe cut Hiram off. He paced in front of the vid-wall, but I didn't think it was the four troublemaking humans that were on Rafe's mind. He'd been practicing his speech for the Senate when I'd staggered into the pizzeria, and even now he still occasionally mouthed random phrases. "I'm sorry that happened to you, Syd, and I assure you that the people of Little Earth will make restitution to the Ossho. But that doesn't matter now."

I sat forward, ice crunching between my fingers. "What do you mean it doesn't matter? We know what Reno is doing. She's got Aela, which means she's got the record of the Origin. She stole technology from you that allows her to control the Ossho. Her people are rampaging around Primclef capturing wisps. She's going to spread the Origin. And you know where that's going to happen, right? Not exactly playing three-dimensional chess to see that all of Little Earth's humans and the Denzan Senate make a pretty enticing target."

"What's three-dimensional chess?" Hiram asked, scratching the back of his neck.

Rafe stopped his pacing and turned to face me. "First of all, the technology Reno is using to capture the Ossho is highly unstable. I doubt her or any of her compatriots know how to properly work it."

"Worked fine for Hiro," I countered.

"Second," Rafe continued, "rumors of the Origin are already spreading throughout Primclef. The story is going to come out. What difference does it make if Reno is the one to tell it? She doesn't have leverage. She has a foregone conclusion."

"I think it makes a difference," Hiram said quietly.

I nodded in agreement with Hiram, thinking about his experience with Aela versus our experience in the temple. I also remembered the feeling of broken glass under my feet when Aela showed me one of their fractured experiences. It was awful, just like the sense of panic and terror I took from the Origin. Bonding with a wisp—especially when you didn't consent to it—could be seriously traumatic.

"She could do major damage," I said. "Poison the minds of your people, the Denzans . . ."

Rafe actually scoffed at that. "A bitter old woman wielding

technology she doesn't understand? I know you want to retrieve your Ossho friend, Syd, but this is laying it on a bit thick."

"You keep underestimating Reno. First you said you'd track her down in a day. Then you acted like it was no big deal that she busted into your stash of black-market technology and recruited some of your people away. And now you're pretending that whatever she does next is just a distraction from your big speech."

"It *is* a distraction," Rafe replied with more heat than I expected. "Tomorrow, the Denzan Senate will decide the fate of an entire planet. Billions of human lives are at stake. I won't let Marie get in the way."

"That's big talk," I replied. "But I don't actually hear a plan."

Rafe raised his eyebrows, but Darcy spoke up before he could respond. "If Syd's right and Reno does try something at the Senate, shouldn't we at least be prepared? We could equip our people with gas masks."

"How would that look to the Senate?" Rafe asked, his tone gentler when he was speaking to Darcy. "Like we're preparing to wage biological warfare on them? As if tensions weren't already high enough."

"You stole a bunch of ships from the institute," I said. "Whose fault is it that tensions are high?"

Rafe held up his hands. "Please. I know this is difficult for you, but you have to trust me. I know what I'm doing. Tomorrow will be a great day for humanity and Denza as well, so long as we stick together." He glanced in Hiram's direction. "Close up when you're finished."

With that said, Rafe left us in the pizzeria, heading off some-place where he could practice his speech without fielding a bunch of pesky questions. I wasn't at all satisfied by his whole *trust me* shtick, and I looked across the table at Darcy to see what she thought. Until recently, she'd been Rafe's most loyal supporter, but even Darcy was frowning now, picking at a crusted spot of sauce on the table.

"So," Hiram said, breaking the silence. "Grandpa is full of shit, right?"

Darcy sighed. "He's holding something back."

"Or he doesn't want us to know how much is out of his con-trol," I said.

"Could be both," Hiram added. He leaned his elbows on the counter, studying Reno and her three accomplices on the vid-wall. "Captain Reno really recruited all the dicks, didn't she?"

"What were you going to say before?" I asked. "About Hiro's dad?"

Hiram snorted. "Oh yeah. Grandpa likes to pretend this never happened. Hiro's dad was one of the First Twelve. He turned out to be kind of a drunk. How long ago was it, Darcy? Like five years?"

"We aren't supposed to talk about this," Darcy said quietly, glancing at the door to make sure Rafe was really gone. "It was longer than that. We were little when he crashed."

"Whatever," Hiram said, turning back to me. "Old Takagi got wasted and took a skiff out for a joy ride. He crashed it into a moving train. Takagi stumbled out without a scratch on him, obviously. The passengers weren't so lucky."

"Holy shit," I said. "What happened after that?"

"Takagi volunteered to return to Earth, knowing what that would mean," Darcy said.

"Grandpa convinced him," Hiram added. "Hiro's always been a real prick about it. Thought the punishment was too severe. The rest of Denza got over it, though. We all pretend like it never happened. They didn't even take Takagi's statue down. Only place to learn about that is in those Merciful Rampart pamphlets."

I shook my head. "What about the other two?"

Hiram pointed first at a craggy-faced man with slicked-back hair and a thin mustache. Based on the acne scars, I figured he must have grown up on Earth. "That's Luca Sapienza. He served on a ship with Reno back in the day. Didn't really see him as the troublemaking type, but I guess he's loyal."

"The other one is Irena Markov," Darcy said. I took a closer look at the dark-haired woman, who looked like she might have been a model back on Earth, her chin tilted up like even in her ID picture she was managing her angles. "Rafe never liked her."

"The way Grandpa tells it, she's from a well-connected family on Earth who discovered the Consulate when they weren't supposed to," Hiram said. "Irena got to come up here as a result, even though she didn't meet any of the academic or psychological qualifications. You know the Consulate doesn't just send anyone up, right? They're supposed to be useful. And not an asshole."

I thought of my mom back on Earth. "Yeah," I said evenly. "I know they're strict."

Darcy snapped her fingers. "She's the reason everyone calls Rafe the mayor. Remember that?"

Hiram laughed. "That's right. A couple years ago, Irena wanted us to hold an election for who was actually in charge of Little Earth. Of course, she was, like, the only candidate to declare. No one even bothered to vote because Gramps has things on lock."

In five minutes, I'd learned more about the secret history of Little Earth and the humans on Denza than I had in all the months I'd been here. Things weren't as unified and harmonious as Rafe had always made them seem.

"If I were Reno, seems like those three are exactly who I'd try to recruit," I said. "For all his talk about knowing everyone who matters in the galaxy, it doesn't seem like he was even keeping an eye on them."

Hiram cocked his head as if I'd just made him think of something. "Hold up . . ."

He swiped the ID pictures off the vid-wall and loaded up a scheduling grid with names assigned to tasks like "perimeter," "ship maintenance," and "colony prep." These were the duties that Rafe had assigned to all the humans who were stuck on Little Earth now instead of soaring separately through the Vastness. Hiram cycled back a few days on the schedule until he reached the day when Reno had gotten onto Little Earth.

"What is this?" Darcy asked.

"Yeah," I said, squinting at the screen. "Was I supposed to be doing chores since I've been here?"

"Nah, of course not. Grandpa lets you dainty hybrids live the sweet life while the rest of us get assigned grunt work to keep us busy." Hiram highlighted three names on the grid—Takagi, Sapienza, and Markov.

"Wait a second," I said. "They're all assigned to 'perimeter.' What does that mean?"

"Guard duty," Hiram said. "Supposed to walk the edge of the island and make sure nobody sneaks on shore or leaves for Primelef. Never needed guards before all this started."

"And Rafe gave out these assignments?"

Hiram nodded. "Yep."

"I don't understand," Darcy said. "Why would Rafe trust those three to work guard shifts?" She took a closer look at the grid. "Not only that, but why would he trust them to be the only ones standing guard?"

Darcy was right. The three humans who had defected to Reno were the only ones assigned to a perimeter shift that night. No wonder it had been so easy for Zara and H'Jossu to sneak onto the island.

"He let it happen," I said. "He knew that would Reno would be coming, he knew who she'd recruit—and he let it happen."

Darcy tugged at the strings on her hoodie. "Could've been a test. Maybe Rafe wanted to see if those three were loyal."

"Come on, Darcy," Hiram said. "You know Grandpa better than that."

I'd assumed that Rafe was just screwing up—underestimating Reno, making bad choices. But that wasn't what had happened at all.

"He knows what Reno is up to," I said. "And he wants it to happen."

Darcy crossed her arms. "There has to be more to it than that. Rafe's not a bad man. He's not like Reno."

"Whatever they're planning, we're going to be there to stop them," I said. "I'm sure Rafe is monitoring my communications. Can one of you guys get word out to the others?"

Hiram nodded. "Grandpa thinks I'm too much of a dumb-ass to get down with any subder . . . ? Subto . . . ? Uh, sneaky shit," he finished. "What do you want me to tell them?"

I took over the vid-wall, pulling up the route of Rafe's planned march to the Denzan Senate. "Tell them where to meet us," I said. "And tell them to get us some gas masks."

24

I knew from my recent trip that the Denzans were offering Little Earth a private rail line that would connect them directly to the Senate. But loading his people onto a train wasn't dramatic enough for Rafe.

He wanted to march.

At sunrise, the humans of Little Earth crowded onto three pontoon boats and started across the water for Primclef. I'd thought about sneaking out here the night before and punching holes in the bottoms of the boats, but there was no shortage of nautical transportation on Denza. Besides, if I got caught sabotaging Rafe's big moment, he'd make sure to keep me away from the Senate, and that was looking like our only chance to catch Reno.

Better to let it play out. Stay tight with the major players. And be ready.

Everyone was dressed smartly in their freshly ironed institute uniforms, the different insignia on each one a reminder of how spread out humans were across the Denzan fleet. The vibe was upbeat. On my boat, people passed around coffee and pastries. It seemed like everyone was excited to be moving forward; they'd been biding their time on Little Earth for weeks now. Finally, something was happening.

All told, there were only about fifty humans on the three boats. The rest, which numbered about twenty, went back up to the ships Rafe had commandeered. The ISVs finally moved from their positions above Little Earth, shadowing our boats as we streaked across the ocean.

I sat with Darcy and Hiram at the front of the boat, the salt spray cold on my cheeks and forehead. Darcy's hood kept blowing down, and eventually she gave up on pulling it back up and just let the wind whip through her hair.

I gazed up at the ISVs floating above us, eclipsing the moons that still hung in the morning sky. "Does he want it to look like we're invading Primclef?"

"You should know by now, Grandpa doesn't do anything by accident," Hiram replied.

We were greeted with cheering and waves as our boats approached the line of Denzan vessels that had been sending messages of peace and poetry to the sequestered Little Earth. The Denzans got their boats out of the way, clearing us a lane, and then fell in behind us. When they waved, we all waved back, like this was just a friendly outing on the water. I made note of the absence of any Merciful Rampart protesters mixed in with the Denzan craft. They'd probably be waiting for us at the Senate.

I'd caught only glimpses of Rafe since last night. He was busy keeping everyone organized and motivated, shaking hands and being charming, a fresh coat of black dye in his hair. He sported an old but well-maintained flight suit, exactly like the one he wore in the statue of the First Twelve. I watched him as he approached us—patting backs and hugging friends on his way, tipping his head back to laugh at some joke—totally in his element.

"Amazing, isn't it?" Rafe asked, holding his arms open when he finally reached us. "The finest humanity has to offer, all in one place, unified for a common goal. It's beautiful."

Darcy managed a smile while Hiram pretended to be very interested in the choppy waters. I flashed a cheesy double thumbs-up.

"I want the two of you marching up front, right beside me," Rafe said to me and Darcy.

"Sure," I said. "Got to have your hybrid mascots on display."

Rafe put his hands on his hips. "Symbols of unity between the species. Today's not a day for cynicism, Syd."

"What about me?" Hiram asked. "Where do you want me?"

Rafe frowned at his grandson. "Just try to keep up."

Hiram snapped off a mocking salute, shifting uncomfortably on his bad leg. Someone called Rafe's name, and he started to turn away, but I put a hand on his shoulder to stop him.

"We know you set it up so Reno could raid your stash," I said.

Rafe's smile didn't falter. "I've done nothing to help Marie. She chose not to return to Little Earth. She's not one of us."

"Uh-huh," I replied. "Keep going with that plausible deniability shit, dude. I just wanted to let you know that, whatever she's got planned, we're going to stop it. We're going to get our friend Aela back and make sure no one else gets hurt."

"Sydney, my boy," Rafe said, patting my cheek. "I'm absolutely counting on it." Then he pulled me close. "We have to show the Denzans that we can police our own. Make an example of Marie."

I recoiled from him, keeping my voice low. "Jesus. This is all a big publicity stunt to you. Don't you care about the damage she could do? The . . . the trouble she could start?"

I wanted to say "war," but figured Rafe would just fluff me off as being dramatic. The amped-up glimmer hadn't left his eyes. To him, everything was going as planned.

"Billions of human lives hang in the balance. There's no amount of damage Reno could do that outweighs the suffering of our people on Earth." He patted my shoulder. "We all have a role to play, Syd. Me, Reno, even you."

"I'm not playing your game," I said weakly, but Rafe had already broken away from me.

And anyway, that was bullshit. I was absolutely playing his game. I was going to stop Reno just like Rafe wanted me to.

Who better than den *Eastwood*? A couple of hybrids and their diverse crew.

"What did he say to you?" Darcy asked.

I shook my head. "It's like we thought. He wants Reno to make a scene, and he wants us to bring her down."

"Then that's what we'll do," Darcy said with a certainty that I didn't share.

The jocular atmosphere of the boat died down when we reached Primclef's docks. Rafe was clear that he wanted us to look serious, but not threatening. Resolute, but not angry. It was seven miles from the docks to the Senate, and we were supposed to do the whole walk in silence.

"Well," Hiram said. "See you guys at the party." He slipped into the ranks of humans, leaving me and Darcy to take up our positions next to Rafe.

We set out. Rafe offered to link arms with Darcy, and, after a sheepish glance in my direction, she looped her arm through his. When he offered his other arm to me, I pretended not to notice. I stayed a half step behind him as he led the procession of humans in an orderly column down the thoroughfare.

Right from the start, there was no shortage of onlookers. Denzans crowded along the edge of the pathways or watched from windows and rooftops. Mixed in with them were Vulpin and Panalax, but I didn't see a single Ossho. Strange that there wouldn't be here to observe this moment. Hopefully Reno hadn't captured every wisp in Primclef and they were just lying low until it was safe for their kind again. I smiled sadly to myself, thinking of Aela, who would probably be like, *Oh, I've never been captured by an insane boomer before; sounds like a neat experience.*

"Why does he look so weird?" a small Denzan boy asked his mother as we passed. It took me a second to realize that he was pointing at me.

"He's a hybrid," his mother explained with an apologetic smile when she saw that I'd noticed them. "'Different' doesn't have to mean 'weird.'"

I waved to the kid and he hid his face against his mother's leg.

As we marched on, it started to feel like I was a part of a very awkward parade. It was often uncomfortably quiet, with the murmuring Denzans going silent as we approached. I tried to read their faces to see what they thought of Rafe's demonstration. For every encouraging smile or waving Denzan in the crowd, there was one with their brow nervously furrowed or who shook their head judgmentally when I made eye contact.

"Hey, big boy!" a swaggering Vulpin with his fur done up in fancy curlicues yelled at Rafe. "Good idea to walk! Your belly's gonna get to the Senate a half hour before you do!"

"How'd you get so fat when your pizza sucks shit?" a second Vulpin heckled.

"Well, can't disagree with that," I muttered.

Rafe didn't respond, and soon those Vulpin were behind us, replaced by a new section of crowd. Despite the fact that our little group was composed of the most fearsome species in the galaxy, I still started to feel small and exposed. The onlookers only seemed to grow in number the closer we got to the Senate. Maybe there was a message in that, too, even if the Denzans hadn't sent it purposely. As powerful as the humans were individually, there were only like fifty of us. But there were tens of thousands of Denzans and their allied species watching. We were just a small part of a larger galactic society.

We were about halfway to the Senate when the ships that had been gliding along above us veered off. A murmur went through the crowd—humans and Denzans alike—as the stolen ISVs coasted in formation toward the Serpo Institute's mountainside spacecraft dock.

"Where are they going?" I asked Rafe. With all the chatter created by the moving ships, there was no reason to worry about being overheard.

He glanced back at me. "I'm returning them. I think we got our point across."

A few blocks later, a flash of light hit my eye. Someone was catching the sun with a mirror and reflecting it into my face. I squinted up at the rooftops, trying to identify the source.

It wasn't a mirror at all. It was a knife.

Once Zara was sure that I'd seen the signal, she stepped back from the edge of the rooftop she'd been perched on.

I slowed my walk. Rafe was so focused on the archway entrance to the Senate that I don't think he noticed. I could tell Darcy saw me out of the corner of her eyes, but she didn't say anything. I wasn't ditching her. We'd talked this through last night.

The crowd of humans overtook me, one man jostling my shoulder when I got in his way. Pretty soon, I'd made it to the back of the demonstration, where Hiram was limping at a slower than normal pace. Walking alongside him—and earning no shortage of quizzical looks from the rest of the bystanders—were H'Jossu and Melian.

"Look who I ran into," Hiram said.

"Yeah, what a coincidence," I said. We'd gotten in touch with the rest of our crew last night and asked them to meet us during the protest. If we were going to play defense against whatever Reno had planned, we needed help. And we needed supplies.

"Man, there was no way I was going to miss this," H'Jossu said. "Solidarity with humanity! They make the best TV shows!" He pumped his furry fist in the air. "More streaming options! In the institute dorms! More streaming options! In the institute dorms!"

H'Jossu's dumb chant got a lot of confused looks both from the humans ahead of us and the bystanders. It was a good distraction, though. Melian took the opportunity to reach into her backpack and hand over some gear to me and Hiram. We each got an earbud that would link our crew via a private comm channel and a breathing apparatus. I took an extra set for Darcy. The contraption that Melian handed out wasn't exactly a heavy-duty gas mask like I'd envisioned. Instead, it was basically a strip of plastic with an elastic band that would fit over my mouth and nose. The Denzans used them to supplement their oxygen during high-altitude work.

"Will this thing really keep out a wisp?" I asked, stuffing the breather into the front of my uniform. Hiram did the same.

"Can't say for sure," Melian said. "Best we could find on short notice. Not a lot of gas masks just lying around the institute."

I shuddered at the thought of having to endure the Origin again. If Reno did try to deploy the Ossho like I expected her to, I'd be relying on a piece of equipment not much sturdier than a snorkel.

"Once we're inside, spread out and keep your eyes on the entrances," I said. "If you see anything weird, use the comm to shout it out."

H'Jossu had stopped his chanting to amble along beside us. "What are we supposed to do if Captain Reno does show up? Besides, um, wave our arms and shriek."

"Leave her to me," Hiram said.

"Or me," Zara piped in over the comm.

"I'll race you to her, you annoying furball," Hiram said with a grin.

"We don't have to fight Reno," I said, trying to impress this upon the others. "We just have to derail whatever she's planning. Focus on keeping the Denzans safe."

"Be the tapeworm in the yogurt," H'Jossu said. "Got it."

I caught up with Rafe and Darcy as our procession marched through the Senate's cavernous entrance. The opening was so huge that the humans behind me didn't even need to break ranks; they could fit in shoulder to shoulder, ten across, with room for more Denzans to file in alongside. Once we passed under the archway and its carvings of linked hands, there was an equally wide passage with branching switchback staircases that led to the higher levels carved directly into the rock. We passed the staircases and kept going straight down the main passage and the Senate floor was just right there. No gates or security or even a velvet rope. Security wasn't something the Denzans worried about.

Yesterday's visit to the Senate hadn't prepared me at all for what the place would look like when full. Four rings of stadium seating extended up from the floor, and every section was packed with Denzans still hustling up and down the aisles in search of a bench they could squeeze onto. My brain zipped through some math—a head count of a bench, multiplied by benches per row, multiplied again by the number of sections—there had to be almost fifty thousand people here. A huge holographic projection floated above the proceedings and—oh, hey, there I was, caught on video as the camera drones focused on Rafe's grand entrance.

"Holy shit," I said to Darcy as we bumped together in the crowd. When we got close, I handed off her breather and earbud and she slipped them into her hoodie's pockets. "Is it always like this?"

"Never bothered to come before," Darcy replied. "But no, I think it's pretty rare for a Senate hearing to look like a hyperball final."

Our human contingent was ushered toward an empty section in the lower bowl. Rafe gave one last look at me and Darcy before we parted.

"Front row, you two," he ordered, raising his voice to be heard over the roar of conversation that echoed throughout the cavernous chamber.

With confident strides, Rafe walked directly onto the Senate floor. Darcy and I took seats in the row we were instructed to, although I made sure to grab the aisle so that I could dip out at the first sign of trouble. The rest of the humans filled in the benches behind us, Hiram a couple rows back with them.

My eyes skimmed across the crowd. Thousands and thousands

of faces. I tried to ignore gray-skinned Denzans as I looked for humans sitting where they shouldn't be, but at a certain distance everyone blurred together.

"Too many people," I muttered to Darcy.

"No kidding." She slouched low, taking the opportunity to put her earbud in.

I touched my ear to activate the comm. "Did you guys all get in okay?"

"Covering the top level," Zara reported. "By the trains."

"I'm in the institute section," Melian said.

"Too crowded for me in there, so I'm patrolling the main entrance," H'Jossu said. "Is it too late to assign code names or . . . ?"

"Has anyone seen my uncle?" I asked. "Melian?"

"There are a lot of Serpo instructors here and some captains, but I don't see Tycius," she replied.

My eyes settled on the section directly across the chamber from ours. Nothing but Denzans there, all of them clad in the same red-and-black webbed uniform. They stared determinedly at us, unblinking, like their glares would scare us out of the room.

"How'd the Merciful Rampart get a whole section to themselves?" I asked. I scanned the group for familiar faces and spotted Batzian sitting in the last row. Maybe it was wishful thinking, but I didn't think his stare was as cold as the rest of his crew's.

It was Melian who answered in my ear. "That means they've been given time to address the Senate."

"Oh," I said. "Great."

The high-backed chairs spread across the map of Denza were all occupied by senators now. There was a pretty even distribution of genders and ages among the senators, although my new friend Senator Formachus looked to be the youngest. I noticed one senator, seated atop the northern islands, where Batzian and Melian were from, who wore a Merciful Rampart pin on the breast of his formal robe. While the senators were a varied bunch of Denzans, they did all have one thing in common.

They looked pretty uncomfortable with Rafe Butler slowly walking through their ranks.

Rafe didn't go for the lectern in the center of the floor. Instead, he came to a stop in a stretch of ocean not far from where Senator Forma sat on the island of Primclef. He clasped his hands behind his back and squared his shoulders. Gradually, a hush fell across the amphitheater.

"Am I standing in the right place, senators?" Rafe asked. A flea-size mic drone hovered close to his face, amplifying his words through the chamber's sound system.

Most of the senators realized this was a rhetorical question, but one older man, whose robe was wrinkled and tea-stained, pointed shakily at the lectern before awkwardly dropping his hand.

"I'm standing on Little Earth," Rafe said, glancing down at the painted ocean beneath his feet. "An island too small to add to the map, I suppose. Certainly not important enough to merit its own chair." He glanced to the senator on his left. "Do you represent me, Senator?" He glanced to the right at Forma. "Or you?"

Forma studied Rafe through her ever-flashing glasses, but

didn't respond. There was some disgruntled muttering from the humans around us.

"Humanity is approaching its fiftieth year on Denza," Rafe continued. "In that time, our species have grown close. We have fought for each other. Learned from each other. Discovered the universe together. Loved one another." He gestured toward our section, where Darcy and I were conveniently plopped front and center. "Raised children together."

"Ew," Darcy said and tried to slouch even lower.

"And yet there is still no Little Earth on the map, no senator here to represent me," Rafe continued. "For fifty years, we have served as champions of the Denzan people. You have honored us with statues and granted us an island to remake like our home. But you have stopped *seeing* us. We needed to commandeer your ships before you would even *notice* us."

Some of the Denzans in the crowd grumbled at that, while others went as far as to shout out denials. Rafe let those words hang in the air as he finally approached the lectern.

"We cannot be physically harmed by conventional methods, but we can be hurt," Rafe continued. "The apathy of our Denzan brothers and sisters hurts us. The lack of a true home hurts us. The memories of our kin, stranded on Earth, ignorant of the universe beyond the borders of their home system—that hurts us most of all." Rafe stood behind the lectern now, his hands clutching its sides. "For fifty years, we lucky few who were selected to come to this paradise, we have never once turned away from our true home. Yearning for a time when the Wasting that afflicts our kind could be cured and the bulk of humanity could be lifted up to a place beyond poverty and war and misery."

Without realizing it, I'd scooted to the edge of my seat. Even though I knew where this speech was going, Rafe had still gotten his hooks in me. I leaned toward him as he paused, waiting for him to deliver the gut punch.

"But there is no cure for the Wasting," Rafe said quietly. "We know that now. I can never return home to shepherd my people into a new era. Every day, for the rest of my life, I will mourn the loss of Earth. I will mourn every human who has needlessly lost their life there over the last fifty years while we blessed citizens of Denza *did nothing*. But now I ask you, how long will the Denzans let this suffering continue? How many humans must die before you finally *see* us? Fifty years ago, we came here to help you, Denza. Now we need your help. We need you to give us a home."

Rafe hit a button on the lectern. Above him, the holographic image of a world much like Earth appeared, casting the whole chamber in a light blue glow as it slowly rotated.

"This is Illaria," Rafe said. "An uninhabited planet with qualities similar to Earth. I humbly request that the Denzan Senate set it aside for the urgent relocation of humanity. We must . . ."

Rafe kept on talking, but I wasn't listening. I'd seen his images of Illaria once before, in his pizzeria, but my brain had been too tired from my surprise return to Denza to really *see* it. Having the planet projected above me like this, the details blown up huge—it suddenly clicked into place.

A tightness on my arm from the metal sleeve.

A ring of fire.

World killer.

The blue oceans boiling. The landmasses I'd seen wreathed by clouds of toxic ash. So similar to my home planet, I'd just assumed . . .

The vision that Goldy had shown me, it was never fully clear. I thought the planet I destroyed was Earth.

But it might have been Illaria.

25

Just when my eyes had started to water from staring, Darcy dug her elbow in my ribs. I blinked, broke out of my trance, and looked at her. She tapped her ear and mouthed, *Are you hearing this?*

I hadn't been hearing anything. I'd been lost in that vision. Earth. Illaria. My destiny. Was any of it true? Now I wasn't even sure I could trust my own memory. Hadn't I already broken the chain by leaving Goldy trapped aboard the *Cavern*? If that was the case, why did I feel so much dread in the pit of my stomach at the sight of that planet? Maybe this was all part of Goldy's plan, my destiny. By trying to prevent a war, I'd thrown my lot in with Rafe, potentially securing him a new home world for humanity. A world that I would kill.

I shook it off. Needed to stay in the moment. The future would have to wait.

"Syd?" That was H'Jossu coming over the comms. I wondered how many times he'd said my name. "Do you read? I found Tycius. I think you better come back to the entrance . . ."

I popped out of my seat with maybe a bit more speed than necessary and got some startled looks from the humans around me. However, most eyes were still glued on Rafe, who had begun fielding questions from the senators.

"To begin with, we would abide by the immigration standards already set by the Serpo Institute and the Consulate . . . ," I heard Rafe say as I jogged down the aisle and backtracked toward the entrance.

The passage to the street was completely empty now, with everyone packed into the chamber, so I spotted H'Jossu's broad back right away. He'd drawn himself up to his full height, looking like a big mold-covered bear, his hairy arms extended out from his sides. H'Jossu blocked the path of a floating cargo platform that was loaded with a massive object hidden beneath a black curtain.

"Let us pass, you carrion-eating fool!" Arkell shouted. "We are expected on the Senate floor."

"Um, first of all, rude," H'Jossu said. "Second of all, I'm not moving until my captain tells me I should."

Of course, here was the rest of the Merciful Rampart contingent, ready to make a grand entrance of their own. Arkell stood just out of H'Jossu's swiping distance, his eyes narrowed to slits. I could tell that Arkell's red-and-black uniform had been freshly ironed for the occasion, and I could also tell that he was tremendously irritated by H'Jossu's interference. He blotted at his forehead with a handkerchief, probably furious that he was going to have to face the Senate looking sweaty.

Behind Arkell were a couple of Rampart lackeys operating the floating platform. Nearby, Ayadora leaned on her cane at a safe distance from the fracas. Her cataract-sealed eyes were pointed at the scene, her lips pursed impatiently.

"Oh, hey, Syd," Jamdora said.

The hybrid was who I focused on as I skidded to a stop beside H'Jossu. Jamdora had hold of my uncle. One of his arms was wrapped around Ty's waist, Jamdora squeezing my uncle like they were posing for a prom picture. His other hand pinched the spot where Ty's neck met his shoulder. It must have been some kind of pressure point, because my uncle looked frozen, completely locked up, his jaw clenched like he couldn't even speak.

"Let him go," I said.

"He took a run at Captain Arkell," Jamdora explained. "I was just keeping the peace, my friend."

"Be careful," H'Jossu loudly whispered to me. "He moves like a ninja."

Jamdora let my uncle go with a gentle push that sent him stumbling into H'Jossu's outstretched arms. Tycius coughed and did a full-body shudder and then a half second later was back upright and pointing a finger at Arkell.

"This is madness!" he yelled. "You have no idea the danger you're exposing our people to!"

I glanced up at the massive object covered by a curtain and took a halting step backward.

"Hold up," I said. "Tell me that's not what I think it is."

I'd just been sitting in the Senate stands, staring up at the projection of Illaria and revisiting the vision Goldy had given me for the thousandth time—and now, there he was, with only a curtain separating the two of us.

"Denza needs to understand that they are free from the Etherazi menace," Arkell said. "Seeing is believing."

"Oh, no way!" H'Jossu exclaimed as he caught on, too. He put both his paws atop his head in disbelief. "That's the Eye of Sauron under there?"

"No," Ayadora said. "It is an Etherazi."

"Have you guys never seen a single monster movie?" H'Jossu rumbled, shuffling from foot to foot in agitation. "They always escape from their cages! Man gets all arrogant that they've tamed the beast, and then—*splat*."

Arkell eyed H'Jossu, his scarred face twisted with derision. "This is a waste of time," he said, turning to look at my uncle. "I allowed you to board the *Cavern* last night in the spirit of cooperation. I thought we had finally put our differences behind us."

"That was before I knew you planned to bring that creature here," Tycius replied. "As if this hearing weren't combustible enough, here you are walking in with a bomb."

"Go hide on Earth for another decade. It suits you," Arkell replied. "Denza will enter its new era without you."

Ayadora stepped forward, leading with her cane. She bumped it against H'Jossu's toes. "We are already late," she said. "Are they going to move, Arkell? Or must my son move them for us?"

I exchanged a look with Jamdora. He shrugged at me apologetically, like *What are ya gonna do?* I could empathize with a guy being dragged into tough situations by his mother. On the other hand, his whole chill-buddy vibe and pretty face were immensely punchable. Maybe he knew some lost Denzan martial art, but I doubted he'd ever had to fight Earth dirty.

Basically, I was preparing to kick him in the balls when my uncle put a hand on my shoulder.

"Let them go through," Tycius said. He glared at Arkell. "But if something happens, Arkell, it's on you."

"Yes, yes, I know," Arkell replied. "I'm perfectly willing to bear the burden of Denzan liberation."

H'Jossu and I stepped aside, allowing Arkell to lead the floating platform down the tunnel toward the Senate floor. Jamdora stuck out his arm for his mom, and she looped her hand through the crook of his elbow. With a nod in my direction, he led Ayadora after Arkell and the others.

"I could've taken him," I muttered.

"Ehh," H'Jossu replied.

"The two of you brawling here on the concourse wouldn't have changed the outcome," Tycius said. "It would've created a scene, and, one way or another, Arkell would've gotten to show off his pet monster."

"I thought it would be bigger," H'Jossu said.

I remembered back to the *Cavern* and the giant hourglass containment unit they'd had Goldy imprisoned in. "It *was* bigger, wasn't it?"

"The Gold One has gotten smaller. Shriveled up. If I had to guess, I'd say he's dying," Tycius replied. "Come on. We should stay close to them, in case we need to step in."

We followed the Merciful Rampart crew down the passage toward the Senate floor. Snatches of discussion reached me—it sounded like Rafe was outlining a set of commitments to preserving the native species of Illaria.

"I've got our crew spread out around the Senate," I told my uncle. "Watching out for Reno."

"Good," Tycius said. "I knew you'd be prepared."

Funny, I didn't feel prepared at all.

"Some constructive criticism, if I may, Captain Tycius," H'Jossu said, "but I think if we were truly prepared, we'd have code names."

I shot him a look. "Do you want me to call you Maverick? Is that what this is about?"

"Maybe."

Shaking my head, I turned back to my uncle. "What were you doing on the *Cavern*, anyway?"

"I . . ." Ty's mouth tightened in a way I'd come to recognize as him not wanting to talk about something. "When I learned they were docked here, I asked Arkell if I could see the Gold One."

"Really? Why?"

"I wanted to try to communicate with him, like we did before," Tycius said. "I wanted him to tell me how . . . how I . . ."

I held up a hand so Tycius knew that he didn't need to finish that sentence. As obsessed as I'd become with Goldy's prophecies,

I should've known that they would gnaw away at my uncle, too. He wanted to know how he failed me. How he died.

"It wouldn't talk to me," Tycius concluded. "The eye wouldn't even open."

"Good," I said. "It's a liar. We don't have to believe anything it says."

From the floor of the Senate, one voice rose up above the others in a shout. "As representative of the Noros Islands, I cede my time to the Merciful Rampart contingent!"

That must have been the senator from up north who was rocking the Rampart apparel. Of course. Arkell had said they were expected. The crowd murmured—and no small amount of Denzans actually groaned and hissed—as Arkell and his team made their way across the floor. Tycius, H'Jossu, and I watched from the tunnel as Arkell ascended to the lectern where Rafe still stood. Rafe, to his credit, seemed completely unsurprised by the disturbance and cleared the way for Arkell with a gentlemanly bow.

"My name is Arkell, and I speak for the Merciful Rampart."

Arkell's voice was scratchy and small even in the mic, and it took me a moment to realize that he was actually nervous. His arrogance and his stern lecturing technique worked in a one-on-one setting, but with thousands of his fellow Denzans looking down on him, Arkell didn't seem so sure of himself. I noticed him reach for his bony shoulder as if to rub the place where his metal binding used to be. Meanwhile, Rafe lingered by the podium, looking sturdy and confident, his patient smile never faltering. I almost felt bad for Arkell.

"It may surprise some of you to hear that we at the Merciful Rampart support the human proposal for a new home world," Arkell continued. "Humanity does not belong here. Recent events have shown that they cannot be trusted to live among us, to respect our laws and culture, to be model galactic citizens. In your hearts, buried beneath your survivor's guilt for humanity's service during the Etherazi invasion, I know many of my fellow Denzans feel the same. Humans come from a violent place, an unenlightened place, where might dictates right—and they have brought those values with them to Denza."

"I was born here, you old bitch-ass," Hiram grumbled over the comm.

I scanned the audience to see how they were responding to Arkell's rhetoric. The crowd seemed split—many shook their heads or booed his rundown of humanity, while others sat in respectful silence. The senators seemed similarly divided.

"We Denzans are generous of heart and spirit," Arkell continued, "and so our natural empathy has long stood in the way of simply sending humanity back to Earth. The so-called Wasting that Rafe described, the certain death that awaits his people—it has kept us from deporting these humans to preserve our own safety. A new home world solves that problem. It is morally imperative that we Denzans help humanity relocate. We should then destroy the wormhole to their galaxy and let them continue their society's development without interference, as we should have some fifty years ago . . ."

Arkell wasn't the skilled orator that Rafe was, but he was really good at sneaking insults into his offers of assistance. I watched Rafe, unsurprised to see how he nodded along with Arkell's words. A new home for humanity was his prime concern. He'd probably already stolen the technology to create a new wormhole if Denza thought to cut off humanity from the rest of the universe. And, I realized, if he needed someone to use a Wayscope—he had Darcy. And me.

"But," Arkell said, raising a finger that trembled slightly in the air, "before we can do what must be done to safeguard the galaxy, we must overcome the issue of Denzan cowardice."

That certainly got the crowd's attention, a ripple of grumbles and yells passing through the audience.

"Oh, good," I whispered to Tycius, "he's going to have a go at your people now. Thought he wasted all his best burns on humanity."

"What will we do without humanity to protect us from the Etherazi?" Arkell asked, affecting a weak, mewling voice. "Who will save us if those nightmares return?" He pounded his fist on the lectern, the sound hollow and flat. "We can protect ourselves! The Merciful Rampart can keep Denza safe!"

That must have been the signal because the Rampart guys manning the platform whipped the curtain away, revealing the hourglass-shaped containment unit that held Goldy. Tycius wasn't kidding before when he said that the Etherazi had shrunk. The last time I saw the Etherazi's core it had looked like a peach pit the size of a car. Now he was no bigger than a refrigerator, the bark-like carapace shriveled and flaky in a way that it wasn't before. I didn't need to be a theoretician to tell that Ayadora's machine was slowly killing the Etherazi.

It seemed like a horrible way to go. Trapped, starved, put on display—ugh, what was I doing? Pitying an Etherazi now?

But it was my fault he was in there. I was supposed to save his life. And I hadn't.

The Denzans—senators and spectators alike—leaned forward to get a better look at Arkell's monster. None of them had ever seen the inside of an Etherazi before, but the flickering whorls of temporal energy were unmistakable as they curled off Goldy's shell, only to be eradicated by the container. Next to me, Tycius winced and rubbed his temples. Even this limited exposure, while tolerable, messed with the Denzans' brains.

It took the crowd a few heartbeats to realize what they were looking at, but when it finally sank in, the response was visceral.

They screamed—some in terror, others in rage. Some shouted at Arkell, others at Goldy. Some began to cry, or hugged their neighbor and buried their faces in each other's shoulders, hiding their eyes.

". . . train coming in . . . ," a voice said over the comm. I think it was Zara. I couldn't really make out what she was saying through all the shouting.

I cupped my hand over my ear. "What? Zara, repeat."

Meanwhile, at the sight of the Etherazi, Rafe's composure finally broke a bit. He took a halting step away from Arkell and the lectern and cast his eyes about, almost like he was looking for

315

a battle-anchor to climb into.

". . . third level . . . think it could be them . . ."

I scanned the upper tier for a sign of danger, but there was already too much commotion. Denzans hugged themselves and rocked in panic, while some directly fled for the exits. The three of us standing in the tunnel had to dodge to the side as Denzans pushed and shoved to get away, even the sight of a captive Etherazi too much for them.

"This is not what we agreed upon!" bellowed the senator from the Noros Islands. I noticed that he'd taken off his Rampart lapel pin. "Remove that monster at once!"

A few of the other senators were on their feet as well, some filtering toward the exits with the spectators and others staring with terror and awe at Goldy. Senator Forma put her hands in the air, trying to get their attention. "Please! We have a responsibility to continue! Cover that thing and retake your seats!"

"It can't hurt you!" Arkell yelled into the microphone. "We have it trapped! Us! The Denzan people have overcome the Etherazi, not with brute force, but with science and ingenuity!"

I tried to push my way up the nearest staircase, but there was no way up that wouldn't mean bodying a bunch of Denzans. Better to let them get the hell out of here than to stand in their way. I edged back toward the Senate floor.

"Zara," I said into the comm. "Where you at? Does anyone have eyes on her?"

She didn't reply.

"This is a mess," Hiram observed.

The whole chamber wasn't fleeing, though. A not-insignificant portion of Denzans remained calm, listening to Arkell, their curiosity overtaking their trauma. They started to push their way closer to the floor for a better view, welcomed forward by the Denzans in the Merciful Rampart section. Even more jostling, even more bottlenecks.

"Got to clear this crowd," Melian said, grunting as someone bumped into her.

I pushed my way toward the senator floor so as not to be in the way of the Denzans running for the exits. H'Jossu followed me, while Tycius paused to help an elderly man who'd been tripped up and nearly trampled.

"Zara?" I tried again. "Come on! What did you—?"

"Reno is here!" Zara yelled over me. "Coming from above!"

I looked up in time to see Zara hopping through the third-level section that I'd sat in when I'd met with Forma. She was moving against a tide of Denzans trying to run for the trains, bouncing from bench to bench, glancing over her shoulder like she was being chased. At the same moment, I noticed how the Denzans in that section had stopped retreating up the stairs and were now backing up toward the benches like they were afraid of something on the concourse.

"Shit," I said. "Here we go."

I glanced to my left, where H'Jossu stood with his claws flexed and ready. I glanced to my right, where, in the human section, Darcy and Hiram were both on their feet. Everyone was on their feet, though. I quickly scanned the opposite sections for Melian or

Batzian, but I'd lost them both in the crowd.

"I don't see them, Zara," Hiram said. "Where are they?"

"Thought they were chasing me . . . ," Zara said breathlessly. "Not sure now . . ."

As I watched, Zara did a graceful dive over the edge of the third level and landed in a stairwell on the second level. She rolled out of sight from there, hidden behind a group of gawking Denzans.

I searched the upper deck for any sign of Reno or her allies. The Denzans up there had stopped moving. In fact, of all the sections, that now seemed to be the calmest. For a moment, I thought I saw a flash of magenta up there, but I was soon distracted by the scene at the lectern.

"The humans can leave! We can protect ourselves!" Arkell shouted, still giving his speech. "The Merciful Rampart can protect you!"

"That's enough, I think, Arkell," Rafe said, the mic picking up his words as he held a hand out toward the Denzan. "We need to let things calm do—"

Sppsht.

It was a literal splatting sound, no other way to describe it, the noise a body made when it was crushed. Like dropping a package of ground beef on the kitchen floor. Amplified by the lectern's microphone, it echoed throughout the Senate. The panicked scene actually calmed for a moment as everyone looked to see what happened.

Rafe blinked. He took a startled step backward and stumbled off the lectern, his face covered in Arkell's blood.

Arkell was a smear. He was liquid.

Reno stood up from where she'd landed on top of Arkell, dripping with him, covered with him. She'd launched from the third section and come down feetfirst on top of his head. Like a nail dropped off a skyscraper onto a melon.

"Okay, hon, go ahead," she said, brushing a bit of Arkell off her shoulder. "Protect them."

26

Now everyone was screaming. If they weren't screaming, they were running. Mostly, they were doing both. Seeing a body crushed by a falling meteor-woman tended to get that reaction.

"They aren't telling you the truth!" Reno screamed into the microphone, her words directed at the human section. "The Denzans have stolen from humanity! They have crippled us and imprisoned us! And we *will* have our reparations!"

The humans hadn't panicked like the Denzan spectators, who were already freaked out from the reveal of Goldy, but they also didn't exactly spring into action. Most of them stood there, staring at Reno, looking confused or horrified.

And then the capsule landed among them.

The silver football-size object had been flung down from one of the upper levels. Things were happening too fast for me to accurately trace its source. But I'd seen that object before, back at Remembrance, when I'd caught Takagi filling them up.

"Masks!" I shouted. "Hiram! Darcy!"

The capsule broke up with a hiss and an Ossho cloud came spilling out. The humans in the closest row barely had time to backpedal a few steps before the gas was on them—flowing into their mouths, snaking up their noses. Once the Ossho was in them, they collapsed like their strings were cut, landing on the benches or tumbling into the aisles. Through the magenta haze, I saw Darcy stagger forward and roll onto the Senate floor. Even if she'd gotten her breather on in time, we weren't sure if they would keep out the Ossho.

"I will show you the truth!" Reno screamed.

A moment later, Darcy popped to her feet, her breather securely fastened on her face. Hiram followed her out of the cloud, waving a hand in front of his breather-covered face in order to clear the fog. The Ossho cloud had thinned out as it spread to more and more humans. Tendrils were visible from their mouths and noses, swaying like coral growths, almost like they were waiting to connect to something.

"Well, at least the breathers work," Darcy said over the comm. "What no—?"

"Look out!" Hiram shouted and shoved Darcy to the side, pushing her out of the way of a human who had dropped from the upper level.

The human landed with enough force that he cracked the stone floor, sending rifts through the painting of the Denzan ocean.

That was Sapienza, one of Reno's old buddies who had joined her cause. He wore a breather of his own—way more heavy-duty than the kind we had. Sapienza lunged for Hiram's mask, but Hiram caught him by the arm and twisted him to the ground with a judo throw.

"Reno!" Meanwhile, at the lectern, Rafe had charged forward to deal with his fellow First Twelve. "This bloodshed! What have you done?"

I wondered if Rafe had rehearsed that line. He'd known this was coming. And now he thought he could put on a show.

"What you don't have the stomach fo—"

Their words had been broadcast over the Senate's sound system, but that was cut off when Reno ripped the podium clean from the stage and swung it like a baseball bat. I think the sheer violence of the act caught Rafe by surprise, because he barely got his arms up to cushion the blow. Rafe was sent flying off the small stage, crashing into a chair that a senator had luckily abandoned.

"Syd!" H'Jossu said from beside me, his breather barely stretched across his plump snout. "Did you see?"

I nodded. When Reno had attacked Rafe, I'd caught sight of something strapped across her back.

Not something. *Someone.*

Aela.

Reno wore the stick-figure exo-suit like a backpack, although, just as I started forward, she pulled Aela loose from the straps and stood them up on the upraised dais. Aela looked inert, lifeless, and Reno handled them with all the care a photographer would use on their tripod. To Reno, Aela was simply equipment. She had done something to my wisp friend's faceplate, attached some kind of cylindrical contraption made of the same glass and silver as the capsules. I thought I could see magenta flowing around in there, held at bay by streaks of artificial lightning.

I glanced over my shoulder to where Hiram and Darcy were struggling with Sapienza. I'd lost track of Tycius, Melian, and Zara and it was hard to hear anything over the comms but chaos. There were swelling crowds at all the exits and also growing piles of unconscious bodies as more Ossho capsules were released around the Senate. Takagi and Markov—Reno's two other underlings—must have been moving through the sections doing that. I focused on Reno. She was at the center of all this.

"We have to help Aela," I said to H'Jossu.

"I'm right behind you!" He said, punching one of his paws into his palm. "Let's try not to die!"

"Deal."

As we ran toward the dais, for a moment, we ended up alongside Jamdora. He was hunched protectively low, and it took me a moment to realize that he was carrying his mom in front of him. Ayadora had lost her cane in the commotion. Her white eyes were narrowed at Jamdora's rough handling.

"You're going in the wrong direction!" I yelled at him. "Get out!"

"Can't!" Jamadora replied. "We have to secure the Etherazi. It's our responsibility!"

Shit. In the mayhem caused by Reno and company, I'd almost forgotten that Goldy was sitting in a box in the middle of the Senate floor. The Merciful Rampart guys that Arkell had operating the platform had fled, probably when their leader got squashed by a bug. The rest of the Merciful Rampart section had collapsed, a bloom of Ossho spreading among them. I saw Batzian's unconscious body halfway up the stairs; he'd almost made it to the exit. Luckily, the fog hadn't yet reached the floor, or Jamdora would've been knocked out.

I winced when I noticed Goldy's eye was open. Even in its diminished form, it was still hella unnerving to realize that molten gold pupil was fixed directly on me.

"No time for you," I grumbled, then said to Jamdora, "Good luck!"

"Winds at your back!" he replied and veered off toward Goldy.

"He's kind of nice, actually," H'Jossu said.

We were almost to Reno when another capsule burst on the lower level. Some Denzans who had been sheltering there ended up sprinting across the Senate floor, getting in our way. The group was led by Forma and, I quickly realized, was nearly all senators.

Forma grabbed on to my arm. "You have to stop this!"

"I'm trying," I said. "Get your people somewhere safe."

That seemed like a ridiculous thing to say, considering the circumstances, but then my uncle's voice came in over the comm.

"South exit!" Tycius yelled. "Send them that way, Syd!"

I glanced over my shoulder. Tycius and Melian stood near a tunnel that had stayed clear of Ossho clouds and maniac humans. They were helping to usher Denzans to safety there, struggling to keep things orderly.

"That way—!" I told Forma, pointing her toward Ty.

I didn't even get to finish my sentence. A capsule landed at our feet. I kicked the container away from us but wasn't quick enough—it split open, expelling an eager cloud of Ossho that immediately swarmed into the mouths and noses of Forma and the other senators. I caught Forma as she fell, and H'Jossu snagged two others in his burly arms, but the rest collapsed in a pile around us. H'Jossu and I gently set down the senators we'd caught next to the others. There was nothing else we could do.

A tendril of Ossho tried to push into my breather. I caught a whiff of the burning ozone smell that I always associated with Aela, but it passed quickly as my breather kept me safe.

"What are they seeing . . . ?" I muttered.

Forma's eyes were rolled back in her head, magenta ripples popping across the whites. Up close, I saw how a tail of Ossho mist fluttered from her nostrils, almost like it was reaching out for more. I waved my hand over her face, thinking maybe I could shoo the wisp away or something, but it did nothing.

H'Jossu hit my shoulder. "Look!"

On the dais, Reno had snapped a silver circlet around her forehead. There were diamond-shaped nodes at each of her temples that sparked with the same electric energy as the capsules that were getting chucked everywhere. I got the sense that her preparations were almost complete as she was entering a code into the module attached to Aela's faceplate. Distracted as she was, I don't think she noticed that Rafe had recovered. He charged for her, ahead of me and H'Jossu, his mouth and nose buried in the crook of his elbow.

The arrogant old man—he should've listened to me. He thought he could manage this catastrophe, that he could twist it to his advantage. But I could tell by the grim way his brow furrowed that this was way worse than he'd expected.

The cylinder on Aela's faceplate flashed with electricity and snapped open. A cloud funneled out, thicker and more voluminous than what had been contained in the capsules—this was bright magenta streaked with the sooty black corruption that Aela had picked up back on Ashfall. That was my friend. But they weren't in control.

Reno braced herself before the exo-suit with her mouth wide open. The device attached to her head flared at the temples. As if commanded to do so, the entirety of Aela's gaseous form hurtled up Reno's nostrils and then passed out through her lips. Reno convulsed, her head tilted back—the whole process wasn't gentle like when I connected with Aela. It looked painful. Forced.

From Reno's mouth, the cloud began to expand. It fanned out across the Senate chamber, seeking the groping tendrils that rose up from the people who had already passed out from the capsules. Soon, it blanketed the entire area, connecting every person there to Reno.

Rafe never made it to the dais. Aela washed over him, and his upraised arm did nothing to stop his mind from being pulled into the collective. He fell onto his knees and went comatose like the others. I turned back to check on Melian and Tycius, on Darcy and Hiram, on Jamdora, but I couldn't see any of them through the thick cloud.

"This is bad," H'Jossu rumbled. "Aela would never do this."

"I know," I replied. "Come on. We have to—I don't know. Turn it off!"

We only made it a few more steps before a shadow blocked our way. The magenta mist was so thick that I didn't see him coming until he was right on top of us.

Hiro Takagi's dispassionate gaze settled on me through the visor of his own breather.

"You again," he said. "Huh."

I made a move—I wasn't even sure what I was going for, maybe a punch, maybe a shoulder tackle—but Hiro was much too fast. He drove his fist into my gut with enough force that I ended up partially draped across his forearm. He shucked me off onto the floor.

With a roar, H'Jossu raised up to his intimidating full height, his claws poised to rake down. Takagi lunged forward and grabbed him around the waist, hoisting H'Jossu's full bulk over his shoulder with ease. He spun once to gain momentum and then smashed H'Jossu down over the back of one of the empty chairs. H'Jossu's spine made a sickening cracking sound as his body twisted into an impossible arc. His legs flailed for a moment and then went still.

"H'Jossu!" I yelled, scrambling to my feet.

Takagi was there to meet me. He grabbed me by the front of the shirt.

"Enough," he said with a sigh. "You don't need this."

With his free hand, he ripped off my breather.

Almost immediately, the Ossho cloud hanging in the air

flooded my nostrils and everything went black. I was powerless to stop it, like being dragged into a bad dream.

A vision filled my mind. It was just like back on Ashfall—my mind was slammed with images that I didn't want, that I couldn't turn away from.

The Tytons. Golden and powerful. Godlike in their power. I'd seen these snippets of memory before, in the warning that the ancient Denzans had left in the temple. But now the context had changed. What had been meant in the last vision to invoke fear and intimidation now carried a sense of glory and awe.

"We were great once," Reno's voice said in my mind. "Powerful. Beautiful."

She was in control, I realized. The Origin was playing out again, but this time it was Marie Reno's version. I could only assume that the same vision was playing out in every mind connected to Aela.

"The Denzans stole that from us," Reno declared. "We must take it back."

27

My mind was assaulted with a highlight reel of how glorious the Tytons were before the Denzans betrayed them, wiped most of them out, and then trapped the few survivors on a prison planet. It was similar to the vision I'd experienced back on Ashfall, but where that had been a warning about the Tytons, now those same memories had been recast to celebrate them.

We were once a beautiful and unstoppable species that lorded over the galaxy . . . and look how bad they treated us!

The vision also felt more jumbled than the one I'd experienced on Ashfall—less controlled. The memories were flowing through Reno and sometimes felt cluttered and haphazard.

I caught a glimpse of the First Twelve statue on Little Earth, young Denzans posing for pictures in front of it.

We're nothing but mascots to them, Rafe.

A flash of dead Vulpin strapped into the bridge seats of a space-craft.

Look what they made me do!

And then, suddenly, I was back in my grandfather's cabin. I stood in the middle of the living room, looking out the open front door at the porch. A gentle rain fell, a storm just breaking up. Denza's three silver moons sliced through the clouds to cast every-thing in a hazy light. The air felt warm and smelled sweet. Two people sat in wooden deck chairs, holding hands as they watched the drizzle die down. I could only see the backs of their heads, but I knew that was Reno and my grandfather out there.

I took a step toward them, then froze as Reno turned her head. She was younger, her face unlined and hair blonder. She didn't see me. Instead, she whispered some private joke to my grandfather, and he chuckled, squeezing her hand tighter.

It was strange that I could move here. In the vision of the Tytons, I didn't have any agency at all. My mind wasn't being pummeled by someone else's memories now. This was more like the visions Aela had pulled me into in the past where I was free to look around and explore.

"Yes, exactly like that. Reno holds this memory dear, and you are familiar with this place, so we were able to redirect your con-sciousness here. We don't have long, Syd."

I spun around to find Aela standing behind me. They were in their familiar form of a tall, vaguely humanoid streak of quicksil-ver, although there were some disturbing new elements to their appearance. The edges of Aela's form were darkened, the inky stain most noticeable on their fingertips and on the ends of their comet's tail of magenta hair. There was also what appeared to be a collar around Aela's neck, a chain made of electricity running back to the cabin's fireplace and disappearing up the chimney.

"Aela!" I exclaimed. I closed the distance between us and scooped them into a hug. "You aren't erased!"

For a split second, the cabin disappeared and I was once again stuck watching a Tyton try to shield their child as an ancient Denzan attack cruiser sprayed them with toxic black ichor. The vision lasted for only a moment, but it made me shudder.

"Ah, we have never experienced the pleasing sensation of a reunion before," Aela said when the cabin was restored around us. "It distracted us."

I held up my hands and carefully stepped back. "Sorry. I didn't realize that would happen."

"Neither did we," Aela said. "We have never been enslaved before either. Many new experiences. Some empirically better than others."

It struck me for the first time that Aela was using the plural now instead of the singular. "You're not just Aela anymore, are you? Reno combined you with the wisps she kidnapped from Remembrance."

"Yes, and with others she hunted down in Primclef," Aela said. "We are her collective now, all beholden now to her projector. That is the device she wears. It connects her to our exo-suit and to the capsules they've trapped pieces of us in. We were forced to spread into every available mind and sedate them until Reno activated the projector. Then we flowed through her and she used her mind to direct us, forcing us to show the Senate . . ."

"Got it," I said. "So you can't stop it? You're not in control?"

Aela shook their head. "We are very familiar with your mind, Sydney Chambers, so we were able to pull you into this place, but we cannot do that for everyone. Our best method of resistance so far has to been to slow down the pace of Reno's vision. The memories she wishes to share, the context she has built around them—they are poisonous. We are relaying them at a reduced time signature in the hope that our crew will stop her in the real world."

"So time is moving slower in here than in the physical world?"

As I asked the question, the view through the doors and windows of the cabin changed. It was like I was looking out through my own eyes from where I'd passed out on the floor. I could see one of H'Jossu's furry arms twitching. Beyond that, the magenta fog had started to thin as Aela had forced their way into every unprotected mind in the Senate, delicate tendrils crisscrossing the room and leading back to Reno and the exo-suit.

A blur of motion crossed my vision—Hiram and Takagi taking swings at each other. It was like watching a fight in fast-forward. Instinctively, I took a step toward the cabin's door, thinking that I could help Hiram.

"Shit," I said, glancing back at Aela. "You can't wake me up, can you?"

Aela shook their head. "I'm sorry. Reno won't allow that. But I believe help is on the way."

I'd lost sight of Hiram and Takagi duking it out, but now I

saw Darcy zipping toward me in fast motion. She carried one of the heavy-duty gas masks that Reno's crew of psycho humans was using. Hiram and Darcy must have ripped it off Sapienza, which hopefully meant that at least he was out of the fight.

"He is indeed," Aela answered my thought. "Our orders are to afflict the minds of everyone except Reno."

Darcy skidded to a stop next to my body. She held me by the back of my head, tilting the view through the window. The cabin's furniture slid across the floor; the picture frames tumbled from the mantel and broke. This pocket vision that Aela had pulled me into would end once Darcy got the breather on me and cut me off from the cloud. It was already unraveling.

"How do I stop this and set you free?" I asked Aela hurriedly. "Smash the thing Reno's wearing?"

"Yes, smashing would work," Aela replied. "Taking control would be even better."

"You mean I should put that thing on my head?"

"Yes," Aela said. "With a friendly mind linked to our collective, I could show the humans and Denzans something different. Something uncorrupted by Reno's madness."

I reached out and snagged Aela's hand, their touch electric against my skin. "I'm going to fix this, I promise. I wasn't able to bring you home before but this time—I won't let you down. And then we can hit the beach, okay?"

Aela's lips curved into a gentle smile, but I detected a bit of melancholy underneath it. "Sounds like one of your better plans, Syd. Good lu—"

Darcy pulled the mask over my face and I regained physical consciousness with a painful gasp. The inside of my mouth tasted like I'd been sucking on an exhaust pipe, and my midsection ached from where Takagi had walloped me.

"Thanks for the save," I said.

Darcy nodded. "What did you see?" she asked. "What's Reno showing them?"

"The Origin. Her version of it, anyway."

"That can't be pretty," H'Jossu rasped.

I was relieved to hear the Panalax talking. I knew his species couldn't be killed without destroying the brain, but his bulky body was still bent in a sickening rainbow over the chair back. I stumbled over to him and tried to gently ease his massive frame onto the floor. Darcy came to help, although she kept glancing across the chamber to where Hiram was backpedaling away from Takagi's methodical punches.

"Hang in there, buddy," I told H'Jossu.

"Good one," he replied. "Don't worry about me, Syd. I think my host body might be ruined. Going to need a lot of fresh water and sunlight to repair it."

We managed to get H'Jossu off the chair he'd been speared on, but his mammoth frame wouldn't bend back to normal. I quickly took stock of our situation. Hiram had his hands full with Takagi. The last I'd seen Tycius and Melian they'd been back by the entrance, but they were out of sight now, hopefully having retreated somewhere safe. We hadn't heard from Zara since Reno's crew arrived. Markov, Reno's third lackey, was also missing; although she had to be responsible for some of the capsules that exploded in the crowd, she hadn't shown her face. I couldn't decide if that was a good sign or a bad sign.

Everyone else that hadn't fled from the Senate was unconscious and under Reno's influence. All the humans and thousands of Denzans, enduring her vision.

"We have to disconnect Reno from Aela," I told Darcy. I spoke loudly in case any of our crew were listening over the comms, but that was probably unnecessary. The room had gone eerily silent. "Put an end to this shit."

Darcy shot a look at the unconscious humans piled in the bleachers. "Are you sure we even want to wake them up? Right now we've only got Takagi to deal with. But if even half of them wake up with a bit of Reno's madness . . ."

"Aela said if we can get that device Reno is wearing, they can control what the humans—what everyone—sees. They helped Hiram through it—"

A sharp grunt sounded over the comm. "Yeah. *Help Hiram.* Good damn idea."

About thirty yards away, Hiram was struggling to defend himself against Takagi's assault. He wasn't moving around very well on his bad leg and so wasn't able to launch much offense of his own, focusing instead on deflecting Takagi's punches and kicks. As I watched, Takagi feinted high and then lanced out with a kick that struck Hiram's bad leg. I heard his cry of pain over the comm.

I started toward the fight, but Darcy put a hand on my

shoulder. "He's already beaten your ass twice," she said. "You deal with Reno. I'll help Hiram."

Darcy charged Takagi while I sprinted toward the dais. Takagi must have seen what we were doing, though, because he broke away from a staggering Hiram to meet Darcy halfway. He was fast and, although Darcy tried to juke aside, he kicked her dead center in the chest and sent her flying right into me.

We tumbled together and quickly hopped back to our feet. Takagi was on us in an instant.

"You don't learn," he said to me, backhanding me with enough force that I felt my teeth loosen. As I fell, I clutched the front of my mask to keep it from flying off.

Darcy fired off a punch at Takagi's throat, but he lowered his chin and absorbed the blow with a smirk. He grabbed her by the front of the uniform and drove her backward, slamming her against a wall. Once. Twice. The back of her head cracking against the hard surface.

No. I was disoriented. That wasn't a wall.

That was Goldy's enclosure.

I sprang to my feet as the hourglass-shaped containment unit teetered and tipped. Just as it went over, I managed to slide under it with my arms up. The thing was heavy, but I was strong enough to slow its descent and lower Goldy gently to the ground.

"Are you insane?" I yelled, as if I didn't know the answer.

"I don't understand why you insist on fighting," Takagi replied as he dropped a slumping Darcy. "You've seen the Origin. You know Marie is right."

"We know you guys are assholes!" Hiram shouted as he leaped onto Takagi's back. He looped his arm under Takagi's chin and squeezed with all his might, at the same time hooking his legs around Takagi's torso to try to pull him to the ground.

"Hold him," Melian said over the comms. "I can get there!"

I saw Melian start her sprint out of the corner of my eye. She must have been waiting in one of the tunnels, looking for her chance to help. She kept her head down, running straight for the dais.

Takagi broke one arm free of Hiram's grip and lashed backward with his elbow—once, twice, three times—each one smashing into Hiram's mask. His breather broke apart on his face. As if it could sense the opening, the thinning Ossho cloud curled out a tendril toward Hiram.

"Wait . . . wait!" Hiram yelled.

Aela didn't listen. The wisp flowed into Hiram's nostrils, his eyes rolled back into his head, and he went limp. As soon as his grip loosened, Takagi hefted Hiram over his head and flung him like a javelin. His body struck Melian just as she reached the dais, slamming into her, crushing her against a chair. She cried out over the comm and then was still.

"Fuck this," I growled.

My hand slid into my pocket and came back tipped with the knife Zara had given me. The black coating on the blade shone dully.

I lunged at Takagi.

He spun and grabbed me by the wrist.

"Ah," he said, eyeing the push dagger. "What do you have there?"

I grabbed Takagi by the shoulder for leverage and tried to drive the blade toward him, but he wouldn't budge. He shoved me backward, and I fell onto my back with Takagi's knee pinning down my free arm.

"A union of two species," Takagi remarked casually. "Some people think you hybrids are the future of galactic society. I, frankly, do not see it."

One by one, he started to pry my fingers loose from the knife. Worse than that. He snapped them, bending them against the back of my hand. I cried out with each digit that Takagi broke.

The only comfort in that moment was a raspy voice over the comm. A raspy voice quietly singing at an extremely inappropriate moment.

"Now, this is a story all about how my life got flipped—turned upside down . . ."

I made sure to keep my cries of agony loud and dramatic. I mean, they were sincere. It was not a pleasant sensation getting your fingers broken. But I needed to keep Takagi distracted. Because, behind him, H'Jossu had scuttled up the dais. He needed to walk on his hands and feet, stuck in a backbend, his floppy ears brushing the floor. But he made it up there.

H'Jossu booted Reno in the side, knocking her stiffened comatose body over. The tendrils of Ossho continued to flow from her, although the stream began to lose its coherence as H'Jossu fumbled with the circlet around her forehead.

"And I'd like to take a minute, just sit right there," H'Jossu sang. "I'll tell you how I became the prince of a town called Bel-Air."

With a yelp, H'Jossu rammed the circlet down onto his own massive dome and then ripped off his mask. He tumbled over, lying there prone on his side, his feet scrambling uselessly.

He'd done it. The Ossho funneled out of Reno and into H'Jossu, connecting the Panalax to every mind on the Senate floor. I could only imagine what he was showing them.

Meanwhile, the push dagger fell from my grip. I didn't even have a grip anymore. The fingers on my right hand were crooked and bent, my knuckles bulging and howling with pain. It somehow hurt more when I looked at it. I wasn't sure how much more I'd need to endure, how much longer I'd have to keep Takagi distracted. He didn't even seem interested in the knife anymore. Instead, finished with my fingers, he started to bend my hand back at the wrist.

"I had heard you hybrids inherited our invincibility," he said. "Doesn't seem entirely true."

"Takagi! What the hell are you doing?"

For a moment, I felt relief as Takagi's grip loosened on my arm. That faded quickly as I saw Irena Markov—the third member of Reno's group—power-walking across the Senate floor toward us. I was seeing spots from the pain of my busted hand as Markov approached, her appearance blurred at the edges.

"Where have you been?" Takagi asked as he stood, using my ribs to push himself up.

"I did my part," Irena replied, motioning to the dais. "But you let them get to Reno."

Takagi looked over his shoulder and snarled at the sight of H'Jossu now plugged into the Ossho flow. Reno's body lay nearby. It worried me that she was stirring. It also worried me that Markov had picked up my push dagger.

"We need to get her back in," Takagi said. "Come on."

Takagi glanced back at Markov for a response. That's when she slipped the knife in between his ribs. She stabbed him three times—the black-tipped blade piercing impenetrable human flesh and chipping unbreakable human bone—before Takagi batted the weapon away and grabbed her around the neck.

Not her. Him.

Tycius.

It felt like a long time since the railyard in Washington. That's when my uncle had first introduced himself in the guise of Humphrey Bogart. I hadn't seen him use the holographic projector since—it was a device that was only effective on human eyesight, not a Denzan's more advanced vision. But once a spy, always a spy.

My uncle had broken the Denzan code of nonviolence to save me. I didn't know what that would mean if we survived this.

Dark circles of blood appeared on Takagi's shirtfront. He seemed more perplexed than anything, staring down at his injuries as he held my uncle by his neck.

"What did you do to me?" Takagi asked. "I'm hurt."

"I am sorry," Ty replied, his eyes bulging as he gasped for air. "But this must stop."

Takagi sank to his knees, taking Tycius down with him. I rolled to my feet and rammed my shoulder into Takagi, trying to break his grip on my uncle's neck with my one good hand.

"Syd!" That was Darcy's voice. "Syd, look!"

Darcy had only just regained consciousness after Takagi had slammed the back of her head against Goldy's enclosure. She'd been slumped there, against the glass, but now she hurriedly crab-walked away from it.

There was a crack in the containment unit, probably made by Darcy's skull. Without any of us noticing, that hairline fracture had been slowly growing, spreading, golden energy trickling forth like the last warning before a dam burst.

Goldy's eye locked onto me.

"Shit," I said. "Get back!"

Wait. Not me. He wasn't looking at me.

Darcy.

The hourglass exploded, spraying everyone in the vicinity with shards of glass and flecks of ultonate. I raised my arms to shield my face, and when I brought them back down, Goldy floated above me. His core was still shriveled and reduced, but molten gold energy was beginning to pour slowly from his pupil, like a reactor coming back online, gradually covering him in the mind-bending maelstrom of Etherazi energy. I had the vague impression of an egg trying to hatch, little wings and a fanged mouth trying to break through into our reality. I felt a splitting headache spread from the base of my skull to my molars.

Behind me, my uncle cried out in pain and confusion, whether from Takagi's strangling grip or Goldy's brain-melting appearance, I couldn't be entirely sure.

I tried to face the creature. With one bad arm, no weapons, and a brain that was struggling to comprehend what I was seeing—I didn't stand a chance. Maybe I could launch myself at Goldy's core before too much of the temporal energy gathered. Maybe it was still vulnerable.

The eye stared at me. I glared back. In the end, I'd helped set him free. I hadn't changed anything.

"Come on, then," I said. "Do your worst."

Goldy surged toward me. I dove to the side.

Totally unnecessary. He wasn't going for me.

The Etherazi enveloped Darcy in a tentacle of temporal energy. Lifted her? Swallowed her? It was hard to fathom exactly what was happening. Darcy floated above the Senate floor, pulled close to Goldy's unblinking core, the energy swirling around her.

Was this what it looked like when he'd taken me?

For a moment, I thought I heard his booming voice.

THEY LEFT YOU BEHIND.

Goldy streaked toward the ceiling, taking Darcy with him.

28

You have seen the path that brought you here, Darcy Ward. That brought you to ME.

Now see where your path leads.

You cannot run like you used to. You are older now. Your knees ache. There is a deeper ache within you as well. A longing that you've never felt before. You miss your child. You are worried that you will never see her again. That this is the end.

That feeling of dread pushes you to move faster. You are sprinting up a twisting staircase, floor after floor passing as you take the steps two at a time, desperately trying to make it to the roof of the tower. The walls are cold stone reinforced with steel. You don't recognize the place, but you also know that you've been inside the building before.

The air is muggy and reeks of sweat and blood. The power here has been knocked out, and so the stairwell's only illumination is the occasional flashing red emergency light. There was a fight here. A battle. There are scorch marks on the walls. And there are bodies. You don't check their identities as you pass; you aren't even sure whose side they were on—humans, Denzans, Vulpin, Panalax, every species represented in the dead. You hop over the corpses, knowing that their lives are beyond saving, but that if you can only make it to the roof, you might save the others.

The rest of the planet.

There is a weapon at the top of the tower. A surface-to-air energy cannon capable of destroying a spacecraft in the upper atmosphere. You know the code to activate it, and you know exactly where to aim it.

"Darcy!" a breathless voice yelps from behind you. "I can't keep going!"

You glance over your shoulder. You didn't even realize that there was a Denzan woman running with you, doing her best to keep up. Her white hair is pulled back in tight braids, and she wears a strange metallic covering across her knuckles. There is a dark slash across her abdomen, a fresh wound. She stops in the landing below you and sinks down against the wall. Even though you know you should keep going, you hesitate.

"Melian . . . ," the future you says. You are just a passenger in this timeline, watching the events unfold through the eyes of one of your possible selves. You feel the regret welling up inside you, the cold understanding that you need to leave your old friend behind.

"Go," Melian says, waving you away. "I'll be fine."

She won't be fine. You know this.

You take off running again, sprinting up level after level.

"He won't do it, Darcy!" Melian yells after you. "He knows we're down here! He won't do it!"

It sounds to you like she's trying to convince herself. You hope that she's right, but you aren't willing to take that chance.

Doom is gathering in the sky above, and your ascent up the staircase begins to feel more and more like a nightmare. The floors seem to be unending. The heat, the smell, the bodies—you learned a bit about hell during your studies of Earth culture at the Serpo Institute. Now you understand what they meant.

Finally, you burst onto the roof of the tower. You need to shield your eyes from the sun—bright and red, more vivid than the one you grew up with on Denza. There aren't any moons in the sky. You have never been to this place, this planet—and yet you have, you will. From your vantage point, you can see the foaming gray ocean in the distance and, closer still, the blocks of smaller buildings and homes that fan out around the spire.

You have lived here, you realize. For how many years? You're not sure.

But in that time, you never heard the birds stop chirping. Until now.

Everything is quiet, as if the planet knows what is coming.

A shadow hangs in the air, like an ink stain on the cloudless sky. The spacecraft is literally one of a kind. No one had ever built a ship like it before, and no one has dared to build another since. It floats there like a fang waiting to sink down into the planet's exposed throat.

The world killer.

The cannon atop the tower has never been tested. It was built to defend the planet from threats like the one floating overhead, but has never actually been fired. It looks like such a simple thing—a barrel that points up to the heavens, a mechanized platform to swivel it around, a computer terminal to control it. You know that it is so much more than that. The cannon draws power from the planet's core. As tall as the tower is, its foundations sink even deeper underground. The structure is a testament to strength and ingenuity.

And yet, where did that get the people of this planet? There are more corpses strewn across the roof. The attack may have even started here. You recognize some faces as you sprint toward the cannon's controls—unguarded, dormant, alone.

You're one of only a handful of people with the codes necessary to fire the cannon. There's a distinct possibility that you're the only one still alive.

With shaking fingers, you punch in the twenty-digit code. You committed it to memory even though you long doubted you'd ever need to use it. Beneath your feet, the entire building begins to hum with energy.

But above you, there comes a flash of light. The ship has disappeared, hidden from sight by the wave of destruction it just unleashed.

He did it. He really did it.

You have only seconds.

You see the ocean bubble and boil. You see the sky turn red with crimson.

In that moment, you wish that you'd think about your daughter or her father or your father or Rafe Butler or Melian or any of the others that you've loved over the years.

But all you can think about is him.

You should've killed Sydney Chambers when you had the chance.

29

Even in his depleted form, Goldy was nearly impossible for me to look at. Still, despite the feeling like my brain was trying to expand out through my skull, ignoring the hot tears that streamed down my cheeks, I forced my eyes to track him. I had to at least try to help Darcy.

I crouched low and leaped into the air with all the power I could muster. I left cracks in the floor of the Senate where I took off, but my best jump was still well short. Goldy had already floated up to the third level, hovering right above the rotating hologram of Illaria. Somehow, despite all the insanity that had gone down, the projector was still on, broadcasting an unpleasant reminder of what Goldy expected me to do. Perfect.

With the Etherazi out of reach, I was powerless to do anything but watch. My mind tried to interpret what I was seeing.

Darcy's limp body was tangled in a web of temporal energy, the flow nothing like what Goldy produced when I'd met him in space, but growing with every second that passed. It occurred to me that with one surge of energy, Goldy could probably wipe out this whole room. He either didn't want to or didn't have it in him. I think he was still regaining his strength.

The unblinking eye at the Etherazi's core stared down at Darcy. For a moment, I saw the draconic form I'd encountered before. It looked almost like Darcy was cradled in one of the monster's wings.

Darcy changed. Her shape cycled in and out of our reality. Darcy as a child. Darcy as a middle-aged woman. Darcy covered in ash. Darcy holding a baby. Darcy disintegrating into particles. None of it made any sense, and, if I stared much longer, I felt like I might pass out. My mind had begun to rebel and was preparing to shut me down for my own good.

And then Goldy's carapace of energy coalesced behind him like a comet's tail and he streaked out of the Senate chamber, blazing a path through one of the third-level train tunnels. In the distance, I heard the wail of Primclef's Etherazi warning system. Too late for all that, guys.

Goldy didn't take Darcy with him. He simply dropped her.

Finally, I could do something useful. I lunged to get under Darcy and caught her in my arms. She was unconscious but alive. Streaks of gold ran through her hair, much like the ones that were only now beginning to fade on mine. She was going to hate that.

I lowered her gently to the ground. "What did he show you?"

I whispered, although even that sounded incredibly loud in the quiet of the Senate chamber.

Darcy didn't respond. She was in a deep sleep. A coma, maybe. It had taken me a few days to recover from my exposure to the Etherazi, but I did recover eventually. I had faith that Darcy would, too.

She wasn't the only body that I needed to check on.

I raced back to where my uncle had fallen in a tangle with Hiro Takagi. I shoved Takagi's hands off my uncle's neck—those hands were cold now, lifeless—and checked Ty's pulse. Steady but worryingly slow. His eyes were open, staring into nothingness, rings like dark mascara around them that I knew were singe marks. Tycius had looked directly at Goldy. The sight had damaged him, wrecked his mind. I had no way of knowing how bad the damage was.

"Ty? Can you hear me?" I gently shook his shoulder.

"What did you do?"

That wasn't my uncle who answered. It was Reno.

I shot to my feet to face my former captain. We stood with the painted ocean between us. Reno was slightly hunched, still shaking off the disorientation of her experience with Aela. We were both about the same distance from the dais, where H'Jossu's contorted body slumped with control of the Ossho cloud running through him. She took a step in that direction, and I matched her.

Me and Reno. The only two left standing.

I tried to stop cradling my broken hand against my stomach. I didn't want her to see how clearly overmatched I was.

"I was showing them the truth," Reno continued when I didn't reply to her first question. "They have a right to know what the Denzans did to us."

"Your truth isn't the whole truth," I replied. "And these Denzans didn't do anything to you."

"They tricked us into fighting for them," Reno said. "All while they let our families and friends rot on Earth, dying slowly when they could've been so much more."

"What does that even mean—*so much more?*" I asked, happy to keep her talking to buy time. We'd both taken a few more steps toward the dais, but I was still hoping to avoid a fight that I was almost definitely going to lose. "You think humans should be running things like the Tytons did? Dominating everyone? Look at what you've done, Reno. You killed those Vulpin. Enslaved the Ossho. And I'm sure you'd do worse if we let you keep going. You're pretty much proving Denza's point."

While I spoke, I noticed Reno's glare soften a bit. A sad, longing smile spread across her face. I wasn't sure what to make of that look, but it made me really uncomfortable.

"Goddamn, you're just like him," she said wistfully. "Always with an answer for everything. Running his mouth with some philosophical bullshit. You know he went back to Earth for you, right?"

I swallowed. "My grandfather, you mean."

Reno nodded. "He wanted to hold his grandson and the Denzans wouldn't let your mother leave Earth. Can you believe that? We could've had *everything*! We *should* have . . ."

"That's not how I heard it," I replied. "He wanted to go back. He wanted to help with my father's research. He was trying—they were both trying—to fix the Wasting. My grandfather wanted to be with his family. I don't think there was anything left for him on Denza."

Of course, I couldn't resist the opportunity to throw in a little dig. Reno's eyes widened a fraction, and her mouth tightened.

"You're a fool like he was," she said quietly. "Soft. Afraid. That's the Denzan in you, Cadet."

There were only about thirty yards separating us now, the dais in between us. Reno's eyes flicked in that direction. She must have known I was distracting her, keeping her from resuming control of Aela and the collective. I angled my body and dropped my shoulder, ready to at least put myself in her way.

"Reno—!"

Irena Markov clambered down the stairs from one of the upper sections, nearly tripping over unconscious bodies on the way. There was no juddering to her appearance this time; that was no holographic projection. It was the real Markov, and she was covered in blood.

My stomach dropped. I didn't think I stood much chance against Reno, but I could at least use our shared history to try to gain an advantage. Alone against two humans, though? There was no way.

Markov held something out in front of her. A scrap of fabric, I thought, at first. But no—it was furry and grisly. It looked like a chunk of scalp that she'd torn right from Zara. My heartbeat quickened, and I took a sharp step in her direction. Zara had been off comms since the humans first started their attack. If Markov was carrying around a piece of her like a trophy . . .

"Reno, I don't understand," Markov said, her voice oddly wobbly. "I don't understand what she did to me."

Markov took a few steps closer and then collapsed onto her knees. There were knife slices all across her shoulders and arms, her chest and face. Wounds inflicted by one of Zara's sludge-tipped blades.

"Am I dying?" Markov asked Reno, sounding frightened. She pitched forward, landed on her face, and was still.

"The bitch ripped my ear off," Zara said. The Vulpin was suddenly at my side, having crept over while Markov distracted both me and Reno. She was hunched and breathing hard, her uniform splattered with blood, a good-size chunk of her pelt missing. "But she'll live. I didn't catch any of her arteries. Figured you wouldn't approve."

"Zara!" I was so relieved that I almost reached out to hug her. When my arms twitched toward her, Zara tossed one of her daggers in the air. I reflexively caught the weapon in my good hand. "I was worried. You weren't answering on comms."

"You're smart. I'm sure you can figure out why," Zara replied, rolling her eyes. I winced as I took a closer look at the torn scalp where her ear used to be, but Zara responded by grinning. "What a story it's going to be. Zara den Jetten. Defeater of humans."

"Cocky pup," Reno said. "You won't be telling any tales."

The initial shock of Markov's appearance had worn off, and

Reno was focused on us again. I clutched the dagger Zara had given me in an overhand grip, shielding my busted hand against my side. Next to me, Zara took a few deep breaths, wheezing slightly, having probably endured a worse beating in her fight with Markov than she was letting on.

"Think we can take her?" Zara asked.

"Don't have a choice," I replied. "You go low, I'll go high. Try not to die."

Zara's tail flicked back and forth, then tightened against her body. "Didn't realize you knew Vulpin poetry."

Reno shot toward the dais. We charged forward to meet her.

Run, lie, fight. I'd used every one of those methods since entering the Denzan Senate. In those few seconds before impact, I wondered—wasn't there a better way? I told myself that Reno had come unglued, that the Origin had unlocked something angry and bitter within her. She had to be stopped, and we were the ones that had to do it. Would she be the last, though? Or would there always be others like her and Takagi? Would it be *Run, lie, fight* forever?

At least, as Reno cocked her fist back to take my head off, in this very specific case, I was running toward something instead of away from it. I was going to get killed, probably, but at least I'd progressed as a person.

Just as we were about to come together, a blur grabbed hold of Reno's arm with enough force to completely knock her off course and also save my face from getting mashed.

Hiram.

"Enough," he said. "That's enough, Captain Reno."

Reno turned on Hiram, grabbing him around the neck. "I had such hopes for you, Hiram! And you choose to side with these . . . these lesser creatures . . ."

Before Reno could really get a grip on Hiram, another set of arms fought to secure her shoulders, pulling her backward.

"It's over, Marie," Rafe Butler said. "Stop."

"Let me go!" Reno shouted. "All your words, Rafe! Nothing but hot air! Meaningless!"

I jumped into the scrum with my one good arm, trying to weigh down one of Reno's thrashing arms as she wrestled against the Butlers. The more we tried to contain her, the harder Reno thrashed and the more incoherent her screaming became. For a moment, I wasn't even sure that the three of us would be enough to stop her.

But we weren't alone. Other humans regained consciousness and joined us—ones I'd seen on Little Earth, who had marched with us to the Senate. One by one, as they were released from Aela's grasp, they came forward to help us subdue Reno. Soon, there were dozens of hands holding tight to Reno's arms and legs, keeping her pinned, not letting her do any more damage. I glanced over my shoulder and saw that the Denzans were waking up, too. They were helped to their feet by humans, or huddled in small groups, or watched wide-eyed as we took care of Reno.

"You're weak!" she screamed. "You're all so goddamn weak!"

"You're wrong," Hiram said, meeting my eyes across the huddle of bodies. "This is strength. Real strength. We all saw the truth."

* * *

I was one of the only people in the Senate that day that didn't get to experience the vision. The masterwork of the newly formed Aela Collective. I would always feel a little jealous about that, like I had missed out. Maybe experiencing the vision with all the others would have healed something in me like it did for many of the Denzans and humans connected to Aela. I'll never know. I only heard the details secondhand, and it was always like having someone try to explain a dream.

Reno had already forced the Origin upon everyone, so Aela had no choice but to start there. In Reno's version, the Tytons were proud and mighty and glorious, an intergalactic certainty, and their downfall only came as the result of the deceitful machinations of lesser, jealous species.

Hers wasn't the whole truth, though. That was history filtered through the lens of anger and resentment.

When Aela regained control, they showed every mind what it was like to live under the looming presence of the Tytons. The fear and the powerlessness. The Tytons had misused their great strength for domination. They had betrayed themselves. They had failed the moral imperative of the powerful. Aela tapped Hiram's mind for this, letting everyone feel the disgust he harbored for his ancestors when he saw how they treated those weaker than them. Humans were better than that.

We could be better than Tytons.

In Reno's version of the Origin, the Earth was a punishment. A cruel trick played by the Denzans on generation after generation of human. That, too, was true, but it wasn't the whole story. Aela guided hundreds of minds through the guilt the Denzans felt for what they'd done. So much shame that hundreds of thousands of years later they were still binding their limbs in penance.

And if Earth was so terrible a place, why had so much beauty emanated from there? Here, Aela tapped into H'Jossu's encyclopedic knowledge of the planet—not just the nerd stuff and the sitcoms, but the art and the music and the words. H'Jossu described it later as "a very special episode."

Then, Aela took them beyond the Origin. Because that was ancient history, and we were more connected to the present. Aela let the network of minds experience the sense of awe that Rafe felt when he first set foot on Denza and also let them feel his longing for home. Aela pulled other experiences from other minds—a human and Denzan leaning close for a nervous first kiss, a Denzan aching with jealousy as he watched a human scale a wall with ease, a human gasping for air in the ocean and laughing as his Denzan friends tickled his feet below the waves. So many memories and shared experiences, so many connections.

The message was clear. We weren't beholden to our pasts. History would only repeat itself if we let it.

Instead of the fear and anger Reno had meant to stoke, Aela left the minds that were connected to them feeling calm and hopeful. Uncertainty remained, sure. But it was an uncertainty we could face together.

After that, H'Jossu told me, Aela asked him for release. They instructed him in how to turn off the mechanism that had enslaved the Ossho. The vision ended.

While we were subduing Reno, while the Denzans were picking themselves up, while the cavernous chambered recovered—Aela rose above us. They gathered all the wisps into one great black-streaked magenta cloud. They floated up, up, and out, leaving their ruined exo-suit behind, and Denza with it.

They had shown us what they could. There was more out there to experience.

We would have to figure out the rest on our own.

THREE MONTHS LATER

THE MOON

30

The next time I saw Marie Reno, she was feeding the birds. She cupped a pile of seeds in her palm and tried to coax a sparrow forward, but the little bird was too skittish, and so Reno just tossed the seeds into the dirt and smiled as the little sparrow and all his friends went to town. Reno looked much older now. Her face was lined and her hair had grayed and she walked with a cane. She tilted her head back and let the sun hit her face, and when she lowered her gaze, her eyes landed right on me.

I took an involuntary step back.

"She can't see you," Rafe said. "Not unless you want her to."

"I'm good," I replied.

It looked like Reno had a small cabin surrounded by miles of pristine forest. But what she really had was a cell augmented by Denzan holographic technology. Reno's prison was a peaceful illusion.

"I don't blame you," Rafe said. "I tried to visit with her once. I watched her for a while beforehand. She seemed at peace. But as soon as she saw my face . . . ?"

He trailed off. "She wasn't happy to see you," I said.

"That's an understatement," Rafe said with a snort. "You seen enough?"

I nodded. "I'm glad she's in there. And I'm glad moon prison seems pretty chill. Can't believe the Denzans were able to build this place in only a couple months."

"The Luna facility? Syd, it's been here for more than a decade," Rafe replied. "Only a few of us knew about it before now. Reno isn't the first human to lose her head. When our people become dangerous, we needed a humane place to store them."

"One of your solutions," I said.

He smirked, then coughed into his shoulder. "I'm an equal opportunity schemer, Syd. You should know that by now."

The former pizza maker led me by other cells, most of them unoccupied, but some tuned to peaceful holographic realities. Irena Markov, Luca Sapienza, Hiro Takagi's father—they were stored here, too. As we passed them by, my eyes lingered on Markov, whose face and arms were covered with horrible scars from the wounds Zara had inflicted upon her. In her cell, she sat on a beach, sunning herself, not worried about anyone staring at her markings.

I was surprised when Rafe reached out to steady himself on my shoulder. He'd been trying to hide it, but I still heard the rattle in his lungs when he spoke. His knees were shaky as we walked, the vigor gone from his strut.

The prison facility was buried beneath the surface of Earth's moon, hidden from human sensors by Denzan stealth technology. We were close enough to the toxic planet to strip a human of their extraordinary abilities, but far enough that they wouldn't waste away and die. I'd felt flu-like since getting here, my first time this close to Earth in almost a year. I couldn't imagine how bad the symptoms were for Rafe.

"Are you sure you should be here?" I asked. "This close to Earth?"

Rafe squeezed my shoulder with a fraction of his old strength. "I wouldn't miss this for anything, Syd. I've dreamed of this moment. I'm glad this place could be used for something other than storing the worst of our kind. And I'm even gladder that you are here to see the exodus begin."

"I heard you asked personally for the *Eastwood*," I replied.

"Well, of course," Rafe said. He led me into the elevator that would carry us back to the Luna facility's main level, where my shuttle was docked. "I think your friend Senator Formachus would've sent you regardless. I hear she's quite fond of you."

"I don't know about all that," I replied, feeling the back of my neck get warm.

Forma had kept her promise and gotten our crew restored to the *Eastwood*, with my uncle named the captain for real. And all we had to do was keep reporting back to her.

Only Batzian had chosen not to return. I hadn't seen him since that day at the Senate and didn't think Melian and he were on speaking terms. As far as I knew, Batzian was still with the Merciful Rampart. Even after the experience with Aela, the group hadn't changed their minds about humanity, especially not after word of Arkell being crushed by Reno spread around Primclef. If anything, their membership had swelled.

Even so, the senators sympathetic to the Merciful Rampart had joined Forma and voted to allow humanity to colonize Illaria. It was a process that would take years. The Serpo Institute was supervising both the initial building of a colony on Illaria and the first contact with the greater population of Earth.

"I hope you understand how crucial your role will be here, Syd," Rafe continued as the elevator rose. "The time to keep you hidden from the people of Earth is over. You're a bridge between our two species. I can't tell you how envious I am of what you get to do. Returning home, to our planet, to lead our people into the future."

"Yeah, about that," I replied. "I'm not sure I'm ready to lead anyone anywhere."

Rafe grinned at me. "My boy, of course you are. You've been leading since you came up the gravity well."

The elevator opened up, and we stepped into the docking bay. Shuttles were always coming and going from the Luna base, Denzans using the port as a way station to ferry supplies. There were a handful of Denzans taking a break to stare up through the domed glass ceiling above. Rafe and I joined them.

Earth. I'd gone so far, seen so much, and still the sight of my home planet took my breath away. A blue orb partly enveloped by shadow.

A dozen ISVs floated in a neat line between Luna and Earth. The *Eastwood* was among them. The ships had started arriving a few days ago, making no effort to hide themselves from humanity. It had been agreed upon that the best way to approach the Earthers was to make ourselves known and then let them come to us. We didn't want them to feel threatened. Let them get used to the fact of alien life at their own pace. Let them approach us peacefully before we made the offer to evacuate them from their poisonous planet

Of course, the Consulate was monitoring humanity's response. It was wall-to-wall news coverage. Some fear, for sure. But mostly, as my mom told me in our last call, there was curiosity and amazement. She'd seemed honestly surprised that the Earthers hadn't immediately tried to nuke us.

"Maybe we can change," she said to me. "But I'm not holding my breath."

It still wasn't clear what was going to happen with my mom. Forma dodged the topic whenever I brought it up. She was allowed back to the Consulate only for her weekly calls with me. Otherwise, she wasn't welcome among the Denzans. Rafe had agreed that only a certain amount of humans would emigrate from Earth to Illaria every year, and he'd also agreed that the Consulate would be able to deny relocation to anyone they viewed as a threat to galactic society. I figured that meant my mom. I wasn't even sure she wanted to leave Earth. That was another conversation we were avoiding.

I half expected her to end up in a cell on Luna, so just the fact that she was free felt like a victory. We could figure out the rest later.

"Never thought I'd get to enjoy this view again," Rafe said. "I wish Hiram were here to see it."

"He'd probably just talk shit," I replied. "Ruin it for everyone."

"True," Rafe said with a chuckle.

Hiram was still officially part of the *Eastwood*'s crew, but he had begged off the mission to Earth, instead choosing to join an infrastructure team that was setting up the first encampments on Illaria. He threatened me with a beating if I told anyone this, but the planet frightened him. After the damage done to his leg by that sludge-covered bullet, he didn't want to chance getting too close to his ancestral home world. I think a part of him also worried that, if he saw Earth in person, he, like his mom, might not be able to resist the planet's pull.

"He sent me a message today," Rafe continued. Since the Senate, I'd noticed a change in the way that Rafe talked about his grandson. There was pride in his voice now. "Things are going smoothly on Illaria. And he said a friend of yours showed up to watch."

I raised an eyebrow. "What friend?"

"The Aela Collective," Rafe said. "It's hanging in Illaria's atmosphere. Observing."

This was probably selfish of me, but I was still smarting a bit that Aela had dipped out after everything that went down at the Senate without so much as a good-bye. Aela had been inside my brain. They probably knew me better than anyone else in the universe. I'd thought we were friends. But was Aela even Aela anymore? They had absorbed all the other wisps that Reno had captured and fled Denza. I'd kind of expected them to return to the Ossho Collective like we talked about, but Aela didn't go in that direction. Apparently, their aimless travels through the galaxy had eventually brought them to Illaria.

I wondered if Aela had gone to Illaria because they figured out what I did. That it might not be Earth I was prophesied to destroy, but humanity's second home world. Had they gone there to watch?

I shook those thoughts away. I'd proven that Goldy's prophecies weren't set in stone when I'd left him trapped aboard the *Cavern*. Sure—he'd gotten free anyway. But I hadn't been the one to save his life. Score one for choosing your own fate.

Rafe walked me back to the shuttle, where Zara was waiting. She sat on the roof of our spacecraft, legs crossed, staring out at the Earth. There were surgeons on Denza that could've fixed Zara's ear, but she'd chose to leave it as a tattered nub atop her head. She wore the injury like a badge of honor. Before we left Primclef, during a visit to Keyhole Cove, I swore I saw some young Vulpin who had purposefully chopped off the tip of an ear. Everyone knew who Zara den Jetten was and what she'd done in the Senate. No one talked about her father the whoremaster anymore.

"Ah, there's one other thing I wanted to talk to you about," Rafe said.

By now, I knew Rafe well enough to know that this *one last thing* was really the *only thing* he was interested in talking about. "What is it?"

"My people finished doing their sweep of Ashfall," he said.

367

"Your original report mentioned a cache of antihuman weapons in the sniper tower. My team reported that it was empty. Any idea what might have happened to those?"

I raised my eyebrows. An armory's worth of antihuman weaponry had disappeared into thin air. That couldn't be good. Tensions between Denzans and humanity had eased in the last three months, but the galaxy was still a very dangerous place.

"No idea, Rafe," I said. "Honestly. I hope you find them. We don't want that stuff getting out."

It wasn't until me and Zara were on the way back to the *Eastwood* that I realized I did have an idea. Something that had been in the back of my mind for months now that I'd never gotten a satisfactory answer to.

"Zara," I said, "back on the Torrent, you traded Ezziah den One-Left a vial of that sludge."

"Half a vial," Zara corrected me.

"And something else," I said. "Something you said had nothing to do with the *Eastwood*."

"Yeah," Zara replied.

"What was it?"

She reclined in her seat, twitching her good ear in amusement. "Come on, Syd. You already know. Considering how the old chef made sure to ask the question in front of me, he's probably figured it out, too."

I pinched the bridge of my nose. "Shit, Zara. I don't know how I feel about Ezziah having an arsenal of antihuman weaponry."

She shrugged in response. "You don't have to feel anything

about it. Already done and dusted." I shot Zara a flat look, and she sighed, flashing her fangs. "Look, the humans have their strength. The Denzans have their Wayscopes and wormholes. But what did we Vulpin have, huh? Now things are a bit more even."

"It's not a competition, Zara."

"Of course it is," Zara replied. She flicked the flap of skin where her ear used to be. "You think everyone holding hands and getting along will last forever? We've got to be ready, Syd."

I wanted to roll my eyes and fluff Zara off. I wanted to believe that fighting and bloodshed didn't have to be inevitable. We'd saved a lot of lives back at the Senate compared to what might have happened if Reno had been allowed to drive everyone as mad as her. It didn't have to always be brute force that prevailed. Not everywhere had to work like Earth or even Stonelea.

But I'd seen my future. I knew there was more violence to come.

"I wish you'd told me," I said, leaning back and crossing my arms. "We didn't even get anything good out of that deal except captured."

Zara smirked. "Seemed like a fair trade at the time."

Back on the *Eastwood*, things were more crowded than they had been in a while. The Serpo Institute allowed us all to remain cadets, but the *Eastwood* was still supposed to be a training vessel. There were some open slots to be filled now that Aela and Batzian were off the ship and Hiram was taking some time away. That meant we had three new cadets, plus a new first officer, chief engineer, and lead proctor to replace the staff that had gone crazy, gotten stabbed, or been crushed. I'm not sure it's a job I would've signed up for. Surprisingly, there were a ton of applicants.

I hadn't really gotten to know the newcomers. They were on the *Eastwood*. But they weren't really den *Eastwood*. Not yet, anyway.

Zara and I passed by the seminar room, where H'Jossu was in the middle of an impromptu lecture on Earth culture, the newbies all seated in a semicircle around him. My Panalax pal had recovered from the injuries he suffered during the Senate blowup, although the spine that originally came with his body was pretty much shot. That meant growing a new carapace of mold across his back to support him, almost like a spongy white turtle shell. Essentially, he was bigger than ever.

"On Earth, ''Sup, bro' can be used as a greeting," H'Jossu told our crewmates. "But it can also be used as a combat challenge, especially between young males, when repeated over and over again—''Sup, bro. 'Sup, bro.' Do you hear the difference?"

All but one of the new cadets hurriedly scribbled down notes. The third was too busy waving at me. I wasn't sure exactly what sort of string had been pulled or by who, but Jamdora was now aboard the *Eastwood*. He'd traded the black-and-red Merciful Rampart garb for one of our uniforms, and he was constantly, unbearably chill and nice, never talking about how humanity was the scourge of the galaxy or bombarding us with Rampart propaganda. He avoided the topic of his mother, but I heard that despite the stunt at the Senate, the Denzan government was extremely interested in her technology.

"That one's a spy, you know," Zara said, her eyes narrowed at Jamdora.

"I think they could *all* be spies," I replied.

Zara pinched my arm approvingly. "There's the Chambers paranoia I love and respect."

As we continued along the corridor, we bumped into Melian coming out of the med-bay. She held a vial of small white pills that I recognized immediately.

"Did he have another episode?" I asked.

Melian nodded, touching my shoulder for a moment. "Right after you left. He tried to work through it, but . . ."

I took the pills from her. "Thanks, Mel. I'll go check on the captain."

When I entered, Ty's room was dark, like it was supposed to be after he had one of his episodes, but he was sitting up in bed staring down at his tablet's screen, which completely defeated the purpose of resting somewhere peaceful. His left eye was half-lidded and twitching like it always was these days—he still hadn't regained full sight out of it, and the doctors in Primclef worried his vision might continue to degrade. Ever since the encounter with Goldy, my uncle had been prone to headaches, disorientation, and fainting spells. Obviously, we kept all of that out of the reports we filed to the Serpo Institute, although with all the new crew on board it probably wouldn't be long until rumors of my uncle's infirmities reached the higher-ups.

"Six more messages today," he said as soon as I entered. "All of them asking the same thing. It's unbelievable."

I went to his bedside and took the tablet away from him. "You're supposed to be resting."

"I'm fine, Syd. Just a little headache. Melian overreacted." He said all that but didn't fight me on taking his screen away. In the near darkness, the metal bindings that covered his arm from fingertips to elbow shone dully.

"Take your pills," I said, holding them out. "And I told you before, stop reading those messages."

"They're calling me Tycius the Merciless now," he said, throwing back the pills with a sip of water. "Can you believe that?"

I shook my head. "Tell me you've at least stopped responding."

"I have to respond, Syd," Ty said. "These Denzans all know what it felt like—what it felt like to kill a man. They think what I did was brave. They need to know that it haunts me. That I wish I'd had another choice. That I see his face every time I close my eyes."

I'd long given up on trying to convince my uncle to forgive himself. Hiro Takagi was a total psychopath, and he probably would've murdered us both and taken his time doing it. But those details didn't make it any easier on Tycius. He had broken the biggest taboo in Denzan society. Considering the circumstances and knowing how valuable he was—how valuable I was—the institute and the Senate had given him a pass. But I saw the looks they gave him before we left Primclef. They were afraid of him. It was like Tycius belonged to a different species of Denzan now. The ones who had come before. The ones capable of wiping out the Tytons.

And, in a way, that was my fault.

"Won't be long now until we get to go down to Earth," I said, trying to change the subject. "Diner food awaits, right? I'm going to need a ton of pancakes and bacon to make up for losing my strength. And you'll get to be Bogey again."

Ty's smile was shaky in the dark. The pills he took for his migraines worked quickly, and he was already dozing off.

"Yes," he said. "It will be nice to be someone else."

After my uncle dozed off, I wandered up to the *Eastwood's* observation deck. My mind was troubled. It always was, these days. The Origin was public knowledge now, and yet we'd avoided any real bloodshed between humans and Denzans. We were on the verge of uplifting humanity, offering the masses an opportunity to relocate to a new world—one where they could start from scratch and hopefully not repeat the mistakes of the past. It should've been a hopeful time.

But I couldn't shake the dread that the worst was yet to come.

I flopped into a couch on the observation deck, once again staring out at the bright blue marble where I'd been born. It took me a second to realize that I wasn't alone. Darcy sat in a chair in the back of the room, gazing out at the planet, too.

"Oh, hey," I said. "You were just leaving, right?"

I had thought that Darcy and I had buried the hatchet back on Little Earth, but ever since the Senate she had been cold to me. When I came into a room, she made a habit of clearing out. I'd tried to talk to her about her experience with Goldy—the effects of which were still evident from the streaks in her hair, which, of course, she kept hidden under her hood—but she said she couldn't remember anything. I swore he spoke to her. She told me he hadn't.

Darcy did get up. But, to my surprise, she didn't leave the room. Instead, she came over to sit next to me.

"That's where you grew up, huh?" She pointed her chin at the Earth.

"That's it," I said with a sigh. "Home sweet home."

"You don't sound very excited to be back."

I sighed, trying to put my thoughts in order. "The Earth doesn't really feel like home anymore, I guess. I mean, I never really had a home there to begin with. We were always running. I never got attached. The humans there . . . my mom, the ones Rafe wants to save . . . they aren't even really my people, I don't think. Not anymore. I can't stop thinking about Reno and those others. How she looked at me. I think I'm a little afraid of what we're doing here, Darcy."

Darcy was staring at me, and I realized I was babbling.

"Sorry," I said. "Didn't mean to unload on you."

"It's okay," she said. "I never really felt at home on Denza either. I never fit in. Or maybe I never allowed myself to fit in. I don't know. Anyway, I get what you're saying. We don't belong anywhere. And yet we're needed everywhere."

I nodded in agreement. "We've got each other, at least. We hybrids have to stick together, right?"

"Right," Darcy said, her voice quiet at first, then firmer when she continued. "Right. Let's stick together. Although I'm not too sure about that Jamdora guy."

I chuckled. "Yeah. Me neither."

We sat there in silence for a while and, slowly, our orbital position shifted so that the sun was behind the Earth. The flare of orange put what looked like a halo of fire around the planet. I shivered, and I'm pretty sure Darcy did, too.

"Do you ever worry about the future?" I asked her. "About what we might have to do?"

Darcy shrugged. "I don't know. Sometimes."

"My dad thought he was right when he trapped himself on Ashfall. Reno thought she was right when she tried to stage her coup. I wonder about how they got to those points. All the things that happened during their lives that twisted them up and made them into . . ." I trailed off for a moment, then steeled myself. "If I ever get like that, Darcy, promise you'll stop me. Okay?"

Darcy turned to lock eyes with me. For a moment, I thought I saw a flare of fire in her pupils, like I was an explosion and I was expanding in her direction, but it must have just been a trick of the light.

"I swear," Darcy said. "I swear I'll stop you."